SWITCHING GEARS

CHOOSING PROVIDENCE - BOOK 2

JILL BURRELL

First edition: November 2022
Library of Congress Control Number: 2022918474

ISBN: 978-1-955507-10-3 (eBook)
ISBN: 978-1-955507-11-0 (pbk)

To all of my writing buddies and critique partners. You guys help keep me sane and moving forward when I want to give up.

CHAPTER 1

A twinge pulled at Scott's low back as he dropped into the chair opposite from Stan Wright in the small waiting area in the corner of the convenience store. The chair looked more comfortable than it actually was.

He gave Stan a tight smile before giving him the news. "The AC compressor in your truck is bad."

Stan scooted to the edge of his seat. "I thought compressors went bad from non-use. I've been using it all summer. Why did it suddenly give out?"

"Probably hasn't worked all summer. You said it hasn't been cooling well for the last few months. This heat wave made you realize how bad it really was."

"What's it going to cost me?"

Scott hesitated for a heartbeat before answering. "A thousand dollars."

"A thousand!" Stan scowled at Scott. "That's absurd."

"A new compressor runs about seven hundred and eighty dollars."

"So, you'll make over two hundred dollars on labor?"

"There's also a fee to dispose of the coolant from the old compressor." Scott squared his shoulders. "And it'll take me the better part of a day to replace it when the part comes in."

"Great! Just great." Stan got to his feet and propped his hands on his hips as he shook his head. "How long until the part arrives?"

"Three days tops. But I won't be able to get to it until next Tuesday."

"A whole week? Why so long if the part will be here by Thursday?"

"I've got a line of cars ahead of you." Scott hated saying this, but unfortunately, he'd had to say it way too often over the past three weeks. Even though Eli had only worked part time at the shop, he'd been a huge help.

"You're going to make me continue to drive that toaster oven for an entire week in this heat?"

Scott shrugged. "Sorry, man."

"This is ridiculous. I may as well take it to Pasco."

Stan wasn't the first customer to threaten to take his car elsewhere. The tiny town of Providence had one other shop. However, Decker's only specialized in oil changes and tires. Pasco was almost an hour away, so the people who could still drive their cars that far did. Scott hated losing business, but he worked twelve-to-fourteen-hour days as it was.

He stood. "That's your choice."

"I don't have time for this." Stan sprang to his feet. "Get me my keys."

Irate and impatient, Stan didn't even wait for Scott to pull his truck out of the shop; he followed him into the garage and backed out as soon as Scott handed him the keys.

Scott attempted to push the whole ordeal from his mind as he laid on the creeper and rolled himself under Mr. Moore's car. Even though he enjoyed the peace and quiet of working in the shop alone, he sure could use an extra set of hands, especially while replacing a fuel pump.

He should have hired help weeks ago before Eli left for college, but he simply hadn't had the time. Nor did he want to face the overwhelming task of creating an intelligent-sounding job posting. His family would have helped if he'd asked them, but despite struggling with dyslexia all his life, asking for help never got any easier.

Ten minutes later, Scott rolled out from under the car to grab another wrench. Again, he wished he had an extra set of hands as he rolled back under the car. He'd barely made the wish when someone kicked his boot.

"Need some help today?"

He rolled out to find Ben Young, a former coworker here at the shop, standing over him.

Scott let his head fall back on the creeper. The tension that had kept him wound tighter than a coil spring released inside him. "I won't say no to that."

Within minutes, Ben had pulled on a pair of coveralls and joined him underneath Mr. Moore's car.

"Aunt Charity said you've been burning the midnight oil quite often lately," Ben said, reaching up with a wrench. "Yet the lot is still crowded out there?"

"I know. I swear everyone needs something fixed lately." It was good for business—when they stuck around, that is—but Scott was overwhelmed. The heat of the late August sun shining through the open bay door on his legs drove his body temperature up.

I should have backed this blasted car in.

"When are you going to hire some help?" Ben asked.

"When I find time." Scott's response sounded like a growl.

"You're going to burn yourself out before that ever happens."

"I know, I just…" He let his words die off, because even though Ben knew of Scott's struggles, he still hated admitting them out loud.

"Would you like me to run an ad and do the interviews for you?"

Scott stopped what he was doing and looked at Ben. Was this Ben's way of letting him save face? Simply saying yes, was so much easier than having to ask for help.

"I'd appreciate that. Thanks."

"No problem."

They worked in silence for some time with the clink of their tools and the nearby traffic the only sounds in the shop. Ben knew he wasn't much of a talker, and Scott appreciated that the other man didn't feel the need to fill the quiet.

The men fell into a comfortable rhythm that felt like old times. Scott had worked with Ben for less than a year before the other man decided to return to practicing law. Ben had made a lasting impression on him, however. The way the man selflessly served others, despite grieving the loss of his wife and his daughter, impressed Scott.

Feeling the need to act friendly, Scott forced himself to ask Ben about his family.

"They are growing like weeds." Warmth filled Ben's voice as he talked about his kids. "Little James is nine months old already. Can you believe it? And Cassey and Kallie will start kindergarten next year."

After all Ben had lost, it was great to see him happy again.

"That's great, man." Scott wasn't sure what else to say.

"Amy's excited," Ben said but didn't elaborate. He used to do that all the time to Scott. Instead of telling him what he intended to say, he left him hanging, just to make Scott talk.

"Oh yeah? About what?" It wouldn't surprise Scott if Ben announced they were expecting again.

"Aunt Charity agreed to sell us the diner."

Scott dropped his wrench and looked at Ben. "She did? Is it just because she's ready to retire, or are the Knights downsizing their holdings?"

The Knights owned the only grocery store in town as well as the diner across the street and the repair shop Scott had been managing for the past three years.

"A little of both, I think. Amy mentioned to Charity years ago that she'd love to have her own place someday. So now that Aunt Faith finally convinced Charity to retire, she's giving Amy first dibs on the diner."

A spark of hope shot through Scott, making his toes and fingertips tingle. Did Charity agree to sell to Amy because she was related? Or would she be willing to let go of the repair shop too?

Scott's only goal—since he walked away from his dream of being a forest ranger almost eight years ago—had been to own his own garage. He'd painstakingly saved every penny he could for the past seven years and had what could be a sizable down payment on his own shop.

Having to build his own place would take that much longer and end up adding to his costs. Besides, he hated the idea of leaving Charity in a lurch with the repair shop that had been her late husband's pride and joy.

But if she'll sell me the garage...

Taking slow, even breaths, Scott picked up his wrench and tightened the final few bolts. "Do you think the Knights are interested in selling the repair shop?"

It was Ben's turn to stare at Scott. "Are you interested in buying it?"

Scott shrugged. "Maybe."

"I suppose it's time you owned your own shop. What are you now? Twenty-nine?"

"Just turned twenty-eight last month." Scott looked away from Ben's piercing gaze. "Do you think I can handle it? I mean with my…"

Ben nodded. "You've managed to keep the place running well the past few years. As long as you focus on your strengths and continue to let others help you out, you'll make a great repair shop owner." Ben went back to tightening the bolts on his side. "I say go for it. I honestly don't know whether my cousins plan to let the repair shop go, but I never thought Charity would sell the diner either. Wouldn't hurt to ask."

A lightness filled Scott's chest as he rolled out from under the car a few minutes later. He stood and stretched, and Ben did the same. He grabbed two water bottles from the small refrigerator in the shop and tossed one to Ben.

Ben caught it and took a long swig. "You know, after you purchase your own shop, the next step is to get married and settle down."

Scott spewed the water he'd been guzzling all over Mr. Moore's car.

~

KENNEDY SLIPPED into her apartment and closed the door softly behind her. What were her chances of being able to slip into her room without her roommate Eden noticing?

The scent of buttery microwave popcorn hit her just as Eden stepped out of the kitchen, hugging a bowl. She stopped and frowned at Kennedy. "I thought you had a date with Nate tonight?"

"So did I." Kennedy's lip trembled as she fought back tears.

"Have you been crying? What happened?" Eden wrapped an arm around Kennedy's shoulders and pulled her into the living room. "What did that jerk do now?"

Eden didn't like Nate because he had an ego the size of Mount Saint Helens, but Kennedy had had a crush on her dad's partner's son since she was twelve. When she was sixteen, he started flirting with her, and she'd let all of her girlish daydreams of someday marrying Nathan Cooper take root. He finally asked her out after she turned eighteen, and within a year, they were dating steadily. It felt like they were always meant to be together.

Kennedy's throat tightened, and she swallowed hard. Her body grew hot as her heart pounded in her chest. So many emotions tumbled around inside her—humiliation, contempt, resentment—she didn't know how she was supposed to act or what to say. She finally settled for, "He dumped me."

Surprisingly, she didn't feel all that sad or depressed. She felt... rejected. Even that emotion surprised her, since deep down, she'd known this day would come. She'd just been too stubborn to admit that Nate wasn't the man she wanted him to be. She was angry and hurt over the way he'd strung her along for so many years, but she wasn't all that sad to see the relationship end.

When did I fall out of love with Nate?

"What?" Eden's delicate eyebrows rose. "I thought he was getting ready to propose?"

After nearly six years of dating, Kennedy had feared he'd never fully commit to her. It wasn't until she pressed the issue last spring that he started talking about marriage.

"I thought he was, back before my dad got sick, anyway. But he's been kind of distant since Dad…died." When she'd needed Nate the most, he'd started canceling dates and finding excuses to work in a different bay from her.

She'd known something was going on with him, but she'd been too devastated by the loss of her father and having to settle his estate and deal with his hospital bills, that she hadn't taken time to analyze Nate's behavior.

"So, he just decided he was done after all these years?"

Kennedy had often told Eden in the past how Nate flirted with many of their female customers—yet another reason her friend didn't like him. But she hadn't shared with her how often he hung around Olivia's desk lately. The new receptionist dressed much nicer than was expected for an auto repair shop, and her short skirts and plunging necklines had caught the attention of most of the mechanics, including Nate's.

Kennedy squeezed her eyes shut as the scene she'd interrupted in the parts room this evening filled her mind. The room grew suddenly hot, and Kennedy's ribcage squeezed the air from her lungs as her stomach churned. Technically, she'd dumped Nate after finding him and Olivia together, but she felt rejected all the same.

She dropped onto the couch and propped her elbows on her knees. Scrubbing her hands over her face, she recalled the things she'd learned from Nate tonight. She couldn't decide what hurt worse; the fact that he blamed her for his infidelity because she refused to sleep with him before they were married, or that he'd only dated her all these years to keep her from marrying someone else and eventually taking half of the shop with her.

Tears pricked Kennedy's eyes again. "He said he wants a real woman."

"What? How can he say that?" Eden rubbed Kennedy's back. "You are just as smart and beautiful as any other woman out there. Even more so because you have so many talents most women will never have." Eden shook Ken's shoulders. "You are gorgeous no matter how you dress. I'd kill to have your curves, and don't even get me started on how jealous I am of your long hair."

Even though Kennedy always wore t-shirts and jeans for work, she tried to make an effort to dress up for Nate when they went out. She wanted him to see her as a woman and not just another one of the guys. She had Eden and her nanny to thank for teaching her how to curl her hair and put on make-up.

Tonight, she'd even put in a little extra effort. Even though she had enough curves to make wearing the men's mechanic uniforms uncomfortable, she didn't have the kind of assets Olivia flaunted. Nor was she the type to flaunt the assets she did have.

Kennedy lifted her head and looked at her friend. "That's not even the worst thing he said to me tonight."

Eden's eyes widened, and her nostrils flared for an instant before she masked her features and hugged Kennedy tighter. "You deserve better than him. You realize that, don't you?"

Kennedy nodded as tears filled her eyes. She'd hardly dated any other men. Nate took what many would consider to be the best years of her life, and she had nothing to show for it. Nothing to build a future on. No boyfriend. No financial security. And no job.

Because after what she learned tonight, there was no way she'd go back to T&J's Auto Repair Shop.

She chewed on her lip for a moment before speaking. "You know how my mom's battle with cancer lasted three years before she finally died?"

"Yes, but what does that have to do with Nate being such a jerk?"

"Well, I didn't realize it back then because I was only ten, but there were a lot of medical bills, plus the funeral expenses. Dad ended up selling half of his share of the garage to his partner, Joel Cooper, years ago."

"Didn't Coop just help you out with the expenses for your dad's funeral?"

Kennedy rubbed her hands on her skirt. "Yes, but I never told you how bad it really was."

Eden pulled back to study Kennedy's face. "What do you mean?"

"Well, between the hospital stay after my dad's initial stroke, the long-term care center, then additional hospital visits with each stroke, and the fact that he was no longer working, not to mention all the funeral expenses…" Tension built, in Kennedy, stealing her breath, just like it had when she realized how many hospital bills there were. And boy, were caskets and burial vaults expensive. At least she hadn't had to buy a headstone. She'd only had to pay to have her dad's death date added beside her mother's.

The finality of it all hit her again, as it had many times over the past two months, and a sense of abandonment swept over Kennedy. Despite the amazing support of her best friend, she felt so alone. Even more so after everything that had happened tonight.

"So, you're saying Coop paid for more than just your dad's funeral expenses?"

"Yes, but it came from my dad's share of the shop. Once everything was taken care of there was so little left, he asked me to sign over the remaining portion."

Eden scowled. "That was supposed to be *your* inheritance."

"I know, but there were a lot of expenses, and Coop paid them all plus enough for me to pay off my truck." He'd wanted her dad's motorcycle too, but Kennedy refused to sell it. It was all she had left of her father now. Kennedy sighed. "I'm debt free. Which is a good thing because I no longer have a job."

Eden jerked back. "He fired you?"

"No, but after finding out tonight that the only reason Nate dated me all of these years was to keep full ownership of the garage in the family, there's no way I'm going back to T&J's."

Eden frowned and tilted her head. "I don't understand."

"He was only going to marry me if he needed to to keep ownership of the garage. That's why he's been so aloof since my dad died."

Eden's jaw dropped. "What?"

"He never loved me," Kennedy's words came out as a whisper through a tight throat. "He only dated me to keep me from falling in love with and marrying someone else and taking half, well, a quarter of the shop with me."

Eden sucked in a sharp breath. "Did Coop push him to do that?"

"I don't know. Nate's selfish enough to want control of the whole shop himself, but you know Coop has never really approved of me working in the shop. He won't be sad to see me go."

A heaviness descended over Kennedy, and the weight of an anvil settled on her chest. Everything she'd built her dreams on was gone. Everything.

"Oh, Ken, I'm so sorry." Eden wrapped her arms around Kennedy and squeezed.

"I can't go back to the shop." Her throat ached with another onslaught of tears at the thought of never again setting foot in the building where she grew up; the place where she'd worked side by side with her father since she was a young girl.

"What are you going to do?" Eden loosened her hold.

Kennedy blinked back tears as she shook her head. "I have to find another job, but it can't be with a garage that's in any way associated with T&J's." Which meant she might have to leave Spokane.

Eden would hate that, so Kennedy kept the thought to herself. She turned to Eden. "No matter what happens, don't let me fall for another arrogant mechanic."

CHAPTER 2

"Scott?" a feminine voice called. "Are you in here?"

Scott rolled out from under Mrs. Howard's car to find Ben's wife, Amy, carrying a to-go bag from the diner. He pushed himself to his feet and wiped his hands on a grease rag.

"Charity's worried about you." She held the bag out. "She says you're working too hard. You're not even taking lunch breaks anymore."

He took the bag with one hand as he reached for his wallet with the other.

Amy held up her free hand palm out. "Charity said no charge. The least she can do is take care of her employees. I mean, we servers get a free meal every shift."

"Tell her thanks." Scott's voice came out deeper than usual and a little rough. He hadn't spoken to anyone since this morning when he told Mr. Hodges he needed a new carburetor.

He didn't usually mind the quiet, but without Eli coming in every afternoon, talking up a storm, the garage had become extra quiet. He'd taken to turning on the old boom box that had sat on the shelf above the workbench since before he started working at the garage years ago.

"How's your family doing?" Amy asked.

"Good."

"I can't believe Debbie and Austin brought back that adorable little baby with them from their honeymoon."

Neither could he or the rest of the family. His sister and her new husband had surprised everyone when they extended their honeymoon by four days only to return home with a new-born baby they planned to adopt.

"Yep." Scott hated having to make small talk with people. He never knew what to say.

"Well, I'd better get back to work." Amy waved and headed back across the street to the diner.

Scott deposited the food that was giving off the most amazing aroma of garlic and butter on the small table in the corner of the office and went to the bathroom to wash up. As he scrubbed the grease and grime from his hands, he noted how filthy the sink had become. He couldn't remember the last time someone had cleaned the bathroom.

Probably before Eli left.

He ate a solitary lunch of lasagna and garlic bread, hoping the whole time that Ben found him some help soon.

Hours later, Scott straightened when his brother Rudy strolled into the garage. "Hey."

"Need help today?" Although Rudy still wore his deputy's uniform, he'd shed his gun belt. A sure sign he was off duty.

A small weight lifted off Scott's shoulders. He'd been hoping Rudy would make it in soon to help with the paperwork since Mary, the manager of the convenience store who often helped him, hadn't been around much the past few weeks.

Scott nodded. "Yes, Mary's still at the hospital with Chase."

Rudy's gaze became distant as he shook his head. Like Scott, Rudy had suffered the loss of a good friend in a terrible accident years ago. Hearing about the horrible motorcycle accident that left Mary's son paralyzed and his friend dead haunted them. One minute they were two teenage boys having one last hurrah before school started; and the next, Chase's life was forever changed.

Rudy squared his shoulders. "I know he probably won't be released from the hospital for a few weeks still, but we need to help Dad build that wheelchair ramp for Mary this weekend. She's got enough to worry about right now."

Scott nodded. It didn't matter if he fell further behind at the garage and people took their cars elsewhere. He owed Mary. Not only was she like a second mother to him, she'd helped him keep up with all the paperwork since he took over management of the repair shop almost three years ago.

If Scott had known there would be so much paperwork, he might have refused when Ben and Charity asked him to manage the shop. Ordering parts was one thing, but typing up quotes, invoices, and receipts were not among Scott's strengths. Not to mention keeping the books and making quarterly reports. He just wanted to work on cars.

Fortunately, Rudy and Mary checked on him frequently and kept him on track. Until Chase got in the accident, that is. Now, he relied on Rudy more than ever.

After going through the list of parts that needed to be ordered with Rudy, Scott went back to work while his brother typed away on the computer, preparing tomorrow's invoices. Scott had been jealous of his younger brother most of his life. Rudy was incredibly intelligent and especially good with computers. He'd tried to explain all the technical ins and outs to Scott multiple times, but that stuff made no sense to him.

Scott also admired how easy it was for Rudy to talk to people. He could converse with anybody about anything for hours. Scott's mind usually went blank in social situations. Rudy had explained that it was just a matter of listening and asking follow-up questions. Scott had no problem with the listening part. He preferred that over talking any day. But he never quite knew how to respond to the things people said.

What he lacked in personality and brains though, he made up for in size and strength. He took after his mom's side of the family, who were all tall and solidly built, whereas Rudy took after their dad; tall, lean, and wiry.

Rudy left an hour later, but Scott kept at it. He needed to put in at least another two hours tonight.

A text from Ben came through on his phone as he finally decided to call it a night.

Ran an ad today with several papers throughout eastern Washington. Hopefully, we'll get some hits soon.

Ben must have copied the ad in the text because the next words read:

Automotive Technician needed for a small but busy shop in Providence.

Scott continued to read for only a moment, because after the third line, the words started to jump around on his phone screen, and he had difficulty distinguishing between words like brakes and batteries and emissions and electrical.

He scrolled down, catching more big words like suspension and transmission. Judging by the length of the ad, Ben was thorough.

Most employers, when they ran an ad, rarely ended up hiring individuals who matched all the requirements, but if Ben found somebody who could do even half of what the ad listed, Scott would finally be able to catch his breath.

And then maybe he'd find the time to talk to Charity about buying the repair shop.

TEARS FILLED Kennedy's eyes as she hugged Eden goodbye. She blinked them away before releasing Eden, because if her best friend saw her crying, then she'd start, and the two of them would look like a couple of hormonal females.

"Are you sure you have to go?"

"I start my new job tomorrow morning. I need to get settled in before my first day."

Not that she had more than a couple of suitcases and boxes to unpack. That's why she'd waited so late on Sunday afternoon to leave. A new job *and* leaving Eden and the apartment they'd shared for the last six years kind of terrified Kennedy. Especially now that her dad was gone. Her roots in Spokane felt precariously shallow.

Eden pouted. "I know but why does it need to be in Providence?"

"I need a fresh start far away from Spokane and T&J's. You know that. I can't take the chance that I'll run into Nate." Kennedy would never admit to her best friend since fifth grade how terrified she was to move away from the only home she'd ever known. Especially since she wasn't sure who she was anymore or what she wanted out of life.

Nate had not only shattered her self-esteem, he'd triggered an identity crisis in her. Everything she'd planned for her life had been built on lies and deceit. She felt like she was floundering in her efforts to start over.

Who willingly moves to a small town to work at a dinky, two-bay repair shop?

Even though her new job paid well, she couldn't picture herself owning her own shop—or even a portion of a shop—any time soon.

"I know," Eden said, "but that doesn't mean I'm not going to miss you like crazy. Do you realize we've seen each other or talked on the phone every single day since we were ten years old?"

"We can still talk every day. And I'll only be an hour and a half away. We can even visit each other on the weekends."

Kennedy had a feeling it would take her a while to make new friends, especially of the female variety. She tended to get along better with guys than she did women. Her relationship with Eden was an anomaly. They couldn't be more different from one another, but they shared a bond stronger than most best friends because of their shared loss.

They'd been friends since fifth grade when they both lost their moms. Kennedy's mother had died at the beginning of the school year after a lengthy battle with cancer, and Eden lost her mom in a tragic car accident the following spring. When Tommy Price teased Eden about not having a mom, Kennedy couldn't help herself. She beat him up. She and Eden had been best friends ever since.

The loss of their mothers and being only children were the only things they had in common. Kennedy was raised in an auto repair shop, while Eden grew up in a veritable mansion. Kennedy was a classic tom-boy, but Eden was a socialite, often sharing the limelight with her wealthy businessman father. It was only because of Eden's—and her nanny's—influence that Kennedy even owned anything remotely feminine and knew how to apply makeup. The most important lesson she'd learned from Eden, however, was how amazing a hot bath felt after a long, strenuous day at work.

"And you're sure this job is going to work out?" Eden caught Kennedy's arm as she turned to get in her truck that was already packed and loaded with her dad's motorcycle in the back. The only meaningful thing she had of her father's now that T&J's was lost to her.

"The guy I interviewed with earlier this week seemed knowledgeable about the garage and thinks I'll be a great fit. It's a small shop. Apparently, there's only one other full-time mechanic that works there—the manager—but Ben said he's a good guy."

Kennedy wasn't sure why Ben Young, a lawyer, had interviewed her for a job as a mechanic for Knight's Repair Shop, but he seemed to know cars inside and out and had been very thorough in his questioning. He'd repeatedly quizzed her on diagnosing engine problems with only a list of irregular car behaviors. She wasn't worried about the work as much as she was about who she'd be working with. She'd had her fill of working with sexist, chauvinistic men who thought women belong in the kitchen and not under a car.

Eden must have seen the trepidation on Kennedy's face because she said, "At least you'll only have to prove yourself to one man and not a whole shop full."

Sometimes it was creepy how well Eden read her mind. "That is a relief."

Ben had warned her Scott was the strong silent type. Kennedy could handle that as long as he was willing to let her do the work she'd been hired to do and didn't try to coddle her and mansplain everything to her.

CHAPTER 3

*K*ennedy's stomach churned as she dressed for her first day of work the next morning. She hadn't slept well last night, knowing that if she didn't make a good impression today with the manager, she might find herself out of a job.

That's why she wore a simple gray t-shirt that said, *Never too old to play with cars,* instead of the brighter colors she usually preferred. Maybe after she got to know the manager of the repair shop, she'd feel like she could wear her favorite t-shirts with silly sayings.

Although failure wasn't usually a part of her vocabulary, she'd suffered way too many defeats lately to feel like she could bounce back if she had even one more.

"Just be yourself, Ken. You're enough." Her father's voice filled her head and pricked her heart.

He'd repeatedly given her pep talks when the frustration of trying to prove herself in a man's world became too much. Never mind that any of the male mechanics could—and often did—make the same mistakes she did, she was often judged much more harshly.

That's why Kennedy had learned to be thorough and cautious. She rarely made mistakes, anymore, but she'd had to work twice as hard to prove herself.

She stared at herself in the small bathroom mirror. "I can do this. I'm an excellent mechanic. Yes, I'll have to prove myself to my new boss, but I've done it before. I can do it again."

She debated whether to put her hair in a ponytail now and don her baseball cap or wait until she'd met her new boss. Hiding her eyes behind the bill of a cap probably wouldn't make a good first impression.

Deciding to pull her hair back and just strap her ball cap though her belt loop for now, she stepped out of the bathroom and checked the clock on the bedside table.

Seven forty-five.

I don't want to be that early, do I?

All she had to do was go down the back stairs and walk around to the front of the shop and she'd be at work.

After her interview, when she asked Ben about apartments for rent in town, he'd frowned and mentioned there was a housing shortage lately. But then he'd made a phone call and turned around and offered her the apartment above the garage.

It was small, but it was furnished, which was a blessing. Most of the furniture in the place she'd shared with Eden had been provided by Eden's dad, so Kennedy hadn't felt right about taking any of it with her. At least, this apartment had a decent-sized bathtub.

A slight rumble vibrated under her feet.

That must be Scott opening the repair shop.

When a second rumble sounded, she decided she was tired of waiting. She took a deep breath and repeated her dad's words as she walked out the door. "Just be yourself. You're enough." She needed this job, so she'd do whatever it took to impress the manager. Even if it means doing all the grunt work like oil changes and fixing flats."

The walk to the front of the shop passed quickly as Kennedy attempted to squelch the commotion whirling in her stomach. She resisted the urge to press her hand to her abdomen. That's all she needed—to walk in looking like a weak female who had no place in a repair shop.

She rounded the corner to find a tall man with the build of a lumberjack at the back of the shop facing the workbench. She wasn't sure what she'd expected her new boss to look like, but the man with his back to her was not only larger than she expected, he was also younger.

There wasn't a hint of gray in his wavy auburn hair and judging by the way his blue shirt stretched across the taut muscles of his broad shoulders, the guy was in great physical shape.

Pasting on a smile, she cleared her throat and stepped up behind her new manager. "Hi, I'm Ken MacGregor. You must be Scott Wheeler."

Something clanked against the workbench, and the lumberjack tensed before jerking his arm back. He spun around, his eyes widening as he stared at her. His mouth opened then closed again, making no more than a soft grunting sound.

Her own eyes grew big as she tilted her head back to meet his hazel eyes. The man not only had an imposing build, he had striking features, a prominent brow, full lips, and a strong jaw covered in stubble that only enhanced his ruggedness. His broad chest expanded as he sucked in a deep breath.

A surge of attraction coursed through Kennedy, stealing her breath. Why had she hoped her new boss wouldn't be an old chauvinistic, stick in the mud? Working with someone this attractive would be nothing but a distraction.

The lumberjack's jaw clenched, and his fists balled. A reaction she'd seen from disapproving males too many times to count.

Kennedy sighed and braced herself for a fight.

Scott pulled his old pickup truck to a stop behind the repair shop and let out a long whistle as he stared at the red Chevy Silverado next to him.

Now that's a man's truck!

It was exactly the kind of truck he'd love to have, if he wasn't saving to buy his own repair shop, that is. It was a much bigger vehicle than he needed, considering his daily commute to work was only a mile and a half and he rarely needed to haul anything, but it was good-looking, nonetheless.

His gaze lingered on the Honda Goldwing motorcycle in the back as he climbed from his own truck. The only motorcycle he'd ever owned was the dirt bikes he and Rudy rode as teenagers. Even though he was mostly a homebody, he'd always loved the idea of hitting the open road on a bike like this.

Must belong to the new mechanic.

No one would leave a bike like that in their truck if they were dropping it off for repairs. Scott sucked in a deep breath and let it out slowly, letting his shoulders relax as he did so. He had a feeling he and the new mechanic were going to get along great. The relief that filled him Friday evening when he got Ben's text that Ken Macgregor would be here at eight a.m. Monday morning had stuck with him through the rest of the weekend and made him feel lighter and more energized than he had in a month.

He'd hardly bothered to read Ken's resume that Ben forwarded to him. He trusted Ben and figured if this Ken guy passed Ben's scrutiny, then he must be an excellent mechanic. Of course, Scott stopped reading the resume as soon as the words and letters started to dance around on the page.

The relief at finally getting some help had been so powerful he hadn't even minded the next text from Ben, saying Ken would be living in the apartment upstairs. The one place Scott hoped to live one day, if he was fortunate enough to convince Charity to sell the repair shop to him, that is. He'd considered moving out of his parents' house many times over the years, but the nest egg he'd accrued reminded him that even though he was plenty old enough to be on his own, there were perks to living with his parents. Besides, as shallow as it sounded, he'd miss his mom's cooking if he moved out.

He checked the clock as he opened the garage doors, then grabbed a grease rag and began straightening up the workbench. He couldn't believe he'd let it get so disorganized over the past few weeks.

He'd just picked up the new alternator for Mrs. Allen's car to wipe under it when a cheerful, lilting voice startled him.

"Hi, I'm Ken MacGregor. You must be Scott Wheeler."

The alternator slipped from his hand and landed on the fingers of his left hand. It was all he could do to not let loose a string of swear words. His mother had taught him never to swear in a lady's presence and judging by the voice behind him, there was a lady present.

That can't be right. Ken Macgregor is supposed to be an experienced mechanic. A male mechanic.

He shoved the alternator off his hand and spun around, expecting to find an unfortunate young man whose voice never dropped. But the vision standing in front of him was as feminine as they come with big brown eyes framed by thick lashes and a smile that lit up her face, revealing a dimple in each cheek.

Pain pulsed in his fingertips from being pinched by the alternator. He balled his fist to create a counter pressure in the throbbing digits and clenched his teeth together to hold back the cuss words that wanted to escape, now more than ever.

What was Ben thinking?

Didn't he realize Scott needed real help, not a secretary—although he could use one of those too.

She held out a dainty hand. "It's nice to meet you."

"You're Ken?" Scott's voice came out gruffer than usual. She looked more like a Barbie than a Ken. He cleared his throat. "And Ken is short for…" Surely, her parents hadn't named their daughter Kenneth.

"Kennedy."

Kennedy.

The name was as pretty as she was.

Realizing she still held out her hand, he grabbed it. It felt small and delicate, just like he expected, but he hadn't anticipated the warm gentle pressure of her palm to ignite sparks that both burned and energized, sending jolts of electricity racing up his arm. He released her hand as quickly as he'd grabbed it and wiped his palm against his pants.

She turned and looked around, revealing long blond hair that hung halfway down her back despite being in a ponytail. A hint of vanilla and strawberries mingled with the garage's usual odor of oil and grease.

"Your shop is small, but it looks well equipped."

Scott watched her as she wandered. She was dressed normal enough in worn jeans and a gray t-shirt that sported faint oil stains, but that's where the resemblance to a tomboy ended. No, she looked like a model pretending to be a tomboy. She was tall and had more curves than the typical supermodel but still…

Women who looked like they could be on the cover of a magazine did not work in garages. Gorgeous women, who looked like her, didn't crawl under cars and get their hands dirty. No way were her dainty hands strong enough to do the kind of work he needed done.

He grunted. "There's been a mistake."

"Excuse me?" Her voice rose in pitch.

"I know Ben hired you, but you don't have the qualifications I'm looking for."

Something sparked in her brown eyes before they narrowed. She balled her own fists as she planted herself in front of him.

"The ad said you were looking for someone with a minimum of two years' experience. I've worked in a garage since I was sixteen."

"So?" She looked all of seventeen years old.

She propped her hands on her hips and leaned forward a little. "I've worked in a garage for nine years."

Scott's head jerked back as he did the math.

She's twenty-five?

Before he could find the words to argue with her about her own age, she went on. "The ad also said you wanted someone proficient in diagnosing and repairing brakes, steering and suspension…" She ticked off items on her fingers as she continued to speak, her annoyance only making her more attractive. "Electrical and emission systems…"

The vanilla and strawberry scent grew stronger the longer she stood there. So strong he had a difficult time focusing on her words. She continued to talk about air conditioning, transmissions, and certifications then babbled on about self-motivation and customer service, but the rest may as well have been Greek. He was too distracted by her scent and the glossy sheen on her rosy lips to pay attention to her words.

He shook his head. Had the ad said all that? Scott couldn't remember. Maybe he should have read the full listing Ben sent him. Even if he had read it, he still would never have agreed to hire Ken. No, Kennedy—he simply couldn't think of the woman in front of him by a man's name—because a garage was no place for a woman. Especially a woman who was so distracting. Accidents occurred when people got distracted, and he couldn't let that happen again.

"It also said 'Able to lift heavy objects and perform strenuous labor.'" At least he thought it did. If not, it should have.

"I'm stronger than I look." Kennedy propped hands on her hips again and jutted out her chin.

Scott wasn't too sure about that. Okay, so she wasn't exactly petite and delicate, but he doubted her slender arms could do the demanding work often required in the shop.

He shook his head again. She may know a little something about working in a garage but helping around a repair shop was a far cry different than actually doing the work. Scott needed someone who could really pick up the slack.

"If you're not strong enough to do the work, you become a hazard to yourself. And to me."

And I can't let another woman get hurt on my watch.

Her mouth slackened for a moment, and she looked like she wanted to punch him. Then she squared her shoulders, stepped a little closer, and glared at him. "I know how to get the job done." Her words came out clipped, and her voice tight.

Scott felt like a bobble head doll for how much his head shook. He looked up to the ceiling, silently willing her to step away from him. He would move, but he was already backed up against the workbench as it was.

Her feminine scent, and the warmth emanating from her so close in front of him raised the temperature in the garage by at least ten degrees. He balled his fists again to keep from tugging at the collar of his shirt.

"I can't work with someone like you." The words came out all growly, and he repressed a groan as soon as he realized how they sounded.

"Excuse me?" Her delicate eyebrows arched. "I thought Knight's Repair Shop was an equal opportunity employer."

The last thing he needed was Kennedy running back to Ben, crying discrimination. If Charity got wind of Scott giving the new employee a hard time, she might let *him* go and would never consider selling him the shop.

He scooted sideways and stepped away from her. "We are." He sucked in a deep breath. Finally.

"Good." A triumphant smile lit her face. "Are you going to put me to work? Mr. Young said he thought I'd be exactly the kind of help you needed."

What?

Scott's eyebrows shot up. Was there a double meaning in those words? He wouldn't put it past Ben to hire Kennedy just to shake up Scott's world. But surely, they'd had other, better-suited applicants.

He shook his head again. Scott didn't have time to babysit her to make sure she didn't hurt herself, and he couldn't afford for her to make a costly mistake on a customer's car.

"Fine. You can start by cleaning the shop."

"Excuse me?" Her brows lowered over narrowed eyes as her rosy lips pressed into a thin line.

If he was a bobble head, then she was a parrot.

"You heard me." He folded his arms across his chest and dared her to argue with him.

"If all you wanted was a maid, then why didn't you advertise for a maid?"

The fact that she stood her ground and argued showed that maybe she *was* stronger than she looked. At least she had a backbone.

"I don't need a maid. I need a mechanic."

She gave a curt nod. "Then put me to work."

"I don't have time to teach and train you. Heaven forbid you break a fingernail." He couldn't keep that last comment from sliding out.

"Seriously?" She held up her hands, displaying blunt fingernails void of nail polish.

Okay. So maybe she wouldn't break a nail, but her small hands didn't look strong enough to remove a lug nut, let alone an oil filter. Nor did she have grease and grime soaked into her cuticles and every crack and crevice of her skin.

Scott resisted the urge to shake his head again. "I'm not sure we have a uniform that will fit you. We'll have to order—"

"If it's all the same to you, I'd rather just wear my own jeans and t-shirts. Men's clothes don't fit me all that well."

Scott's gaze scanned her figure again. He noted the white lettering across her gray t-shirt. Hoping he didn't look like a creep, he took a moment to process the words then bit back a smile as his mind put them together. *Never too old to play with cars.*

Kennedy was about the same height as Eli, but that's where the resemblance ended. She was busty enough that she'd need a shirt two sizes larger than Eli wore. And pants... Well, men's pants weren't made to curve around hips like hers and taper in at the waist.

"Fine, but get yourself a pair of steel-toed—"

"Boots." She kicked out a foot, revealing a boot whose rounded toe was no doubt lined with steel.

Scott didn't know they even made steel-toed boots that small. For a tall woman, she had surprisingly small feet.

Having run out of patience and reasons to tell her to take a hike, he shook his head one last time and turned his back to her. Hopefully, she'd stay out of his way so he could get some work done. So much for getting some breathing room. He could hardly take a deep breath without her strawberry vanilla scent filling his lungs.

He paused before bringing the Honda in to change the timing belt and pulled out his cell phone. He sent Ben a text.

Dude. So. Not. Funny.

CHAPTER 4

A freaking maid.

Kennedy slipped on her hat and picked up the grease rag from the workbench. She grabbed a wrench to wipe down.

I can't believe I've been relegated to cleaning the shop.

She'd spent more years than she could count at T&J's acting as a maid and gopher. She hung the wrench on its hook, letting it bang against the pegboard as she grabbed another one. Although her dad had been willing to let her work at his side, Cooper had been stricter about having her out on the floor until she turned fifteen. Even at that point, she'd done little more than fetch tools and hold things. It had taken years to get Cooper to agree to give her a real chance as a mechanic.

She hung up the next wrench on the well labeled—but nearly empty—pegboard and grabbed a screwdriver. The workbench held more tools than the pegboard.

How does Scott find anything in this mess? No wonder he's so far behind.

She looked over at the man now bent under the hood of a Honda Pilot. Despite the plain navy-blue pants, his backside was as attractive as his front, which just made her blood boil a little more. She'd spent her whole life having to prove herself to the men she worked with, but it always irritated her when a man she found attractive was as big of a chauvinist as the rest of them.

Nate had been that way. Many times over the course of their relationship, he'd suggested she try a job more suited to women, like waiting tables or becoming a librarian. He'd even pushed her to take the secretarial position when it opened a few months ago.

Within a matter of minutes, Kennedy had all the tools wiped clean and back where they belonged. She sucked in a deep breath and turned toward Scott.

She stepped closer, trying to see what he was working on under the hood of the Honda.

"Would you like some help?"

Scott jumped, hitting his head on the underside of the hood. "Da—"

He cut off the swear word he'd been about to let loose and stepped back and rubbed the back of his head.

Well, that's a change.

Most men didn't bother to curb their language around her. And the few times she'd actually asked a man to stop using foul language around her, she'd gotten a lecture about if you can't handle the heat of working in a man's field, then get out.

Scott pointed a finger at her. "Don't do that!"

"Do what?"

"Sneak up on me."

"Sorry, I wasn't trying to sneak up on you. It's not my fault you're so jumpy."

"I'm not jumpy. I'm just used to working here alone, most of the time."

"Got it," she said with a smile. "No sneaking up on you." She motioned to the car. "I was just wondering if you could use some help."

"I don't need your help. I asked you to clean the shop."

Kennedy's whole body tensed, and she clenched her jaw to keep from letting go of a few choice words of her own. Was he saying he didn't need any help? The cars out in the lot said otherwise. Or did he mean he didn't want *her* help?

She waved toward the workbench. "I cleaned and organized all the tools."

He studied the workbench for a moment before letting his gaze roam around the shop. "The tools are only part of the shop. There's still plenty more for you to do."

"Yes sir, boss." She gave him a mock salute and a tight smile. "But you might want to mark some notches on the cogs before you pull that timing belt off. You don't want to get the new one lined up wrong." She turned toward what she assumed was a janitorial closet.

I'll clean your shop. I'll get it so clean you can eat your lunch off the floor.

The small room Kennedy stepped into was indeed a janitor's closet, but it was also a bathroom. One that hadn't been cleaned in a long time. She stared at herself in the small mirror for one long moment. She'd spent her whole life having to prove herself in a man's world. She could do it again.

Don't give him a reason to fault your work, even if it is just cleaning.

She took stock of the cleaning supplies then went to work.

An hour later, with her back aching, and the sparkling bathroom smelling like lemon-scented Pine Sol, she walked out, carrying a broom and a bucket of cleaning supplies. Now to tackle the shop. The bathroom had been filthy by most peoples' standards, but it was easy compared to the work the rest of the garage would require.

Scott now had his head under the hood of a Dodge Charger.

She stepped to the opposite side of the car so she wouldn't startle him. "Do you mind if I turn on the old boom box on the workbench?"

He didn't hit his head this time, but he still startled. He gave his head a quick shake, whether in answer to her or to rid it of unpleasant thoughts about her she wasn't sure.

"Fine." The single word was rough, as though his tongue was made of sandpaper.

"Thank you," she said in a cheerful voice. She turned the dial on the radio to her favorite pop station.

"Just don't change—"

Music cut off Scott's words.

She turned it down. "I'm sorry, what did you say?"

His lips pressed together, and his eyes narrowed. Finally, he shook his head again and ducked back under the hood of the car.

Kennedy rolled her eyes and turned up the radio. The man could hardly even bear to look at her, let alone speak to her.

Well, if he wasn't going to make an effort, neither was she!

MUSCLES PULLED in Scott's back. He'd been bent over one engine or another for almost four hours now, and he needed a break, but he didn't feel like he could take one. Not until he got caught up, but without real help, he wasn't sure he'd ever get there.

At least the phone had been relatively quiet today and he hadn't had any new customers drive up.

"Hellooo?" Charity Knight's chipper voice filled the garage.

Scott stood upright, wincing at the pinch in his back. He'd been neglecting his core exercises too often lately, and his back was feeling it.

"Hey," Scott greeted the owner of the repair shop as Kennedy walked out of the office.

"Oh, you must be Kennedy MacGregor." Charity turned a smile on Kennedy. "It's so nice to meet you."

Of course, Ben told Charity the new hire's full name but couldn't be bothered to tell Scott that he'd hired a woman.

While Kennedy and Charity exchanged greetings, Scott pulled a water bottle from the small fridge and chugged it.

"I'm glad Scott finally has some help." Charity winked at Kennedy. "Maybe now he'll spend less time in this shop and more time out finding himself a woman."

What?

Water spewed from Scott's mouth toward the two women before he managed to suck in a sharp breath. First Ben and now Charity.

Scott had no idea so many people were concerned about his love life. Or lack of one. As if his parents weren't bad enough.

Kennedy and Charity jumped away with a shriek, but their pant legs and shoes still ended up speckled with dark spots. They turned shocked faces to him.

He backed up a step and held out a hand toward them as his face flamed. "I'm sorr—" The remainder of the water in his mouth slid down his bronchial tubes, and he turned to the side fighting the urge to cough. The noise that came out sounded like a snort of laughter.

Great. Now they think I'm laughing at them when really, I'm dying.

Charity stared at him with an arched eyebrow as he gave into a fit of coughing. Kennedy looked at her pant legs and boots then scowled at him like he was some sort of freak of nature.

For all he knew, he was. Judging by the heat in his cheeks, his face must be beet red, and he feared his eyes might be bugging out by how hard he coughed to rid his lungs of a few measly drops of water. Seriously, he couldn't have sucked in more than a few drops because a lot of wet spots covered Kennedy's legs below the knees.

He gave another small cough. "I'm terribly sorry, ladies."

Charity laughed. "Serves me right, I guess. That's what I get for teasing you." She handed the bag she'd brought with her to Kennedy. "I'm sorry you got the brunt of it, dear. Maybe this will make up for it. I'd better get back to the diner. Enjoy your lunch."

Charity gave a short wave and exited the garage.

Kennedy still stared, dumbstruck.

"Charity, wait." The last thing Scott wanted was to sit down at the tiny table in the corner of the office and eat lunch with the woman he'd just spit water all over.

Charity stopped just outside the garage and looked at him expectantly.

For the past week, Scott had been meaning to talk to her about buying the repair shop. But he'd been so busy that she'd already left the diner each evening by the time he quit work, and he hadn't felt right about bothering her at home. Because for all her spouting that he worked too hard, she worked just as hard, starting long before the sun came up.

"Did you need something, Scott?"

"Yeah, uh, sorry…again about the water." His lungs continued to tickle as his chest tightened.

I can't do it.

He couldn't come right out and ask her right after spitting water in her face.

He tugged at his collar. "I uh… Can I schedule a time to meet with you to discuss…some uh…business?"

A time when I feel less like an idiot.

She grabbed his arm. "You're not quitting on me, are you?"

"No. No, nothing like that."

She leaned closer and lowered her voice. "It's not Kennedy, is it?"

Scott's body turned warm as he thought about the pretty blond who had spent the last few hours dancing around the garage with a broom and a mop. The woman knew how to move her hips. That's part of the reason why his back hurt so bad; he'd kept his head down in order to keep from ogling her.

Now more than ever, he believed Kennedy didn't belong in the garage. But he wouldn't complain to Charity, or Ben for that matter, about her. It would only make him look whiny and sexist.

"No."

"Good. I know working with a female mechanic will take some getting used to, but Ben assured me Kennedy was well qualified."

He'd essentially told Scott the same thing. Not only when he hired Kennedy, but also when he responded to Scott's text this morning, saying: **Give Kennedy a chance. She knows her stuff.**

Scott didn't want to give her a chance because he wasn't sure he could stand to work with someone who was so distracting again.

Charity patted his arm. "Stop by the diner any afternoon around two, after the lunchtime rush, and we can talk."

Scott nodded as Charity walked away. He'd have to keep an eye on the clock because he was usually elbow deep in his work at two. He turned and walked into the garage.

Kennedy had set the bag Charity brought on the workbench and untied the top. "Does Charity always bring lunch over?"

The scent of Charity's potato salad and something with bacon wafted out of the bag, subtly overpowering the odor of grease, oil, and lemon cleaner.

"She usually sends one of the waitresses." Scott peeled off his latex gloves. "Guess she wanted to meet you today."

"But she always feeds the mechanics lunch?" Kennedy's eyebrows arched.

"Started a couple of weeks ago, when she realized I was working late and not taking a lunch break."

Kennedy gave a little nod. "So, will this perk stop once I help you get caught up and you're no longer having to work late?"

He shrugged. "Dunno."

Could she really help him get caught up? Ben said give her a chance, but he couldn't let go of his belief that auto repair work was too dangerous for women. Sure, it wasn't the same as cutting down trees, but he couldn't count the number of times he'd pinched, scraped, and cut himself over the past seven years.

As Kennedy carried the food into the office, he went to the bathroom to wash his hands. He stepped through the door and came to an abrupt stop.

Wow!

He'd never seen this bathroom so clean or smell this good, although the lemon scent was a little overpowering. He'd noticed the smell of the cleaner grow stronger as Kennedy moved around the garage, and guilt had eaten at him. No matter how much she scrubbed, she'd never be able to get the shop truly clean. It was a repair shop, after all. Oil and grease stains didn't come out.

He didn't expect her to clean away decades of grime, but she'd done an amazing job here in the bathroom. He scrubbed his hands, then returned to the office and slipped into the seat across the small table from Kennedy. Warmth filled his face again as he took in the wet spots that still dotted her jeans.

"Sorry about the water…earlier."

Kennedy smiled and shrugged. "I can think of worse things to have spit on me."

Unsure how to respond to that, he stayed quiet. He considered thanking her for cleaning the bathroom and the shop, but he wasn't very good with words. Kennedy no doubt already had a low opinion of him. He didn't need to make it worse with a poorly phrased compliment, especially when cleaning wasn't the kind of work she wanted to do. Instead of speaking, he simply dug into his turkey bacon club sandwich, figuring the sooner he finished, the quicker he could get away from her and back to work.

"So…" Kennedy said after a full minute of silence. "I take it you're not married?"

"Nope." Scott kept his gaze on the other half of his sandwich.

"And since Charity is so concerned about you finding a woman, I assume you're not dating anyone?"

Was Kennedy just trying to make conversation? Or was she actually interested in his relationship status? This was not a topic he'd ever broach with a new acquaintance. Of course, he usually didn't bother to start conversations with people period.

He shook his head. "You?"

Scott wasn't sure why, but he really wanted to know if she was single. Not that it mattered. He wouldn't get involved with another coworker, no matter how pretty she was.

She gave a tight smile. "Newly single after a six-year relationship."

What was he supposed to say to that?

I'm sorry? Congratulations?

Whoever let her go after stringing her along for six years was an idiot.

"Is that why you moved to Providence?"

Her gaze dropped to the food she'd hardly touched. "That and other reasons."

Though he was curious about what happened with her long-term relationship and what other reasons made her uproot her life, he held his tongue. Her tense posture and distant expression said she didn't want to talk about it. Judging by the way she twisted one of her small pearl earrings, she'd lost more than a boyfriend recently.

He should probably express condolences or something, but without knowing more about what she'd been through that would sound stupid, maybe even offensive. He tried listening like Rudy said, but he never knew what to say to people, especially women. The one thing he had no problem talking about was cars.

Kennedy lifted her chin and smiled, but it didn't reach her eyes. "So, how long have you worked at Knight's Repair Shop?"

"A total of nine years." He took another bite of his club sandwich.

"A total of?" Her eyebrows rose. "Did you work somewhere else in the middle of those nine years?"

Scott swallowed, but the food stuck in his throat. He didn't talk about the three years he worked away from the garage. In fact, he tried not to even think about them, because every time he did, the grief and guilt crept back in, consuming him.

He lifted his water bottle to his mouth to dislodge the food stuck in his throat.

Kennedy gave a dramatic flinch as though bracing for another shower.

He forced the water down before chuckling. "I'll never live that down, will I?"

She laughed. This time, her smile met her eyes. "It takes time to rebuild trust when it's been lost."

"Fair enough." He gave a tight laugh before answering her question. "I started here when I was sixteen, but I worked with the Forest Service for three years after high school."

"Ooh, that sounds fun. I considered doing that years ago."

Scott shook his head. The blasted bobble head was back, but he couldn't seem to stop his head from jerking back and forth. He felt too strongly about women working in dangerous jobs and working for the Forest Service certainly qualified as dangerous.

"What? Why are you shaking your head?" A glint of challenge sparked in Kennedy's eyes.

Any other time, he might find it attractive, but not when it came to talking about something that had nearly destroyed him. "The Forest Service isn't a good place for women, unless it's on the recreation crew."

Kennedy's eyes widened, and her mouth dropped open. She leaned forward in her chair. "You think the only thing a woman is good for is scrubbing toilets and cleaning fire pits?"

"I didn't say that." Scott squared his own shoulders, but his gaze rested on the table. "But the Forest Service has too many dangerous jobs that aren't appropriate for women. Just like here."

Kennedy's eyebrows arched, and her lips turned down. "No wonder you're still single."

CHAPTER 5

"*H*e's so chauvinistic, he makes Nate and his dad look like women's lib advocates," Kennedy said to her phone as she dumped frozen veggies into her chicken stir fry. Normally, she took time to cut up fresh veggies, but she was too hungry tonight.

She'd thrown away her lunch after only taking a few bites because she couldn't stomach eating across from Scott after he'd made such a rude, degrading comment about women. She was usually quick to admit that there were plenty of things men did better than women, just like the opposite was true, but when a guy had the kind of attitude Scott did, it just rubbed her wrong. It only made it harder to have to ask for help on those occasions when she wasn't strong enough to do what a man could with ease.

"Seriously?" Eden scowled at her from her phone screen. "I didn't think they got any worse than Nate."

"I didn't either. Until today." Kennedy couldn't wait to escape the garage this afternoon and talk to her best friend.

As it was, Scott was still there when she left, working on his fourth car of the day. She'd repeatedly offered to help with the repairs, but even after the garage was as clean as it was ever going to get, he'd insisted she straighten up and organize the office.

So, she'd spent the afternoon trying to figure out the filing system. At first, she'd thought it was alphabetical by customer name, but then parts of it were filed by dates. In the end, she'd emptied the drawers, creating stacks of files all over the small office. After getting the okay from Scott to weed out files that were more than three years old, she'd reorganized the rest. Tomorrow, if Scott refused to let her work on cars again, she'd start making sure everything was digitized and further clean out the filing cabinet.

"So, he didn't let you touch a car at all?"

Kennedy rolled her eyes. "Not one. He said I was a liability—a hazard to myself and to him—and he relegated me to cleaning the shop."

Eden looked up from painting her nails. "Cleaning? As in dusting and sweeping?"

Kennedy gave a dramatic head bob. "Oh, I cleaned that shop. I ruined the broom and mop in the process." She rubbed her aching back. It had been a long time since she'd mopped such a large area. She couldn't wait to sink into a hot bath after dinner.

"You mopped the floor of the repair shop?" Eden laughed.

"I would have pressure washed it like we always did at T&J's. But I couldn't find a pressure washer anywhere."

"And this Scott guy is the only other employee that you work with?"

"Well, there are cashiers that work in the gas station and mini mart, but I don't think they associate much with the mechanics. Scott's not exactly the type to sit around and shoot the breeze. The actual owner, Charity Knight, is super nice though. She brought lunch over from the diner that she owns across the street." She didn't bother telling Eden she hadn't eaten much of it. Instead, she told her friend how Scott spit water at her and Charity when the older woman teased him about finding himself a woman.

"Wait. He's single? How old is he?" Eden gave the phone her undivided attention.

Kennedy stirred the vegetables and chicken in the frying pan one last time before turning off the burner. "He started working at the garage when he was sixteen and he's been there a total of nine years, but he worked with the Forest Service for three years after he graduated from high school. So, that would make him..."

"Twenty-eight. You didn't tell me he was only a few years older than us."

"What does it matter? In my mind, that makes his chauvinism that much worse. I mean shouldn't our generation be more accepting, instead of stuck in the Dark Ages?"

Scott reminded her of a lumberjack the first moment she saw him, so Kennedy had almost laughed out loud when he'd said he used to work for the Forest Service. That is, until more sexist comments came pouring out of his mouth.

Eden nodded. "True but is he attractive? I'm guessing not, since he's twenty-eight and still single."

Kennedy didn't want to get into exactly how good-looking Scott was, because her irritation with the man was already at its peak.

"He's single alright, and I know exactly why. He basically thinks the only thing women are good for are scrubbing toilets and cleaning."

"What a jerk!" Eden sighed. "I bet Coop would let you have your old job back, if you wanted to move back to Spokane. It would save me from having to find a roommate."

They both knew Eden didn't need to find a roommate to help pay the rent. She made good money working for her father.

"And have to work every day with Nate?" Kennedy rolled her eyes as she scooped her dinner onto a plate. "No thanks. I'll take my chances with this male chauvinist over that cheating jerk." Bitterness filled Kennedy's voice, but after the day she'd had, she didn't care.

"Cheating? What do you mean?" When Kennedy looked away from the phone, Eden went on. "Kennedy, what are you not telling me?"

Kennedy sighed. She hadn't meant to let that slip, but she was just so fed up with the male race today, she needed to vent. As she waited for her food to cool, she told Eden about walking in on Nate and Olivia in the parts room last week.

"I'm so sorry, Ken. I always knew Nate was a jerk."

"I know. I guess I'm just lucky to be able to make a clean break. This job may suck, but at least my coworkers—correction, coworker —doesn't look at me with pity because he knows the boss's son dumped me, and that I've lost everything I've worked my whole life for."

"How do you do that?" Eden stared into the phone meeting Kennedy's eyes.

"Do what?"

"Always find a silver lining. You've had a really crappy day, you've been mistreated, and discriminated against, yet you find a reason to decide you're better off there than you were here."

Kennedy sighed again. "Honestly? Since my dad died, and Nate dropped that bomb on me, it's been really hard to find the silver linings."

"I know, but you're better at it than anyone I know. And I'm confident you'll win Scott over. He just needs time to see what an awesome person and mechanic you are."

Just be yourself. Her dad's words echoed in her head again.

"You know what? That's exactly what I'm going to do. I'm going to win him over." Kennedy grimaced. "Let's just hope my big mouth doesn't get me fired before I achieve my goal."

FORTY-EIGHT...FORTY-NINE...FIFTY.

Scott dropped to the floor and sucked in deep breaths of air. That was his second set of push-ups and his arms now felt like jelly.

"Ah, there you are." Rudy's voice filled the basement room they'd converted into their personal gym.

It wasn't much of a gym with only a treadmill, a Bowflex machine, and a set of barbells, but he and Rudy had spent countless hours here working out together over the last ten years. Sometimes the weights provided the therapy and other times the conversation with one another did what the strenuous exercise couldn't.

It was part of the reason Scott and Rudy still lived with their parents, besides the fact that there was a shortage of apartments around Providence, and they were both saving for a down payment on a house—or in Scott's case, his own shop. Deep down, he didn't want to move out, and he figured Rudy didn't either.

"Judging by the sweat soaking your shirt, you either had a rough day at work or a very light day and needed to burn some excess energy." Rudy pulled off his uniform shirt and loosened the Velcro straps on his bullet-proof vest.

Scott rolled onto his back and grunted.

"Rough day. Got it." Rudy nodded. "What happened? I thought the new mechanic was supposed to start today."

"The new...hire started today alright." Scott couldn't think of the pretty blond who'd danced around the shop with a mop as a mechanic. "That's the last time I trust Ben to hire a mechanic."

"What do you mean? What's wrong with the new guy?"

Scott rolled his head side to side on the mat.

Blast it!

He couldn't seem to lose the stupid bobble head today.

"You mean besides the fact that Ken MacGregor's real name is Kennedy?" He tilted his head to the side and looked up at Rudy.

"Kennedy?" Rudy's furrowed brow lifted as understanding filled him. "Oh, ho-ho. Ben hired a female mechanic?" Rudy's laughter filled the small room. He doubled over for a moment before dropping onto the end of the bench press as his laughter continued.

Scott grunted as he pushed himself to a sitting position and propped his arms on his knees. "Are you done yet?"

Rudy gasped for air as he wiped tears from his eyes. "Sorry, I'm just picturing you working with a woman who could probably bench press you."

"Think again." Scott's voice was tight as he recalled Kennedy's big brown eyes, long blond hair, and curves.

No way could she bench press me.

But she sure did something to him. All day, he'd struggled to take a deep breath that wasn't filled with the scent of strawberries and vanilla. Until she'd filled the garage with the smell of lemon and pine, that is.

But her ponytail hanging out of the back of her baseball cap—man, he loved it when women wore their hair that way—swayed as much as her hips as she danced around the garage while she cleaned. And his breath had repeatedly hitched as attraction surged in him. It had been over seven years since he'd been this attracted to any woman.

Rudy sobered. "You mean she's not..." He looked at the opened door before lowering his voice. "An *unattractive* stocky tomboy?"

Mom would totally box Rudy's ears if she heard him say anything derogatory in reference to a woman's looks.

"Not even close."

His brother's grin grew as he leaned forward. "So, what does she look like?"

Scott chewed on his cheek for a moment, debating how to answer. If he came right out and told Rudy Kennedy looked like Barbie, he'd sound as sexist as Kennedy no doubt thought he was. But if he described Kennedy's pretty features and enticing curves, would his attraction for his coworker be evident?

He cast his own glance at the door before speaking. "Not unattractive and stocky, that's for sure."

"So, she's pretty?"

Gorgeous! Scott bit his tongue to keep from blurting out the word.

Rudy laughed again. "I'm going to take your silence as a yes. But come on, bro, give me an idea of what she looks like."

He gave a little laugh of his own, before propping his feet under the barbell he planned to bench press in a few minutes. He leaned back and started a set of sit-ups. There were better core exercises, but he couldn't talk through them. Doing sit-ups, he'd be able to continue to talk until he hit thirty or forty reps.

Scott honestly couldn't think of another woman that he and Rudy both knew to compare Kennedy to other than their sisters, but that felt weird.

"Tall, probably five ten, but with curves. Kind of an hourglass figure."

Rudy nodded. "So, she's shapely? What color hair does she have?"

"Blond. Long." Scott's breath came in little puffs. Okay, maybe he'd only make twenty reps while talking.

"Eyes?"

"Of course, she's got eyes." He knew that wasn't what Rudy was asking, but he couldn't resist.

"Very funny." Rudy laid a ten-pound weight against Scott's chest. "What color?"

"Brown." Scott wrapped his arms around the weight and continued with his sit-ups. "Big. Brown. Eyes."

Rudy unbuckled his gun belt. "So basically, the new mechanic is a curvy, brown-eyed Barbie. No wonder you're working out so hard. You must be feeling all kinds of sexual tension."

Scott dropped back so fast, his head hit the mat. "That's not—"

"Hold that thought. I'm going to change my clothes, so I can join you."

Rudy was out the door before Scott could finish his protest.

It's not sexual tension.

That only happened when there was attraction on both sides. Scott was pretty sure Kennedy thought he was the biggest jerk on the planet.

Rudy returned just as Scott wrapped up his sit-ups. "So, does Barbie actually know anything about cars?"

"Don't call her that." It was bad enough Scott couldn't help thinking of Kennedy as a Barbie, but having Rudy call her that rubbed him wrong.

"Why? It's not like I'd call her that to her face." Rudy started the belt on the treadmill and continued to jab the button until he was at a jog.

"It just feels…" Scott didn't know how to finish that sentence without giving away the turmoil raging inside him.

"Feels what? Sexist? Misogynistic? It is, but it irritates you, so I just can't help myself." Rudy punctuated his words with a laugh.

Scott scowled at Rudy. Half the time, he didn't even understand the big words his little brother used. The fact that he used them to annoy Scott irritated him even more. He grunted as he lifted the loaded barbell onto the bench press. He laid down under the bar. "Kennedy definitely thinks I'm a chauvinist."

Rudy stopped the treadmill. "Man, why do you always do your bench presses when I'm on the treadmill?" He walked over to spot for Scott.

"Why do you always get on the treadmill when you know I'm going to bench press?" Scott raised the barbell and brought it down to his chest.

"Why does Barbie—I mean *Kennedy*—think you're a chauvinist?" Rudy grinned as he emphasized her name.

Scott raised the barbell. "Probably because I made her clean the shop today." He lowered the bar again.

Rudy leaned over to make eye contact with him. "Why?"

Scott's stupid bobble head kicked into gear again, and he swore under his breath.

Rudy grabbed the barbell, yanked it up, and set it in the rack.

"Hey, what are you doing?" Scott asked.

"What do you mean what am I doing? I'm saving your life. Why were you struggling after only two reps?"

Scott scoffed. "I wasn't struggling. I just..." He bolted upright, full of tension and pent-up energy. How did he explain to Rudy something he didn't understand himself? "I just couldn't let her get under a car."

"Why? Doesn't she know her stuff when it comes to cars?"

"Ben said she does, but I was afraid she might get hurt."

Rudy walked around the bench and grabbed a nearby stool. He parked himself in front of Scott. "Stop it, you hear?" He leaned forward, getting right in Scott's face. "Stop. Right. Now."

"I can't be responsible for—"

Rudy punched Scott's shoulder, sending a jolt of pain through him. He sucked in a deep breath, welcoming the physical pain over the mental and emotional anguish he was spiraling into.

"Listen, the repair shop isn't the Forest Service."

"Doesn't matter. The garage can still be dangerous. Accidents happen all the time in repair shops."

"That's right, accidents." Rudy gave Scott's shoulder a shake. "It was an accident, remember. There's nothing you could have done."

Yes, there was.

He should have insisted on bringing the tree down himself when Hannah didn't cut her hinge properly. He shouldn't have let her continue with the back cut. He was the supervisor. It was his responsibility to keep his crew safe. And he'd failed.

"Yes, accidents can happen anywhere." Rudy's voice pulled him back to the basement of their parents' home. "But Kennedy shouldn't be deprived of doing her job just because you have a hang-up about letting women work in a situation that could potentially be dangerous."

Rudy was right. Scott knew that. So why had he been such a jerk to Kennedy today?

He wanted to blame it on the shock of having a female mechanic show up when he'd expected a man, but it was more than that.

It was the attraction.

Scott hadn't been this attracted to a woman in years, and the reaction was so strong it apparently sent massive amounts of testosterone to his brain, making him act like a caveman. If Ken Macgregor had been a stocky tomboy, like Rudy guessed, would he have reacted the same?

Just having a woman in the shop made him anxious. He didn't want anyone, especially a female mechanic, getting hurt because of something he asked her to do.

Rudy smacked Scott's shoulder. "You'd better put Barbie to work, or you'll lose her and be right back where you started."

"I suppose." Scott laid back down, and Rudy positioned himself back at the head of the bench again.

"So, how long are you going to wait to ask Barbie out?"

Scott's elbows sunk to his sides, pressing the full weight of the bar against his chest. He looked up to find Rudy grinning at him. Sucking in a deep breath, he pushed upward. The bar wavered as he lifted. He placed it back in the rack. Lifting so many pounds while he was distracted probably wasn't a good idea, but he'd loaded the weight on hoping to burn off some off his frustrations.

"I'm not going to ask her out. And don't call her that."

"Sorry." Rudy grinned again, looking anything but contrite. "Why aren't you planning on asking Kennedy out?"

"Because we work together. I don't need that kind of distraction at work."

"I doubt she'll be any less distracting just because you're not dating her." Rudy laughed. "But if you aren't interested, then you won't mind if I come by and introduce myself to the new mechanic and welcome her to town."

Scott absolutely did mind, but if he protested too loudly Rudy would know just how attracted he was to Kennedy, and then everyone in town would know, because Rudy couldn't keep his mouth shut for anything.

"Your paths will cross eventually. Why don't you just leave it at that?"

A mischievous glint filled Rudy's eyes. "I'm sure I can find a reason to come into the shop tomorrow."

Scott swore under his breath and grabbed the barbell again. Maybe a freak accident would happen here in his parents' basement. Then he wouldn't have to worry about facing Kennedy again. Nor would he have to worry about Rudy showing up at the garage and flirting with his very pretty coworker.

CHAPTER 6

"Good morning," Kennedy said as she greeted Scott with a smile the next day. "I figured I'd finish organizing the office, unless you have something else you'd like me to do."

She held her breath, hoping he'd say, "Sure, you can change out the starter on the Nissan." She'd gone through the paperwork for each of the cars waiting for repairs and knew that they were still waiting on parts for two of them, but parts for the others had arrived yesterday afternoon.

Scott grunted and shook his head.

Of course, as long as there was anything for Kennedy to do that could be considered women's work, he wouldn't let her get near a car. That's why when she finished organizing the office and updating the digital documents, she went straight to the oversized closet that served as the parts room and did a thorough cleaning and inventory of all the parts there. It was only an eighth of the size of the parts room at T&J's, so it didn't take long.

She'd just walked out of the oversized closet, intent on demanding Scott let her do something worthwhile when a tall buxom woman came through the door joining the repair shop to the gas station.

"Scott Wheeler, get out from under that car so I can give you a hug."

Kennedy froze with her back pressed to the wall. She wasn't sure what surprised her more. The fact that this older woman wanted to hug a man who was half her age or that Scott immediately obeyed.

He rolled the creeper out and got to his feet so fast, Kennedy almost got whiplash.

"Mary," Scott said in a gruff voice as he pulled the older woman into his arms. "How's Chase doing?"

Mary sniffled as she pressed her face to Scott's shoulder. "He's going to live. That's the important thing. But he's got a long road ahead of him."

Scott's biceps bulged as his arms tightened around the older woman. "He's strong. He'll figure it out."

Mary nodded as she pulled back and wiped her eyes. "I know he will, but I can tell he's struggling. Some days more than others." A fresh flood of tears filled her eyes. "I can't thank your family enough for building that handicap ramp into the house. He probably won't come home for a few more weeks, but I'm glad I don't have to worry about that."

"Debbie and Austin want to help with the addition of the handicap suite."

"Oh." Mary let out an exclamation before pressing a hand to her mouth. Her eyes were as round as hubcaps.

Scott grinned, and Kennedy's heart stalled.

Holy moly! The man was attractive!

"Meaning, they'll pay for the whole thing, obviously. With Austin and my dad in charge, I bet we get it built in no time."

Mary pulled Scott in for another hug.

He mumbled something to her that Kennedy couldn't hear, and Mary nodded.

The older woman brushed away more tears when she finally let Scott go. "I'm only here for a few hours today, but it looks like Sherry's managing the convenience store just fine. What about you? Do you need any help?"

Why would this older woman want to help in the repair shop?

Scott cleared his throat and looked at Kennedy for the first time since rolling out from under the car. "Kennedy, I'd like you to meet Mary, the manager of the convenience store and gas station. Mary, this is Kennedy. She's the new...hire. She's been helping out with the office work."

New hire? Really?

Yes, she was newly hired, but she was the new mechanic.

If Scott couldn't even refer to her as a mechanic, he'd never start thinking of her as one. Besides, as far as she was concerned, cleaning was a step down from office work.

Kennedy held out a hand to Mary. The only good thing about not doing any dirty work was not having to wipe her hands clean when meeting someone new. "What Scott meant to say was I'm the new *mechanic.*"

Mary's eyes widened. "Mechanic, huh?" She turned to Scott. "You hired her?"

"Ben did."

"Ah, that makes sense." Mary looked back and forth between Kennedy and Scott again then chuckled. She patted Scott's arm. "Good for you. That Ben is a smart man, you know."

A low rumbling sound came from Scott.

Mary sobered. "So, now that you've got Kennedy to help with the paperwork, you're good?" She gave Scott a pointed look that spoke volumes of something Kennedy couldn't interpret.

Why does Scott need help with the paperwork?

He angled his body away from Kennedy and scratched the back of his neck. "We'll figure it out."

Figure what out?

Hadn't Scott said that same thing about Mary's son who was apparently in a severe accident that left him disabled? What did Scott and Kennedy have to figure out, other than how to get him to trust her to work on cars?

"Good, now I won't have to worry about how you're getting by while I'm at the hospital with Chase."

Why would the manager of the convenience store worry about the manager of the repair shop *getting by*?

Scott lowered his voice, but Kennedy still heard his next words. "Don't worry about me. I'll bring in Rudy if I need to. Tell Chase 'Hi' for me."

Who's Rudy? And why would Scott need to bring him in?

Mary nodded and made her way back inside the convenience store.

Kennedy stared at Scott as he watched the other woman go. He had a soft spot a mile wide for Mary and her son. For some reason, she had a hard time equating that with the sexist lumberjack she'd worked with yesterday.

He shot her a quick glance before turning back to the car he'd been working on.

But Kennedy had too many questions tumbling around inside her head to let him go back to ignoring her. "What will we figure out?"

Scott's shoulders slumped, and he let out a heavy sigh before turning back to her. "I'd like you to take over...the paperwork." His words came out strained, as though he measured them carefully.

"Paperwork?" Kennedy folded her arms across her chest as she studied him. Either asking her to do the paperwork made him horribly uncomfortable, or he realized that asking her to do office work made him appear just as misogynistic as he did yesterday.

"Yeah, you know, order the parts, prepare the quotes and invoices?"

"I know what kind of paperwork we do in a garage." Kennedy fought to keep her voice level even though she seethed inside. "So, you're saying that not only do you want me to be your maid, you want me to be your secretary as well?"

Scott's face flushed. "No. Well, sort of." He scratched the back of his neck again.

"Only sort of? When do I get to do real work?"

"Hi, guys."

Kennedy and Scott both turned to find a tall, lean sheriff's deputy striding into the garage. Leaving his cruiser parked just outside the empty bay.

The deputy offered his hand to Kennedy. "You must be Kennedy MacGregor."

She pasted on a smile and grasped his hand. "That's me. And you are—"

"What are you doing here, Rudy?" Scott asked, his voice again making that deep rumbly sound.

Rudy? This is the guy Scott said he'd bring in if he needed to.

Kennedy studied the officer. He looked very familiar. In fact, he looked like a younger, leaner version of Scott.

Rudy laughed and held up his hands in a sign of surrender. "I know what you're thinking, bro, but I swear I didn't come in just to check out the new mechanic." He shot Kennedy a wink. "I brought my cruiser in for servicing."

"You know I'm swamped." Scott took a step toward Rudy, who retreated a step, but never lost this grin.

"According to the logs, it's a month overdue. I bet Bar— I mean Kennedy wouldn't mind changing my oil." Rudy shifted his gaze from Scott to her. He gave her another wink. "Would you?"

What had he almost called her before he correcting himself? Whatever it was, his slip seemed deliberate and set the muscle in Scott's jaw working as he took another step toward Rudy. His fists balled much the same way they had yesterday.

Kennedy didn't know what was going on between the brothers, but this was her opportunity to get Scott to give her a chance. Not that changing the oil and checking fluids was a great way to prove oneself, but at least it was better than cleaning and paperwork. She stifled a sigh. She'd had to start at the bottom at T&J's; she could do it again here.

She stepped between the two men. "I can service the deputy's cruiser, boss."

"Boss?" Rudy mimicked with a smirk and a laugh that sounded like a snort.

Scott advanced on his brother, sandwiching her in the middle.

Fearing they might come to blows, she put a hand on each man's chest and...

Holy moly!

Her hand met solid muscle behind each shirt. She suspected Rudy's was enhanced by a bullet proof vest under his uniform, but it was the firmness and curvature of Scott's pectoral muscles that short-circuited her brain. From the moment she first laid eyes on him yesterday, she knew he was built, but feeling his rock-hard chest through his shirt...

The muscle beneath her palm twitched, and she jerked her hand back as though she'd been burned. Her gaze jumped to Scott's.

A spark of something lit his hazel eyes. If she didn't know better, she'd guess it was desire, or at the very least interest.

How do you know what desire looks like, girl?

The voice in her head had a point. Apparently, despite being in a relationship for the past six years, Nate had never truly desired her, or even been particularly interested in her, for that matter. Her stomach sank as she realized she was probably a lot more attracted to Scott than he was to her.

Why am I even attracted to such a jerk anyway?

Kennedy had never felt so shallow in her life. Was that why she'd stayed with Nate for so many years? Because he was good looking, and she liked being seen on his arm?

She shook her head to clear it of the depressing thoughts. Folding her arms again, she faced Scott. "I'll make you a deal."

He folded his own arms and locked gazes with her. "What?"

"I'll do *all* of the paperwork and I'll keep the garage spotless, *if* you'll let me do the oil changes." She couldn't believe she was begging for the most menial task in the shop.

"Just the oil changes?"

"And the other easy, *safe* tasks." She fought the urge to roll her eyes as she added emphasis to the word safe. "You know, like spark plugs, batteries, flats and rotations." She forced herself to shut her mouth. If she pushed for too much, he might not agree to let her do anything.

He stared at her for a long moment with that muscle twitching in his jaw as his brow crept lower and lower. Rudy snickered beside him, and Scott shot daggers at his brother before saying, "Deal."

Kennedy grinned, but he held up a finger before she could even think about calling this a win.

"Let me know if you need help." Deep furrows formed between Scott's brows. "I don't want you hurting yourself."

"Oh, puhhlease." This time she did roll her eyes. She turned away before he could change his mind. "Deputy, get that car in here."

THE MOMENT KENNEDY rolled under the cruiser to remove the oil plug, Rudy sidled up to Scott and whispered, "She definitely looks like a Barbie."

Scott refused to talk about Kennedy with his brother when she was only a few feet away. So, he said. "Mary's here today."

That's all it took to get Rudy to go into the convenience store. It's a good thing too, because the last thing he needed was his brother catching him ogling his coworker.

Now that Kennedy bent over the engine of Rudy's cruiser to remove the oil filter, Scott had to look away. He'd never once admired a fellow mechanic's backside. Of course, he'd never worked with anyone with such an attractive backside before either.

Stop being such a creep.

He shifted his body, so it wasn't so easy to let his gaze drift in Kennedy's direction.

"Nuts!" Kennedy stamped her booted foot.

He raised his head. "What's wrong?" The words came out sharper than he'd intended.

He didn't have time to help her. Nor did he want to stand close to her again. He could still feel the warmth and pressure of her palm against his chest. She smelled like peaches and cream today, and it drove him crazy. It was a good thing Rudy had been close by, or he might have done something stupid like push Kennedy up against the Honda and kiss her.

"Nothing." She gave him a dazzling smile and turned to the workbench, returning a moment later with oil filter pliers.

Scott watched out of the corner of his eye as she fitted the pliers onto the oil filter. She'd shifted so her backside was no longer to him, thank goodness, but the sight of the lean muscle in her slender bicep straining did nothing to dampen his attraction to her. She *was* stronger than she looked.

"Peanut butter balls!" She stamped her foot again.

Scott straightened and looked at her. It was all he could do not to bust out laughing at her version of a swear word. Just one more reason he couldn't think of her as a real mechanic.

"Problems?"

She grinned again, her smile a little tighter—a little faker—this time. "Nope. No problems at all."

Scott gave up any pretense of trying to work and watched her grab the wrench, whose sole purpose was to remove stubborn oil filters.

She took another shot at the filter. The tip of her tongue peeked out of the corner of her mouth as she once again strained for all she was worth.

"Fudge nuggets!"

Scott burst out laughing as he walked over to her. "Peanut butter balls and fudge nuggets?"

"Oh, shut up. My mom taught me not to swear, okay?"

His mother had taught him to watch his mouth too, but that hadn't kept Scott from throwing out the occasional swear word now and then. Never around his mom, of course.

Pink colored Kennedy's cheeks, making her even more attractive. "I'm sure it gives you great pleasure to see me fail already."

He bit his tongue to squelch his laughter. "No, it doesn't."

"Well, what are you waiting for?" She propped her hands on her hips.

He wished she'd stop doing that. It only drew his attention to her curves just like every time she crossed her arms over her chest, it drew his gaze to her ample bust line. Propping her hands on her hips also caused her t-shirt to stretch tighter across her chest.

And here I am being a creep again.

He'd glanced at her shirt several times already this morning trying to make his mind decipher the words written there. The picture of an engine block helped him put all the pieces together. *I still play with blocks.*

The light blue t-shirt complimented her complexion, and Scott marveled that she could look so feminine despite wearing an oil-stained t-shirt. How did she make it look so good?

He'd been so stunned by the surge of attraction that shot through him this morning when he first saw her, he couldn't think of a single thing to say when she asked him if he had something he'd like her to do besides finish in the office. When his tongue stuck to the roof of his mouth and his pulse kicked into high gear, he'd totally forgotten his resolve to be nicer to her today.

He gave himself a mental shake. "What do you mean?"

"Aren't you going to help me? Obviously, I can't get the stupid oil filter off by myself."

She looked so blasted attractive admitting defeat; he couldn't resist a little teasing. He propped his hands on his own hips, mimicking her posture. "Are you going to actually *ask* me for help?"

Something flashed in her eyes.

Probably anger, since he doubted she found this situation as entertaining as he did.

Her grin this time looked like the Cheshire cat from *Alice in Wonderland*. Toothy, a little maniacal, and possibly dangerous. "Would you mind removing the oil filter for me, please, boss?"

"Why do you keep calling me that?"

She shrugged. "You're the manager here. That makes you my boss."

He couldn't tell if that was sarcasm in her voice or resentment. He really wasn't very good with people in general, and he was even worse with women.

He finally grunted and waved her aside. If he was going to help her, he couldn't do it with her standing so close. Her peaches and cream scent lingered in the air, making him crave his mom's peach pie. Most people probably wouldn't notice such a subtle smell amid the typical odors of oil and grease, but he was so accustomed to the smell of the garage that her delicate scent stood out as much as she did.

He wrapped his hand around the oil filter in a tight grip and twisted.

Nothing. The blasted thing didn't budge.

Her lips turned up in a smirk as he grabbed the oil filter pliers and twisted for all he was worth.

Still nothing.

Pretending he wasn't totally embarrassed, he casually slipped his other hand around the handle of the pliers. His biceps strained against the sleeves of his shirt, cutting off the circulation. Which hardly mattered because, judging by the pressure in the veins in his forehead, he'd probably have an aneurysm before he actually lost feeling in his arms.

He swore under his breath as he released the pliers.

"Problems?" Kennedy said in a syrupy sweet voice.

A small growl rumbled through his chest as he glared at her. Grabbing the oil filter wrench, he tried again. Just when he feared he'd have to admit defeat, the filter budged.

Yes!

He tightened his grip and pulled with renewed effort.

"Aha!" Kennedy patted his shoulder. "You did it!"

Scott let go of the wrench and sucked in a deep breath as he stepped back. Kennedy could take it from there.

"I can't believe how tight that was. I wonder who the hulk was who put that filter on."

Scott turned away before she could see the result of the heat rushing to his face.

"Do we have a contract to service all of the sheriff department's vehicles?" She grabbed his arm and pulled him back before he could answer. "Were you the last one to change the oil on the deputy's car?"

That twinkle was back in her eyes again, lighting up her whole face, and her hand felt like it might burn a hole into his arm.

He scratched his neck, subtly disengaging her hand.

She laughed as she turned back to the car. "Well, *you're* definitely as strong as you look."

Scott froze.

She thinks I look strong?

What else had she noticed about him? Could she tell he was attracted to her?

He tucked his head back under the hood of the Honda before she could see how she affected him.

Two hours later, he rolled out from under a Nissan Sentra and got to his feet as yet another male voice filled the garage.

"Hello?"

The open bay had been like a revolving door today. Less than an hour after Rudy left, Kyle, the youngest deputy on the force showed up with his car needing servicing. The kid had followed Kennedy around like a puppy dog and flirted with her until Scott told him he could wait inside the convenience store.

Then right after lunch, Mr. Wilson showed up, requesting an oil change. Even though the older man was surprised to see a female mechanic, he hadn't tried to flirt with Kennedy. Scott still planned to give Rudy a piece of his mind for spreading the word about the new mechanic at Knight's Repair Shop.

His shoulders hiked up as he realized who the latest customer was.

Travis Brooks. Providence's biggest womanizer.

The other man's eyes lit up when Kennedy stepped out of the office. "Well, hello there. I heard Knight's had a pretty new mechanic, but no one said how truly gorgeous you were." He stepped close to Kennedy and offered his hand. "I'm Travis Brooks."

Kennedy gave Travis a tight smile. "Kennedy Macgregor. How can we help you?"

"Oh, I can think of half a dozen ways you could help me, beautiful." His gaze roamed over Kennedy's figure.

Scott's fists balled, and he took a step toward the pair.

"Perhaps I should rephrase that." Kennedy's smile faded, and her words came out strained. "How can we help you with your *car*?"

Travis gave a flirtatious smile that Scott was sure had won many women over. Hopefully, Kennedy was smart enough to see through his smarmy charm.

"My truck," he motioned outside the bay door to a black F350, "needs an oil change."

Kennedy shifted toward the open bay before responding. "Well, bring it in then."

Scott stepped between the two of them and glared at Travis. "Or I can sell you the oil filter and you can change it yourself, like you usually do."

Travis laughed. "Being territorial, I see." His gaze followed Kennedy as she walked to the supply closet. "Can't say that I blame you, Wheeler."

Scott repressed the growl that wanted to escape. "Get your truck in here."

The sooner they finished with Travis's truck, the sooner he could be on his way.

When it looked like Travis intended to stand around and watch Kennedy work, Scott got right in his face, blocking his view of Kennedy. "You can wait inside, just like everyone else."

"Thanks, but I'd like to make sure she gets the filter on nice and tight, you know."

Scott squared his shoulders and folded his arms. "That wasn't a request." He was half a head taller than Travis and had at least twenty pounds on the other man. "If you don't trust my mechanic to change your oil, you're welcome to buy a filter and do it yourself."

My mechanic? When did I start thinking of Kennedy as a mechanic? And she's definitely not mine.

Travis glared at him for a long moment before finally stepping toward the door that led into the convenience store. "Fine." He held up a finger. "But make sure she puts in the right kind of oil and gets the filter on tight, you hear."

"I will personally tighten the filter."

Hulk-style.

Scott walked up to Brooks's truck as Kennedy rolled out from underneath. He located the filter and fitted the wrench around it.

"Hey, what are you doing? Oil changes are supposed to be my job, remember?"

"I know. But there's no way you're getting off a filter Travis put on himself."

Kennedy scoffed and rolled her eyes. "Are you going to step in every time you think I can't handle my job?"

Blast.

He'd done it again. Except this time, he wasn't trying to protect her from hurting herself, he wanted to protect her from Travis Brooks and his womanizing ways.

"No. I just want Brooks's truck finished and him gone."

"Do I detect some bad blood between you two?"

It was Scott's turn to scoff. "The only bad blood here is the blood that runs in that man's veins."

She put a hand on his arm, sending an electric shock through him. "Don't worry about me. I know how to handle guys like Travis."

Scott stepped away from her. While he didn't doubt that Kennedy had put up with plenty of unwanted attention at her last job, he wasn't sure she was savvy enough to fend off Brooks for long. The man could be relentless.

"I doubt that. Brooks isn't the kind of guy who takes 'no' for an answer."

Scott's blood simmered as he thought about how Travis had hit on first Joy, then Sheila in high school. He recalled hearing Sheila crying to their parents one night that Travis had tried to force himself on her. Fortunately, she'd managed to get away from him. They had called the police, but nothing ever came of it.

After Scott loosened the oil filter, he returned to the Nissan. "Let me know when you're ready for me to tighten the filter."

Kennedy planted her hands on her hips. "I may not be freakishly strong like you, but I know how to tighten an oil filter." Irritation tinged her voice.

"I didn't say you didn't. But I promised Brooks I'd personally ensure his oil filter was tight."

"Fine." She turned back to the truck with a huff, and Scott bit back a grin.

She was kind of sexy when she was annoyed. Okay, she was sexy all the time, but he loved it when she had that spark of defiance in her eyes.

Stop it. She's your coworker. You can't go there again.

After Scott ensured the oil filter was tight, he waited for Kennedy to inform Travis his truck was finished and take his payment before he returned to the Nissan.

As expected, Travis asked Kennedy out. "How about I thank you over dinner tonight?"

Kennedy gave a short laugh. "Do you always thank your mechanics with dinner?"

Travis smiled. "Only the pretty ones."

"Well, Mr. Brooks, I'm flattered, but I don't date clients."

Scott watched out of the corner of his eye as Travis stepped a little closer to Kennedy. "In that case, consider this my last oil change. I won't bring my truck in for servicing ever again."

She stepped away from him as she spoke. "That's too bad. We have a lot of services to offer here at Knights. But I also don't date playboys." She held up a finger when he opened his mouth. "And I can tell you're as big of a playboy as they come. Now, if you'll excuse me, I have work to do." She turned and walked into the office and closed the door behind her.

Travis looked like he might try to follow her, but Scott stepped between him and the office. "You heard her, Brooks."

Travis's fists balled as he glared at Scott again. He smirked. "Keeping her all to yourself, huh?"

It was all Scott could do to not punch Travis's smirking mouth. "It's time for you to leave."

"First, you take my job, then you go all territorial with the sexy new mechanic. Don't worry, Wheeler, there'll be plenty of opportunities for me to get to know her outside the garage." Brooks stalked to his truck and climbed in. With a roar of the engine and a squeal of rubber on asphalt he was gone.

Before Scott could return to the Nissan, the office door opened a crack, and Kennedy poked her head out. "Is he gone?"

"Yes."

"What was that he said about you taking his job? I thought you said there wasn't bad blood between you."

"There isn't on my part, other than he's a jack—" Scott bit off the cuss word. "He's a jerk. My late boss, Rich Knight, fired him for repeatedly showing up to work drunk and stealing money for booze, then he hired me back after I left the Forest Service."

Scott's stomach hardened as he recalled the way Rich had stormed into his bedroom six weeks after Hannah's accident and dragged him out of bed. "Life's too short to live it wallowing in grief. There are too many people who need your help, and I'm one of them."

It had been the hardest thing Scott had ever done, but he'd gotten up that day and every day after that because Rich had needed him. Eventually, he'd moved on and he'd healed. Mostly.

"So, he's holding a grudge because the boss hired you instead of taking him back?"

"Something like that." Scott turned back to the Nissan.

Kennedy moved with him. "Hey, uh, do you want some help with that catalytic converter? I have small hands. I can get down in tight spots." When Scott didn't respond, she kept talking. "I finished cataloging the parts that arrived earlier, and the paperwork is done for now." She waved her arms. "And the shop is still clean." She gave him such a hopeful look he was tempted to give her anything she wanted.

He could use an extra pair of hands, but he didn't relish working so close to her. His stomach tightened, and he swallowed down the anxiety that spiked in him at the thought of letting her get under a car to do anything more than remove an oil drain plug.

"Fine." He stepped to the radio on the workbench and set the dial to his favorite country music station. He needed all the distraction he could get if he was going to be working close to Kennedy.

CHAPTER 7

Scott straightened and pressed his hands into the small of his back. He rubbed at the tight muscles there for a moment before closing the hood of the Ford Taurus. He and Kennedy had just finished repairing a leak in the radiator.

He caught the water bottle Kennedy tossed to him and unscrewed the cap. She stepped back as he raised it to his mouth. He chuckled and shook his head before taking a long swig. "Ah, that tastes good." He looked around the shop. "And this feels good."

"What feels good?" She gave him a cheeky grin, flashing her dimples. "Working with me?"

Other than the constant tension that sat coiled somewhere between his midsection and his chest, it did feel good working with Kennedy. He couldn't take a deep breath without getting the scent of something fruity and delicious, but he enjoyed having another set of hands helping around the shop.

He returned her grin. "Feels good to almost be caught up." They'd be busy again once the backordered parts arrived for the three cars still out in the lot. "It's been a month since the lot has been this empty." And surprisingly it had only taken three days with Kennedy's help to get to this point.

"You would have been caught up sooner if you'd let me help with that air conditioning system this morning."

"You were busy changing the oil on those three cars that came in."

They'd had one more customer, an older woman, bring her car in yesterday afternoon for an oil change, and then three additional cars this morning. Scott was certain he had Rudy to blame—or thank, in Kennedy's case. His brother had forced him to put Kennedy to work, because Scott could barely keep up as it was. He didn't have time to do mundane things like oil changes.

"Yes, but those were a piece of cake compared to a whole AC system. I'm just glad you finally came to your senses and let me help with this." She nodded to the Taurus.

The screech of tires and the honk of a horn drew Scott's attention. He looked up to see a truck slam on its breaks to avoid hitting a car that pulled out of Charity's Diner. As the cars went their way, his gaze shifted to the corner of the parking lot. Charity's car was still there. He turned and looked at the clock above the workbench.

The lunchtime rush was long over, and Charity would be leaving soon. This was his chance to talk to her.

He turned to Kennedy. "Can you hold down the fort for a few minutes?"

"Sure." The pitch of Kennedy's voice reflected her surprise. "It's not like we have any work at the moment."

"Call Mrs. Martinez and let her know her car is ready." He headed to the bathroom to wash up. "If she comes to pick it up before I get back only charge her half of the usual labor fee."

"Why?"

Scott stopped and turned back. "Because she's an older lady with a fixed income."

"Ah, the Granny Discount. Got it." Kennedy smiled. "Is that why we repaired the leak instead of replacing the radiator like we should have?"

"Yep."

Scott stepped into the bathroom, intending to wash his hands but then he took one look in the mirror at his grimy clothes and decided to change to a clean uniform even though the day was almost over.

Judging by her arched eyebrows, as he walked out of the bathroom, Kennedy noticed his change in clothing, but he kept on walking.

The diner was relatively quiet when he entered, and he caught Charity's eye right away. Within minutes, he found himself seated at a table across from her with a glass of water and a slice of peach pie in front of him.

"How's work at the shop going?" Charity asked before Scott could find the words he wanted to say. "The lot's not nearly as crowded as it used to be."

"Good. We're caught up, for now."

"And Kennedy's working out okay?"

Kennedy drove him crazy on a daily basis. If it wasn't the way she smelled different, yet amazing, every day, it was the way she danced around the garage. She'd been the first to turn on the radio this morning, and she'd set it back to her favorite pop station, turning to him with a challenge in her eyes after she did so.

Scott let it go, mostly because he had a feeling Kennedy enjoyed riling him, and he didn't want to give her the satisfaction of letting her know she drove him crazy.

"Kennedy's...fine."

She was more than fine, but he wouldn't admit that to Charity, or anyone else for that matter. He bit back a grin as he thought about the t-shirt she wore today. It said, *I'm here because you broke something.* Tools surrounded the words. If he thought she looked amazing in blue yesterday, it was only because he hadn't seen her in red yet.

Kennedy would probably be delighted if she knew the stress she caused him with her t-shirts that were always covered with words. He'd made it his goal each day to figure out what her t-shirt said without appearing to stare at her chest. Today, it took him almost until noon.

"Good, so what's up?"

Scott pulled his mind away from Kennedy and rubbed his palms against his thighs. Good thing he'd put on clean pants. "I…uh…"

"Scott Wheeler, you'd better spit it out. You've had me on pins and needles for the past three days. You said you're not planning on quitting, and this isn't about Kennedy, so I can't fathom a single other reason you'd want to speak to me privately. Especially since you haven't done so once in the three years you've been managing the garage."

"I know. I just…" He drew in a deep breath. "I heard you're planning on selling the diner to Amy, and I wondered…if you'd consider selling the repair shop to me?" He was out of air by the time he got the words out. He couldn't help holding his breath as he waited for Charity's response.

Her eyebrows rose, and her mouth dropped open as she sat back in her seat. "You want to buy the garage?"

"I've been saving for a long time to buy my own place, but I thought I'd see if you were interested in selling first."

"So, if I don't sell the shop to you, I might lose you?"

"Well, not right away." If she wasn't interested in selling, he'd have to look for a place to build and that could take a while.

Charity's eyes grew misty as she looked out the window at the repair shop. "I remember the day Rich surprised me with this diner. Damon, our youngest, had just started school, and I felt at a loss while the boys were at school. Rich knew I'd always dreamed of owning my own restaurant."

She smiled as she looked back at Scott. "He told me he'd sold this piece of land to some developer from out of town. I was so envious when it became obvious they were building a restaurant here. One day, he asked me to bring his lunch to the shop, instead of coming home, like he usually did. They'd just finished installing the sign when I showed up." She pressed a hand to her chest. "I was both livid with him for deceiving me and thrilled at the same time. He'd built it exactly as I wanted it."

"I loved working across the street from him for so many years." Her voice grew husky as she continued. "I'd be lying if I said it hasn't been a challenge these past four years without him." She dabbed at her eyes with a napkin.

"I'm sure it has," Scott said. He too had struggled to go to work each day after his boss, who'd been a downright good guy, passed away from a sudden heart attack.

"But I'm no spring chicken anymore. It's time to let the younger generation take over." She met his gaze. "I'll talk to my sons and see if they're interested in letting the garage go, since it's part of the family holdings along with the diner and the grocery store."

The air whooshed from Scott's lungs as his heart accelerated.

Yes!

He smiled at Charity. "Thank you!"

"If they agree, we'll discuss a price, and I'll let you know."

Scott barely had time to nod before Charity was summoned to the kitchen. He grinned so big while he ate his pie, he probably looked psychotic. He was in such a good mood that he took a piece of pie back to the garage for Kennedy.

When he returned to the shop, he found Kennedy in a standoff with Wes Miller. She stood with hands on her hips, her chin jutted out, and a flash of anger in her eyes.

"What's going on here?" He set Kennedy's pie on the workbench and stepped between the two who looked like they were about to come to blows.

"I'm glad you're back." Wes stopped towering over Kennedy and turned to Scott. "I brought my truck in to have my brakes replaced and this young lady is saying that I need new rotors *and* wheel bearings. She wants to charge me twelve hundred dollars to get my brakes replaced."

Kennedy handed Scott the service quote. Heat filled his face as he tried to focus on the words written there. He scanned the page, spotting the words brakes, rotors, and bearings, but there were a lot of other words there too, and they all started floating around.

He turned to Kennedy. "You sure about this? This seems excessive if he's only having problems with his brakes."

She folded her arms and cocked her head to the side. "Did you read the part about the groove in the rotors and the grating in the bearings?"

Scott tensed. No, he hadn't read all of that and he wasn't about to in front of Kennedy and Wes Miller. Wes was a stubborn man and often critical, finding fault with everyone and everything. Scott didn't need either of them staring at him while he struggled to read Kennedy's diagnosis of Wes's truck.

There was only one way to save face here. Unfortunately, he'd offend Kennedy in the process. He turned to Wes. "Why don't you wait inside while I check your brakes myself?"

Kennedy's eyes widened and her mouth dropped open for a split second before she snapped it closed. She pressed her lips into a thin line and balled her fists at her side as she raised her chin.

"Be my guest." She turned and walked into the office, slamming the door behind her.

Wes shook his head. "What possessed you to hire a woman?"

"I didn't hire her." The words were out before Scott realized how negative they sounded.

"So what? Charity decided to punish you? My condolences, man. I've worked with enough women to know they can be downright impossible to work with, especially when they're hormonal."

Scott didn't figure Wes—with his constant criticism and negative attitude—was all that pleasant to work with either. There was a reason the man was forty-five and twice divorced.

He nodded toward the door to the convenience store. "Have a seat inside."

Since the front tires were still off the truck, it didn't take Scott long to see that not only were the brake pads worn clean to the metal, they'd dug a groove into the rotors. He took more time to read through Kennedy's diagnosis than he did to inspect the brakes. When he came to the part about the bad bearings, he put the tire back on and did a few simple tests; feeling the wobble and hearing the grating, humming noise Kennedy had no doubt heard.

Sure enough, Wes needed new bearings as well as brakes and rotors.

Squaring his shoulders, he walked into the store and sat opposite Wes. "How long have you been having trouble with your brakes?"

Wes gave a sheepish shrug. "I don't know. A little while, I guess."

"Judging by the damage to your rotors it's been longer than a little while." Scott held the paper out to Wes. "Kennedy's spot on. How much longer would you have waited to bring your truck in if your bearings hadn't started to grind. That's what they were doing, right? Making a loud grating noise?"

Wes lowered his gaze as he gave another sheepish nod. Then his gaze must have focused on the paper he held, because he cursed. "I can't afford this kind of work on a truck that's nearly twenty years old."

It was no secret that Wes Miller was a penny pincher, but Scott supposed paying alimony to two ex-wives made unexpected expenses a challenge.

Scott sat back in his seat and folded his arms. "Can you afford a new truck or a lawsuit when you cause an accident?"

"No."

Scott had seen this kind of thing again and again. People ignored the little problems until they became big problems, then they got upset when it cost so much to fix what they broke.

I'm here because you broke something. He grinned as he thought about how appropriate Kennedy's shirt was today. People like Wes gave him and Kennedy job security.

"I'm sure my office manager can help you work out a payment plan."

"You mean that woman?" Wes hooked a thumb over his shoulder toward the shop.

"Yep." Scott didn't even try to hide his grin.

"No thanks." Wes hastily folded the statement and shoved it in his pocket before pulling out his phone. "How long will it take to fix my truck?"

"Part should arrive tomorrow morning, so by late afternoon."

"Let me know the minute it's finished." Wes shook his head in disgust as he jabbed at his phone before walking away.

Scott walked back out to the garage. Now for the really unpleasant task. Apologizing to Kennedy. Apologies in general were hard enough but having to do it to someone who made him as nervous as Kennedy did him was even harder.

He rapped on the office door before opening it.

Kennedy sat at the computer, a furrow between her brows. She barely gave him a glance before turning back to her screen.

He cleared his throat. "I'm sorry. I know making my own diagnosis of Wes's truck made it look like I wasn't confident in your skills as a mechanic."

She turned away from the computer. "Yet you did it anyway. How *could* you know what my skills are? You've hardly let me do anything independently, except change oil. You didn't even read the statement."

"I know. I'm sorry. But guys like Wes won't admit when they're wrong. I knew he wouldn't leave unless I did my own assessment."

She shook her head, her brow furrowing again. "It's always the same story. I don't know why I thought it would be any different here." She pinned him with her gaze. "Do you even have any idea what my skills are?"

Scott scratched the back of his neck. "Ben sent me your resumé."

She leaned forward in her chair. "But did you read it?"

Heat rushed to Scott's face again, and he resisted the urge to fidget. "I uh, haven't exactly had a lot of time."

"If you manage your time the way you manage your shop, it's no wonder."

"What's that supposed to mean?" The muscles in Scott's shoulders bunched. One minute he was trying to apologize and now, he was under attack.

"It means your files were a mess. It's almost as if two different people do the paperwork around here; each with their own system. And most of the work orders and invoices have barely any description and are disjointed at best."

"I um… I'm not very good with the computer and…the paperwork. Mary and Rudy sometimes help me out."

She sat back in her seat again. "No wonder. And they obviously don't communicate very well with each other."

"Anyway, I told Wes that your assessment was correct." Scott said to deflect her attention away from the fact that he hadn't been doing his own paperwork. "He complained about the cost, of course."

"Figures."

He bit back a smile. "I told him he could discuss a payment plan with my office manager."

"You have an office manager?"

Scott scratched his jaw. "I was kind of hoping you'd take on the title."

She rolled her eyes before throwing her hands up in the air. "Why not? I'm obviously doing the work of an office manager." Sarcasm deepened her voice. "Wow. I've only been here three days, and I've gone from being the maid to your secretary and now the office manager. Maybe by next week, I'll get to do real mechanic work. You know, the work I was hired to do?"

"Or maybe I'll let you replace Wes Miller's brakes, rotors, and bearings." Scott walked out of the office to the sound of another car pulling up outside.

"Wait!" Kennedy followed him. "Are you serious?"

He stopped and turned back to face her. She must have had some good momentum because she ran right into him. Her arms flailed as she fell backward. He reached out and grabbed her shoulders to steady her.

Although she was hardly petite, her shoulders felt slender and fragile under his large hands. His pulse skyrocketed as her fruity scent hit him again. An urge to pull her closer filled him.

How did the woman always manage to smell so good despite working in a garage?

As soon as he was certain she was steady on her feet, he released her and stepped away. "I don't want you to tell me how good of a mechanic you are, I want you to show me."

"But won't Wes have a fit if he finds out I'm the one who worked on his truck?"

Scott grinned. "Probably. Isn't it the office manager's job to soothe the client's ruffled feathers?" He picked up the box he'd left on the workbench. "Consider this an apology for doubting you."

Kennedy's brows shot up, and she froze. "What is it?"

"Open it and find out." He held out the container waiting for her to take it. When she finally did, he turned and greeted their newest customer. "Good afternoon, Mrs. Allen."

"I DON'T GET IT, EDEN." Kennedy said to her phone as she laid it on the closed toilet lid. She tossed a bath bomb into the full tub. This one was called citrus spectacle. "It was like he was a totally different person when Mary walked through the door." She slipped into the steaming bath and let out a long sigh. "The growly, chauvinistic lumberjack of a man was gone, and he hugged Mary like she was his own mother. He was all concerned about her son, who was apparently in an accident."

"Maybe he's not such a jerk after all." Eden's voice, coming through the speaker on Ken's phone, echoed through the bathroom.

"Maybe. Especially since he agreed to let me do all the oil changes, and he actually let me help with some other projects."

"But you hate doing oil changes."

"I know, but it's better than sweeping and mopping." Kennedy slid down until the water covered her shoulders. "But Paul Bunyan left me alone in the shop today for a little bit while he went over to Charity's Diner. During that time, a Sid came in."

"Sid as in that old guy who refused to let a woman work on his car? Or someone literally named Sid?"

"This guy's name was Wes, but he was totally a Sid. He freaked out when I told him he'd damaged his rotors because he'd waited so long to get his brakes replaced. And his bearings were bad as well." Kennedy raised up and tucked her knees under the water as she grabbed the little brush she used to clean her nails.

She wore gloves like most mechanics, but the dirt and grime still managed to get in her cuticles and every crack and crevice of her skin. She didn't really care what her hands looked like, but she needed to do something while she soaked. Otherwise, she fell asleep in the tub, and waking up in cold water was no fun.

"Wes said there was no way I knew what I was talking about and kept demanding to talk to Scott."

"Did Scott tell him you were spot on?"

"Not at first."

"What?"

"He hardly read the quote when I handed it to him. He just told Sid —I mean, Wes—that he'd do his own assessment."

"You're kidding."

"Nope." Kennedy swallowed hard to remove the lump from her throat. Scott had apologized to her—with the best peach pie she'd ever tasted—but he had no idea how badly he'd hurt her by questioning her work in front of a customer.

She took a deep breath. "Get this, today he promoted me from maid and secretary to office manager."

"Office manager? Isn't that just a glorified name for secretary and gopher?"

"Yes. But I've gotten the impression that he really doesn't like paperwork." So much so he'd hardly bothered to read the statement she'd printed out for Wes. She didn't mind doing the paperwork, as long as she got to do some real work too. "He did agree to let me do the repairs on Wes's truck though."

"That's great, Ken, but it feels like he's just throwing you a bone. You know, giving you just enough attention to keep you happy without ever really treating you like an equal."

"I know," Kennedy sighed. "It'd be easier to prove myself if he wasn't so averse to letting me actually work on cars. Hopefully, once he realizes I know my stuff, he'll trust me to take on more projects."

Although she'd enjoyed working with him on the radiator this afternoon, working so closely with him had made her even more aware of his size and strength. She'd had a difficult time catching her breath as they worked together because his nearness kept her heart rate slightly elevated.

Working day after day with a man who drove her so crazy in a such contradictory ways made working at Knight Auto Shop the hardest job she'd ever had.

CHAPTER 8

*S*cott nearly laughed out loud the next day when he finally deciphered the words on Kennedy's shirt. *I'm a mechanic. I can't fix stupid, but I can fix what stupid does.* It had taken him a lot longer to read than he'd like to admit, but he couldn't wait to see the look on Wes's face when he came in to pay for the services Kennedy did on his truck.

Scott was learning her t-shirts not only fit her personality, they also matched her mood. Today's shirt was full of sass and sarcasm.

Her fidgeting and organizing showed how eager she was to get to work on Wes's truck, and as soon as the parts arrived, she did exactly that.

Anxious for her to succeed, Scott walked up behind her as she prepared to remove the tire he'd had to put back on yesterday. "Make sure your jack is secure under there and don't forget—"

"Look," She spun around on her low stool and glared at him with raised eyebrows. "I don't need you to *mansplain* anything to me. You want me to show you how good of a mechanic I am? Then let me show you."

Scott held his hands up in surrender and backed away where he could no longer smell her lemony-orange scent. He turned his attention to Mrs. Allen's car where he needed to replace the fuel filter. Well, most of his attention.

Seeing Kennedy crouched next to Wes's truck wasn't nearly as distracting as watching her bend over an engine, but he still had a hard time keeping his eyes off her. And yes, he may have been checking to make sure she was doing her job right, but he was more concerned about whether she was endangering herself in any way.

Once again, Kennedy beat him to the radio that morning. Her pop music filled the air, and she frequently sang along. It shouldn't surprise him that she had a nice voice, but something about how perfect she seemed to be grated on his nerves.

They worked on their separate projects mostly in silence, except for the music and Kennedy's singing and her occasional outbursts of "Nuts!" or "Fudge nuggets!" every time she struggled with a stubborn bolt or part.

Scott repeatedly bit back a laugh at her ridiculous non-profanity.

When lunch arrived, and he found himself sitting across the small table from her again, where their knees practically touched, he decided he wanted to know more about her.

The thought made his palms grow clammy, and he hurried and finished his hamburger before his sweaty hands made his bun soggy. Why did talking about something other than cars with his coworker make him so nervous? It's not like they hadn't conversed over lunch before. But usually, it was just about work stuff.

Finally, he found the courage to open his mouth. "Why a mechanic?"

"Excuse me?"

"Why'd you become a mechanic?"

Kennedy dabbed her mouth with a napkin and sat back in her seat. "I grew up in an auto repair shop. You may have heard of T&J's Auto Repair in Spokane?"

"Yeah, I've heard of it."

"I grew up in that shop. Thomas, my dad, was the T in T&J's."

"Was? As in..."

Her eyes glistened as she gave a sad smile. "He passed away two months ago."

"Sorry to hear that," Scott said in a gentle voice. "That must be difficult, but why did you leave Spokane? Didn't you inherit his half of T&J's?"

"I always thought I would someday, but my mom passed away years ago after a lengthy battle with cancer. Dad had to sell half of his portion to Joel, his partner, to pay off all the medical bills and funeral expenses."

"Don't you still own a quarter of the shop?"

Kennedy picked up a French fry and swirled it in her ketchup. "Unfortunately, I had to sign over the remaining quarter to Joel, so I could afford my father's hospital bills and burial fees."

A vice tightened around Scott's chest. Kennedy had not only lost her father, she'd lost her livelihood. She'd come here, hoping to make a fresh start, and he'd been a jerk to her.

"That's rough. I still don't understand why you left Spokane though. Did Joel let you go?"

Kennedy's gaze remained on her plate as she continued to drench the French fry in ketchup. "He didn't let me go. I chose to leave." She glanced at him before lowering her gaze again. "I loved that shop. I was there every day after school and all day long in the summers. I dreamed of raising my kids there, teaching them everything I know about cars. But when I walked in on—" She chewed on the side of her lip for a moment as though choosing her words with care. "My dreams practically vanished overnight, and I couldn't stay in a place that was full of so many memories of my dad. It just wasn't the same without him."

Scott had a feeling there was more to Kennedy's reason for leaving than she was letting on, but as an introvert, he'd never been one to push if somebody didn't feel like talking. He hated when people did that to him.

"What about you?" Kennedy asked. "What made you want to be a mechanic?"

He tensed. Even though he enjoyed working on cars, he hadn't always planned on becoming a mechanic. He'd wanted to be a forest ranger.

He shrugged. "I like working with my hands. I never did very good in school, so college wasn't really an option."

Kennedy finally discarded the soggy fry. "But you worked for the Forest Service for a time. You must have wanted to do something else?"

Scott didn't talk about his time with the Forest Service with anyone. He balled up his napkin and dropped it on his Styrofoam tray. "Yeah, well, I guess we've both learned things don't always turn out the way we want." Picking up his garbage, he stood and left the claustrophobic office.

He should have known better than to ask Kennedy questions he didn't want to answer himself. Of course, she'd reciprocate. She was friendly like that and for some reason, that irritated him.

THE NEXT MORNING, Kennedy found Scott at the workbench scrubbing the dirt and grime from a vacuum pump. She took a moment to admire his broad shoulders and trim waist before greeting him.

"Good morning!"

"Mornin'." Scott barely looked up from the vacuum pump. The light layer of stubble on his face at the beginning of the week had thickened to a full-blown beard that looked great on him.

Kennedy didn't realize she found beards so attractive. Most of them men she'd worked with—Nate included—hadn't been able to grow more than scraggly scruff.

If Scott wasn't so broody, she'd think he was downright handsome, but there was something to be said for personality. Scott didn't seem to have much of one. Ben hadn't been kidding when he said Scott was the strong silent type.

Yesterday at lunch was the first time he made an effort at conversation that wasn't directly related to work. And then he'd clammed up and walked away when she tried to reciprocate. The rest of the afternoon had been quiet and strained.

Scott finally paused his efforts to clean the pump and looked at her. His gaze raked over her, before settling on her shirt. His brow furrowed a little, and she wondered if she'd gone too far with today's sunflower yellow shirt that said, *Just pretend I'm not here. That's what I'm doing.*

There was something about her broody, grumpy boss that made her want to push his buttons. That's why she always changed the radio station when she got the chance, even though she didn't mind country music.

After a long moment, a small smile touched Scott's lips before he squelched it and muttered, "Impossible."

She considered it a personal goal to get her grouchy boss to smile. And she'd almost succeeded.

"What's on the schedule today, boss?" Kennedy asked as she propped her hands on her hips.

"You tell me. You're the office manager." The gruffness of his voice sent a little shiver down her spine.

Even his voice was sexy. It was unfair to have to work with someone so perfect. Okay, so he wasn't exactly perfect, but he made her feel things she hadn't felt since she was a teenager and Nate first started paying attention to her. She was determined not to fall for another arrogant mechanic though. Even though Scott's chauvinistic side had mellowed, he still acted plenty arrogant.

She grabbed the spreadsheet she'd created yesterday afternoon from the office and returned to the garage. He'd only given her the title of office manager to pacify her, but she kind of liked the idea of being able to boss him around.

Being caught up had only lasted for an afternoon. Yesterday, while she replaced Wes's bearings and rotors, and Scott worked on Mrs. Allen's car, they'd had four customers show up with a variety of car problems, plus a handful of oil changes.

The quick and easy work of oil changes was great for business, but Kennedy kind of wished there weren't so many cars in Providence needing servicing right now. It always pushed back other more exciting jobs. Besides, she was beginning to feel like a circus sideshow. Everyone couldn't wait to meet the new female mechanic. Of course, the men were much more interested in watching her work than they were about the oil going into their car.

Thankfully, Scott, even though he muttered something about killing Rudy every time a new oil change customer came in, always insisted they wait inside while she serviced their car. That hadn't deterred a couple of the men from asking her out though.

She'd easily deflected their invitations. They were either much too young—like right out of high school—or much too old for Kennedy to take their invitation seriously. Fortunately, none of them gave off the creepy womanizer vibe Travis Brooks did.

As she went over the list of repairs they needed to do, including the parts they had and the ones they were still waiting on, Scott's gaze stayed focused on her hands. The man rarely made eye contact. She assumed that went along with not being much of a talker, but he seemed strangely fascinated with her hands today.

"And then we have the transmission rebuild for Oliver Daniels," Kennedy said, wrapping up her list.

"Make Oliver's transmission the priority." Scott said, still staring at her hands.

"Why? He came in after at least two of these other customers."

"His family only has one car, and he works in the Tri-Cities area. He's either going to have to take time off until his car is fixed or pay someone to drive him to work. He can't afford either."

Then he definitely couldn't afford a new car or even a new transmission. Hence the reason they were rebuilding the tranny. No wonder Scott offered to drive Oliver home yesterday after he brought in his car.

He often surprised her with the thoughtful little things he did for people that were in sharp contrast to the grumpy-growly persona she saw each day.

She pointed at the paper. "I can take care of these jobs, if you want to work on the transmiss—"

"No, we'll work on the tranny together." He lifted his gaze and met her eyes. "To get it done quicker. Those other jobs can wait."

Kennedy's brows rose. Did Scott just invite her to work on a major project with him?

No. He demanded *I work with him.*

She bristled as the glimpse of the compassionate mechanic vanished. Too bad the rest of the time, Scott was the same arrogant jerk she met that first day. Why make her the office manager if he didn't intend to let her manage how the work got done? Why did he even bother asking what she had planned for the day, if he didn't intend follow her plan?

She had no problem with working on the tranny with him—it'd be much more rewarding than anything else she'd do today—but she needed to give him a piece of her mind.

"I don't apprec—"

Without warning Scott grabbed her hands, causing the spreadsheet to fall to the floor. A warm tingling sensation raced up her arms as his strong hands cupped hers.

"How?"

"How what?" her voice squeaked.

"Your hands were as grimy as mine yesterday."

Despite wearing gloves while she worked on Wes's truck, her hands had still ended up filthy, as they did most days. The cleaners they used to cut through the grime only did so much and didn't really clean the cuticles and crevices.

Scott released one hand and slid his palm across the other. "And they're soft. How do you do that?"

He rotated her hand again, and his calloused fingers rasped across her knuckles in a gesture that probably wasn't meant to be seductive but sure felt that way. The sensations he elicited in her were electrifying, arcing through her nervous system, short-circuiting her brain, and stealing her breath.

The temperature in the garage skyrocketed as awareness filled her. Scott stood so close. She looked up at him, searching his face. What was he doing to her?

Her gaze was drawn to the alternating spokes of brown and green in his irises, creating the prettiest hazel eyes she'd ever seen. Funny how she'd never noticed how unique his eyes were before now.

Kennedy sucked in a deep breath. "I uh…"

He'd asked her a question, she was sure of it, but for the life of her, she couldn't find an answer. She licked her suddenly dry lips, wondering what it would feel like to have Scott kiss her.

His gaze jumped from her hands to her face, zeroing in on her mouth. His eyes widened, then he released her hand as quickly as he'd grabbed it and stepped away. He rubbed his palms against his thighs as he backed toward the open garage door.

"I um… I need to get…some parts…I mean tools from the storage shed out back." He turned, then quickly pivoted back and grabbed the key that hung above the workbench before disappearing outside.

Kennedy picked up the spreadsheet and used it to fan herself as she retreated to the parts room. She leaned against the wall and took deep steady breaths. What just happened?

I cannot fall for my boss.

Falling for a coworker again could be disastrous. She needed this job. The last thing she wanted was to have to uproot her life again—not that she had many roots here—and move to another town.

Trying to push Scott and what just happened out of her head, she hid out in the parts room for as long as she dared, making sure they had the gaskets and seals they needed to rebuild a transmission.

Scott returned to the shop, making all kinds of noise, but still she lingered, not ready to face him yet.

Deciding she couldn't hide out any longer, she grabbed the bags of seals and gaskets and walked out of the storage room. Right into Scott.

She let out a little shriek and pressed a hand to her chest as her heart leaped to her throat. "Oh, my fudge nuggets! You scared me to death. I nearly punched you."

Scott scoffed. "Like you could hurt me."

"Hey, I used to do Taekwondo and kickboxing at my gym back in

Spokane." She glared at him. "I could take you down if I wanted to. So don't sneak up on me again."

He shook his head in disbelief. "I didn't sneak up on you. I was just coming to see what was taking you so long." A smile pulled at the corner of his mouth. "My mom always says you only startle when you don't trust someone or you're guilty of something. So, which is it?"

Heat filled her face. She didn't trust *herself*. At all. Her hyper-sensitive body was totally out of control! Why on earth had it responded like that to a man she could barely tolerate.

"Neither. I just startle easily." She shrugged and stepped further away from him.

Kennedy did her best not to react to every little bump and brush of his arm or head against hers as they worked together under the car, but his natural, musky scent mingled with soap and fabric softener were a heady contrast to the smell of oil and grease surrounding her.

She kept reminding herself what a chauvinistic jerk he was only a few days ago in an attempt to dampen her attraction. She doubted his opinions concerning a woman working in his garage had changed much, but rather he'd just chosen to keep them to himself. For that, she was grateful. Proving herself in a man's world was hard enough without your boss's constant disapproval.

As the morning dragged on, his proximity only made her more anxious, and Kennedy often found herself chattering about anything and everything as they worked. Scott's only responses were nods or grunts. Even then, she only got a response when she asked him a direct question. Most of the time, he appeared to be ignoring her.

Relief filled her when she had to stop helping him and do an oil change. She was grateful to put a little distance between them so she could catch her breath. Unfortunately, she didn't get another break from working side by side with him until lunch arrived.

Kennedy loved having a gourmet meal show up at noon every day. Okay, so the hamburgers and club sandwiches with fries or salads weren't gourmet, but they were much better than the frozen dinners she usually ate for lunch.

Scott was about as talkative as usual while they ate, and Kennedy didn't want to say anything that would cause him to walk out like he did yesterday, so she stuck to discussing cars and their owners.

They'd only been back at work for an hour when a redheaded woman with a grandmotherly figure walked into the garage. "Hellooo."

Scott and Kennedy both straightened. She watched as he rubbed at the small of his back. He'd been doing that a lot lately. The man needed a massage. He'd been under too much stress and working too hard.

"Hey, Mom."

Mom?

The woman turned to Kennedy. "You must be the new mechanic. I'm Alice Wheeler. I've heard so much about you from Rudy. Welcome to Providence. I'm so glad Scott finally has some help."

She's heard about me from Rudy? Not Scott?

"Thank you." Kennedy held up her hands then shrugged an I'd-shake-your-hand-but-mine-are-dirty gesture. "It's nice to meet you."

"I can't wait to get to know you better. You should come to our Labor Day barbecue on Monday."

"That's kind of you, but I wouldn't want to intru—"

"Oh, I insist." She put a hand on Kennedy's arm. "You need to make some friends and get to know people around town. We have a big family and a few more are always welcome."

Kennedy looked at Scott out of the corner of her eye. How did he feel about his mom inviting her to their family barbecue?

He focused on scrubbing the grime off one of the parts they'd removed. Either he hated the idea, or he couldn't care less whether Kennedy showed up at the family party.

She smiled at Alice. "Thank you. It sounds fun."

Alice patted Scott's arm. "Your dad's gassing up the car. I just wanted to let you know we're headed to the Tri-Cities this afternoon, and we'll probably make a night of it. So, you're on your own for dinner. Rudy starts the night shift this evening, so he won't be around either."

"Alice, let's go," a man called from the open window of a gray sedan.

"Coming," she called and started toward the car before turning back. "Scott, make sure Kennedy knows how to get to Debbie's house." Her gaze shifted to Kennedy. "We'll see you at five on Monday."

Kennedy turned toward Scott after waving to Alice. His cheeks had bright rosy spots on them. She couldn't help the laugh that erupted from her. "You still live with your parents?"

He shrugged. "There aren't a whole lot of places to rent in Providence. Besides, it seems like a waste to throw money away on my own place when my parents have plenty of room."

His logic was sound, but Kennedy still couldn't resist teasing him. "Yes, and if you moved out on your own, you might have to fix your own meals. Does she do your laundry too?"

More color flooded his cheeks. "She likes taking care of her family."

"That's great, but you're how old?"

One side of his mouth quirked up in a grin. "My sister's thirty-six, and my mom's over there almost daily, even though Debbie has a cleaning service and a part-time nanny."

Alice Wheeler certainly seemed like the doting, helicopter-parent type, but Kennedy had a feeling there was more to Debbie's situation than Scott was letting on.

"Do you mind that your mom invited me to your family barbecue?"

"Why would I?" He turned back to the transmission they were still dismantling.

Why indeed? If he didn't care, he obviously wasn't as affected by her nearness as she was his. He viewed their relationship as purely professional.

"Debbie has a pool," Scott said.

"Okay?" What was Kennedy supposed to make of that statement? "So, you're saying I should bring a swimsuit?"

"Only if you want to swim. The grandkids usually end up in the pool."

"Do the adults swim?" The thought of seeing Paul Bunyan in a pair of swimming trunks made her breathless all over again even though she wasn't working all that close to him at the moment.

She focused her attention back on taking apart the transmission.

He shrugged. "Sometimes."

As Scott explained how to get to his sister's house, Kennedy realized she'd passed by the mansion last night when she'd taken her dad's motorcycle out for a ride. With a house like that, a cleaning service, and a part-time nanny, Debbie certainly didn't need her helicopter-mom hovering every day.

She studied Scott out of the corner of her eye as she worked. Why hadn't he moved out of his parents' house yet? According to Ben, the apartment above the garage had been empty for a while. Scott didn't strike her as the type who couldn't bear to leave Mommy and Daddy, so what was he saving his money for? A house, maybe?

As five o'clock rolled around, Scott made no signs of wrapping up for the evening even though they were far from done with the transmission.

At five thirty, Kennedy finally faced him. "You're planning on finishing this tonight, aren't you?"

Scott glanced at the clock. "If we— I mean, if I finish it tonight, then Oliver can have his car for work tomorrow."

"I know you're strong and all, but do you really think you can put all of this…" She waved at the partially rebuilt transmission. "…back in the car by yourself?"

"Probably, with the help of the T.J."

"T.J.?"

"The transmission jack."

"You name tools too?" Kennedy asked with a grin.

His brow furrowed, and he cocked his head.

"I've always named inanimate objects." She pointed at the tool she used yesterday to remove the lug nuts from Wes's tires. "For example, I call the impact drill Tina."

"Tina?"

"Yeah, you know because it's noisy and kind of whiny." She grinned. "And I call the air compressor Bubba."

The edges of Scott's mouth quirked up along with one eyebrow. "Why Bubba?"

"Because he's full of air and has an over inflated sense of self-importance."

Kennedy caught a glimpse of a full-blown smile before Scott shook his head and turned away.

Well, what do you know? Paul Bunyan does have a sense of humor. It's small but at least he's got one.

What would Scott think if he knew she'd nicknamed him after the famous lumberjack? She wasn't sure she was ready to find out, so she reached for another gasket. "Well, guess what, Mr. Do-It-All-Myself, you don't have to do it all yourself anymore." She nudged his arm with her elbow. "I don't mind sticking around and helping. I don't have any plans tonight, except a long hot bath."

Scott's movements froze except for his head that swiveled her way. His eyebrows were raised again, but he looked more surprised now rather than confused.

"That's my secret." She wiggled the fingers of her gloved hands. "I enjoy soaking in the tub after a long day at work. It helps clean my hands, and the minerals in the bath bombs soften my skin."

"Bath bombs?"

"Never mind." She doubted Scott would appreciate all the things she enjoyed about soaking in a tub of hot perfumed water.

The next three hours felt like five. Mostly because she grew tired and hungry, and she figured Scott was exhausted too, because his normally clipped speech became terser and more impatient. They both heaved an audible sigh of relief as they tightened the final bolts.

Surprise filled her when he asked her to take Oliver's car for a test drive while he put the tools away. "Really, you want me to drive it?"

"You know how to drive, don't you?"

"Of course."

"And you know what to listen for in the engine and transmission?"

"Yes."

He tossed the keys to her. "Well, what are you waiting for?"

Kennedy didn't hesitate. She got in the car and started it up. Test driving a car was much more enjoyable than cleaning up.

Relief and satisfaction filled her as she made a quick trip around town and then headed out on the two-lane highway past Scott's sister's house. She picked up speed, carefully listening as the automatic transmission shifted through the gears. When she heard nothing amiss, she returned to the shop.

"Good as new," she said as she walked back into the garage. "Well, as good as can be for a twelve-year-old car with two hundred and fifty thousand miles."

"Good." The word was barely more than a grunt. "Will you follow me over to drop it off at Oliver's?"

"Sure. Let me run upstairs and grab my keys." She skidded to a stop at the door. "Do you want to ride back in my truck or on my bike?" For some reason, Scott struck her as the type of man who would be comfortable on the back of a bike.

He froze like a deer caught in the headlights, eyes widening again, like they had when she mentioned the bath bomb. When he hesitated longer than she expected, she made the decision for him.

"I'll just grab my truck keys."

She should have known with his reaction—or lack of—when his mom invited her to the barbecue that he wouldn't be interested in riding a motorcycle with her. She should have known that just because they'd worked well together today, and she'd proved herself knowledgeable, his opinion of her and attitude toward her wouldn't magically change.

She didn't even know why she mentioned her bike. That would force them to practically touch, and after her reaction to him this morning, that was the last thing she needed.

Ten minutes later, after dropping the car off to a grateful Oliver and him promising to stop by the garage tomorrow to set up a payment plan, she parked behind the shop. As she and Scott climbed from her truck, she decided she wasn't quite ready for the day to end.

Hooking a thumb over her shoulder at the back stairs, she said,

"I've got some leftover lasagna, if you'd like to join me for dinner." When he froze and got that wide-eyed look again, she smiled and rushed to add, "You know, since you're on your own for dinner tonight."

She held her breath as he stared at her across the truck bed.

I'm such a glutton for punishment.

But she was also lonely. She and Eden had been planning to spend the weekend together until her father sprung an important business trip on her that he insisted she needed to accompany him on. The thought of eating dinner alone again sounded about as appealing as a root canal.

When Scott continued to hesitate, scratching his neck like he had poison ivy, she considered withdrawing her offer again. But he spoke before she could.

"You know how to cook?"

"Of course, I know how to cook. You think because I enjoy doing 'guy things,'" she made air quotes, "I don't know how to do 'girly things'?"

"No, that's not—" he shook his head and lowered his gaze to her truck bed. "I just didn't know you could cook."

"There's a lot of things you don't know about me."

He nodded. "Okay," he said, surprising her for the second time this evening. "Let me make sure the shop is locked up first."

Kennedy's heart lodged in her throat as she walked up the stairs. Now she had to figure out how to make conversation with the handsome broody lumberjack over dinner without feeling like a rambling idiot like she had been most of the day.

CHAPTER 9

*B*last!

Why had he accepted Kennedy's invitation to dinner? It felt too much like a date, and he hadn't been on one of those in years. Not since Hannah pulled him out of his shell. His breaths came a little quicker as he climbed the back stairs, but it wasn't because of the physical exertion.

Kennedy made him nervous, especially when she talked about bath bombs and riding a motorcycle together. Visualizing her in a bath had left him struggling to stay focused on his work, and the thought of her riding a motorcycle...

Phew!

That was even sexier than the way she wore her ponytail pulled through the back of her baseball cap. Kennedy drove him crazy. She'd looked so enticing acting the part of a bossy office manager this morning. He still couldn't believe his moment of insanity when he grabbed her hand and stroked her palm. The contact had caused fire to race along his skin, and his mind had completely short-circuited. It was all he could do to not pull her into his arms and kiss her.

He rubbed his damp palms against his thighs, realizing belatedly that he still wore his dirty work pants.

Blast! Now I need to wash my hands again.

Despite working together all day, he'd barely spoken to her. He enjoyed listening to her sporadic chatter, but he never knew what to say. He liked the sound of her voice, though. It's light lilting cadence was almost melodic. He could listen to it all day.

She probably thought he was the rudest person on the planet because every time she asked him a question, he usually nodded or grunted in response. It wasn't all that different of a response from what he gave most people, but it felt different, because every time he looked at Kennedy, his tongue stuck to the roof of his mouth and his mind went blank.

He scratched his neck once, then twice more before finding the courage to lift his hand to knock.

"Oh, there you are," Kennedy said, poking her head out. "I thought I heard someone on the stairs."

Yep. Here I am. Standing out here like an idiot.

Kennedy waved him in, and he sucked in a deep breath before easing past her. She still smelled faintly of coconut and pineapple like she had all day, and her proximity made it difficult to breathe. She'd shed her work clothes and now wore an oversized, hot pink t-shirt that said *No Guts No Story* and shorts that showed off her long shapely legs.

"You can use the kitchen sink, if you need to wash up."

"Thanks."

The smell of garlic and tomato permeated the air as he washed his hands, and she moved around the small kitchen. Even though his back was to her, Scott was all too aware of her every move.

"So, do you think Oliver will actually show up tomorrow to set up a payment plan?" Kennedy asked as she pulled the lasagna from the microwave and placed it on the table.

"Yes." He took a seat at the table that was slightly bigger than the one downstairs in the office. Three chairs sat around the table, instead of two.

Kennedy set garlic bread and a salad on the table before sitting across from him. "He's too young to qualify for the granny discount, but I have a feeling you're not planning on charging him the full labor fee."

"No, I'll wave my portion."

Kennedy stared at him for a long moment. "You just keep surprising me."

"What do you mean?"

She shook her head as she dished up two plates of food. "Nothing. I guess when you live in a small town, you know everybody's sob story, and you have to take pity on them."

He shrugged as he picked up his fork. "Something like that."

Scott could explain that not only was Oliver supporting five children, he'd brought his mother who has muscular dystrophy to live with them last year, and his wife had quit her job to stay home and take care of her mother-in-law, but that was a lot of words to get out. Words that he might stumble over and make a fool of himself with.

"So, how do you make a living if you're constantly giving people a break on their repair bills?"

"I still live with my parents."

She laughed, and he allowed his lips to turn up in a grin. The motion felt strange. Not because he was smiling, but he'd kind of made a joke, and he hadn't bumbled it.

He took a bite of his lasagna. It wasn't as flavorful as his mom's, but it was better than having to cook for himself.

Kennedy laughed. "Right. Your mom still cooks your meals and washes your laundry."

Scott bristled at her mocking tone. He wanted to argue and explain that he paid rent to help his parents out in addition to working with them in their huge garden and on their endless home improvement projects. His dad was notorious for overdoing it. He even assisted his dad occasionally with the remodeling jobs he did for other people. When he wasn't swamped at the garage, that is. But such an explanation felt like too much work.

He gave a soft grunt and kept his mouth shut.

"So, what does fending for yourself usually look like?" Kennedy asked before taking a bite of her garlic bread.

He lifted one shoulder. "Leftovers. Sometimes, Rudy cooks."

"Why does Rudy cook? Are you that adverse to doing…" She grinned as she made air quotes again. "…women's work?"

"No. I can cook if I want to, I just don't…care to." As far as he was concerned, any cooking that required reading a recipe wasn't worth the effort. It left him too stressed out to enjoy the food, assuming it turned out edible.

He tapped the corner of the cardboard lasagna tray that was obviously store-bought with the end of his fork. "Thought you said you could cook. Anyone can bake a frozen meal."

"Touché." Kennedy laughed, and the light-hearted sound caused a ripple of pleasure to flow through him. He liked her laugh.

The tension he'd almost forgotten about coiled tighter in his gut. For a moment, he'd actually conversed with Kennedy about something other than cars, and he'd enjoyed it. But now, the collar of his shirt threatened to choke him despite being unbuttoned, and his tongue felt too big for his mouth.

"I do know how to cook, and I do it often, but lasagna is one of those meals that requires too much work when you're only feeding one person."

"You're feeding more than one now."

She laughed again. "Yes, and I'm glad you're helping me eat it. Otherwise, I'd end up eating it for a week. As much as I like lasagna, I don't like it that much."

They lapsed into a silence that grew more uncomfortable by the second. Scott knew he should say something, but for the life of him, he couldn't think of a single intelligent thing to say. All he could think was how nice it was sitting in this small apartment—that he'd imagined living in someday—across from Kennedy. And that kind of terrified him.

Why after all these years, when he finally found himself attracted to another woman, did it have to be a coworker?

"So, tomorrow is Saturday. I assume the shop is open?" Kennedy speared a piece of lettuce with her fork.

"Yes, until two or whenever I get around to closing it."

SWITCHING GEARS

"Do you need me to work?"

He kept his eyes on his plate. "Nah, maybe down the road, we can take turns covering Saturdays."

"Down the road...when you finally decide I know what I'm doing?"

Was that a note of hopefulness in her voice or irritation?

He'd seen for himself the past couple of days that Kennedy really did know her stuff. He hadn't once needed to tell her where to place a part or what to do next. She'd kept her head held high yesterday when she explained to Wes the work she'd done on his truck, and thankfully, Wes had been smart enough to keep his opinion of female mechanics to himself.

Scott admired Kennedy's spunk in standing up to him and her determination to prove herself. But that was his problem... He admired her too much.

Working so close to her all day had been torture, and then she'd gone and offered him a ride on her motorcycle. He'd much rather be the one to give her a ride and have her wrap her arms around his waist, but either way, that kind of contact would drive him crazy. It would distract him.

He shook his head to clear it of the direction his thoughts kept traveling around Kennedy. "That and when I figure out how to let go a little."

He'd had to work so hard for every little success in his life, it was difficult to consider letting someone else take over in the only area he'd succeeded. If you could call it that? He was only a mechanic, but he knew cars.

His phone buzzed in his pocket. Even though pulling it out at the table was rude, he did it anyway, because he needed a distraction from trying to make conversation with Kennedy.

His heart lodged in his throat when he saw the text was from Charity. His thumb hovered over the text box icon. If her family wasn't interested in selling the shop, he didn't want to read that in front of Kennedy. He didn't need a spectator to his disappointment.

Unable to stop himself, he tapped the text box anyway. He stared

93

at his phone, willing his mind to find the words he wanted to read. Despite Kennedy sitting nearby, he kept his gaze focused on the words of the text, intent on interpreting them correctly.

Letting the shop go is hard but hanging on to it is harder because it will never be the same without Rich there. We can't think of a more deserving, harder worker to hand Rich's pride and joy over to.

Scott let out the breath he'd been holding. The text went on, mentioning Andy Giles—Providence's only real estate agent—and something about an official appraisal and fair market value. Finally, he came to the bottom line. The Knights were asking fifteen thousand less than he figured it would take to get his own shop.

"Everything okay?" Kennedy asked.

His face split into a grin. "Everything's great!"

"That must have been some good news."

"The best."

He wanted to lift Kennedy out of her chair and swing her around the small apartment while he cheered, but then he'd want to kiss her pretty smiling lips, and that wouldn't be good. She was his coworker, for goodness' sake. He subdued his smile and settled for tucking his phone back into his pocket.

"You're not going to share?"

"Not yet." He grinned at her. "But I need you to open the shop on Tuesday morning."

Monday was Labor Day, so he'd have to wait until Tuesday to go to the bank and apply for a loan.

Kennedy pointed at her chest. *"You* want *me* to open the shop?"

"Why do you sound so shocked? You've proven to me you know your stuff." He lifted one eyebrow. "So, can you open the shop or not?"

"Of course, I can." She grinned so big, her dimples creased her cheek.

"I'll probably be about an hour late."

"Okay." She drew out the word as though waiting for him to tell her why he needed her to open the shop.

But he didn't plan to tell anyone just yet. His family knew he wanted a shop of his own someday, but they didn't know he'd talked to Charity. He didn't want to have to hide his disappointment from them if she said no. Now, he liked the idea of keeping it a secret until it was a done deal, and he could surprise his parents.

They'd helped him through so many struggles in his life, especially while he was in school, that he wanted to make them proud. Some parents might not be excited about their son buying an auto repair shop, but he knew his mom and dad would be thrilled for him.

Conversation grew stilted again, and Scott kept shoveling food into his mouth to keep from having to find something intelligent to say. Before long, his plate was empty, and he didn't know what to do other than take it to the sink.

Feeling like an idiot for eating so fast, he filled the sink with soapy water. The least he could do was wash his own dishes. Mom still did a lot for him and Rudy, but she'd taught them to help out around the house and clean up after themselves.

Kennedy joined him a minute later, and her arm brushed against his as she slid her plate into the soapy water. "You don't need to do the dishes."

Warmth swept over him at her nearness. Not even the smell of the lemony dish soap blocked her tropical feminine scent. "Um... I don't mind."

Her hand brushed his again as she took the plate from him to rinse, and Scott stilled.

She did too.

He should pull away, but he didn't want to. The sparse square footage of the small kitchen seemed to shrink around them, until there was nothing but him and Kennedy. Side by side. Touching hands.

He bumped hands with her a lot at work, but it wasn't the same when they both wore gloves. Here, now, he felt the warmth and softness of her skin against his. The tingling that raced up his arm heightened his awareness, and an overwhelming desire to pull her into his arms flooded over him.

Kennedy looked up at him with wide brown eyes. She blinked

once, then twice and licked her lips. She leaned toward him a little. Or maybe he was the one leaning.

The air in the small apartment grew unbearably hot, and Scott forgot how to breathe. All thoughts fled from his head except how amazing it would be to kiss her.

He jerked his hands from the hot, soapy water and backed away.

What am I doing?

Kennedy was a good mechanic. He needed her. Kissing her would only screw things up.

Grabbing a nearby dish towel, he dried his hands before patting the beads of perspiration from his forehead.

"I uh… I'd better go." He threw the dish towel at her and backed toward the door.

Her mouth dropped open, and she scowled as she caught the dish-towel that glanced off her shoulder.

He fumbled with the doorknob, unable to make his fingers work properly.

"Scott."

He stopped with the door halfway open. "What?"

"Wait a second." She disappeared into the bedroom then returned several seconds later. "Catch." Before he realized that she even held anything in her hand, she launched it at him.

He caught it an inch from his chest. "What is it?"

"It's a bath bomb."

"What am I supposed to do with it?"

"Duh, take a bath and put it in the water."

His eyebrows hiked up. "I'm not using some girly bath—"

"Relax." She walked toward him, and the cool night air coming through the open door did nothing to lower the rising temperature in the apartment. "It's only eucalyptus, peppermint, and lavender. It won't make you smell too girly." She grinned. "But it will help relax the sore muscles in your back."

And now, she stood too close again, looking much too kissable. He needed to get out of here. Fast.

"Okay." Gripping what felt like a ticking time bomb in his fist, he stepped out onto the metal landing. "Thanks for your help today a-and for dinner."

He hurried down the stairs so fast, he was lucky he didn't fall. Walking straight to his truck, he drove home still gripping the bath bomb in his left hand. It wasn't until he walked into the house and remembered that neither his parents nor Rudy were home tonight that he took time to actually look at the small ball he held.

He read the words relaxation and sore muscles on the plastic wrapper.

Hmm... Why not?

He'd have to use his parent's garden tub, since the one in the bathroom he and Rudy shared was too small for him to relax in.

Ten minutes later, he slid into the hot, blue-tinted water and sighed. He couldn't remember the last time he took a bath. Maybe when he was eight? Or when he was achy with the flu when he was twelve?

The scented water reminded him more of his grandmother's homemade muscle rub than it did Kennedy, but thanks to the lavender, he had a feeling he'd still come out smelling much more feminine than he'd like. Good thing he was home alone tonight.

He scooped up a handful of water and let it trickle through his fingers. The minerals made his calloused hands feel almost slimy. No wonder Kennedy's hands were soft despite the hard work she did every day.

Never in a million years would he have thought he'd work with a female mechanic who knew as much about cars as he did. Especially not a woman who looked like Barbie. A lot of tomboys tended to display masculine traits, but there was very little about Kennedy that could be considered masculine other than her chosen profession.

He couldn't believe he'd almost kissed her tonight. He finally had a helper who could take care of all the paperwork and help pick up the slack in the shop. He couldn't drive her away by coming on to her. She deserved to be respected in her place of employment, no matter where she worked.

But he also couldn't stop thinking about her. Was she taking a bath right now too? What scent was her bath bomb tonight? The temperature in the bathroom spiked as Scott's imagination took control.

Nope. Stop.

He couldn't go there. He had to keep his mind out of the gutter if he expected to continue working with her. And if he was indeed successful in purchasing the shop, he needed a competent mechanic like her to help run it.

He leaned his head back and closed his eyes, letting his mind wander over the changes he'd like to make to the shop. Maybe someday, he'd even add on and expand Wheeler's Repair Shop. Or should he call it Scott's Auto shop?

His head snapped up sometime later when someone called his name.

How had he fallen asleep? This tub wasn't near big enough or comfortable enough for a man his size to take a nap in. The water was still warm, so he hadn't been asleep that long, but his hands looked like the prunes his grandma used to eat every day.

"Scott? You here?" Rudy's voice grew louder.

Scott sprang to his feet so fast he nearly slipped and fell thanks to the silkiness of the minerals in the water. Heat filled his body at the prospect of being caught in the bathtub by his younger brother. He pulled the plug and grabbed a towel to wrap around himself.

Rudy stepped into their parents' bedroom just as Scott exited the bathroom. "What are you doing?" His brother's eyebrows shot so high they almost met his hairline.

"Nothing." Scott pushed past Rudy and headed down the hall to his own room.

"Were you taking a bath?" Rudy asked in surprise as he followed Scott. "Since when do you take a bath? And why does Mom and Dad's bathroom smell like Grandma Wheeler's bedroom?"

Scott ignored him and closed his bedroom door in Rudy's face.

Rudy gave him exactly enough time to pull on some underwear and a pair of sweatpants before knocking and opening the door. The brothers respected each other's privacy, but they were close enough they didn't keep many secrets from each other.

Rudy leaned against the door frame and folded his arms across his chest. He grinned. "So, is this some sort of new kinky thing you do when you're home alone?"

"What? No!" Scott picked up the towel he'd dropped and threw it at Rudy's head. "I had a backache, so I took a bath. No big deal."

Rudy caught the towel and sniffed. "It is a big deal, because one, I've never known you to take a bath. Ever." He held up one finger followed by another as he stepped closer to Scott. "And two…" He sniffed again. "You smell…pretty." Rudy busted out laughing, and Scott took a swing at him. He dodged the punch easily and continued to laugh. "Seriously, who are you? And what have you done with my brother?"

Scott ignored him and walked into the kitchen to get a drink of water. Despite spending who knows how long in a steamy bathroom, his throat felt incredibly dry.

"Don't you have streets to patrol and pedestrians to harass?"

"I'm starving, so I'm taking my lunch break early. What did you have for dinner?"

Scott froze. Rudy would tease Scott mercilessly if he knew he had dinner with Kennedy.

Rudy opened the refrigerator. "I saw your truck at the garage less than an hour ago, so I know you haven't been home long." He snapped his fingers and grinned again. "Oh right, I guess you were too busy taking a bath to eat dinner." Rudy pulled out a container and peeked inside. "So, what are we eating?"

Scott cleared his throat. "I've eaten."

"So eager to take a *bath* that you scarfed your dinner, huh?" Rudy drawled out the word bath, and Scott itched to throw another punch at him.

Rudy put the container back and pulled out another one. "So, what did you end up eating?"

Scott downed his glass of water before answering. "Lasagna."

Rudy ducked his head into the fridge. "Mom made lasagna?"

"No. Um… Kennedy invited me over for dinner."

Rudy straightened and let the fridge door swing close. "Kennedy invited you to dinner?" His face split into a grin, and he punched Scott's shoulder. "Way to go, man. I have to say, I didn't think you had it in you. She's only been here a week and already you two are dating!"

"It wasn't a date." The words came out through clenched teeth. He liked the idea of dating Kennedy though. "She just…" Scott scratched his neck. "We worked late, and she offered me dinner."

"She worked late with you *and* fed you dinner? She likes you, man!"

"No, I'm pretty sure she can barely tolerate me still." He'd seen the fire in her eyes when he told her she'd be working on the transmission rebuild with him, despite her carefully laid plans.

"No way. She wouldn't offer you dinner if she hated you." Rudy opened the refrigerator again. "Pretty sure she had ulterior motives for inviting you up. Question is… did you give her what she wanted?"

Scott grabbed Rudy in a head lock and rubbed his knuckles against his brother's head.

Hmm…my back feels better.

Rudy struggled but Scott not only had a height and weight advantage, he'd surprised Rudy by grabbing him while he was bent over.

"Ow!" Rudy tapped against Scott's arm even though he could take him down if he wanted to. "Let go, you brute!"

Scott released Rudy with a little shove.

His brother rubbed his head for a moment before smoothing out his hair. "What did you do that for?"

"Your comment was totally inappropriate, and you know it."

"Chill. I only wanted to know if you gave her a goodnight kiss. Geez."

No way would Scott admit to how close he'd come to kissing Kennedy.

"Nothing's happening between me and Kennedy," he insisted.

"Isn't there a line in some Shakespeare play about protesting too loudly?" Rudy asked with a grin. He took a quick step back to get out of Scott's reach.

Scott had no idea what Rudy was talking about, but his brother was right. The more Scott protested, the more obvious it was that he liked Kennedy.

Rudy's grin grew wider. "Nothing's happening yet. But it will."

His brother's words were so confident, Scott had to wonder if Rudy was right. Had Kennedy's invitation been a more-than-friends thing? For a moment there, standing beside her at the sink, he could have sworn she wanted that kiss as badly as he did.

CHAPTER 10

"You have to help me, Eden. I have no idea what to wear." Kennedy looked at her best friend on her phone screen.

"You definitely need to dress up a little, above your usual standards," Eden said, and Kennedy rolled her eyes. Eden always wanted Kennedy to put in a little more effort than her usual jeans and a t-shirt. "But it's just a barbecue, so I wouldn't go too dressy."

"Except it's at Scott's sister's house. She lives in a mansion. Although his mother seems pretty down to earth."

"Jeans and t-shirt won't cut it then." Eden tapped her lips. "Turn your camera around and show me your closet."

Kennedy did as she asked and walked over to her closet.

"You should wear one of your summer dresses. Fall is just around the corner, and you won't be able to wear them much longer."

A dress was always Eden's first choice for every event and usually Kennedy's last choice. It wasn't that she didn't like dresses, she just felt like she was screaming for attention when she wore them.

As Eden weighed the pros and cons of each dress in the closet, which were few, Kennedy debated whether she really wanted to wear a dress or not. Did she want to draw attention to herself?

She wouldn't mind having Scott look at her again with that little spark of interest she'd seen in his eyes Friday night, right before he bolted. For one brief moment, she almost thought he was going to kiss her, and even though she was crazy for thinking it, she'd wanted him to. But then he'd darted for the door.

It was probably for the best. The last thing she needed was to get mixed up with another cocky mechanic. Scott didn't strut around the shop like Nate did, but he had a brashness about him that rubbed her wrong. But then he did things like bring her pie, wash her dishes, and give a struggling father a break on his transmission rebuild, making her question whether he was really as bad as she thought.

"Ooh, the blue one," Eden said from her phone. "It brings out the natural highlights in your hair and compliments your complexion. You're going to curl your hair, aren't you?"

"Maybe." Kennedy pulled the blue summer dress with tiny yellow and white flowers from her closet. It was one of her favorite dresses because it didn't cling too tightly to her curves but was still flattering.

"Yes. Curl it." Eden insisted as Kennedy flipped her camera back around.

"You should come curl it for me."

Eden groaned. "I wish I could. Believe me, I'd rather be anywhere but here."

"Must be rough spending the weekend on one of the biggest yachts on the Pacific Ocean." Kennedy let sarcasm fill her voice.

Eden had felt bad for canceling their weekend plans, but Kennedy couldn't fault her friend for doing her job. Her dad called the weekend jaunt down the coast a business trip, but it was little more than a bunch of social activities—that could be written off as business expenses—designed to rub shoulders with other wealthy, influential businessmen.

"With one of the biggest egos on the whole Pacific coast." Drama filled Eden's voice. "It's amazing any of the rest of us could fit on the boat with the size of Tristan Jourdain's head."

This wasn't the first time her friend had something negative to say about the playboy son of the tech billionaire that her father had been doing a lot of business with lately. Kennedy had never met Tristan, but his face showed up in the tabloids occasionally. He and Eden would make an attractive couple, but if even half of the things the tabloids touted about him were true, she didn't blame Eden for disliking the man.

Kennedy painted her toenails a glossy red while they continued to chat about their weekends. Kennedy's had been mostly boring except for the long ride she'd taken on her father's motorcycle on Saturday. And Eden's had been filled with trying to avoid Tristan.

Heaviness settled over Kennedy when Eden had to end the call to catch her flight home. She missed her friend, and she'd wanted to talk to her about Scott, but she hadn't been able to bring up the subject. What was she supposed to say?

I think I'm falling for him, even though he's kind of a jerk.

There'd been times when she'd caught Scott looking at her with a different light in his eyes than his usual glare that hovered somewhere between annoyance and disdain. On Friday morning when he grabbed her hand and again that evening after dinner, she thought maybe he felt the attraction too. Both times, he'd shut down and walked away though, which meant he probably didn't feel the things she did.

Falling for someone again, who wasn't interested in her, was something only a desperate woman did. Kennedy may be floundering, wondering where on earth her life was headed, but she wasn't desperate. Yet.

She took the time to apply a little makeup but decided against curling her hair. Instead, she pulled it to the side in a loose French braid before picking up the cookies she'd made that afternoon and walking out the door.

Alice hadn't asked her to bring anything, but Kennedy felt weird showing up to a party empty handed. Her stomach tightened as she parked her truck beside Scott's in his sister's wide driveway. Meeting new people and having to be social without Eden by her side always made her nervous. What if Scott's family shared his opinion about female mechanics?

Following the sound of children's laughter, she walked to the open back gate instead of the front door of the massive house. She took in the large backyard with colorful flower beds, a fancy gazebo, and a stone path leading here and there. A pack of young boys yelled and laughed as they chased a soccer ball, and a group of teenage girls blew bubbles for two dark-haired toddler girls.

Kennedy walked far enough into the yard to see several tables set up near the back of the house and a cluster of adults sitting around visiting. Although there were at least three other men present, her gaze went straight to Scott's broad-shouldered frame. He'd shaved last week's beard off and now sported a hint of dark stubble. The man was incredibly good looking when he wasn't glaring at her. He looked almost happy and content. Her gaze dropped to the small bundle in his arms.

He's holding a baby.

Her footsteps faltered as her heart rate kicked into overdrive. Her pulse hammered out a rapid staccato at the base of her throat. She'd never seen anything quite so attractive. Kennedy wasn't one of those women who felt like their biological clock was ticking, but she'd always wanted a family of her own, even more so now that her dad was gone. That's why she resented the years she'd wasted with Nate.

Until now, she'd never really pictured Scott as a father. He seemed too grumpy, but the way he smiled at the infant in his arms did something to her.

"Hey, Kennedy."

She jumped at the boisterous voice behind her. Spinning, she found Rudy dressed in his deputy uniform.

"You look like a stalker hiding here by the bushes." He grinned as he took her arm. "Come on. I'll introduce you to the family."

Kennedy allowed herself to be led to the group of adults where Scott's sisters and brothers-in-law introduced themselves. Everyone took turns pointing out their children from the kids that roamed the yard. So many names were thrown at Kennedy there was no hope to remember them all. She gave up even trying.

She did catch that six of the kids—three of the redheads, the dark-haired toddlers, and the infant Scott held—all belonged to Debbie and her husband Austin. No wonder Alice Wheeler came to Debbie's house almost daily to help. Debbie had her hands full.

Her eyes locked with Scott's when Rudy joked about her already knowing her slavedriver of a boss. He gave her a tight smile and a quick nod before one of his nephews tugged on his arm, begging him to come play soccer with them. He passed the baby off to his dad and walked away without a backward glance.

It was all she could do to keep her jaw from dropping open. She hadn't expected Scott to welcome her to his family's party with open arms, but he'd hardly even acknowledged her. That stung.

"So, Kennedy, what's it like to work in a male dominated field?" Scott's sister—was it Joy? —asked. "I bet you meet all kinds of men who think women don't belong in a garage."

Kennedy nodded, but bit her tongue to keep from saying, "Yeah, and your brother's one of them."

"Ugh!" the other sister said. "Chauvinistic men are so annoying."

Rudy laughed and winked at Kennedy. "Yeah, good thing there aren't any of those in this family."

Rudy had seen his brother's reluctance to let her do a simple oil change, but did he know how truly horrible Scott was that first day?

Kennedy laughed. "Yeah, good thing, or I might not have a job."

Debbie rolled her eyes. "Male chauvinism is right up there with stubborn male pride. Two of the things the world could do without."

Debbie's husband, Austin, wrapped his arms around her. "Hey, I've got male pride in spades." He kissed her cheek. "Our pride is what make us so good at getting all of the things done on our wife's 'Honey-Do' list."

The rest of the men chimed in with a chorus of, "That's right," and "Amen."

A squeal out in the yard caught Kennedy's attention. She turned to find Scott swinging one of Debbie and Austin's sons up in the air. He set the boy down, only to have him turn and beg Scott to make him fly again. Scott erupted in full-bodied laughter as he lifted the boy again.

Kennedy resisted the urge to fan herself in front of Scott's family. There was something about that man that spiked her blood pressure, in good ways and bad. Like he did on Friday when he abruptly changed the plans she'd so carefully made for the day only to turn around and grab her hand, throwing her off kilter.

"Kennedy!" Alice Wheeler gave her a side hug. "I'm so glad you made it." She took the plate of cookies from Kennedy and pulled her into the house.

For the next twenty minutes, she visited with Scott's mom and sisters while they put the finishing touches on veggie trays, salads, and more desserts than Kennedy had seen in a long time.

The women were friendly and attempted to include her in the conversation, but it flowed from one topic to another so fast Kennedy could barely keep up. They jumped from talking about raising kids, to hormonal teenage girls, to little league sports, to attending church.

Scott's mom took Kennedy by surprise when she asked her if she'd like to attend church with them next Sunday.

"Um…maybe. I might make a trip to Spokane to visit my friend next weekend."

Alice put a hand on Kennedy's shoulder. "Well, you're always welcome to join us."

"Thank you," Kennedy said, even though she wasn't sure she'd ever take Alice up on her invitation, especially if Scott attended church with his family. Sitting by him at church would feel weird but sitting alone wasn't appealing either.

When dinner was served, she sat at an empty table that soon filled up with teenage girls. She couldn't keep herself from searching out Scott in the crowd. He made eye contact with her, and for a moment, she thought he might sit in the one remaining seat beside her. That is until one of his brothers-in-law said something to him, drawing him into a conversation. He cast a brief glance her way, his lips lifting in a half smile or maybe it was a grimace—hard to tell with that man— before sliding into a chair across the table from Liam—or was it Mason?

Disappointment settled heavy in her stomach, stealing her appetite.

"Hey, Kennedy, thanks for saving me a seat." Rudy winked as he sat beside her.

She couldn't help smiling at Scott's friendly brother. Although he was attractive in his own way, he didn't make her heart race and her insides turn to jelly every time he was near. But at least he paid attention to her and smiled at her, which was more than she could say for Scott. She was beginning to think the man really didn't like her.

Kennedy had dressed up for this party—something she didn't do very often—with the intention of having a good time. Just because Scott refused to acknowledge her presence didn't mean she couldn't still have fun. With his brother.

KENNEDY'S LAUGHTER filled the air, and something twisted in Scott's midsection. He looked over Mason's shoulder at Rudy and Kennedy sitting at the next table.

Seeing her glide so gracefully into the backyard when she first arrived totally knocked the wind out of him. She'd almost looked like an angel. Except she wore blue. Didn't angels always wear white?

Either way, there was something ethereal about Kennedy. Every day at work, he saw the stubborn tomboy who was determined to prove herself, but behind the grease-stained jeans and t-shirts with ridiculous sayings, he couldn't help but see the woman she tried to hide. And he struggled to treat her like just another mechanic. But tonight, with her pretty dress, side braid, and strappy sandals she was all woman.

She reminded him of that ice princess in the Disney movie his nieces had watched over and over again several years ago. Elsa, was it? It was probably still sexist of him to think of Kennedy as Elsa, but it sounded better than the clichéd Barbie.

Like a teenage boy with a crush, she did things to him. Things that made him feel anxious and excited all at once. Unfortunately, like usual, the anxious part won out and left him speechless. He hadn't even been able to spit out a proper greeting when she first arrived. It hadn't helped that she'd caught him with a baby in his arms.

Shortly before Kennedy arrived, Debbie dropped baby William in his arms when one of the twins fell and scraped her knee. He hadn't minded holding the cute little infant, but he'd been psyching himself up to talk to Kennedy about something other than cars tonight, and the baby had been a distraction. Then when Kennedy smiled at him with raised eyebrows, he'd felt self-conscious and completely tongue tied. Dallas begging him to come play soccer gave him a chance to escape awkward conversation, so he took it.

Kennedy laughed again, and a coiled spring tightened in Scott's abdomen. Why couldn't he be more like Rudy? Outgoing, witty, funny, and able to converse with anyone about anything?

Rudy bumped shoulders with Kennedy and said something that made her smile again.

Scott gripped his plastic fork so tight, it snapped. Austin and Mason laughed, and when Kennedy looked up, she caught him staring at her. He tried to smile, but he wasn't sure his lips moved, and when her smile faded, he looked away again.

Blast! She probably thinks I don't like her.

Nothing could be further from the truth. He'd only known her a little over a week, but he liked her more than any woman he'd met in a long time.

"Green's not a very good color on you," Austin said quietly beside him.

Scott startled. "Don't know what you're talking about."

Austin gave him a sly grin. "Your mom caught me looking at Debbie that same way, only without the jealousy, at the barbecue after we built the gazebo last spring."

And now Austin and Debbie were married with six children. Scott lowered his gaze to his plate. He wasn't looking to get married, was he? He didn't plan on being single his whole life but putting himself out there was hard. Harder than most extroverted people realized. Especially when he'd already lost one woman he cared about.

He grunted but otherwise ignored Austin's comment. Thankfully, his brother-in-law got the hint and dropped the subject.

After dinner, Rudy pulled him and Kennedy out onto the grass with several of the others—kids and adults alike—to play Nine Square. He pushed Kennedy toward Scott and said, "Explain to Kennedy how to play the game, will you?" Then he walked away to recruit two more players.

Kennedy turned toward him and smiled. "Is this game hard?"

Scott's mouth went dry at the sight of her double dimples. His tongue stuck to the roof of his mouth, and he couldn't find the words to respond. He finally managed to shake his head about the time her eyebrows crept up.

"So how do we play?"

Uncomfortable with the direct eye contact, he looked down at the grass and spotted her bare feet with ruby red toenails, and all thoughts fled from his mind.

"Um…"

Blast! Why can't I speak around her?

He didn't have this problem at work. But at work, she didn't look like an angel—or a princess. Besides, they only talked about cars and work stuff at work.

Gah!

Even his thoughts sounded stupid in his head. How was he supposed to explain a game to this pretty woman?

Again, her eyebrows rose, and he felt the heat creeping up his neck. "Hit the ball!" he blurted.

"Okay, but where do I hit it?"

"Up."

"Any particular direction?"

"Nope."

"Any other rules besides hit the ball?" Kennedy asked with a chuckle.

"Don't let it hit the ground."

"What happens if the ball hits the ground?"

Scott scratched at the back of his neck as the heat continued to build there. Explaining how a player had to rotate back to the beginning if they let the ball hit the ground, felt like too many words to get out without stumbling over them.

His niece Savannah stepped close to Kennedy. "It's like volleyball, but each person is playing against every other person in the nine squares…"

Scott wanted to hug his new niece for saving him and explaining something he would have bungled for sure.

Kennedy nodded after Savannah answered all her questions. "Sounds easy enough, but I'm not sure I want to start out next to Scott. He's so tall, he'll get me out in no time."

An odd mixture of relief and disappointment hit him as Kennedy stepped into the empty square on the other side of Savannah. Then she turned and smiled at him, and his heart beat a little harder against his ribcage.

The game got under way, and Scott did his best not to step on any of the little kids around him while defending his square. Shortly after he reached the center and became king, Kennedy ended up in the next highest square. He'd been taking it easy when his nephews were there, and he found himself wanting to go easy on Kennedy too. He couldn't seem to talk to her, but he could at least attempt to play nice.

Kennedy thought otherwise and took his coveted center square within seconds with an unexpected spike of the ball. She grinned at him as he walked back to square one. "You're not supposed to let the ball hit the ground."

The game became more intense and aggressive over the next forty-five minutes as the younger kids wandered off and more adults joined in. Rudy's competitive streak came out, and he and Kennedy seemed to team up against everyone else to keep one or the other of them in the king's position.

They flirted and laughed, giving each other high fives so often Scott wanted to rip his brother's arm off. A burning sensation shot through Scott's chest every time Rudy's hand touched Kennedy's.

Why couldn't Rudy dial it down a notch?

Either his brother had developed a thing for Kennedy, or he was trying to goad Scott into admitting how much he liked her. It wouldn't work though. Scott wouldn't give him that satisfaction. As much as Scott hated to admit it, Rudy was a much better match for Kennedy than he was.

She deserved someone who wasn't broody and critical of her desire to work in a garage. Someone who could make her laugh. Like his brother did.

CHAPTER 11

Scott tugged at his collar to get a little more air into his lungs. Why had he thought it'd be a good idea to wear a tie to meet with Ezra Patterson, loan officer? Sure, he wanted to make a good impression, but he might have gone overboard with the suit *and* tie.

He checked the clock on the wall in the bank's lobby for the tenth time. He'd only been waiting five minutes, but it felt like an eternity. What if Ezra decided Scott didn't qualify for a loan?

Scott rubbed clammy palms on his suit pants.

I'll qualify. I have good credit, a steady job, and a sizable nest egg.

But what if Ezra handed him a loan application and told him to fill it out?

That was partly the reason he'd come in person to apply for a loan; he probably could have filled out an application online, but he kind of hoped Ezra would ask the questions, so Scott could give the answers, and the loan officer could fill out the form for him. He was so focused on not getting up and walking out that he didn't see Ezra step out of the small glass office and cross the equally small waiting room.

"Scott?" The older man's voice was filled with surprise as he called Scott's name.

He bolted to his feet so fast, Ezra fell back a step.

"Yeah, that's me," Scott said.

Of course, it's me.

Not only was he the only Scott Wheeler in this small town, he was also the only customer in the waiting area.

"I didn't recognize you in your fancy duds there." The short balding man waved a hand, motioning to Scott's attire.

Scott adjusted his suit coat that seemed to squeeze his shoulders like a vice and resisted the urge to pull off his tie.

Yep. I definitely overdressed.

He didn't even go to this much effort on Sundays. He either wore a suit jacket with no tie and the collar of his dress shirt unbuttoned or wore a tie with no suit coat. Rarely did he ever wear both.

Scott grabbed the loan officer's extended hand and squeezed as he pumped his arm up and down.

Ezra winced.

"Sorry." Scott released the other man's hand and shoved his into his pockets. He followed Ezra into the small office and sat in a chair that was extremely uncomfortable and too small for his large frame.

As if I'm not anxious enough.

"What can I do for you, Scott?"

"Um… I'd like to apply for a loan."

"That should be easy enough. Generally, all we need is two forms of ID, a quick credit check, and proof of steady employment. Your tax statements for the last two years should suffice. I don't suppose you brought them with you?"

"No." Scott wasn't even sure where to find his tax information. Rudy often helped him file online and organized that kind of stuff for him. He had no idea where his brother might have saved the documents.

"Well, let's get started on the application, shall we? And you can email me the tax documents later." Ezra clicked his mouse a few times then looked at Scott with his hands poised over his keyboard. "What's your account number?"

Scott rattled off his account number, and Ezra's fingers flew over the keys. The older man's eyebrows rose as he studied his computer screen.

"It looks like you have a substantial amount in your savings already. How big of a loan are you needing?"

Scott pulled his phone from his pocket and opened his notes app where he'd already done the math and recorded the amount he needed to borrow. He didn't struggle with numbers quite as badly as he did with words, but he didn't want to take the chance of messing something up. He told Ezra the amount he wanted to borrow.

The other man's eyebrows climbed toward his hairline again. "That's a large sum for a personal loan."

"Well, it's not really personal. I'm purchasing a...business."

"Oh? What business?"

Could he qualify for the loan without actually telling the loan officer what the money was for? He might not be able to keep his purchase of the shop a surprise from his family if he had to tell Ezra. The older man wasn't a known gossip, but news had a way of traveling in small towns.

Scott glanced over his shoulder as if there might be someone eavesdropping in the empty lobby. "Charity Knight has agreed to sell the repair shop to me."

"Is that so?"

Scott couldn't tell if it was disbelief or surprise that drove Ezra's eyebrows upward this time.

"Yes, but I need to get qualified for a loan before Andy Giles can start all the real estate paperwork."

"True, but I'm afraid this type of business loan isn't as simple to apply for as a personal loan."

"It isn't? Why?" Scott's tie seemed to tighten like a noose around his throat, cutting off his air supply, and his suit jacket felt like it had shrunk across his shoulders.

"Well, between me and Andy, we'll need a lot more documentation."

"What kind of documentation?" The question rasped out of Scott's dry throat.

"For starters, both you and the Knights need to sign a letter of intent that includes not only the agreed upon price but also an itemization of which business assets and liabilities will be included in the sale. Are the convenience store and gas station included in the sale?"

Scott nodded. Wait. Had Charity understood his offer to buy the repair shop as a package deal with the convenience store and gas station, like he'd meant it?

Liabilities?

Scott's rattled mind jumped to the next big word Ezra had said. He doubted the Knights carried any debt or liabilities on the garage since it had been in their family for over thirty years, but it would be good to have a clear list of assets—like the gas station, the acreage behind the shop, and the tow truck. He made a mental note to talk to Charity about a letter of intent.

Should be easy enough. Especially if the Knights draw it up, then all he had to do was sign.

Ezra went on. "You'll need to review the contracts and leases the Knights currently have with their vendors and employees for the repair shop as well as the gas station. And isn't there someone living in the apartment above the garage right now? Will you maintain those contracts?" Ezra barely waited for Scott to nod before continuing. "I suggest you ask for a copy of their business financials."

"Financials?" The word squeaked out of Scott's throat.

"Yes. Tax returns, budgets, cash flow statements, accounts payable and receivable, debt disclosures, that kind of thing. I know you've worked there for years, but do you really know what their bottom line is?"

Scott shook his head. With Mary's and Rudy's help, he put information into a balance sheet each month and made quarterly reports, but that was all. He knew the shop was profitable—since it was one of only two repair shops in Providence—but he had no idea how profitable. Nor did he have a clue what he was supposed to do with business financials.

What am I getting myself into?

"In addition to the appraisal and inspection, you may want to schedule a boundary survey, and of course, make sure the property is ADA and OSHA compliant."

Repair shops are supposed to be OSHA compliant?

Scott's ears began to ring, and he felt like he was breathing through a straw. The kind you stirred your coffee with. No way could he figure out that kind of paperwork by himself.

Completely oblivious to Scott's impending panic attack, Ezra kept talking. "And of course, you'll need to obtain your own business license and all the appropriate permits associated with operating a gas station and a store that sells alcohol. You'll be required to register with the state, secure an insurance policy on the business, and will you operate the business under an LLC or a sole proprietor—"

Scott bolted to his feet.

It's all too much. I can't do this!

"I've got to go." The words came out gruff and sharp.

Ezra looked up at him, surprise once again filling his face. "Wait, we haven't even finished the loan application to get you pre-approved."

Scott raked his hands through his hair then clasped his fingers behind his neck. The pull of his suit jacket against his elbows and across his back only added to his agitation. "I can't—" He sucked in a deep breath. "I don't have time for all of this right now."

"Well, give me your email address and I'll send the loan application over. All you need to do is fill it out and attach the tax documents. We'll work with Andy once he starts the paperwork for the sale to get all the other stuff taken care of."

Scott gave a curt nod and rattled off his email. Taking long strides, he crossed the foyer of the bank in three steps and hurried out to his truck. He climbed inside and took a few steadying breaths, feeling his heartbeat pound against his ribcage. All the things Ezra rattled off tumbled around inside his head. Scott had no idea buying a shop required so much paperwork. How was he supposed to make sense of all the reports and documentation and what not that would be required of him?

Perspiration pricked his brow as feelings of frustration coupled with dread and helplessness swept over him. It was the same feeling he got every time a big essay or project was assigned in high school. It was so daunting, he felt like a failure before he even started the project.

Sure, he could have the audio software read documents to him, but it wouldn't help him make sense of all the legal and financial mumbo jumbo, let alone supply the information he'd need to provide. If he was ever going to own his own shop, he was going to have to humble himself more than he ever had before.

Hopefully, Rudy could help him make sense of all the paperwork. His younger brother was probably the smartest one in the family. Although Debbie did have a host of lawyers at her disposal. Scott hated using his sister and her money like that though.

GREAT! *Just great!*

Kennedy hurried up the back stairs behind the garage and let herself back into her apartment. It was just her luck that her period would start—a whole week early—on the one day Scott asked her to open the shop.

She'd left the bay doors open because she didn't want Scott to arrive and find them still closed, but she didn't want him to show up and have her nowhere in sight with thousands of dollars of expensive tools on display either.

It's fine. Scott won't be here for at least another half hour.

She quickly changed and grabbed the small, gray with pink trim cosmetic bag from under the sink. After checking to make sure it had plenty of tampons, she hurried back to the empty shop.

It felt strange being there all alone, but it gave her ample opportunity to stash her "girly bag" somewhere Scott wouldn't notice. This was the worst part about working in a male-dominated career. Some men, usually the married ones, had no problem with her leaving her personal stuff in the bathroom, but most men were embarrassed or freaked out by it.

Thankfully, the bathroom doubled as the janitorial closet, and she was able to tuck it on an upper shelf behind some cleaning products. Scott was tall, so he'd probably still see it, but hopefully, he wouldn't notice.

She looked over her shoulder to double check that her bag wasn't visible as she walked out of the bathroom.

"There you are." A deep agitated voice came from a large dark figure that filled the doorway. He blocked the light coming in through the open bay doors, shrouding his face in shadows.

Kennedy's heart leaped to her throat as a surge of adrenaline shot through her. Her brain screamed at her to run as buried memories of being cornered in the parts room by Leo, a burly coworker with a record, surfaced. A cold chill swept over her. Her heart raced so fast, she feared it might burst.

Her escape route was blocked, so she chose fight over flight. Doubling her fist, she struck out hard and fast at the threat.

The looming figure's head flew back before snapping upright again, "Ow! What did you do that for?" A familiar low grumbling sound punctuated the words.

Kennedy caught a glint of light against auburn hair, and recognition dawned on her. She gasped and clapped a hand over her mouth.

Oh no! I just punched Scott.

Her stomach plummeted. She should have recognized his voice, but it had been deeper and more guttural than usual, as though he were angry or frustrated.

His eyes widened as his fingers flew to his nose.

"I'm so sorry! I didn't realize it was you. You scared me to death."

"Of course, it's me. Who else were you expecting?"

"No one. That's why you scared me so badly. I wasn't expecting *you* for a while yet." She took in his dark suit. No wonder she hadn't recognized him. She'd never seen him dressed up before. He sure cleaned up nicely. "Why are you wearing a suit?"

Scott sniffed and let out a little groan. "I had an appointment." He sniffed again. "Oh no, no, no." He pushed past her to get into the bathroom. Stepping in front of the sink, he pulled his hand away from his face.

Bright red blood filled his palm and dripped from his nose.

Kennedy let out a cry of alarm. Had she really hit him hard enough to give him a bloody nose?

Scott swore and grabbed a handful of paper towels.

"I'm so sorry. What can I do to help?"

"Duh-thig." The word was a muffled nasally groan.

Kennedy hovered in the doorway of the bathroom, guilt eating at her, and watched as he leaned over the sink repeatedly dabbing at his nose. The blood kept coming.

"Pinch the bridge of your nose," she said.

"I ab." His groan rumbled through the bathroom.

Right.

He squeezed his nose with his left hand while blotting with the right, and Kennedy stood helplessly by.

"Try tipping your head back."

"Why? So I choke on my owb blood?"

"Well, if you're not careful you'll get blood all over your clothes."

"Do't you think I knowb that?" Scott shifted his hands from his face long enough to inspect his clothing, which allowed the blood to flow with renewed vigor.

He swore under his breath and cast a quick glance her way. "I deed your help."

Biting back a grin at the nasally sound of his voice, Kennedy stepped to his side. "Of course, what can I do?"

"Take my clothes off."

"What?" She jerked back. Despite the flat tonal quality of his voice, she had no problem understanding his words.

"I don't want to get blood all over my suit, but I can't take my hands away from my nose to change my clothes."

Her amusement at the funny sound of his voice fled. "But…"

"At least help me get this blasted suit jacket off." He pulled his left hand away from his nose and attempted to shrug out of his jacket.

Kennedy stepped behind him and took a hold of the collar. "Why are you wearing a suit?"

"Told you. I had an appoi'tment." He pulled one arm out then shifted the paper towels to the other hand. "Wait. I need to wash this hand. It's all bloody."

"Did you have a court hearing or something?" The only time Kennedy had ever known mechanics at T&J's to dress up was when they had to go to court for a DUI or speeding tickets. Of course, none of them had ever looked this nice when they dressed up.

And boy did Scott look nice! Except for the blood streaming from his nose.

He'd shaved today, making him look less like a lumberjack and more like a model on the cover of GQ. Kennedy couldn't decide which look she liked better. It's no wonder she didn't recognize him when he stood in the doorway with his face in the shadows.

"What?" He scowled at her in the mirror. "Of course not. I just had…an important meeting."

"Must have been trying to make a good impression," Kennedy said, fishing for more information.

"Obviously." At least that's what Kennedy thought he said with his muffled nasally response.

Hiding a grin, she tilted her head and studied him while he dried his hand. He was being secretive. Why?

He shifted and freed his other arm from his suit jacket. She held it and looked around, searching for a clean place to lay it. Finally, she hung it on the corner of the rack that held the cleaning supplies. She turned back to find him unbuttoning the cuffs of his shirt with one hand. When his movements caused the towels to slip away from his nose, blood gushed as though it didn't intend to stop anytime soon.

"Blast!" He grabbed a fresh handful of paper towels and pressed them to his face. "Come take my shirt off."

Kennedy froze. Was he serious?

She'd never taken a man's shirt off before. She wasn't that kind of girl and even though she knew Scott wasn't suggesting something sexual, the thought of standing close to him and unbuttoning his shirt made her hot all over.

"Kennedy, please." He turned pleading eyes to her. "If I get blood on my shirt, my mom will never let me hear the end of it."

Momma's boy needs help.

She snickered, and Scott scowled at her again.

"If you insist." Hopefully her voice sounded more put out than breathless, like she felt.

He turned away from the sink as she stepped close to him. She grabbed his necktie and tried to loosen it by tugging on the bottom strap. Wasn't that how her dad used to do it?

"Not like that," Scott said in a strained voice. "Are you trying to kill me today?" His hand—warm and strong—wrapped around hers and pulled the knot from side to side to loosen it.

Warmth, delicious and electrifying, raced up her arm. It was all Kennedy could do not to jerk away.

"Now pull from here." His voice was much lower and deeper than a moment ago as he released her hand and tugged one side of the tie.

She looked up at his face as she followed his instructions. His hazel eyes were darker than she'd ever seen them before. The striking mossy color looked both mysterious and inviting. Focusing on what she was supposed to be doing, she slid the tie from around his neck and folded it before slipping it into the pocket of his suit coat.

Scott already had the collar of his dress shirt unbuttoned when she turned back, but he stopped his efforts as soon as she approached. His gaze locked with hers as she slid the first button from its hole. His chest pressed out with his inhalations and her knuckles brushed against the hard muscles behind the fabric.

The beating of her heart pulsed in her ears as her breath caught in her lungs. Her hands trembled as she fought the urge to splay her palm across his chest. A fantasy filled her mind of Scott taking her in his arms and holding her tight against him before lowering his lips to hers

"Kennedy?" Scott's voice was rough and gravelly. "What are you doing?"

She startled and sucked in a ragged breath, checking to make sure she hadn't accidentally caressed his pec. She hadn't.

Thank goodness.

She cleared her throat. "I-I'm unbuttoning your shirt."

"Are you going to finish sometime today?"

Heat filled her face. "Sorry, I've never…" Did she want to admit she'd never taken a man's shirt off before? That felt like too much information to share with a coworker. "I-it's backward from my shirts."

It's backward? Really?

How lame. Could Scott tell how affected she was by touching him?

His only response was a soft grunt.

She hurried and finished the remainder of the buttons, trying to keep her eyes from lingering on the expanse of skin that became more visible with each button. And trying in vain to ignore the fact that his abs were as taut as his pecs.

Warmth emanated off his body, and his breathing sounded a little more ragged than it had moments ago, making her pulse keep a frantic pace. As soon as she released the final button, he turned and shrugged out of the shirt.

She took it from his shoulders and draped it over his suit coat before turning back to him. Her breath hitched. She'd seen a few bare-chested men in her life, but she'd never seen one quite so sculpted. She told herself to look away, but her eyes didn't want to obey.

"Holy fudge nuggets!" Her thoughts rushed out of her mouth, sounding every bit as breathless as she felt.

"What?" Scott pulled the towels from his face and looked at his chest in alarm.

"You… You're kind of ripped." Warmth rushed to her face again. "I mean, I knew you were built, but I've never seen anyone quite so…" At a loss for words, she waved her hand at his bare torso.

Blood dripped onto his chest.

He swore and pressed the towels to his face again. Without thinking, Kennedy grabbed a paper towel and dabbed at the blood on his chest. This time, she let her fingertips linger on his skin. The dusting of hair there wasn't near as thick or as course as she expected a man of his size to have.

He froze except for the involuntary twitch of the muscle beneath her fingers.

So did Kennedy. Her gaze jumped to his again. His hands blocked most of his face, but she could see a spark of something in his eyes. Something darker—and more enticing—than what she'd seen in his eyes last Friday when she'd thought he might kiss her.

It was probably a good thing he held a wad of paper towels to his face, or she might have been tempted to rock forward on her toes and press her lips to his. Her legs grew weak as she imagined what it would be like to be kissed by Scott and held in his strong arms.

Scott staggered back a little. "I think I need to sit down," he said in a raspy voice.

Right. She should sit down before she lost strength in her legs altogether.

"Me too," Kennedy said with a rush of air. "I mean, I think you should sit down too. Y-you've lost a lot of blood."

She grabbed a roll of shop towels and followed him to the office where he dropped into a chair. He tipped his head back and closed his eyes.

"Are you going to pass out on me?" She hovered near him.

Scott's only response was a shake of his head.

Blood already soaked his latest handful of paper towels. This wasn't normal, was it?

Her stomach clenched, and tension lifted her shoulders. How would this affect her job?

I just assaulted my boss.

She set the paper towels on the table and rubbed her palms against her thighs. She chewed on her bottom lip while studying the toes of her boots.

Scott could fire her if he wanted to. He'd probably jump at a valid reason to get rid of her.

She'd have to pick up and move again, because she doubted she could find any other work in Providence. Eden would welcome her back in a heartbeat, but no way would Kennedy go back to T&J's.

CHAPTER 12

Scott took a deep breath and counted to five before letting it out. The woman standing over him was driving him crazy in a whole new way. If his nose hadn't been bleeding, he'd have grabbed her and kissed her senseless right there in the bathroom.

Of course, if his nose hadn't been bleeding, he wouldn't have needed her to help him undress and therefore been tempted to kiss her.

"Do I need to take you to the hospital?"

"No, it happens all the time," he said as his head began to pound. "My capillaries are really close to the surface, and I often burst a blood vessel just blowing my nose."

"Does it always bleed this bad?" Kennedy handed him a fresh handful of paper towels.

He threw the soaked ones in the trash can she carried over and pressed the new ones to his face. "They're worse when the weather is dry."

It had been a while since he'd had one this bad. Of course, it had been a while since they'd had rain too. And even longer since he'd been punched in the face.

Kennedy shifted from one foot to the other as she rubbed her knuckles.

She was definitely stronger than she looked. He still couldn't believe how hard she'd hit him. He'd seen stars there for several seconds after she punched him.

"How's your hand?"

"Um…it hurts a little." She tucked her hands behind her back. "I'm so sorry, Scott. I never should have hit you. You just scared the fudge nuggets out of me."

He chuckled at her version of swear words. The action made his head pound harder. Between the trauma to his face and the loss of blood, he was going to have one whopper of a headache this afternoon.

"I thought you were joking when you said you'd studied Taek-wondo and kickboxing." He shook his head. "But hey, you didn't actually take me down."

"That's because I wasn't really trying. It was just a reflex thing." Kennedy wrapped her arms around herself as she spoke, and Scott sensed there had been a specific motivation behind her studying self-defense and the martial arts.

After another minute or so, she handed him fresh paper towels.

"Are you sure you don't want me to take you to the doctor?"

"So I can tell them I was punched by a woman? No thanks!" If even one person at the hospital found out the truth, it would be all over town by afternoon, and people would question whether he'd done something inappropriate that warranted being punched. Small towns were funny that way.

"I've heard serious nosebleeds can sometimes be a sign of Leukemia or a brain tumor."

"I don't have a tumor. I have ITP."

"What?"

"Idiopathic Thrombocyto—something. I can never remember how to say it, let alone spell it. Basically, it means I have low platelets in my blood, which makes it slow to clot."

"Between having surface capillaries and your blood not clotting well, doesn't that make nosebleeds—or any injury for that matter—really dangerous?"

"They can be, yes. Normally, my nosebleeds aren't caused by being punched in the face though, so they aren't usually this bad."

"I feel terrible." Kennedy continued to hover over him. "How do you usually stop a bad one like this?"

Scott didn't want to tell her because it meant going to the ER.

She propped her hands on her hips. "Well?"

"The doctor either cauterizes it or puts a rhino rocket in."

Kennedy snorted. "A rhino rocket?"

"It's a long skinny cottony thing."

"Like…a tampon?"

"What? No. I don't know." The one and only time the doctor had used a rhino rocket on Scott, it reminded him of the feminine hygiene product his older sisters kept in the bathroom drawer. Even though he'd had the thought, he'd never been curious enough to find out just how similar the two were.

"I'll be right back," Kennedy said before hurrying out of the office. She returned with two small, slender, pink and white packages. "We could try these."

"What are those?" Scott asked even though he already knew the answer.

Kennedy rolled her eyes. "What do you think they are?"

"Where did they come from?" She hadn't been gone long enough to run clear upstairs.

"They're mine. I uh…stashed some in the bathroom earlier."

Was that why she was so jumpy and overreacted when he startled her? He leaned away from her as much as his chair allowed. "No thanks."

She dropped the packages on the table and pulled more squares from the roll of shop towels. "It's that or I take you to the ER. You've soaked through already."

Blast! This one is a doozy!

He did not want to put tampons up his nose, but he didn't want to go to the hospital either. And he definitely didn't want to explain how he got the bloody nose in the first place. He swallowed hard as heat enveloped his face, ears, and neck.

He locked gazes with Kennedy. That stubborn glint he'd seen so often in her eyes sparked, and he knew she wouldn't give up. He continued to scowl at her.

She picked up one of the pink packages. "Let's try this." He shook his head, but she went on. "It's a small size so…"

"I don't care what size it is, you're not sticking that thing up my nose. I'm pretty sure the ones the doctor uses are medicated or something."

"Great, let's go then. I'll drive you to the hospital." She pulled her phone from her pocket. "Or shall I call 911?"

"No!" the word came out a growl. "Fine. Let's do this."

She held the slender package out to him.

"Why are you handing it to me? I don't know what to do with it?"

"Well, I don't either. I've never put one in my nose before."

Scott shook his head and glared at her. "Neither have I."

"We're smart people. We can figure this out together." She ripped open the package. "It'll probably be more comfortable if we remove the applicator."

Scott wasn't sure what she was talking about, but he had no desire to discuss the process with her. "Whatever. Just do it already."

Kennedy straddled his knee and leaned over him.

Her proximity elevated his blood pressure and raised the temperature in the small office to something close to a sauna. Well, a dry sauna, as his nosebleed attested. Was there such a thing as a dry sauna?

Yes, the desert.

Man, his mind felt muddled. Was it because of the nosebleed or the woman standing over him?

Her stance in front of him put her chest at eye level, and for the first time today, he focused on her shirt. Again, it took him so long to read the words that Kennedy probably thought him a pervert. *Admit it. Life would be boring without me.*

He would have burst out laughing, except doing so after staring at her chest would be horribly inappropriate. He raised his gaze to the ceiling. Life had certainly been anything but boring since she came to work at the garage. Had it only been a little over a week ago? Life had also become a heck of a lot more stressful too, in some regards.

"Okay." She took a deep breath. "Do I go upward or what?"

"No, straight back." At least that's how he thought he remembered the doctor doing it years ago. "I think." He growled. "I don't know. Just don't shove it in too far."

This is a stupid idea. We don't even know what we're doing.

She chuckled as she stepped closer. "I can't believe I'm doing this."

Kennedy put her fingertips on his cheeks, poised ready to stick the wad of cotton in his nose. Her long hair brushed his bare shoulder, and he sucked in a sharp breath.

He pulled the towels away from his face and braced himself. To keep from looking at her chest, he focused on her big brown eyes, spotting tiny golden flecks in her brown irises. His gaze jumped back and forth from one eye to the other, and he noticed something he'd never realized before. Her left iris was darker than her right, but the right eye was slightly larger and opened wider than the left.

The woman he found so attractive and thought was perfect in so many ways had a flaw. Despite the little discrepancy, her eyes were still the most beautiful he'd ever seen. The tip of her tongue peeked out of the corner of her mouth as she gently pushed the cotton in his nose, and the urge to kiss her hit him like a Mac truck. He squeezed his eyes shut.

"Am I hurting you?" Kennedy asked in a soft voice that felt like a caress.

He opened his eyes and noted the furrow between her brows. "No."

"Good. When you closed your eyes, I thought maybe I was hurting you."

"I'm fine. I just… Never mind." He couldn't tell her he'd closed his eyes because she drove him crazy in a very nonprofessional way. "I hardly feel anything."

Except the throbbing ache in the middle of my face.

"That's because it's not really going in."

"What?"

"Well, I'm trying not to push too hard because I don't want to hurt you. But it's not really moving."

He reached up and took hold of the tampon. Gingerly, he pushed in an upward direction rather than back as he rolled his top lip down over his teeth. He felt it shift in his nostril, creating a sensation of fullness. When the cotton met resistance, he twisted and wiggled it a little until it moved again.

Finally, he reached a point where he wasn't sure he should go any farther. He looked up to find Kennedy biting her top lip to keep from laughing.

A small giggle escaped her, and he grabbed the second slender package off the table. "You're doing this one." The string from the tampon tickled his lips, and it was all he could do to keep from swearing.

"Why me? You did it better than I could have." She giggled again.

"Because you gave me the bloody nose." And because he wanted to see her squirm a little.

Once again, his attraction skyrocketed as she stepped into his personal space. He focused on taking steady breaths and keeping his hands in his lap and off her hips while she put the second tampon in his nose.

Finally, she stepped back. "How does that feel?"

"Like there's a whole lot of something in my nose that doesn't belong there." His voice sounded more nasally than ever.

Kennedy must have thought so too, because the corners of her mouth quirked, as though she held back a smile.

"So, what made you decide to take up kickboxing and Taekwon-do?" he asked.

Her smile vanished, and she wrapped her arms around herself in a protective gesture again. "I um…had trouble with a guy at work years ago."

"What kind of trouble?" Scott wasn't sure he wanted to know, but he hated the idea of anyone hurting Kennedy.

"Leo was an ex-con. He was big; six-four, two-eighty. He cornered me late one afternoon in the parts room at T&J's." A tremor filled her voice as she continued. "He tried forcing himself on me."

Now Scott balled his fists because he wanted to hit something. "I'm so sorry, Kennedy."

She shook her head and shrugged as though trying to shed the memories. "Fortunately, my dad heard me scream and came to my rescue. He fired Leo on the spot, but I hated how weak and powerless I felt in that moment. I promised myself I would never feel that way again. And I haven't, until today."

"I didn't mean to scare you." He gingerly touched his nose. "You are anything but weak."

"I guess I was just jumpy. I'm not used to being here in the shop alone." She rubbed her hands on her thighs again. "I'm really sorry I hit you. Do we need to fill out an accident report or something?"

"Are you kidding? I'm not documenting this." He pointed to the ends of the cotton sticking out of his nose.

She sighed and her shoulders seemed to relax. Then she grinned, and his heart jolted at the dimples that creased her cheeks. "I'm guessing you don't want me to tell anyone I gave you a bloody nose?"

He pointed a finger at her. "Not. A. Word." One of the strings somehow managed to get into his mouth again. He spit making a sound somewhere between "ptooey" and a raspberry.

Kennedy burst out laughing, and despite his annoyance, he joined her. She picked up her phone from the table. "So, you don't want me to take a picture right now?"

"Don't you dare."

She lifted the phone up in front of her.

He was out of his chair in a flash, and with a giggle and a squeal, she darted from the office. He chased after her, following her around the Ford Focus in the first bay then toward the bathroom. He stayed hot on her tail, and when she tried to slam the door in his face, he shoved it open.

She backed against the sink still giggling, her phone clasped to her chest.

Scott slowed his pace and blocked her path to the door as he crept toward her like a lion stalking his prey. His gaze locked with hers as he drew nearer. The twinkle of humor in her eyes and the grin on her face made her prettier than ever. He envisioned putting a hand on the sink on either side of her, pinning her there while he kissed her thoroughly.

She sobered, and her eyes darted around, looking for an escape, but he stood right in front of her now, and she had nowhere to go. She inhaled sharply, and he did the same.

Then she busted out laughing again. "Y-you have kind of a sexy and dangerous look in your eyes, but I just can't take you s-seriously with tampons sticking out of your nose."

Scott stopped his advance and looked at himself in the mirror. He looked ridiculous. No wonder Kennedy kept giggling. So much for thinking she was feeling the same charged tension he was.

"Scott! Kennedy!" Rudy's voice came from out in the shop. "Anyone around?"

Scott stepped away from Kennedy and swore under his breath. "He can't see me like this." He brought a hand up in front of his face. "I'll never live it down."

"I'll go talk to him. You…" She waved a hand at his chest. "At least put a shirt on." She stepped to the door.

He grabbed her arm. "Don't you dare tell him how I got the bloody nose."

She grinned before ducking out of the bathroom and pulling the door closed behind her.

Scott looked at himself in the mirror and swore again. He looked absurd. The bridge of his nose was swollen, and a bluish bruise darkened the inside of his eyes. Did he dare pull the tampons out already?

He heard Rudy ask where he was and Kennedy's explanation of helping him clean up from a bloody nose as he pulled a shirt on.

"Was it a bad one?" Rudy asked. "Do I need to take him to the hospital?"

"I offered to do that, but you know how stubborn your brother is."

Scott scowled at the closed door as he buttoned his shirt. It was all he could do to not let his thoughts linger on the way Kennedy's hands had touched his chest as she unbuttoned his dress shirt. Her touch had set off all kinds of electric currents racing every which way in his body.

He doubted Rudy would be patient long enough for him to change his suit pants, so he left the tail of his shirt hanging out and stepped to the sink again. He grabbed some paper towels just in case, and carefully pulled one tampon then the other from his nose. They hadn't been in there that long, but they seemed to have done the trick.

Yes!

He walked out of the bathroom to find Kennedy and Rudy talking quietly each with a hip leaning against the workbench. It was bad enough that his brother flirted with Kennedy all evening last night, now he'd come to the garage to do it again.

Rudy turned to him. "Whoa, dude! What happened to you?"

"Bloody nose."

"Yeah, but did you get punched in the face or something? Your whole nose is swollen, and it looks like you're going to have two black eyes."

Blast! So much for hoping Rudy wouldn't notice the swelling and bruising.

His brother always noticed everything, especially since becoming a cop.

"Are you sure you don't need to go to a doctor?"

"I'm fine," Scott said in a gruff voice. "It's stopped bleeding now."

"But what started it? You look like you forgot to wear your catcher's mask."

Kennedy fidgeted behind Rudy, guilt covering her face as she gnawed on her bottom lip.

"Nothing. I'm fine." He said the words as much for Kennedy's benefit as he did Rudy's.

"Something must have happened to cause bruising and swelling like that."

He stepped closer to Rudy, getting right in his face. "What are you doing here?"

Rudy stared at him for a long moment before grinning and giving him an I'll-get-you-to-tell-me-later look.

Scott cocked an eyebrow, answering with an over-my-dead-body look.

"I crossed paths with Austin this morning. He said he forgot to mention last night that we can start framing Mary's addition this weekend. He wanted me to make sure you left Saturday open. We need your brute strength." Rudy slapped Scott's shoulder before turning to Kennedy. "Hey, you should come help too."

Great.

That's all Scott needed. It was bad enough Kennedy distracted him to no end here in the garage, and as much as he liked the idea of working side by side with her on Mary's addition, the idea of her using power tools caused tension to coil in his gut. Construction work could be dangerous.

"What exactly are you doing?" Kennedy asked.

"Mary is a good friend of our family. A little over a month ago, her son Chase was in a terrible motorcycle accident that left him paralyzed," Rudy said. "We're building an addition onto her house that's fully handicap accessible."

"I'd love to help, but if Scott's going to be there, I probably need to plan on working."

Rudy scoffed. "It won't hurt to close the shop for one afternoon. Scott does it all the time when he's not busy. He just leaves a sign on the door and a message on the answering machine with an emergency number. I'm sure we can find an extra hammer somewhere for you."

"Oh, I have my own tools."

"Of course you do," Scott said under his breath. Kennedy may look more feminine than most tomboys, but she certainly didn't hold back from trying to fit in a man's world. It simultaneously impressed and irritated him.

She spun on him. "What did you say?"

Heat filled his face. "Nothing."

That little spark that Scott found so sexy lit her eyes, and she grinned. "Count me in on Saturday."

Rudy grinned and gave him a knowing look before shifting his gaze back to Kennedy. "Great, we look forward to working with you." He slapped Scott's shoulder again, a little harder this time, which jolted his head, sending pain shooting through his temples and forehead. "Don't we?"

Scott scowled at his brother. "Aren't you off shift? Isn't it your bedtime?"

"I am, and yes, it is." Right on cue, Rudy stifled a yawn. "But first, I want to know why you're wearing your dress slacks with your work shirt."

Stifling the urge to swear, Scott put a hand around Rudy's shoulder and with a firm grip guided him to the open garage door. "Later," he said in a low yet firm voice.

As much as he wanted to keep his purchase of the shop a surprise, he had a feeling he would need Rudy's help with the paperwork the bank requested. And if he distracted him with the paperwork, Rudy might forget to ask how Scott got the bloody nose and black eyes.

Scott groaned when he spotted Rudy's cruiser in front of their parents' house. Of course, his brother hadn't gone to work yet. Why couldn't there have been an emergency today of all days?

He checked his face in the rear-view mirror of his truck and grimaced. The bruising between his eyes hadn't turned out as bad as he feared, but it was still apparent he'd suffered some sort of trauma. He couldn't chalk this nosebleed up to the dry air.

He tugged the hat he'd pulled from his truck after Rudy left this morning low on his head and braced himself for the inquisition he was about to face and let himself into the house.

"Ah, just in time," Mom said. "We're just sitting down to eat. Wash your hands and come join us."

Scott tried to keep his face averted. "Um, I think I should shower first. Go ahead and eat without me." With any luck, the kitchen would be empty by the time he finished his shower.

"How are you feeling after your nosebleed today?" Rudy asked, stopping Scott in his tracks. Rudy's tone was casual enough, but Scott knew his brother's words were calculated.

He turned and glared at Rudy.

The punk just grinned back at him.

"You had a nosebleed?" his parents said in unison.

Why couldn't this be the night his parents decided to go out?

"This morning." Scott kept his tone casual. "I'm fine now."

"So, you didn't end up at the ER?" Mom asked as she placed a salad on the table near the meatloaf. "You could have called me. I could have taken you."

"No need. It wasn't that bad," he lied.

He and Kennedy managed to take care of it themselves. He'd have to remember that little trick with the tampon. At least she didn't get a picture.

"Then why do you have two black eyes?" Rudy asked.

"You have black eyes?" his dad asked, taking his first good look at Scott's face since he walked in.

"Oh no, what happened?" Mom stepped in front of him and swept the hat off his head. She managed to pull a chair away from the table and pushed Scott into it in a single fluid motion. Before he could protest, three heads with peering eyes bent over him.

"Ouch. That must have hurt." Dad said. "You get in a fight or something?"

Or something.

"Nah, I just ran into…something." Scott attempted to stand up, but he was blocked in on all sides.

"What on earth did you run into that caused that kind of bruising?" Mom asked as she gently probed the sides of his nose.

Rudy grinned and folded his arms in an "I'm waiting" pose. His brother didn't need to hound him to find out the truth of what happened, he just needed to sick Mom on Scott. Mom always got to the bottom of things, and she had the uncanny ability to know if you were lying.

Scott had never been good at lying, especially to his parents. And even though he'd had all day to come up with a story that would sound credible, he still drew a blank. There wasn't a shelf anywhere in the garage at eye level that he could have run into, and he hadn't been able to fabricate a good story concerning a car, without making himself sound totally incompetent.

He considered saying he asked Kennedy to throw him a wrench that he failed to catch, but he used to play baseball in high school. As the catcher, he caught the ball in front of his face all the time. His family would never believe that lie.

"What happened, son?" Dad folded his arms over his chest much like Rudy.

Great, now Dad expects an explanation.

Scott managed to scoot his chair back enough to get away from the crowd hovering over him. He stood and squared his shoulders, bracing himself for the mockery that was to come. "I accidentally startled Kennedy, and she overreacted by punching me."

Mom and Dad's eyes rounded, and their mouths dropped open.

Rudy let out a hoot of laughter.

Before long, his parents' shock turned to laughter too. Within seconds, Mom had tears streaming down her face, and Dad wheezed for air.

"I'm glad you all find my pain amusing." Scott raised his voice to be heard over their chuckles. "I could have bled to death, and you all would have just had a good laugh."

Mom was the first to sober. "I'm sorry, honey, but you have to admit it's kind of funny that a girl gave you two black eyes." She wiped tears from her cheeks. "I knew that Kennedy was going to be good for you the moment I met her."

"What?" Scott stared at his mom. "How is her punching me good for me?"

She patted his arm as though consoling a child. "You can't ignore her and block her out, like you do most people. She'll keep you on your toes and drag you kicking and screaming out of your shell."

It was Scott's turn to stare at his mom with his mouth wide open.

I like my shell!

She leaned over and studied his nose again. "I'll bet that caused a bad nosebleed. How did you get it to stop without going to the ER?"

Heat crept up Scott's neck. "Oh, you know, the usual. Lots of paper towels and patience."

"The usual is the ER," Dad said.

"Yeah, but this time he had Kennedy there to help him." Rudy gave him a knowing grin.

She helped me alright. Right out of my shirt.

But Scott would never tell his family that.

CHAPTER 13

*K*ennedy straightened from leaning over Scott's sister's Porsche at the same time he did. She was the one who rubbed at her low back this time.

Man, this car sits low!

Scott looked at her. "What do you think?"

Is this a test?

Was he as hesitant to diagnose what was wrong with Debbie's car as she was? It wasn't like they got a lot of expensive sports cars in the shop. Even T&J's hadn't seen many Porsches.

"Well, I'm not sure we're looking at a single problem. The check engine light repeatedly coming on signifies some sort of leak in the seals, but the fact that the car is leaking oil, I think there's an issue with the positive crankcase ventilation system. Probably causing failure in the rear seals."

Scott leaned back against the workbench and crossed his ankles. "I agree, but that doesn't explain the vibrating and clunking sound under the center of the car."

"True. Porsches are known for their noisy drive shafts, but this car is especially noisy, and the vibration and thumping during acceleration isn't normal."

Scott had surprised Kennedy yet again when he tossed her his sister's keys and suggested she take the Porsche for a test drive to see what was wrong with it. When he climbed in beside her, the small sports car felt about as big as a shoe box. His masculine woodsy scent filled the tiny car, making her all too aware of his hulking presence beside her. And when her arm repeatedly brushed his as she shifted through the gears, electricity raced through her body.

"No, it isn't. So what would cause that?" Scott folded his arms now and studied her face.

So, this is a test.

As confident as Kennedy was that she knew what the problem was —even though she'd never worked on a Porsche before—his scrutiny made her nervous. After glancing down at her lime green shirt that said, *Good things come to those who hustle,* she feigned a confidence she didn't feel. "Well, it sounds like a bad support bearing in the drive shaft."

He gave a curt nod and a slight grin. "I agree." Then his smile faded, and he rubbed the back of his neck. "I've never replaced a drive shaft or a crankcase in a Porsche. Have you?"

"Nope." She made a popping sound as she pronounced the P.

Scott's eyes dropped to her lips for a moment, and her mouth went dry. She recalled the dark hungry look he got in his eyes yesterday when he cornered her in the bathroom.

He'd wanted to kiss her; she was sure of it. If it hadn't been for the tampons sticking out of his nose, she might have let him. Thankfully, Rudy had shown up and given her an excuse to escape the close confines of the bathroom. As much as she liked the idea of kissing Scott, it would only complicate their working relationship.

She was just glad his black eyes were barely noticeable today. Yesterday, despite retrieving a baseball cap from his truck and pulling it low over his eyes, he'd still made her greet all the customers and the waitress who brought lunch over. He didn't want to take a chance on anyone seeing his black eyes.

Scott gave his head a quick shake and stepped back. "Will you see if we can even order the parts while I call Debbie and give her a quick rundown?"

Normally, they waited until they had a full quote, including cost and labor, before contacting the customer, but Kennedy assumed the costly repairs on an expensive sports car wouldn't be a big deal to someone like Debbie and her husband.

Scott dropped into a chair at the table in the office as Kennedy looked up the parts on her computer. His sister's voice came through the phone so loud, he held it away from his ear. Kennedy couldn't help overhearing as he explained the problem with her car.

He finished with, "Are you sure you don't want to take it to a Porsche dealer in the Tri-Cities area?"

"No, I trust you and Kennedy to fix it. And it's no rush, of course, since I mostly drive the SUV nowadays, but Austin and I do like to go for a drive now and then without the kids."

Kennedy smiled. She'd learned at the barbecue Monday night that Debbie and Austin had only been married a little over a month. He brought three children to the family and Debbie had been fostering orphaned twins since late spring. They'd gotten the call about the baby she'd seen Scott holding while they were still on their honeymoon.

It's a good thing they have a big house.

Kennedy didn't care if she lived in a tent, as long as the man she married looked at her the way Austin did Debbie. It was obvious they were crazy in love. It should have been a red flag that Nate never looked at her like that. That man's eyes had always wandered.

Scott's call ended just as Kennedy opened the shop's email to reach out to a company concerning parts for the Porsche. At the top of the inbox still unread was an email from Bank of Washington. The subject line said Loan Application.

She recalled Scott showing up to work yesterday wearing a suit. Had he been applying for a loan? If so, for what? What would a twenty-eight-year-old man who still lived with his parents need a loan for? Was he finally thinking about getting his own place?

She looked up as he rose from the chair he'd been sitting in. "Hey, what's this email from Bank of Washington all about?"

His head jerked up, and his eyes widened. "Nothing. It's…" He shifted from one foot to the other and scratched at his neck. "I should have had it sent to my personal email. Just ignore it."

Kennedy stared at him for a long moment. He was clearly uncomfortable with her even knowing about the email. But why? His unwillingness to confide in her meant he didn't trust her. Her heart sank. She thought by now he would have seen she was competent and trustworthy.

"Fine." She turned back to the computer and opened a new email.

Scott stepped close enough to check over her shoulder before walking out of the office.

Several minutes later, she found him in the garage leaning against the workbench with his ankles crossed. He held his phone in his hand watching a video with the volume on low.

"What are you doing?" she asked.

He jumped and paused his video. "Nothing."

She propped one hand on her hip and cocked her head, giving him an are-you-serious look. She was getting tired of his non answers and evasions. Couldn't he just be honest with her for once?

"You were obviously watching something. So, what was it?"

He looked down at his feet. "Just watching a video on how to repair the crankcase and drive shaft in a Porsche."

"Why not just look it up in the manual?"

"We don't have a manual for a Porsche here in the shop."

"I'm sure we can find one online."

"Probably, but…" Scott rubbed at the back of his neck. "I'm more of a visual person. I'd rather see it than read it."

"Oh. Well, I'm going to look up a manual anyway."

"Okay." He gave a quick nod.

"Okay." She mimicked his nod before returning to the office.

She mulled over Scott's behavior. He'd admitted that he'd never done well in school and for that reason didn't consider college an option. He'd also said he often brought Rudy or Mary in to help with the paperwork because he wasn't good with computers.

Her brow furrowed as she recalled him barely glancing at her diagnosis of Wes's truck last week. And didn't he admit that he'd never actually read her resume? He acted a lot like Tyler, a mechanic she'd known at T&J's. He was brilliant with engines and motors of all sizes, but he had some form of dyslexia and often needed help from the other mechanics and secretary to write up his invoices and work orders.

Did Scott have dyslexia? Was that why he preferred to watch YouTube videos instead of discovering how to do it himself by following the steps outlined in a manual? That would explain why he asked her to do the paperwork and act as office manager.

She was tempted to take a paper out to him and ask him to read it aloud, but if he really was dyslexic that would only humiliate him, and she didn't want to do that. So, how did she get him to trust her and let her help him?

Scott startled and swore under his breath the next morning when Kennedy walked into the office.

"Good morning. What are you up to?"

Why does she always have to be so chipper?

His gaze jumped to the clock. Was it eight o'clock already? He'd been here for an hour, and he'd barely finished the loan application. It had taken him forever to figure out where Rudy had saved his taxes. He'd planned to ask his brother for help with all the paperwork, but Rudy was working nights all month, and their paths rarely crossed, except for when one or the other of them was headed to bed.

So, Scott had arrived early and had done little more than cuss at the computer.

"Nothing." He clicked to another window, hiding the one with the loan application.

Kennedy's gaze caught the movement of the mouse, and one

eyebrow rose. "Yeah, if it's something you feel the need to hide, I probably don't want to know."

"What?" Scott shook his head.

"I'm not judging you." She held up her hands. "I am a little surprised you're using a work computer to get your fix, but I guess when you live with your parents…" She left the sentence hanging.

Great! She thinks I'm looking at smutty pictures.

"It's not what you think."

She propped her hands on her hips. "You've been acting secretive and mysterious. *Something* is going on."

Without trying to make it look like he was staring at her chest, he studied the words on her shirt and took his time processing the letter combinations. *Suck it up Buttercup.*

How did she do that? The sayings on her t-shirts often seemed so applicable to what was going on in the garage. And today's shirt applied directly to him. He needed to suck it up and tell her the truth.

He clicked on the screen with the application. He'd rather Kennedy know of his disability than have her think he had some sort of porn addiction. "I was attempting to fill this out."

He didn't know why he was trying so hard to keep this whole thing a secret. He liked the idea of surprising his parents with the purchase of the shop, but for all he knew, Charity and her sons may have already told people they were selling the shop to him. Heck, even Ezra or Andy could let it slip.

Kennedy stood behind him and looked over his shoulder. "Attempting?"

Telling Kennedy what he was doing went beyond admitting he was buying the shop; It meant confessing he had dyslexia and that he needed help to do some of the simplest tasks when it came to reading and writing. Would she think less of him?

Assuming she even thinks highly of me.

After the way he treated her last week and his gruff responses yesterday when she asked him about the email and why he watched YouTube videos to figure out how to do his job, he wouldn't blame her if she still hated him.

He kept his eyes on the computer as he cleared his throat. "Charity agreed to sell me the repair shop, and I'm trying to fill out a loan application."

"Seriously?" Both of her hands landed on his shoulders, and she gave him an exuberant shake. "That's so awesome. Congratulations!"

Warmth from her hands seeped through his shirt and spread throughout his body. Today, she smelled sweet, like tootie fruity or bubble gum; something sugary and delicious. Tempting and totally edible. He tamped down his attraction and glanced up at her. His tongue felt thick when he spoke. "Thanks, but all this paperwork might be the death of me."

Kennedy stepped away enough to look him in the eye. "Do you need help?"

The serious tone of her voice told him her offer was sincere. He wasn't sure she could make sense of all of the attachments in Ezra's email any better than he could with the help of an audio reader, but more than anything, he wanted someone by his side while he navigated this craziness. He didn't want to do this whole own a garage thing alone. He wanted a partner. A partner willing to do lots of paperwork.

Thinking Kennedy could be a partner in this endeavor—and maybe even in life—was crazy. They didn't have that kind of relationship. Yet he wanted a relationship with her.

Is it totally inappropriate to think of my coworker that way?

With Hannah, they'd developed a relationship before they worked closely together, so it hadn't felt wrong to be involved with a coworker. But would Kennedy view it as sexual harassment if he flirted with her? Not that he knew how to flirt, especially with someone who made him as nervous as Kennedy did. Hannah had been the pursuer in that relationship, and she hadn't cared that Scott wasn't good with words.

Either way, he needed to tell Kennedy the truth. He couldn't expect to build any kind of a relationship—personal or professional—with her if he wasn't honest.

He cleared his throat. "I'd love help. I'm feeling overwhelmed...

because I struggle with reading." Warmth crept up his neck at his admission.

Kennedy gave him a gentle smile. "I figured as much. So do you have some form of dyslexia?"

"Yes. I have Phonological and Visual Dyslexia." He ran his thumb nail along the edge of the keyboard as he talked. "I not only have a hard time processing the sounds of letters and words, but they also float around on the page. I struggle to retain the things I've read." He shook his head. "Wait, how did you know I have dyslexia?"

"I didn't, but I figure it must be something like that, because you barely glanced at my diagnosis of Wes's truck, you have Mary and Rudy help with the paperwork, and you'd rather watch how-to videos than read manuals." Her cheeks turned pink. "To tell you the truth, I'm kind of relieved to hear this, because there have been days, when I thought you were overly fascinated with my chest."

Heat rushed to Scott's face. He turned back to his computer screen, hoping she wouldn't see the color flooding his cheeks.

She laughed. "But I realize now that you were just struggling to read my shirts." She shrugged one shoulder. "Honestly, I think it's pretty smart how you've surrounded yourself with people who can help do the things you can't."

"Really?" He glanced at her out of the corner of his eyes. "You don't think I'm dumb because I can't read and write as well as most people?"

"Why would I think you're dumb? You have a disability that makes you have to work extra hard at something most people take for granted. Admitting you have a weakness and need help makes you smarter and stronger than most people who are too proud to admit they can't do everything by themselves."

Her words made him feel ten feet tall. He folded his arms across his chest. "So, what's your weakness?"

"Me?" She pointed her thumb at her chest and grinned. "Oh, I don't have any weaknesses. I'm practically perfect."

Scott gave a laugh that sounded like a snort. "If you say so, Mary Poppins. But *practically* perfect people have at least one weakness."

Her grin faded. "You're right. I actually have too many to count."

"Tell me one. You know, to make me feel better."

Kennedy chewed on the side of her bottom lip. Scott could see the indecision on her face.

Finally, she said, "My biggest weakness is…believing someone cares when they don't."

He frowned. "What do you mean?"

Did this have something to do with her ex. Is that how he managed to string her along for six years? By making her believe he cared about her when he really didn't. If he didn't care, why did he stick around for so long? And how could he not care about a beautiful, charismatic woman like Kennedy? Despite the questions racing through his mind, Scott couldn't find the words to voice any of them.

She shook her head. "Never mind. So do you want my help or not?"

Even though he was dying to know more, he wouldn't push her to talk about something she clearly didn't want to discuss. He'd pulled away from her plenty of times when he didn't want to talk about his personal life.

He nodded. "Yes, I want your help."

KENNEDY PULLED a chair over to sit beside Scott.

Warmth emanated off his muscular body beside her, making her breath catch in her chest. He smelled woodsy and oh so masculine. Every time his arm or leg brushed against hers, electric shocks raced through her body. It was all she could do to stay focused on reviewing the application with him.

Once she was certain everything was in order, she scooted away. "I think you're good to hit send."

"Really? Are you sure?" Scott's hand hovered over the mouse. When she nodded, he chuckled a little. "I thought, when this day came, I'd feel more excited and less nervous."

"Why are you so nervous?" She was excited for him. And a little jealous. Scott's success was a reminder that she would never have her own shop or even a partnership in one.

He clicked the send button then immediately clicked another link. "Because the loan manager at the bank wants me to request all these documents from the Knights. And of course, he expects me to review them and make sense of them. I'll have to act on some of them right away."

Kennedy's eyebrows rose as she looked at the list. By the names of the documents, she could tell that most of them were financial documents or contracts of some sort. No wonder Scott felt overwhelmed. She'd never had any experience with any of the things on the list. Would she really be able to help him?

She gave him a tight smile. "Wow. That is a lot. I guess we'll have to eat this elephant one bite at a time." She scooted a little closer and took the mouse from him so she could click on the spreadsheet she'd made for the week. "Let's look at the work we have scheduled so we can decide when and how we're going to tackle all of this."

After discussing the car repairs that needed to be done, they determined which tasks would go faster by working together and which ones could be done solo.

"I'll do all of the solo work," Scott said with hopefulness in his voice as he gave her a pleading look. "If you don't mind looking over the paperwork and seeing what we need to act on first."

Normally, Kennedy would fight to do her share of the work, but there was something about the way he looked at her. The fact that he looked directly at her at all was remarkable. Most of the time his words were aimed at the floor, the ceiling, or somewhere beyond her shoulder. He hadn't once grunted or scowled at her this morning, and he looked downright sexy with that puppy dog look in his eyes.

Kennedy's stomach bottomed out. She had a feeling she was developing a whole new weakness when it came to men, or rather a particular man.

As the day wore on, she alternated between long stints at the computer and periods of working side by side with Scott. Her time spent at the computer was mostly boring, so she gladly joined him every time he needed her help.

She enjoyed working with him, but she was also hyper aware of his proximity and powerful body. Each time she returned to the computer, relief flooded over, and she relished the opportunity to catch her breath.

Occasionally, she made him come into the office so she could read documents to him that caused his eyes to glaze over. She did her best to keep him engaged so he could make decisions for her to act on. Most of the items on the list were merely sending a request for documents, but a few had her chewing her lip.

After a solid hour on the computer trying to figure out whether Scott should set up an LLC or a sole proprietorship for his company as a business owner, she felt more clueless and overwhelmed than ever. She needed to fess up that she had no clue what she was doing when it came to this kind of legal stuff.

She took a moment to admire his trim waist and broad shoulders when she walked into the garage to find him working on something at the workbench. The man did things to her insides and made her feel alive in ways that she hadn't experienced since she was a teenager with a crush on an older boy.

"So…I know I promised to help you, but…" Her words died on her tongue when Scott turned toward her with a crestfallen face. She hated disappointing people, and she especially didn't want to make things harder for him. She grimaced. "I have no idea what the difference is between an LLC and a sole proprietorship. I've looked into both, and I can't make sense of any of it." She gave him her most apologetic look.

Scott sagged back against the workbench. "I'm equally as clueless. I planned to ask Rudy to help me with all of this before you offered, but besides the fact that he's working nights all month, I'm not sure he could figure it out any better than you could."

With slow movements, Scott pulled his phone from his pocket and stared at his blank screen for a long moment. A pained expression crossed his face before he tapped the screen and muttered, "Guess I need to swallow my pride and ask for more help."

Something tightened around Kennedy's chest. She hated asking for help as much as the next person, especially when it came to admitting to a man that she couldn't do something as well as he could. Scott must find it extremely frustrating to have to ask for help twice in the same day.

"Hey, Ben. I need your help," Scott said into his phone.

Kennedy's head came up as understanding dawned on her. It all made sense now. No wonder Ben ran the ad for a new mechanic and conducted the interviews. Creating a job posting and reviewing resumés would have overwhelmed Scott.

In her interview, Ben had mentioned that he'd worked with Scott for a time. Of course, he'd figure out—like she had—that Scott had dyslexia.

She loved that even though Ben didn't work here anymore, he was still willing to help Scott. Her mind raced as she considered all the ways she could help him too. She may never have the opportunity to own her own shop, but she could help Scott achieve his dreams.

CHAPTER 14

Scott's mouth went bone dry as he watched Kennedy ride up to Mary's house on her Honda Goldwing. The only thing sexier than a woman wearing her ponytail pulled through the back of her baseball cap was a woman wearing a pair of bib overalls with braids in her hair astride a motorcycle.

Did it make him some kind of creeper to find Kennedy so attractive when she looked like a schoolgirl?

"Hey, Kennedy." Rudy dropped the other end of the beam he was helping Scott carry and walked toward the woman who drove Scott crazy. "If I was still on duty, I'd give you a ticket for not wearing a helmet. But since I'm not in uniform, I guess I'll have to settle for giving you a lecture."

Kennedy laughed and affected a southern accent. "But deputy, I barely drove a mile to get here and didn't go over thirty-five the whole way."

Rudy laughed then asked Kennedy something about her motorcycle.

"It was my father's." A tightness filled Kennedy's voice that Rudy might not recognize, but Scott did. It was the same tone her voice took on the day she told him about her father's death and losing her portion of the garage.

A splinter pricked Scott's chest. Since she'd lost out on any chance of owning a part of T&J's Auto Shop, the bike was probably the only thing she had of her father's. His ribcage squeezed in his chest, and he wished he could somehow right the wrongs done to her.

Rudy straddled the motorcycle and gripped the handlebars as he talked and laughed with Kennedy.

That's it.

Scott was done watching his brother flirt with her. He scowled and shifted to lift the beam onto his shoulder. After depositing it where Austin directed, he returned to the trailer to grab another one while Rudy continued to charm Kennedy.

At the garage, Scott had Kennedy to himself, mostly. And even though he didn't exactly flirt with her, he saw a side of her that no one else did. The side that danced around in grease-stained jeans. Today, he had to share her vibrant personality with others. With his brother.

He didn't want to spend all day watching Rudy charm Kennedy and making her laugh. He wanted her to notice him. Of course, every time she even so much as looked his way, his tongue tied in knots. He hated how he could talk with her when it wasn't personal, but anytime he considered having a non-work-related conversation with her, all coherent thoughts fled his mind.

He'd fought the attraction big time this week. As if he didn't already admire her enough—and in more ways than he should—he'd developed a newfound respect for Kennedy thanks to her willingness to help him with something that was totally outside her job description.

He always did his best to keep their conversations focused on the paperwork or mechanic work, because every time he thought about how pretty and nice she was, he broke out in a cold sweat. Of course, that hadn't stopped him from thinking about how nice it would be to have someone like her as a partner at the shop.

Rudy and Kennedy finally made their way over near the house about the time Scott carried the last load of two-by-fours over. Seeing his brother stand so close to Kennedy chafed him. He dropped the boards on the ground. The short stack toppled and fell toward Rudy and Kennedy.

They both jumped back a step and looked at him with wide eyes.

"Watch it, man!" Rudy scowled at him.

"Sorry." The word came out a growl, and heat filled his face.

Now Kennedy would really think he didn't want her here. He couldn't find the words to make a better apology though, so he walked to his truck to get his tool belt.

He didn't realize Rudy had followed him until he stepped right up beside Scott and leaned an elbow on his truck bed. "What's your problem?"

"What makes you think I have a problem?"

"Because you threw a stack of two-by-fours at me and Kennedy."

"I didn't throw them *at* you."

"Okay, maybe you didn't throw them, but you're being rude and extra surly. You didn't even say 'hi' to her."

"Didn't have a chance with you rushing over there and flirting with her." Scott shook his head and turned away. All he needed was for Rudy to know how jealous he was.

His brother grabbed his arm and pulled him back. Scott tensed, ready to give Rudy a piece of his mind. Better yet, a fist in his face.

Even though Scott wasn't typically a violent man, he and Rudy had had their share of scuffles growing up. They'd learned to work well together and appreciate each other's strengths, but every once in a while, Scott got jealous of his younger brother, and when that happened, he had little tolerance for his friendly, chatty sibling.

Rudy's eyes narrowed. "Are you jealous?"

"Why would I be?" Scott couldn't bring himself to meet his brother's gaze.

"Why indeed? I mean, if I had your strength and brawn to go along with this face…" he grinned, "then you'd have reason to be jealous."

When Scott didn't laugh, Rudy smacked his shoulder. "If you like her, do something about it."

"Like what?"

"Talk to her. Flirt with her."

Scott kicked a small rock under his truck. "She's my coworker. I shouldn't—"

Rudy scoffed. "The world is full of couples who met at work."

Scott scratched the back of his neck. "I don't... I don't know how to flirt."

"I'll say. The grumpy growly persona is a total turn-off for most women."

Scott stifled the urge to let out a growl, proving Rudy's point. Instead, he shook his head and turned away from his brother again while he snapped his tool belt around his waist. Why had he ever thought Rudy could help him?

Rudy sidestepped and stood right in front of him. "Wait. All you have to do is smile and compliment her."

"On what?"

"Anything. Tell her you like the color of her shirt or the way she's wearing her hair. Tell her she smells nice and looks pretty or you think she's funny."

"That's easy for you to say. Every time I look at her my mind goes blank."

"Seriously? How have you worked with her for two weeks and not talked to her?"

"We talk..." Scott dropped his gaze again, "about work stuff."

"You've never talked about anything other than cars?"

Scott shrugged. "Not much." He'd walked out on her a time or two when their conversation turned more personal. It was rude, but it was easier than talking about things he didn't want to discuss. And all of the paperwork she was helping him with had just become another work thing. He didn't struggle to discuss it with her as much now as he did at first.

Rudy just stared at him, shaking his head, hands propped on his tool belt.

Scott tried to push his way past his brother. "Forget it."

Rudy slapped a firm hand against Scott's chest. "Wait. Look, if you get tongue tied when you look at her, then don't look directly at her. Simply look her direction and smile as you give her a compliment."

Not meeting her eyes would make a compliment sound insincere, but it might work. It's what he did most days, anyway, when he talked to her.

I like the color of your shirt and the way you're wearing your hair.

You look pretty. I think you're funny.

Scott looked across the yard where Kennedy stood talking to Austin. She wore a red t-shirt under her bib overalls. His favorite color on her, followed by light blue, like the dress she wore to the barbecue on Monday. All the things Rudy suggested were true, so why did he find them so hard to say?

He looked at his brother again. He'd hate himself for making this admission, because Rudy would never let him live it down, but if he was going to really be able to get Kennedy's attention, he needed his brother's help.

He scratched the back of his neck. "She...she makes me nervous, and then I clam up."

Rudy chuckled as he turned and studied the subject of their discussion. "I can see why. She's smart, skilled, and pretty. Most men are intimidated by women like that. But come on, man, you're strong, smart, and handsome too. You're a perfect match for each other."

Scott fiddled with the tape measure clipped to his tool belt. "We both know I'm not smart."

"Sure you are. The simple fact people pay you to do things they have no idea how to do proves how smart you are."

His brother had a point, but Scott would always be the first to admit his lack of intelligence, especially when it came to bookish things.

Rudy slapped Scott's shoulder. "Hey, she and Austin are coming this way. Remember to smile and compliment her."

Scott's heart started doing a rapid set of burpees in his chest. He wasn't ready to talk to Kennedy yet. His whole body felt jittery as he watched her and Austin walk toward him. She was all graceful and fluid movement. That's why he struggled to see her as anything other than a woman. A woman who made him nervous.

Scott smiled at Kennedy, and she returned it, making her dimples stand out.

Man, she's pretty.

His heart raced a little faster as his rib cage squeezed the air from his lungs.

"Hi," Kennedy said.

"Hey," Scott's voice squeaked a little. He cleared his throat. "Uh… I mean hi."

Rudy nudged Scott's arm before stepping away and talking to Austin.

This was Scott's chance to talk to Kennedy about something other than cars, but for the life of him, he couldn't think of a single thing to say. His mind went completely blank, like Sahara Desert blank, not a tree or bush in sight. Words completely failed him.

Avoiding eye contact, he looked around and scrambled for something to say. His gaze landed on her motorcycle. "Cool bike."

"Thanks. You probably heard me tell Rudy it belonged to my dad."

He bobbed his head. "Yeah, that's cool."

That's cool? What's wrong with me?

"I mean that's cool that you got to keep something of his."

She nodded and shifted from one foot to another. When it looked like she was about to turn and join Rudy and Austin, Scott panicked.

"Kennedy!" The word came out much louder than he intended.

"Yes?" She looked up at him with those big brown eyes.

"I uh…" He scrambled for the words Rudy had suggested as she fiddled with the hammer that hung from her tool belt. "I like your hammer." Scott cringed as soon as the words left his mouth.

Rudy snickered behind them, and tension bunched in Scott's shoulders.

Kennedy's eyebrows arched, and she laughed. She pulled the hammer from her belt and used it to motion toward his. "It looks a lot like yours."

Blast!

Real smooth. He needed to fix this now! Or she'd realize what an incompetent idiot he was.

Smile and compliment her.

Scott forced a laugh and a grin that probably looked predatory. "I think your hair looks pretty funny."

Her head jerked back. "What?"

Rudy snorted.

Scott tried again. "I mean the color of your shirt…smells."

Kennedy's mouth dropped open, and she dropped her hammer.

Austin's chuckles joined Rudy's as heat rushed to Scott's face.

"Sorry. I didn't mean… I just wanted… Oh never mind." He bent and snatched her hammer off the ground and shoved it her direction. He misjudged the distance between them and ended up ramming the handle into her stomach.

A soft "Umph," escaped her lips before she grabbed the hammer.

"Sorry," he said again, his voice a distinct growl this time. He pivoted and rushed over to help his dad untangle the air hoses for the nail guns; the sound of Rudy's and Austin's laughter mocking him.

Could I have made a bigger fool of myself?

STUNNED AND TRYING to make sense of Scott's words, Kennedy turned to the two men who laughed behind her.

They silenced their chuckles, and Austin grimaced at Rudy before walking away. Rudy stepped toward her.

"What just happened?" she asked with her brow still furrowed.

Rudy grimaced and scratched his jaw. "That was my brother's poor attempt at flirting."

"Flirting?"

"Scott's an…introvert."

"Duh," Kennedy said. "Tell me something I don't know."

"He's rather shy in social situations and can be…awkward."

"That was awkward alright."

"He doesn't do small talk. He's always struggled with words and has a hard time expressing himself."

She folded her arms over her chest. "He didn't have any problem telling me I didn't belong in his garage a couple weeks ago."

"He has his reasons for thinking women shouldn't work in a repair shop or any other dangerous job." Rudy pulled the tape measure from his belt and extended it a couple feet only to slide it back in again. "But talking about cars at work is different than socializing outside of work."

"Socializing?"

"Scott's never been good at socializing. With anyone, especially women."

Kennedy's mind jumped back to all the conversations they'd had at the garage. Almost every single one of them had been automotive or paperwork related. Except earlier this week when she gave him a bloody nose. Of course, that had been an unusual circumstance. Then she thought about the stilted and somewhat awkward conversation they'd had when she invited him over for dinner last Friday.

No wonder he'd acted so uncomfortable. That also explained why he hardly talked to her at the Labor Day barbecue.

Kennedy looked over her shoulder at Scott. With his good looks and Paul Bunyan physique you'd never guess he was socially awkward. The strong silent type yes, but awkward, no. Was that why he walked out of the room anytime conversations took a personal turn?

If he was trying to flirt with her—she almost laughed out loud at his botched attempt—did that mean…

Rudy must have read her mind, because he said, "Yes, he likes you, but he thinks dating a coworker is a bad idea."

Kennedy had to agree with Scott, but that didn't keep her heart rate from skyrocketing every time he was near. She watched as he single-handedly lifted a large air compressor from the back of his dad's truck. The muscles in his biceps and shoulders bulged, and Kennedy's breath hitched. The plain gray t-shirt he wore hugged his torso like a second skin, and Kennedy had never longed to be a t-shirt so badly.

"So…how do I make it easier for him?"

Rudy's face split into a big grin. "I knew it. You've got a thing for my brother, just like he has for you, but neither of you want to give in to it."

Kennedy lowered her gaze to the ground where she pushed a rock around with the toe of her boot. "Yeah, well I agree with Scott; dating a coworker is a bad idea—been there, done that—but I admit, I might be interested."

Rudy's grin only grew. "First of all, lower your expectations. Scott will never be an eloquent orator. If you expect flowery words from him, you'll be disappointed. Don't be afraid to ask him questions, and be content with single word responses."

Kennedy frowned. In the past when she'd asked Scott personal questions, he usually shut down and walked out on her.

"And most importantly, be patient with him." Rudy slapped her on the shoulder much like she'd seen him do to Scott. "If anyone can pull him out of his shell, you can."

Kennedy wasn't so sure about that. She watched Rudy walk over to where Austin and Bill Wheeler now studied a set of blueprints on the hood of Bill's truck. Then her gaze drifted to Scott again. He laid out extension cords now. She wanted to rush over and help him, but she knew he was embarrassed at his bungled attempt to flirt with her, so she figured she should give him a little space.

Before long, Bill called everyone to gather around the plans. Scott was the last to arrive and stood as far away from her as he could. Kennedy watched him out of the corner of her eye. He didn't seem to be paying any more attention than she was, but he didn't look her way once.

While Bill talked about measuring twice and cutting once and sixteen-inch centers, Kennedy's mind stayed on Scott. Was this one of those situations where she needed to take the lead and let him know she was interested? Would that make it easier for him?

No. The real question was, did she really want to get involved with another mechanic? She'd determined Scott wasn't as egotistical as Nate, like she'd initially thought, but that didn't mean she'd be able to hold his interest any better than she'd kept Nate's.

"Okay," Bill said, "let's team up, and we'll get these walls up in no time. Scott, you and Kennedy work on the west wall." He pointed to the front side of the house. "Rudy, you work with me on the south wall, and Austin will take the rear." He pointed a finger at Austin. "Holler if you need an extra set of hands, you hear?"

Austin nodded and turned away.

Kennedy looked at Scott. He looked as uncomfortable with the idea of partnering with her as she felt. Normally, she'd look forward to working with him, but after his botched attempt to flirt with her, it all just felt awkward.

He stepped toward his dad and opened his mouth as though to say something, but then closed it again and shook his head. Turning, he walked over to the stack of wood he'd placed on the front side of the house.

Kennedy followed at a much slower pace. If Austin had been the one to assign partners, she'd assume he was forcing them together on purpose, but as it was, she figured Bill was putting her—the weak link —with the strongest. Was it chivalry or chauvinism? Did Scott get his prejudice against women from his dad?

Deciding not to make a big deal of it and show these men she knew what she was doing—thanks to the construction class she'd taken in high school where they'd built an entire house—she helped Scott lay out the boards on the grass. They worked well together—like they always did at the garage—as long as she didn't get in his way. Fortunately, most of the time, she managed to anticipate his actions and was able to help rather than hinder.

He rarely made eye contact with her as they worked, which she was used to. Any time he spoke to her, his words came out clipped and punctuated with a grunt. Much like he spoke at the garage, but there seemed to be an additional layer of tension in his voice today.

She bristled when he insisted on being the one to cut the boards for above and below the window. "I know how to use a circular saw."

"Didn't say you didn't, but it's dangerous," he said before picking up the board and walking away, as though his words explained everything.

Kennedy let out a little growl of her own and turned back to measure and mark the next board. Scott's behavior was totally sexist, but this wasn't the first time he'd mentioned her safety or something being dangerous. Even Rudy had said Scott had his reasons for thinking women shouldn't work in dangerous jobs.

What happened to make Scott act this way?

She couldn't make herself back down so easily, however, when they ended up in a stare down over the nail gun. His fists balled, and that muscle in his jaw twitched, but Kennedy knew what she was doing and refused to let him dictate what she could and couldn't do. Fortunately, he relented, and she didn't need to make a scene.

They almost had their wall finished when Scott's sister, Debbie, arrived with lunch. Scott took his sub sandwich, sports drink, and chips and went over to sit under a large oak tree in the side yard as Rudy and his dad settled on the tailgate of Bill's truck. When Austin followed Debbie back to the SUV with his food, Rudy cleared his throat and gave Kennedy a wide-eyed look. He jerked his head in Scott's direction.

She took in Scott's stiff posture that clearly said, "Leave me alone." The lone wolf vibes he gave off were stronger than any she'd ever seen, even from him. How did one approach a skittish creature with such a domineering presence? More importantly, did she want to?

Yes. I do.

She wanted him to feel comfortable with her. To know he could trust her and talk to her. She'd thought they'd made progress this week while they worked on the paperwork for the purchase of the garage, but he'd distanced himself more than ever after the flirting fiasco.

Most of all, she wanted—no needed—a friend.

She missed her dad and Eden and wanted someone she could hang out with and talk to. Rudy was nice and friendly, but his schedule was crazy. Scott's sisters were also nice, but they were considerably older and in a completely different stage of life than her.

She and Scott had so much in common. They could be good friends if she could just get him to let her in. Walking toward him, she ignored the hitch in his shoulders that said he'd rather she sit anywhere but by him. She plopped down on the grass and leaned back against the tree, putting herself at a ninety-degree angle to him. This way he wouldn't have to look directly at her, and hopefully, he wouldn't feel too uncomfortable because she wasn't facing him.

They ate in silence for several minutes, but Kennedy knew if they were ever going to get beyond this new awkwardness, they needed to address it.

Her gaze remained on the platform where they'd soon be standing up their walls as she asked, "So, you think my hair looks funny?" She made sure to smile as she said the words, hoping he'd hear the teasing in her voice.

He gave a soft groan before saying. "No."

His response sounded self-recriminating and was totally unsatisfying to Kennedy. Rudy had said to be content with single word responses, but she wanted to know what Scott had meant to say concerning her hair. Which meant she needed to ask more questions.

"Do you... Do you like my hair?"

Though no sound—grunt, groan, or growl—came out of Scott's throat, she felt him stiffen beside her. An eternity passed before a single, quiet word sounded beside her.

"Yes."

She wanted to turn her head and look at him to see if he was sincere but figured it might make him retreat even more.

"What do you like about it?"

Was that too open of a question? Maybe he wouldn't answer because a response might take too many words.

"Everything." His gruff response sent shivers racing down her spine.

Her eyes widened, and she grinned. Again, she squelched the urge to turn toward him. "I like your hair, too," she admitted. Heat filled her cheeks at the admission. Flirting was so much harder and more uncomfortable than she remembered.

Was that why Nate had never really been interested in her? Because she hadn't put enough effort into flirting with him?

Scott's head turned toward her. He regarded her with a single raised eyebrow.

"It's true." She met his gaze and shrugged as though she was simply stating a fact, even though the mere thought of running her fingers through his hair made them tingle.

"Why?" he asked, still staring at her.

Trying to hide how flustered she felt, she popped a chip in her mouth and took her time chewing. "Why do I like it or why is it true?"

"Both."

Warmth flooded over her under his scrutiny. She gave another shrug that she hoped looked indifferent. "I like it's dark rich auburn color and wavy texture." She bit her tongue before admitting she wanted to know if it felt as soft as it looked.

With a soft, "Hmph," he turned away again.

Kennedy should be content with this small bit of progress they'd made at personal conversation and end it there, but she wanted to know what else he'd meant to say earlier when he'd jumbled his words.

"And my shirt…?" she wasn't sure how to finish the sentence, and she feared leaving it open like that would prevent Scott from giving her a response.

This time a small groan sounded beside her, and Kennedy bit back a laugh. Scott raised a knee and propped an elbow on it. He covered half of his face with his hand, but the action didn't hide the redness creeping up his neck.

When he didn't say anything, she prodded. "You think my shirt smells?"

"No." There was no hesitation this time. Then after a short pause, he said, "You."

Now she did turn. "Me what? You think I smell?" Certain the shock on her face must look comical, she stared at him.

"Yes."

Her mouth dropped open, and she lifted her arm and sniffed her armpit. She didn't exactly smell fresh, but even after the mild sweat she'd worked up, she didn't smell that bad.

It was Scott's turn to laugh. "No. You... I mean..." he lowered his gaze and let out a quiet growl before sucking in a deep breath. "You smell...good."

"Oh."

"Everyday."

"Oh." Stunned, Kennedy couldn't think of a more appropriate response. She settled back against the tree again, another grin taking over her face. She hadn't expected to get that kind of compliment from Paul Bunyan.

Is that why he tenses every time I get close to him? Because he's affected by my smell?

"I like your...shirts too," Scott said without further prompting. "The colors and the sayings. They're..." he paused so long, Kennedy looked at him again. He kept his gaze on something across the street. "Funny and look good on you."

"Thank you. I like your t-shirt too. I mean, gray is kind of boring, but it looks *really* good on you." Her voice deepened as she added emphasis to her words, and more warmth filled her face.

They ate in silence for a few minutes then Kennedy said, "Thank you."

Scott angled his head in her direction but didn't look directly at her. "For what?"

"For the compliments and for giving me a chance to prove myself in the shop."

He gave a curt nod before turning away again. "I appreciate your willingness to do the paperwork...and all of the other stuff I know you don't enjoy."

Words seemed to be coming easier for both of them now, and Kennedy didn't want their conversation to end.

"I'm glad you're letting me help with your loan stuff."

They lapsed into silence again even though both of them had

finished their food. Kennedy watched Bill and Rudy wad up the garbage from their lunch and knew this moment with Scott would soon come to an end. He must have had the same realization because he shifted toward her a little, causing his shoulder to press against hers.

She sucked in a sharp breath that she hoped wasn't as audible to him as it was to her.

His deep voice sounded closer when he spoke again. "I love that you drive a truck and own a motorcycle."

Kennedy resisted the urge to fan herself. Few women would find those words flirtatious, but his approval spoken in that low tone may as well be a form of seduction, because they did all kinds of crazy things to her insides. And hearing the L word from him even if he was talking about her truck and motorcycle made her want to insist on taking him for a ride. Right now.

"You should take my bike out for a ride sometime."

"I'd rather go for a ride with you." Again, his voice was low and sounded as sexy as could be.

She decided it was best not to question if there was a double meaning in his words. Unable to stop herself, she turned her head and looked directly at him. He lifted his gaze and met hers. When the corners of his lips lifted in a small smile, hers did the same. Then his gaze skittered away.

She was tempted to lay her hand on the grass between them to see if he'd take it but feared that might be pushing things too far. A little successful conversation didn't mean he was ready for a public display of affection. As much as she liked the idea of him taking her hand, she wasn't sure she was ready for a PDA either. Instead, she shifted a little and pressed her shoulder more firmly against his.

"Okay, let's get back to work," Bill called. "We've got walls that need to be put up."

CHAPTER 15

*K*ennedy gathered her garbage and got to her feet right away when his dad called for them to get back to work, but Scott followed at a more sedate pace. He didn't want his time with Kennedy under the oak tree to end, yet he'd never been quite so uncomfortable in his life. Except for when he made a fool of himself a few hours ago.

He wasn't sure why Kennedy went to such lengths to draw him out, but he was glad she seemed more amused than offended by his earlier blunders.

By the time he reached the rest of the group and pitched his trash into the garbage bag Debbie held, Dad was insisting Rudy go home and get some sleep, since he'd come here straight after working the night shift.

Austin waved to Rudy. "Thanks for your help, man. We couldn't have done it without you." Then he turned to Scott and Kennedy. "It's great to have both of you here too. Thanks for being willing to close the shop to help us out. Hopefully, this doesn't make you fall behind again."

Kennedy shrugged. "Between the two of us, we're staying caught up. Besides, Scott will soon be able to set any hours he wants for the shop after the sale goes through."

Scott cringed and glared at Kennedy, trying to tell her to stop talking.

His dad looked up from the blueprints he'd started studying again. "What sale?"

Austin and Debbie both froze, their gazes flying to him. Debbie was the first to speak. "The shop? Who's buying the shop?"

The next thing he knew, Rudy had stepped back to his side. "What's this about the shop?"

Kennedy turned to him, a quizzical look furrowing her brow. "You didn't tell your family?"

"Tell us what?" Dad asked.

"That he's buying the repair shop." Kennedy's voice was little more than a murmur.

Scott rubbed his neck. He knew trying to keep the purchase of the garage under wraps would be difficult, but he hadn't expected Kennedy to be the one to blow the whole thing wide open.

That's what I get for asking for help.

"I uh… Charity agreed to sell the garage to me." Heat filled his face. Now he felt silly for trying to keep it a surprise from his biggest supporters—his family.

A chorus of "That's great!" and "Congratulations!" rang out around him followed by back slaps.

"When did all this happen?" Dad asked.

"I talked to Charity last week, and on Friday, she let me know her sons agreed to sell."

"Last Friday?" Winking, Rudy shook his shoulder. "You told Kennedy before telling us? You sly dog. Was that all an act this morning?"

"What? No. I only told Kennedy because…"

"I walked in on him while he was filling out the loan application, and I offered to help."

"Loan?" Debbie's eyes widened, and her mouth dropped open. She darted a quick glance at Austin, then looked back at Scott. "You're getting a loan from the bank instead of letting us give you the money?" Her brows dipped, forming a V as a look of hurt filled her face.

Scott should have known Debbie would be offended when he didn't ask her for help in purchasing the shop. Ever since she returned to Providence as a wealthy widow, she'd been more than generous with her money. She'd made it well known within the family that she'd gladly give anyone money for anything they needed. But to his knowledge, no one had taken Debbie up on her offer.

The family, in general, didn't exactly approve of the way she came into all her money; by marrying a much older man who was dying of cancer. She'd repeatedly insisted she hadn't married him for his money, rather she'd done it because he didn't want to die alone. Her reason sounded noble, but knowing she was now worth millions because she married a man nearly fifty years her senior felt strange.

A sheen of tears glistened in Debbie's eyes before she turned away and walked to her Escalade. Austin gave him a look that said, you'd-better-fix-this-quick.

Shooting Kennedy, who now looked penitent and chewed on her lip, one last glare, he followed his sister. "Deb, wait."

She stopped in the process of opening the driver's door, but she didn't look at him. "Why didn't you ask me for help? You know I'd happily give you the money, don't you? I wouldn't even expect you to pay it back."

"I know, and that's exactly why I didn't come to you." Scott raked a hand through his hair, bringing it to rest at the back of his neck. "If you'd given me the money, I would feel like the shop belonged to you and not me."

"Well, we could have done a loan with a low interest rate then."

"Yes, but it still would have felt like a handout, and I don't want a handout, Deb."

"You sound like Austin." She stamped her foot. "Why do men have to be so darned prideful and stubborn?"

Scott recalled giving Austin a lecture a few months ago about how he didn't deserve Debbie if he was willing to let his pride get in the way of accepting everything Debbie had to offer.

But my situation is different. Isn't it?

"Listen. People have helped me out my whole life; Mom and Dad, you girls, my teachers. You all made concessions for me, expecting less of me than my peers. I often got special treatment because of my...disability." He squared his shoulders and propped his hands on his hips. "Don't get me wrong, I'm grateful for everyone's help, but this is the biggest thing I've ever done in my life, and I don't want someone making special allowances for me. I don't want someone thinking I don't deserve my own shop." His thoughts turned to Travis Brooks who'd been a burr in his side for years. "I need to do this on my own."

Although, he wasn't really doing it alone. Kennedy had offered to help him. But her assistance didn't feel like as big of a commitment as borrowing almost two hundred grand from his sister.

Debbie smiled, but she shook her head. "Seriously, you men are all the same. Fine, I'll let it go. But..." She pointed a finger at him. "Don't you dare even think about protesting when I give you a down payment on a home as a wedding gift."

"What?" Scott jerked back. "I'm not getting married, so that's not going to happen."

"Are you sure about that?" Debbie cast a glance Kennedy's way as she climbed into the SUV before grinning at him. "I give you six to eight months." She slammed her door closed on his protest and started the engine.

Debbie had barely driven away when Kennedy came up behind him. "I'm so sorry for spilling the beans. I didn't know you hadn't told your family yet."

Still reeling from his sister's prediction, Scott waved away her apology. "It's fine."

"So what was Debbie saying she gives you six to eight months on?"

Scorching heat filled Scott's face.

Apparently, that's when we're getting married.

It probably wouldn't go over well to blurt that out to Kennedy.

Knowing him, he'd bungle it and make it sound even worse than it felt, and he wasn't sure that was possible.

"Nothing."

KENNEDY PLUMPED the pillows behind her before leaning back against the headboard. "And then he said the color of my shirt smells." She said the words to her phone screen. She still missed talking with her best friend in person.

"Are you serious?" Eden's voice climbed an octave. She lay sprawled on her stomach on her own bed in Spokane.

"I know. It shocked me too. But then he turned beet red and walked away. His brother Rudy explained that Scott was trying to flirt with me."

"He calls that flirting?"

"Scott's shy, which I already knew, but apparently, he really struggles when it comes to socializing, especially with women."

"Geez, I'll say. But he's trying to flirt with you… Does this mean there's something happening between you two?"

Kennedy had finally admitted to her best friend that she kind of had a crush on her boss a few days ago when she told Eden about trying to help Scott stop his nosebleed. Of course, she'd downplayed her own attraction and how strongly Scott affected her, but she just needed to talk to somebody about it all, and Eden had always been her somebody.

Kennedy twisted a lock of hair around her finger. "I wouldn't say something's happening, but I think we've finally admitted that we're interested in each other. With his awkwardness around women, I have a feeling things aren't going to go anywhere fast. Which is probably for the best, you know. I mean falling for my boss is the dumbest thing for me to do."

"Why do you say that?" Eden scowled at her phone.

"Look at what happened with me and Nate. I don't want to have to relocate again if things don't work out between us."

"Things didn't work out between you and Nate because he was a jerk of epic proportions, and I think if things hadn't gone south with your portion of the garage, you would have been able to continue to work there despite Nate."

"Maybe, but it's weird to have to work with an Ex." Not that she would know, because she'd bailed and left town.

"I'd say it's weirder to work with someone you're interested in and have to pretend you're not attracted to them."

Kennedy nodded agreement, but she felt Eden's words clear to her core. While working with Scott these past two weeks, she felt like she'd been walking on hot coals. Every time they touched, she struggled to make sure he didn't hear the hitch in her breath. She also found it hard not to reach out and intentionally touch him, especially this past week when he'd been so frustrated with the loan stuff.

Kennedy went on to tell Eden about her and Scott's awkward discussion under the tree and how they'd managed to communicate with short sentences and without looking at each other.

Eden laughed again. "Wow, this guy sounds like a real dork. Are you sure you want to get involved with him?"

Kennedy looked down at her hand—the one that wasn't holding the phone. "I work with him, so I'm kind of already involved with him."

"Wait!" Eden pushed herself up to a sitting position and grabbed her phone. "I know that look. You're already falling for this guy, aren't you?"

Warmth crept up Kennedy's cheeks. "I wouldn't say I'm falling for him, but there's something about him."

She couldn't help thinking about how handsome he looked holding his infant nephew and the way he'd made the other nephew laugh by swinging him in the air. Scott may not be good with women, but he was good with kids. He may not have the greatest communication skills, but he was always very kind to the customers who came into the shop, especially the older women.

"Slow down. We're still talking about the chauvinistic jerk who made you clean the shop and relegated you to doing paperwork?"

Eden was right. Kennedy couldn't believe she was admitting to having a thing for Paul Bunyan who only two weeks ago had been such a jerk. But a soft spot a mile wide opened in her heart when he admitted to having dyslexia and asked her for help. She hadn't told Eden about Scott's disability and didn't plan to for now. Besides, Rudy said Scott had a good reason for thinking the garage was too dangerous for women. She still didn't understand how it was any more dangerous for women than it was for men, but maybe someday Scott would trust her enough to explain it to her.

"He's coming around," she said.

Kind of.

He'd actually let her cut a couple sheets of plywood this afternoon, while he stood nearby with a rigid posture and balled fists as though expecting her to cut off her hand or something.

"He lets me do more work around the shop now."

"Okay, that's it. I'm coming to Providence in the morning."

"What? Why?" Kennedy sat up a little straighter. She loved the idea of seeing her friend in person, but Eden wasn't an impulsive person, so this all felt so abrupt.

"Because I need to approve of this guy before you're totally smitten."

Whether Eden approved of Scott or not, Kennedy feared she was well on her way to being smitten by the big lug. It didn't matter how awkward he was when it came to flirting and personal conversations, there was just something about him that did things to her. Things Nate had never done. Not even when she was a lovestruck teenager.

"But tomorrow is Sunday."

They'd planned to get together again this weekend, but when Kennedy had gotten roped into helping with the construction at Mary's house, they'd had to cancel. Again.

"I'll leave first thing in the morning, we'll go to church together, and then spend the afternoon pigging out on homemade pizza and cookies. What time is church?"

"Um... I don't know."

"You didn't go last week?"

"No, it just felt…weird going to church with strangers."

Attending church services had always been something Kennedy did with her dad, and she'd struggled ever since his death to make herself go. Eden had managed to convince her to go most Sundays, but Kennedy hadn't been able to make herself go alone last week. She recalled Alice's invitation. If she went, she wouldn't be totally alone, but she'd feel weird about sitting by Scott's family, especially if he was there.

"Well, I'll go with you tomorrow, and then next week they won't be strangers anymore."

That was easy for Eden to say; she thought of everyone as a friend the moment she met them.

"Then you can point out Scott so I can figure out why you're all gaga over this guy."

"What if he isn't there? I don't even know if he goes to church."

He probably does.

He owned a suit. Most mechanics didn't own a suit unless they were church goers.

"You better pray he does. Otherwise, we'll have to come up with a creative way for me to meet him."

They talked a little longer while Kennedy looked up the time of the services for the only church in Providence then said goodnight. After plugging her phone in, she laid down and stared at the ceiling. The exhaustion she'd felt when she came home from Mary's house had dissipated, and she felt wide awake now.

The prospect of spending the day with her best friend energized her, yet her mind replayed the conversation she and Scott shared under the oak tree. Would the things they'd said change the way he acted at work?

CHAPTER 16

*E*den nudged Kennedy's shoulder. "There's a tall guy with reddish-brown hair. Is that him?"

Kennedy turned her head in time to see Rudy slide into the pew beside his mom. She'd already pointed out to Eden Scott's parents near the front. It didn't surprise Kennedy that Scott didn't arrive with his parents, but the sharp pang of disappointment that filled her did.

"No, that's his brother." An additional layer of letdown weighed heavy in her stomach when Scott didn't follow Rudy. It wasn't just that Scott didn't come, she really wanted Eden to meet—or at least see—him. Eden was her best friend. Her opinion of the man Kennedy feared she was falling for mattered.

"You didn't tell me his brother was so cute!" Eden said in a voice that was too loud to be a whisper. "If things don't work out with Scott, you could go for his brother."

But Kennedy didn't want to go for Rudy, as nice as he was. She wanted Scott, which was stupid, because even though he let her do a little more work now, he still had a hang-up with women working in garages.

"Shh." An old lady with blue hair in front of them shot them a dirty look over her shoulder.

Kennedy and Eden looked at each other and burst into giggles. The service hadn't even started yet and they were already getting dirty looks.

The service did start though, and an empty place remained by Rudy on the third pew.

Well, peanut butter balls!

Now Kennedy had to find a way for Eden to meet or at least see Scott. Things could get awkward if she left it up to her friend. All she needed was Eden introducing herself to Alice Wheeler and wheedling an invitation to Sunday dinner out of her.

Ten minutes later, the door opened at the back of the room, creating a rush of air through the large room. The hair on Kennedy's arms prickled as unexplained awareness filled her. She knew, even before Eden squeezed her arm, that Scott had arrived. It was as if some sort of electrical current raced through the room, making Kennedy's pulse speed up.

She joined her best friend in watching Scott make his way to the front with long, confident strides.

Man, he looks good in a suit.

Warmth filled Kennedy's body as she recalled taking off Scott's suit coat followed by his shirt only a few days ago.

"Holy moly." Eden's whisper was too excited to be quiet. "Now I see why you call him Paul Bunyan. He's huge and good looking too."

"You should have seen him carrying the air compressor yesterday." Kennedy batted her eyelashes and fanned her face in a dramatic fashion.

Eden laughed. "I can totally see why you're falling for him."

"Do you mind?" Now both old ladies in front of Kennedy and Eden scowled at them.

Kennedy pinched her lips together, but it didn't keep the giggles from returning.

Eden fiddled with her phone in her lap and within seconds, Kennedy's own phone vibrated in her pocket.

She pulled it out.

Why is that man still single?

Kennedy grinned as she responded. **Remember the part about him being awkward?**

Yeah, but I'm surprised women aren't falling at his feet whether he talks or not.

Kennedy had had the same thought herself. Initially, she'd thought it was because he was such a chauvinistic jerk, but she'd since realized that wasn't the case. Well, only partially.

I'm not sure there are that many single women in this town.

Eden stopped texting, and Kennedy did her best to concentrate on the sermon, but her gaze kept drifting to Scott. A small smile lingered on her lips as she replayed their conversation yesterday. Would she ever get to find out if his wavy hair was as soft as it looked?

After the service, she and Eden were still waiting to make their way to the door when Rudy leaned toward Scott and said something while nodding his head in Kennedy and Eden's direction.

Scott looked at her, and their gazes locked. He gave her a half smile and lifted his chin in a nod of recognition. After several long moments his gaze faltered, then returned for a split second only to shift away altogether. He and Rudy got jostled down the aisle, and Scott disappeared out the door without a backward glance.

Kennedy would have liked more acknowledgment than that, but at least it was more than he gave her at the barbecue. Now that she'd given herself permission to be interested in him, patience seemed to desert her.

Eden grabbed her arm. "I see what you mean about the lack of eye contact, but there was something in that look he gave you."

What had Eden seen that Kennedy hadn't? The look he gave her certainly hadn't been heated like the one last Friday night at her apartment or on Tuesday after his bloody nose, but Kennedy desperately wanted to believe Scott was truly interested in her. The idea of falling for another man who didn't reciprocate her feelings made her ill.

Would the awkward yet honest conversation they had under the oak tree change things between them at work tomorrow? Or would Scott still be the same old strong silent type?

With a sinking feeling settling in her gut, Kennedy had a feeling it would be the latter.

Refusing to let disappointment ruin her afternoon with her best friend, she forced a smile and hooked her arm through Eden's. "So, are we making chocolate chip cookies or the double chocolate ones this afternoon?"

~

"Good morning!" Kennedy's arrival and her cheerful greeting brought a little rush of warmth into the shop despite the chill in the fall air.

Scott's mouth went dry as he tried to think of something witty to say.

Blast!

It shouldn't be so hard to say, "Hi, you look great today," or "I love your pink shirt," but it was. Being around Kennedy made him nervous!

Kennedy stood still as his gaze dropped to the lettering on her shirt. She waited patiently for him to decipher the words there. She'd started doing this the day after she found out he had dyslexia.

Scott appreciated her acceptance of the fact that he needed more time than most people to read her shirt, but he still felt weird staring at her chest. The bright pink t-shirt that read, *Another fine day ruined by responsibility*, was completely out of place in the shop, but it fit Kennedy and her vibrant personality.

"Mornin'," he finally managed to mumble.

Kennedy's smile drooped as a flash of disappointment crossed her face, and Scott wanted to smack himself. They'd worked together so well on Saturday, just like they always did in the garage. In fact, they'd gotten their wall completely done.

Despite his and Kennedy's awkward conversation under the tree, Scott was proud of himself. He'd let Kennedy cut all the plywood. His gut twisted as he watched her, even though she did everything right. He kept telling himself not to watch, but he couldn't look away either. He simply couldn't help worrying that she might get hurt.

"Where did the minivan out in the lot come from?" Kennedy asked.

"I towed it in from the freeway yesterday morning. Needs a new timing belt. Make it a priority since the family is staying in a motel."

"Is that why you were late for church?"

He nodded. He wasn't surprised she noticed his late arrival—everybody did—but he couldn't help hoping she'd been watching for him.

Scott lowered his gaze and fiddled with the wrench he held instead of looking at Kennedy. It was stupid that he found it easier to talk to her if he didn't look directly at her.

"You brought a friend."

"Yeah, that was my best friend, Eden. She came down from Spokane to spend the day with me."

"Good." It was a lame response, but Scott didn't know what else to say.

"It was nice to see her again. I've missed her."

Scott could only nod.

When it became apparent he wasn't going to say anything else, Kennedy turned to go into the office.

A little surge of adrenaline opened his mouth, and he blurted out, "You look good in pink."

She froze, then as she started to turn back, he walked into the parts room. He didn't need her seeing the flush that heated his face and neck.

"Thank you." The words were a little more sing-songy than usual, as though she said them with a smile.

His own lips turned up as he stepped into the oversized closet, but he shook his head at himself. Would he ever be able to compliment her to her face without bungling it?

CHAPTER 17

Kennedy waited until Scott stepped out of the office before sucking in a deep breath and fanning herself with the stack of papers she'd just reviewed with him.

They'd just spent the last two hours studying the financial reports the Knights sent over. If the success of the shop and gas station continued as it had for the Knights, Scott would be well off financially.

She was excited for him, she really was, but she also couldn't help feeling jealous. He knew what he wanted and was achieving his goal. Whereas she felt farther away from hers than ever. She figured it would take years to save enough money for her own shop, or to buy-in on an established one, but she wasn't even sure what she wanted anymore. Did she want to work toward owning a large shop like T&J's in a big city? Or should she set her sights on a modest shop like Knight's in a small town? This humble shop and quiet town were growing on her.

The jealousy wasn't what had her so hot and bothered though. It was how claustrophobic the small office felt the whole time Scott sat close to her.

They'd worked together all week, but always on separate repair projects, and she was no closer now to understanding him than she was three weeks ago. Sure, he met her gaze a little more often now and even smiled at her occasionally. And she'd managed to get him to talk about his family a little over lunch, but he hadn't said or done a single thing that could even remotely be construed as flirting.

She'd tried to lower her expectations, like Rudy suggested, knowing any progress they'd made under the oak tree last week wasn't likely to yield quick results, but she couldn't help holding out hope for more. She treasured every compliment and smile he gave her, but it didn't feel like enough.

He'd had ample opportunity to touch her or innocently brush his leg against hers while they'd gone over the financial reports. But he'd made zero contact. If she hadn't been the one explaining the documents to him, he might not have known she was even there. His brow remained furrowed in concentration the entire time with only the occasional nod of acknowledgment that he understood what she was saying.

She'd thought about pressing her leg against his, but she feared she'd scare him away. Besides, she didn't want to pursue someone again who wasn't interested in her enough to make his feelings known.

That's what had happened with Nate. She'd made no secret she was interested in him, so when he flirted with her, she thought it meant he cared about her as much as she did him. It still made her sick to realize how easily she'd let him string her along for so long. Even though he flirted with almost every woman who came into the shop, Kennedy had tried to tell herself that the way he treated her was different than the way he treated them. But it wasn't, and she'd been too stubborn to admit it.

No, she wouldn't throw herself at someone who wasn't interested and committed enough to speak up and say so.

Kennedy turned back to the computer and typed up the work orders for the day. After making a few phone calls, she looked ahead at tomorrow's repairs. She needed to make sure they had a fan belt for the Honda Accord that came in today. The computer said they had one in stock, but Kennedy couldn't recall seeing it in the parts room.

Scott glanced up as she walked out of the office, and their gazes locked. Her heart skipped a beat, like it did every time he looked at her. There always seemed to be so much going on behind his hazel eyes that he never expressed.

It drove her crazy. She wanted to know what he was thinking, even if he was only thinking about cars. And she certainly wanted to know if he ever thought about her. Did he feel the same tension in the air that she did every time he was near? Did he ever sneak a peek at her backside when she was bent over an engine, like she did his? It was horribly inappropriate, but she couldn't seem to help herself. From head to toe, he was a fine specimen of a man.

She gave him a smile as she continued past him to the parts room, and he returned it. Again, her heart stumbled a little. Things might be so much easier if she felt like she could just let him know she was interested, but she still stung from Nate's rejection and felt too vulnerable.

When she reached the parts room, she scanned the shelves, then searched them again, looking for the fan belt. If they had one, she wasn't seeing it. Stepping back until her shoulders pressed against the wall, she looked up at the highest shelf.

Wait. Is that it?

With an ear-piercing scrape of metal on concrete, she dragged the step ladder over. She had to perch on the highest rung to reach the top shelf. Reaching up, she felt only empty space. She leaned back and eyed the shelf again.

Fudge!

She'd pulled the ladder too far to the right. Too lazy to go to the effort of getting down and shifting the ladder, she stood on tip toe and stretched, sliding her hand along the dusty shelf.

Something soft and fuzzy shifted under her fingers, then the unmistakable fluttering of multiple tiny legs crossed her hand at lightning speed and raced up her arm. A shudder shook Kennedy's entire body, and she screamed as childhood memories assaulted her of the mean neighbor boy who put bugs in her hair. She flung her arm back-ward to knock loose the massive, hairy spider with the longest legs she'd ever seen.

The movement dislodged her from her precarious perch, and she fell backward. Swinging her arms, she searched for something to grab a hold of. She found nothing.

So, she did the only thing she could do. She screamed again and prayed she didn't split her head open when she hit the concrete floor.

SCOTT'S HEART clawed its way up his chest at the sound of metal scraping against concrete.

Kennedy's moving the ladder. If she climbs it, she could fall.

He broke out in a cold sweat. It was irrational to stress about every little thing she did, but he couldn't seem to get her—or concern for her safety—off his mind. He'd never forgive himself if something happened to her.

He headed to the parts room to see if she needed help. He suspected she was looking for the fan belt that he'd already pulled down off the top shelf. The least he could do was save her the trouble of searching for something that wasn't there.

He rounded the corner into the parts room to find her precari-ously perched on the top rung of the step ladder. She leaned sideways, searching the top shelf. Then she gave a sudden panicked scream and jerked her arm backward as though she'd been burned. The move-ment threw her off balance, and her arms flailed. She screamed again as she fell backward from the ladder.

The mental image of her cracking her head open on the cement sent his heart to his throat. He darted forward and dropped to one knee, praying as he extended his arms that he'd at least break her fall.

Kennedy's scream ended as abruptly as it began when she hit his arms.

His breath huffed out in relief. He pulled her close to his chest as he stood and brought her upright with him, letting her legs slide to the floor.

She turned wide, terrified eyes on him. Then she wrapped her arms around his neck in a death grip and gasped for air. Her breathing remained labored for several long seconds.

"Thank you." Her breath against his neck sent an arc of desire to replace the adrenaline that seconds ago had been shooting through his veins.

Although she appeared uninjured, her body still trembled in his arms, and he couldn't convince himself to let her go. "What happened?"

She loosened her grip around his neck and leaned back enough to look him in the eye. "There was a s-spider."

"A spider?" He couldn't help himself; he laughed.

"It crawled up my arm. A-and it was huge and h-hairy." She dug her fingers into his shoulders as a shudder rippled through her body.

He tightened his hold around her waist as he stifled another chuckle. He never would have guessed the tomboy who was good at everything would be afraid of spiders. He looked into her gorgeous brown eyes and focused on the golden flecks in her irises. He really should let her go now. But he didn't want to.

He'd tried so hard this week to talk to her and say something witty, but he'd failed miserably. He'd wanted so badly to put his arm around the back of her chair while they went over the financial reports, but every time he considered touching her, his brain shut down, and he couldn't make sense of the words she said. It had taken every ounce of his concentration to stay focused on the reports and keep his hands off her.

His gaze dropped to her full lips—pink and parted—and all rational thought fled from his mind.

"You okay?" His voice was deeper and huskier than usual.

"I don't know." Her lashes fluttered against her pale cheeks. "I can't seem to catch my breath."

"I know the feeling. It happens to me every day." The words were out before he could stop himself.

He tensed when he realized what he'd said, but then he wondered if that had been his problem all along. Did he censure himself with Kennedy because he feared saying something that might tell her how much he liked her? Besides, sounding inappropriate in the workplace, it also made him vulnerable and only added to his anxiety concerning her.

He kept his gaze glued to her lips and tried not to think about what he was doing or the words that might come out of his mouth. If he thought about the situation too much, he'd grow nervous and panic. Then he'd end up making a fool of himself. He didn't want to mess up this moment. He just wanted to hold Kennedy.

And maybe kiss her.

As words came to mind, he told himself to just spit them out. They couldn't possibly sound any more asinine than what came out of his mouth last Saturday. "It usually starts when you walk through the door in the morning and doesn't go away until you leave in the afternoon."

Kennedy gave a soft gasp, and his gaze jumped back up to hers. Her eyes widened, the right one a little bigger than the left. "Really? I thought it was just me."

"Not just you." He continued to hold her gaze for a long moment, willing his mind to not shut down on him and his mouth to continue working. "What do we do?" When a slight quivering started somewhere deep inside him, he forced himself to hold steady. "About it, I mean?"

"I don't know. Trying to ignore it doesn't seem to be working."

"Nope." He looked at her lips again. A mistake? Maybe, but her beautiful brown eyes were too mesmerizing. He could totally get lost for days in their dark depths. "I don't date coworkers." He'd never make that mistake again.

"Me either. Well, not anymore, anyway."

He was curious about what she meant, but he was too distracted to think about that right now. Tamping down the trembling that grew inside him, he asked, "How do we get past this... Whatever this is?"

"Attraction?"

He snorted. "That's stating it mildly."

"Maybe if we...just kiss..." She shrugged like it wasn't a big deal, but it sure felt like a big deal to him. "...we can get it out of our system and move on."

"Doubt it." When disappointment filled her face, he found himself saying, "but it's worth a try."

"Okay." The air from her whispered response hit his lips a fraction of a second before they met the softness of her mouth.

Having granted himself permission to kiss her, he went for it before he could talk himself out of it. All the little sparks of electricity he felt every time Kennedy was near multiplied and shot through his body in a lightning bolt of desire as her mouth yielded and welcomed his kiss.

Her hands slid up behind his neck, and she played with the hair just above his collar, sending tingles skittering across his scalp. She kept a gentle pressure against the back of his neck, letting him know she didn't want the kiss to end.

Neither did he. The nervous quivering he'd been experiencing was replaced by a thrumming vibration that both soothed and energized his whole being.

Groaning against her mouth, Scott tightened his arms around her and deepened the kiss. Her body melded against him as her lips moved with his. She felt so good in his arms. As though she belonged there. Forever.

A fire as hot as any forest fire he'd ever battled blazed in him. How was he ever supposed to keep their working relationship platonic after this? Every time she came close, he'd want to pull her into his arms and kiss her sweet mouth.

Gathering every ounce of willpower he possessed—which didn't amount to a hill of beans right now—he pushed her away from him.

Surprised, her eyes popped open, full of desire that quickly morphed into disappointment. "Did I do something wrong?"

Hardly. She'd done everything exactly right and that was the problem. Her response to his kiss—though normal enough—ignited something in him. Something that filled him full of hope *and* doubts. He wanted a relationship with her. One that lasted forever.

The thought made his ears ring and the room spin a little. He could so easily see himself falling for Kennedy, but he could just as easily see something horrible happening to her. Something that would take her away from him. He couldn't live through that again.

"No, I did."

He hated letting her think he didn't enjoy their kiss, but he couldn't tell her how incredible it had been. And he couldn't stand here and pretend kissing her hadn't just rocked his world. So, he turned and walked out of the parts room, then out of the garage.

He didn't stop until he reached his truck.

CHAPTER 18

*K*ennedy reached out and grabbed the nearest shelf to steady herself, willing her knees to hold her up. She turned and sank onto the bottom rung of the step ladder when they refused to get the message.

Kissing Scott had been a mistake.

Kisses like that—full of passion and pent-up emotions—were addictive and dangerous. They were the kind of kisses that made good girls let their guard down and end up in trouble.

Not that Scott would ever take advantage of her, but it would be all too easy to let him talk her into something she'd promised herself years ago she wouldn't do.

The sensations and desire that he triggered in her were so much stronger than anything she'd ever felt with Nate. Either Nate had always held back, because she'd told him she wouldn't sleep with him before they were married, or he just hadn't desired her enough to let that kind of passion fill his kisses and caresses.

What did that say about Scott? Did he desire her like that?

More importantly, what did it say about her? She'd kissed him as passionately as he had her. As much as she liked him and liked the idea of getting to know him better, she wouldn't say she was in love with him. She wasn't ready for a long-term relationship, was she? She'd only known him for three weeks.

So, why did I kiss him like I'm in love with him?

"Hello?" Amy's voice came from out in the garage. "Scott? Kennedy?"

Kennedy pushed to her feet, took a deep breath, and squared her shoulders before walking out of the parts room.

"Hi," she greeted Amy with a voice that was nearly an octave higher than usual.

"Hi, Kennedy." Amy smiled. "How are you guys making out?"

Heat rushed to Kennedy's face, and she pressed her finger to her lips. Did they look especially red and swollen? Was it obvious she and Scott had been kissing? Their kiss had been kind of lengthy, but it wasn't like they had gotten that carried away.

Amy hooked a thumb over her shoulder. "You guys are keeping the lot mostly empty. That's great!"

Oh. She means how are Scott and I making out with our work. Not literally making out, of course.

"Oh, yeah. We're kiss—keeping up with things well." Kennedy's voice still sounded a little squeaky, and warmth once again flooded her cheeks.

Amy gave her a strange look before laughing at Kennedy's slip. "I'm glad Scott finally has some help." She set the bag containing their lunch on the corner of the workbench and headed toward the open bay door. "A big group of people walked into the diner just as I walked out, so I'd better get back." She turned back before stepping out of the garage. "By the way, I think you and Scott would make a cute couple. Maybe you should think about doing some kissing." She gave a quick wink and a small wave then headed to the street.

Kennedy stood dumbfounded for a whole minute. What did Amy mean by that? Did people think she and Scott were a couple? They hadn't even gone anywhere together in public, so surely people didn't think of them as an item. Had the old ladies in front of her and Eden at church realized they had been talking about Scott and spread gossip?

Although Kennedy liked the idea of being part of a couple with Scott, unless he showed interest in some level of commitment, she'd be better off not getting mixed up with him emotionally. Because if he ever rejected her, she had a feeling it would make Nate's rejection feel like a walk in the park.

She carried the food into the office, expecting to find Scott there, but the room was empty. He'd looked a little shell shocked after their kiss, but he wouldn't leave work, would he?

Maybe he's just out back, looking for something in the storage shed.

However, Kennedy couldn't think of a single thing he'd need from out there today. She leaned around the corner and checked the hook above the workbench. The shed key hung in its usual spot. So, where was Scott?

She pulled out her phone and sent him a text, saying lunch was here. Then she sat down and pulled out the Styrofoam containers filled with chili and grilled cheese sandwiches. Kennedy felt rude not waiting for Scott, but she needed something to focus on other than the amazing kiss they'd shared.

She'd eaten half of her sandwich by the time he slid into the chair across from her. And even though she'd told herself not to make a big deal of their kiss, her heart rate spiked when she looked at him.

He was incredibly handsome in a rugged way, especially with the three-day stubble that darkened his jaw today. Her gaze settled on the lips that had kissed her, and her breath hitched.

Stop staring at him.

He ducked his head and dug into his food, ignoring her.

She kept waiting for him to say something, knowing he probably never would. If they were going to talk about the kiss, she'd have to bring it up.

The question was, would he talk about it? Or would he walk out, like he'd done on other occasions? Maybe she should wait until he was almost done eating.

Her appetite dissipated, and she stirred the remainder of her chili, trying not to stare at Scott, but unable to take her eyes off him.

He must have felt her gaze because he looked up. A small crease formed between his brows before he looked back down at his food. He didn't return to eating, however. Nor did he speak.

"Are we going to talk about it?" Her voice was quiet, hesitant. She wasn't sure she wanted to hear that he regretted kissing her. Or worse, that she hadn't been any good at it. Was that why Nate strayed?

Am I a horrible kisser?

His gaze remained on the table in front of him. "Depends. You going to make me?"

"Is it wrong of me to want a few answers?"

He glanced at her before looking away again. "What if I can't give you the answers you want?"

"What do you mean?"

He rubbed the back of his neck. "Maybe you should just ask your questions."

Not expecting to be put on the spot, she scrambled for a way to get him to tell her where they went from here. Had the kiss meant anything to him?

She'd love to just ask him how he felt about what happened, but she doubted he'd give her a straight answer. He'd probably get up and walk out. Did he prefer to answer with "yes" or "no," like Rudy suggested? Or could she get him to respond with more?

"Did our…" She couldn't bring herself to say the word *kiss* without reliving it. "Did…what we did…get it out of your system?"

Scott snorted and shook his head but still didn't look at her. "Not hardly."

A little surge of relief shot through her. Part of her wanted him to say they could never let that happen again, so she would know there was no point in letting herself fall for him. It would be so much easier if he said he wasn't interested in her like that. But another part of her wanted to hear him say he wanted to do it again. A lot. She wanted to hear that he wanted her.

"Do you…regret it?" She held her breath, waiting for his answer.

He looked at her again, a little longer this time. "No."

A little rush of hope warmed her chest.

He shifted his gaze back to the table. "But it's not a good idea."

And that little flame of hope extinguished.

"What's not?" She knew what he was saying and agreed with him to an extent, but she needed to know what he was thinking. Why didn't he want a relationship with her? Was there something wrong with her? Was she too much of a tomboy?

"You know what I mean."

She lowered her own gaze to the table. "I need to hear it from you. What is it about me that you don't like?"

His head popped up. "What?"

"It's okay." She pasted on a smile. "I can handle rejection, but I'd like to know what I'm doing wrong, so I can stop doing it."

"What are you talking about?" He leaned forward until she looked at him. "You're not doing anything wrong. In fact, it's just the opposite. You're practically perfect, remember?"

This brought a smile to her face, but it didn't last long. "I'm serious. I need to know what's wrong with me."

Scott shook his head again. "Not a da— I mean blasted thing."

She looked down at her hands in her lap, digging in vain at her oil-stained cuticles. "Is it because I'm not feminine enough?"

He swore under his breath. "Hey, look at me." Kennedy looked up to see his hazel eyes boring into hers. "There's not a single thing wrong with you, you hear me?" He scratched at his neck, as though horribly uncomfortable with making eye contact while making such a declaration, but he kept talking. "And whoever told you that is an idiot." Color began to creep up his neck. "Just so you know, I find everything about you…sexy."

Now, he did shift his gaze away. He surprised her when he kept talking. "Your big brown eyes, your colorful t-shirts that match your cheerful personality, the way you wear your ponytail pulled through the back of your hat, and your motorcycle. I like it all."

Kennedy had never heard him say so many words at once, and her chest swelled a little more with each one. If he really liked all of that about her and found her sexy, why wasn't he interested in a relationship with her?

"Then why don't you want to… Why do you think this is a bad idea?"

He let out a heavy sigh. "Dating a coworker makes work distracting and dangerous."

There was that word again. Why did he have such a hang up with dangerous situations at work?

"How does it make it dangerous?" Her question was quiet, inviting him to talk to her.

He propped his elbows on the table and scrubbed his hands over his face before plunging them into his hair. They finally stilled at the back of his neck with his fingers interlocked. He leaned his head back and stared at the ceiling as though searching for answers or sending up a prayer.

When he didn't say anything, she softly asked, "Will you tell me what happened?"

Nearly a full minute passed before he spoke. "Years ago, when I worked with the Forest Service…I dated a girl." He lowered his arms and his gaze. His eyes now focused on the wall behind her, and his arms folded over his chest.

She couldn't decide if his posture was meant to be defensive or protective.

"She worked on the recreation crew when we started dating, so it didn't seem like a big deal to date a coworker. It's not like we worked together very often, but…"

His eyes darken with shadows from the past as she waited for him to go on.

"At the end of that summer, the recreation crew ran low on funds, and they had to cut down on their personnel. Hannah got transferred to the timber crew for our last month of work." One corner of his lips lifted. "I thought I was so lucky; I got to work with my girlfriend in the mountains every day."

He stopped talking, and his Adam's apple bounced. Finally, after several long moments during which Kennedy wondered whether he'd continue, he spoke again. "One day, our supervisor sent us to a specific area to cut down the dead, diseased, and dangerous trees, putting me in charge. Working on the recreation crew, Hannah hadn't had much opportunity to use a chainsaw, so I didn't plan to let her cut down any of the trees, but she insisted she could do it."

He raked his hands through his hair again, and his gaze returned to the ceiling.

"What happened?" she finally asked when he didn't continue.

He looked at her as though surprised to see her still there. "She didn't line up her cuts right when she made her notch, so I told her I would finish bringing it down." His head moved slowly from side to side. "She refused to let me step in. She was stubborn and spunky. I loved that about her, and she looked so blasted sexy running a chainsaw, that I gave in. She started her back cut too low, and I didn't watch the angle she went in at closely enough."

He took several deep breaths before continuing. "The tree shifted, binding her chainsaw. As she struggled to free it, the trunk of the tree twisted and broke free. Because of the rope anchoring it to fall a certain direction, the trunk jerked sideways, knocking Hannah down."

Kennedy gasped and pressed a hand to her mouth.

Scott looked at her again, but his eyes didn't focus on her. His mind was somewhere far away, reliving a nightmare.

"She ended up pinned under the thickest part of the trunk. I sent someone to radio for help, and we went to work as fast as we could, cutting the trunk enough to get it off her, but…she didn't make it." He looked down at his hands, and Kennedy's gaze followed his. Both hands trembled.

He balled them into fists. "It took the EMTs forever to get there, but they said even if they had gotten there sooner, she never would have made it. She had too much internal bleeding."

"Oh, Scott." Kennedy placed a hand over his and squeezed. "You did everything you could for her."

"No, I didn't do enough." Anguish filled his voice. "And it was all my fault. I was in charge. I should have insisted on bringing down the tree." He shoved his chair back and bolted to his feet. "I can't have a relationship with a coworker, it's too distracting, and that makes work dangerous." He turned and walked out of the office, and she suspected, out of the garage again.

Kennedy wanted to go after him, to pull him into her arms and give him the hug he seemed to need. To hold him until he found a way to forgive himself for what happened to Hannah. But she doubted he would appreciate the attention.

Unfortunately, that soft spot that had opened in her heart when he admitted he had dyslexia, had ripped wide open now. What happened to Hannah explained so much of Scott's behavior and his concern for her safety.

It endeared her to him. Which was a bad thing because he didn't want a relationship with her, but now, more than ever, she wanted one with him.

CHAPTER 19

a black, Ford truck parked beside Kennedy's motorcycle as she loaded groceries into the saddlebags. The hair on her neck stood up.

"Well, well, well." Travis Brooks slid down from his truck and hooked his thumbs in his belt loops. His gaze raked over her, lingering on her chest longer than necessary. "What do we have here?"

Kennedy hid the shudder that rippled through her. "Hey, Travis."

"I didn't know the sexy mechanic drove a motorcycle." He stepped closer to her bike and caressed a hand along the curve of the bike's leather seat as his gaze lingered on her hips.

"Well, now you do." Kennedy stepped to the other side of her bike to keep a barrier between her and Travis.

"Wanna take me for a ride?" The low suggestive tone of his voice and the way he eyed her bust again said he wasn't talking about a ride on her motorcycle.

This time, she made no effort to hide the shudder his leering gaze and innuendo-filled words triggered in her. She couldn't wait to get home and take another shower.

Even though she usually climbed onto her bike from the left, tonight she straddled it from the right and slipped the key into the ignition. Without needing to give it much thought, she straightened the motorcycle and pushed back the kickstand with the heel of her left boot while flipping the kill switch with her right hand to the run position before turning the ignition to on.

"Sorry, I'm busy tonight. And every night."

Travis put a hand on her shoulder and leaned in close to her face. "Come on. I'm sure you enjoy having a good time as much as the next person."

His strong breath smelled yeasty with a sickly-sweet odor. Apparently, Travis had been hitting the bottle already tonight—not that she knew when he usually started drinking—but it was only seven o'clock on a Friday night.

She shrugged his hand off her shoulder as she reached up to grip the clutch. "Oh, I do, but unfortunately, your idea of a good time and mine are very different."

"Come on." This time his hand landed high on her thigh. He wiggled his eyebrows as he squeezed her leg. "Give me a chance. I bet I can change your mind."

A wave of disgust and nausea swept over her. Squaring her shoulders and looking him dead in the eye, she attempted to mimic the growl she so often heard from Scott. "The only thing I'm going to give you is a bloody nose if you don't remove your hand." She'd accidentally given Scott a bloody nose. Surely, she could give Travis one on purpose.

He blinked twice then pulled his hand from her leg and took a step back. He grinned as he hooked his thumbs in his belt loops again. "Oh, you like to play hard to get, huh? Want to be wined and dined first?"

"I don't want *anything* from you." She pressed the starter button, and her bike roared to life. Rolling the throttle toward her to rev the engine, she cut off Travis's next words. She pressed down with her right boot on the gear shift and drove out of the parking lot, leaving Travis glaring after her.

She'd managed to make it four weeks without crossing paths with Travis Brooks, but she had a feeling it wouldn't be long before she had another run-in with him. Would she be lucky enough to just drive away next time? She had a feeling he would have gotten much more physical if they hadn't been in a public place. She shuddered again as she turned into the parking lot of the shop. That man made her skin crawl.

Parking behind the garage, she carried her groceries upstairs and locked the door to her apartment. After putting away the half gallon of milk, cereal, bread, peanut butter, and apples she'd purchased, she looked around her apartment forlornly.

Another bleak Friday night stretched ahead of her. She didn't relish the idea of spending it alone again, but with Travis being the only interested party… Alone it was.

Normally, she spent at least an hour on the phone with Eden, but her friend was attending a charity event with her dad this evening. That's why Kennedy had decided not to spend the weekend in Spokane. Well, that and the fact that she volunteered to help at Mary's house again tomorrow with Scott.

Ugh, Scott.

It seemed she couldn't go more than a few minutes without thinking about him. Things between them this past week had been strained to say the least. Kennedy continued to be her cheerful, positive self, and he was his usual quiet, grumpy, surly self.

Okay, that wasn't entirely true. He could be sweet when he wanted to. When Kennedy showed up to work on Monday morning, she found him spraying the shop with one of those home pesticide sprays to kill any more spiders that might be lurking. He even sprayed the apartment for her.

He talked a little more freely over lunch now about things that had little to do with work, but they still avoided personal topics, and they never discussed the kiss. She had been able to get him to talk about his family some, so she felt like she was getting to know him a little better.

She was torn, though. It was stupid to get mixed up with a coworker again, but she wanted to see where things with Scott could lead. Ever since he told her he found all those things about her sexy, she'd been trying to be patient, hoping he would eventually come around.

But he seemed determined to maintain his distance and keep things platonic. She took perverse pleasure every time he tensed up when she stepped close to him. She'd even taken to wearing a little lip gloss, mascara and a spritz of body spray each day. Maybe that's why he'd been especially growly this week. He'd just have to learn to deal with it because she had no plans to stop.

Sighing, she dropped onto the couch and picked up the remote and began flipping through stations. She should try to get out more and make friends. But she'd never been very good at doing that by herself. Eden was the social butterfly, not Kennedy.

She bypassed the romantic comedies that were her usual go to when she had no social life—which was more often than she'd like to admit. She couldn't handle that tonight, not when her own love life looked so bleak. Instead, she chose a suspenseful, action-packed thriller to watch. Changing into pajamas, or rather shorts and an old t-shirt, she grabbed a fleece throw off the bed, and popped some popcorn, before making herself comfortable on the couch.

Two hours later, she released the stranglehold she had on her blanket and grabbed the remote. She pressed the power button, then immediately regretted it when the room was plunged into darkness.

"Fudge sticks!"

She hurried to the kitchen and turned on the light over the stove. She wasn't usually afraid of the dark, but the movie she'd watched left her on edge. It had so many twists and turns that convinced her— right along with the main character—that no one could be trusted. And she'd been right.

Too uptight to go to bed, she opted for a bath to help her relax. Tossing in a cherry blossom bath bomb, she tapped her Feel-Good Classics playlist and sank into the tub. She bobbed her head and tapped her toes against the ceramic as one oldie but goodie song after another played. This had been her dad's favorite kind of music.

He'd always been her hero. She'd been so close to him, his sudden stroke and eventual death had left her floundering. She missed their

Sunday brunches and Monday night football games. She didn't care about the sport as much as he did, but she loved spending that time with him. His house had always been her go-to on Friday nights when Eden had plans and she didn't.

Tears crept down her cheeks. It had been three months since he passed away, and some days, she still couldn't believe he was gone. She tried to stay positive and focused on making a new life for herself, but it wasn't easy.

Twenty minutes later, she climbed into bed, and her thoughts once again turned to Scott. She had a feeling her dad would have liked him. Despite Scott's grumpiness, he was nothing like that jerk Travis, which made her like him all the more. Problem was, how did she get him to let her in?

Eventually, she dozed off only to be woken up by the squeal of tires on asphalt and the rev of a V8 engine. The hairs on her arms stood on end as she bolted upright in bed. Noting the eerie glow cast in her bedroom by headlights in front of the shop, she looked at the clock on the bedside table.

Twelve thirty.

She crept to the window and peeked down through a slit in the curtains. A familiar black truck sat parked only inches from the corner of the building.

Why on earth is Travis Brooks here at this time of night?

He climbed from the truck and yelled something she couldn't decipher. Then he took a swig from a dark-colored bottle before throwing it against the building.

Kennedy jumped at the sound of shattering glass. She jolted again when the roll-up door of the first bay rattled.

"You stole my job, Wheeler!" Travis shouted with a slur.

She pressed her cheek to the glass, but she couldn't see what Travis was doing. After a moment the other door rattled.

Travis yelled something punctuated by swear words that accused Scott of being a lying cheat. Then the door below her rattled again.

Would Travis go so far as to break into the shop or convenience store? There were a ton of expensive tools in there. She wouldn't put it past him to steal them. And if he got into the convenience store, there was no telling what kind of damage he could do. They didn't keep much money there, but he could make a mess and steal all kinds of stuff, including more alcohol.

I should call Scott. He'll know what to do.

She grabbed her phone off the nightstand and found Scott's number just as a loud crash sounded outside. Hurrying back to the window, she watched Travis give the planter he'd knocked over a shove, spilling dirt and chrysanthemums on the ground.

He must have heard her movement because he looked up at her. "Hey, sexy lady mechanic, I wanna ride on your motorbike."

Kennedy jumped back, tucking her face behind the curtain as a band tightened around her chest, stealing her breath.

Nuts! Of course, Travis knows I live here. The whole town does, but why couldn't he forget in his inebriated state?

"Hey, you hear me?" he yelled again. "Come give me a ride."

Kennedy peeked out long enough to see him making an obscene gesture with his hips that told her he was talking about a different kind of ride.

He turned and started walking around to the back of the building, and for the first time in her life, Kennedy swore out loud. Twice.

Scott's words from the first time she met Travis filled her head. *Brooks isn't the kind of guy who takes 'no' for an answer.*

Had she angered him by turning him down earlier this evening?

The thought of what Travis would do to her if he managed to break through her door made her want to sink to the floor and curl up in a ball, but she forced herself to quickly tiptoe to the kitchen to ensure her door was locked.

It was, but would it be strong enough to keep him out if he really wanted in?

As he climbed the stairs at the back of the building, he continued to shout ramblings about getting even with Wheeler and getting it on with the pretty mechanic. All the while punctuating his words with obscenities.

Heart racing, Kennedy hurried back to her room on shaky legs, locked the door, and pressed call on her cell phone. She sank onto the bed then right on down to the floor when her legs refused to support her anymore.

SCOTT BUNCHED his pillow and rolled over and checked the clock for the hundredth time.

Twelve thirty.

Why am I still awake?

He'd exhausted himself with a two-hour workout this evening in an attempt to dispel the pent-up tension he felt after working another whole week with Kennedy. He swore she intentionally stood closer than necessary every chance she got, and she smelled more amazing than ever.

She didn't look like she wore any more makeup than usual, but her eyes looked bigger and prettier lately. And she must be doing something to her lips too because every time he turned around, he wanted to pull her into his arms and kiss her until she was weak in the knees.

He'd had to remind himself a million times this week why dating a coworker wasn't a good idea. But Rudy had been right, not dating Kennedy didn't make her any less distracting. And it didn't make him worry about her any less.

His phone vibrated on his nightstand, and adrenaline surged through his veins, spiking his body temperature. Phone calls in the middle of the night were never good. When he spotted Kennedy's name on his screen his stomach bottomed out.

"'Lo." His voice was deep and rough, even though he hadn't been sleeping.

"Scott?" Panic filled Kennedy's high-pitched voice.

"What's wrong?" He threw back the covers and swung his legs off the bed in one fluid motion.

"T-Travis Brooks is trying to break down my door."

"What?" Scott was on his feet now, scrambling for a pair of sweatpants.

"He's drunk and yelling—" She hiccupped. "Horrible things."

"Is your door locked?"

"Yes, but I'm not sure it's g-going to hold. He's angry because I rejected him earlier this evening." Her voice shook with emotion.

Horrendous images of Travis hurting Kennedy flashed through Scott's mind. He pulled on a t-shirt and grabbed the slippers his mom gave him for Christmas years ago from the back of his closet—slippers he'd sworn to never wear. But he didn't have time to worry about socks and shoes right now.

"Lock your bedroom door and then lock yourself in the bathroom."

Did the bathroom door even have a lock? Or the bedroom for that matter?

"I'm on my way, Ken, but I need to hang up, so I can call Rudy."

"Okay, but hurry please. I think I just heard wood crack."

Scott pulled his phone away from his ear to call Rudy and ended up dropping it on the floor of his dark bedroom. Cussing out loud, he dropped to his knees. He waited until he had his brother on the line before he grabbed his keys and rushed out the door.

The garage wasn't that far from his house, but the drive took forever. He was grateful when Rudy assured him he'd get there in no time, but it still didn't stop the furious pounding of his heart.

After what felt like an eternity, Scott turned into the parking lot of the shop and skidded to a stop. He jumped out, barely taking time to close his truck door, and raced around to the back stairs.

He met Rudy guiding a handcuffed Travis down the steps. "Where's Kennedy?"

"I haven't seen her yet. I need to take out the garbage before I go talk to her."

Travis yelled obscenities at Scott and tried to spit on him as Rudy marched him past. Fortunately, he missed, and Scott took the stairs two at a time, eager to get to Kennedy.

Reaching the top, he stopped to examine the door and its casing. Only a splinter of wood kept the door from swinging open. Instead of forcing his way inside like he wanted to, he pulled out his phone and called Kennedy.

"Scott?" Tension and emotion still thickened her voice.

"I'm here—" he stopped himself before calling her honey. "Rudy's got Travis cuffed. Come let me in."

She didn't bother to say anything else. The line simply died, and he heard rapid footfalls through the apartment. When the door flew open, he wasn't sure who closed the gap between them first, but he found himself just inside with her in his arms, so he suspected it was him.

"I was so scared." Emotion choked Kennedy's voice.

"Sh…" He ran a hand down her silky hair. It was every bit as soft as he dreamed it would be. "I'm here now."

A few sniffles escaped as she kept her face buried against his chest, and her body continued to tremble against him. He tightened his arms around her. He shouldn't be glad she'd suffered something so traumatic, but he couldn't deny he enjoyed holding and comforting her.

A few seconds—or maybe minutes—later, Rudy cleared his throat behind Scott.

Kennedy tried to pull away, but Scott kept an arm around her. She still continued to quiver a little.

Rudy's eyebrows rose, but Scott ignored him. Kennedy needed him, so he was going to be there for her. She didn't have anyone else except a best friend who lived over an hour away.

"Kennedy," Rudy said, "I need to get a statement from you. Do you want to press charges?"

"Yes!" Scott said before Kennedy could answer. Travis needed to answer for the things he'd done.

She looked up at him before nodding her head.

He sat beside her at the small table and kept her hand in his while she told Rudy about Travis accosting her in the parking lot of Knight's Grocery. His blood simmered when she mentioned Brooks touching her shoulder and thigh. Then his own shoulders hunched with tension when she told them about Brooks trying to break in downstairs and knocking over the flowerpot before attempting to get into her apartment.

Scott had been so anxious to get to Kennedy, he hadn't even noticed the flowerpot.

Rudy looked at him. "Do you want to tell Charity or should I?"

"I will, and I'll insist she press charges this time."

"This time? Has he done this before?" Kennedy asked.

"The first time," Rudy said, "was six months after Rich Knight fired him. He showed up at the garage in the middle of the day in a drunken rage. Rich took pity on Travis and drove him home and told him to sleep it off."

"The last time," Scott jumped in, "was a couple years ago in the middle of the night. He was drunk then too. He broke a window to the convenience store. Fortunately, Sheriff Winters drove by on patrol and arrested Travis before he could steal anything or do any further damage. Charity insisted he pay for the new window, but otherwise, Travis didn't get much more than a slap on the hand."

"Why not?"

Scott and Rudy exchanged looks. When his brother shrugged, Scott explained, "Everybody feels bad for Travis, because his mother left when he was young and his dad... Well, his dad's basically an alcoholic."

Kennedy frowned. "So, he's following in his dad's footsteps?"

"Apparently." Rudy shook his head. "This time, we've got him on breaking and entering, driving under the influence, and being drunk and disorderly. Unfortunately, since he never actually hurt you, I can't charge him with assault. Sexual harassment is only illegal in the workplace, but you can file a restraining order against him if you want."

Kennedy gave a small nod. "I'll think about it."

Rudy continued to ask several more questions that Scott found redundant before standing and examining the door frame.

Scott followed him.

"Better get Dad over to fix this in the morning." Rudy looked over his shoulder at Kennedy and lowered his voice. "I'm not sure she should be left alone tonight."

Scott's gaze followed Rudy's to where Kennedy still sat at the table with her arms wrapped around herself. She looked so small and insecure. Even though he knew no one was likely to try and break in again tonight, there was no way he could leave Kennedy alone after such a traumatic experience.

"She won't be."

Rudy grinned and winked before smacking him on the arm. "Attaboy. Take good care of your girl."

Scott scowled as he shoved Rudy out onto the landing and closed the door on him. He didn't even bother trying to lock it, since it wouldn't do any good. Instead, he grabbed the chair Rudy had vacated and braced it under the doorknob. If it had been just him, he wouldn't have bothered—especially in this small town—but maybe it would give Kennedy a little piece of mind.

"You okay?" he sat back down beside her.

She startled and tightened her arms around herself. Whether from fear or just being surprised he was still here, Scott wasn't sure, but it made him more determined to protect and comfort her than ever.

She nodded but her face crumpled as she tucked her chin to her chest.

He scooted his chair a little closer. "Hey, come here." She didn't resist when he reached out to pull her into his arms.

The sniffles returned, but at least she wasn't trembling anymore. After a few minutes, she pulled back a little and gave him a sheepish look. "I'm sorry for being such a cry baby." She swiped at her nose with the back of her hand. "I just got thinking about my dad. He's the one I always called when I needed help, and it just hit me again..." Her eyes welled up with more tears.

Scott grabbed the roll of paper towels off the counter and sat back down beside her. He waited patiently while she wiped her eyes and blew her nose. "Will you tell me about him?"

She gave him a watery smile. "He used to call me Ken. I rarely let anyone else call me that, besides him. He was the greatest. Taught me everything I know from cooking to cars. He was a true artist when it came to automobiles." She went on to talk about his talent with motorcycles and bodywork as well as engines and motors of all sizes. "He was such a patient man, even though he suffered one setback after another. Several years ago, he invested his savings, hoping to recoup enough money to buy back the portion of the garage that he'd had to sell to Coop, but he lost it all when the investment turned out to be a scam."

"Ouch."

"Yes, and one of his good friends—the one who convinced him to invest—lost almost everything too. My dad didn't hold it against him though. In fact, he took Brent's son under his wing and mentored him and helped him get set up in his own shop. Dad was so good with young mechanics, and he stood up for me against Coop, convincing him to give me the chance to prove myself in the shop after I got all my certifications." Her voice grew thick again as she added. "He was always so patient, playing the role of mother and father."

"How old were you when your mother died?" Scott took her hand in his. Relief filled him when she didn't pull away.

His heart hurt for Kennedy as she talked about being a young girl and watching her mother's lengthy battle with cancer and eventual death when she was only nine. How difficult it must have been for her to grow up without a mother?

"I really only have a handful of memories of her. Most of them were when she was sick, but my dad used to tell me all kinds of stories about her." She continued to talk about how pretty and nice her mom was and shared a few stories about how her parents met and where they had their first date.

If Kennedy looked anything like her mom, the woman must have been stunning.

After a while, she gave his fingers a squeeze before pulling her hand from his. "Thank you for calming me down, but it's late. You should go home and get some sleep. We've got a busy day tomorrow."

"I'm not going home." He folded his arms across his chest, so she'd know there was no point in arguing.

Her eyes widened. "What will your mom think?"

She'd probably give him a lecture about how inappropriate it was for him to spend the night at a woman's house, and it'd probably end with something along the lines of what will people think?

Scott didn't care what people thought. Kennedy needed him, so this was where he would stay.

He shrugged. "I'm a big boy and can make my own decisions."

Kennedy stared at him for a long time, chewing on her bottom lip, and Scott's gaze focused on the pink flesh of her lips. It would be so easy to lean forward and kiss her, but he couldn't do that. He'd decided a relationship between them wasn't a good idea, and as much as he regretted that decision some days, he needed to stick to it. Maybe after the purchase of the garage was final, he could consider building a future with her. But tonight…she was too vulnerable.

As though she read his thoughts about wanting to kiss her—or maybe she saw the desire in his eyes—she stood and backed away toward the small kitchen. "In that case, would you like some tea or hot chocolate?"

"Hot chocolate sounds great." He wasn't usually one for sweets unless it was one of his mom's homemade cakes or pies, but he needed something to keep his hands busy, so he didn't pull Kennedy into his arms again. He'd enjoyed having her in his embrace a little too much.

While he waited for her, he settled onto the sofa. It wasn't especially comfortable, but it was a far cry better than the hard chair he'd been sitting on for the past hour. He didn't look forward to spending the night on this thing.

As he watched Kennedy move around the kitchen, his gaze was drawn to her long shapely legs. A wave of appreciation washed over him. He had yet to find something he didn't like about her.

After she handed him a steaming mug of hot chocolate, she settled on the sofa near him, tucking her legs under her and facing him. If he wanted to, he could easily rest his hand on her knee. And he wanted to, but he couldn't complicate their relationship like that when he wasn't sure he could handle continuing to work with her if they were more than just friends and coworkers.

He kept his mug in his left hand and rested the other on the arm of the sofa, so he wasn't tempted to touch her. That did nothing to keep her fruity floral scent from surrounding him and ramping up his desire. It created a hunger in him he couldn't afford to satiate.

Silence—not as uncomfortable as usual but awkward nonetheless —settled around them as they both sipped their cocoa.

Scott's gaze remained on the dark liquid in his mug when he spoke. "So, who was the jerk who told you there was something wrong with you? That you weren't feminine enough."

He found it easier to talk to her lately, but she still made him nervous most of the time because he was so blasted attracted to her. It was easier if he didn't look directly at her.

Out of the corner of his eye, he saw Kennedy lower her gaze to her own mug. "My one and only boyfriend."

"The one you were in a relationship with for six years?" What kind of jerk strung a woman along in a relationship if he didn't think she was feminine enough? And how on earth had he not thought Kennedy was sexy? She may dress in jeans and t-shirts but there was nothing manly about the way her jeans hugged her hips, or the way her bright tees added color to her cheeks. Like the well-worn red shirt she wore tonight that said, *That's a horrible idea. What time?* Man, he loved her in red!

"Yes. Nate was my dad's partner's son."

"Let me guess, he worked at the shop?" When she nodded, a surge of jealousy shot through him. He didn't like the idea of another man working with Kennedy and gawking at her. Especially not some man that could have married her and formed a partnership with her.

"So, what happened?" He looked at her now, watching her features.

Her brow furrowed, her bottom lip trembled, and she blinked several times. Finally, she managed to school her features into a scowl. "Olivia Manwaring."

Scott almost laughed out loud at the other woman's last name. How appropriate for someone who would steal another woman's man.

"And before that, it was Seductive Stacy. Well, I never caught him with her like I did with Olivia, but I'm pretty sure there was something going on between them for a while. And probably with that redhead, Tempting Tina, before that." Kennedy's face paled, and she pressed a hand to her stomach.

Was Nate ever faithful? Was this the first time Kennedy was making all of the connections? Probably not, since she had nicknames for the women. No wonder she thought there was something wrong with her.

"Why did you stick with him for so many years, if he..." Scott wasn't sure how to finish his sentence without it sounding hurtful.

She looked up and gave him a weak smile before setting her half-full mug on the coffee table. She propped her feet up and folded her arms across her chest. Shaking her head, she stared at her feet while she talked. "I just thought we'd always end up together, you know. His dad was my dad's best friend and partner. I'd had a crush on him since I was twelve. He started flirting with me when I turned sixteen, but because he was two years older than me, his dad wouldn't let him date me until I turned eighteen."

Now she studied her fingernails. "We started dating casually at first, but within a year, we were seeing each other steadily. He said he wasn't interested in getting married for a few years, and I was okay with that. I wasn't in a hurry to get married either." Kennedy picked at her cuticles now. "He flirted with just about every woman who came into the shop. It didn't matter how old they were. That was just the way he was, so I tried not to let it bother me. On occasion when I brought it up, he brushed me off, saying he was just being friendly. He told me jealousy was unbecoming on me, making me think I was the one with the problem."

What a jerk!

"Our relationship kind of waned occasionally, since he sometimes worked a second job delivering pizza for his uncle on the weekends."

Pizza delivery? Yeah, right.

"He really only became affectionate and acted committed when a customer or another mechanic showed me a lot of attention."

She shot a quick glance in his direction, and he kept his expression as compassionate as possible despite calling Nate something a lot worse than a jerk in his head.

"I suppose it was my own fault, since I refused to sleep with him until we were married."

209

"No," Scott said forcefully. "A man should absolutely respect a woman's wishes in that regard. If he loved you, he should have been willing to wait for you, instead of skulking around with other—" Scott stopped talking when he realized how hurtful his words sounded.

"Yeah, apparently that was the problem. I don't think he ever really loved me." Sadness filled Kennedy's eyes.

"Then why did he keep stringing you along any time other men showed interest?"

"I confronted him about that after I caught him with Olivia, and he said he planned to marry me someday if need be; to keep full ownership of the shop in the family."

Scott shook his head in disbelief as he put his almost empty mug beside hers and turned his body toward Kennedy. "So what, he just cooled his jets after your dad passed away, and you signed over the remaining portion of the shop?"

She scoffed but it sounded forced. "His jets cooled about the time I refused to sleep with him and stayed cooled unless some other man paid me attention. To be honest, I don't think he found me all that attractive. He always wanted someone more feminine." She tugged at the loose strings of her hem again, more forcefully now.

Instinctively, Scott wrapped his arm around her shoulders and pulled her against his side. "Trust me when I say you are plenty feminine. You have a lot of amazing…assets that grease-stained jeans and t-shirts can't hide."

She turned her head and looked up at him. "You think so?"

The serious expression in her gorgeous brown eyes made his heart rate kick up a notch. With her head on his shoulder, it would be so easy to dip his head and press his lips to hers. But he'd told himself—and her—that they couldn't go there. It made work too complicated and dangerous.

He lifted his gaze to stare at the blank TV screen. "I mentioned a few things I find attractive about you the other day. Those are only the ones that are appropriate to discuss between friends and coworkers. There are others…" His voice deepened in pitch, so he cleared it before continuing. "That I won't bother listing, because I'm trying to only be your friend right now and nothing more. But you're crazy talented with cars. You may not think that's attractive, but it is."

"Right, friends." Out of the corner of his eye, he saw a look of disappointment fill her face. She started to pull away, but he tightened his arm.

"Friends can lean on each other for support sometimes." His voice deepened again, betraying how badly he wanted to continue holding her.

Was he as big of a jerk as Nate for wanting to be close to her after telling her they could only be friends?

Her lips turned up as she settled back against him. "Yes, they can."

They lapsed into a comfortable silence for a time and Scott searched for a topic that would lighten the mood.

"So, you're afraid of spiders, huh?" He chuckled when she shivered. "What's the story behind that?"

"No story, except that I grew up with a horribly mean neighbor boy named Silas who liked to tease and taunt me with all kinds of creepy crawly things. He used to put spiders and grasshoppers in my hair."

"You're afraid of all kinds of bugs then?"

"Only when they crawl on me."

"What about worms?"

Kennedy shuddered, and he laughed. "Do you know how hard it is to get a worm out of long hair?"

"Snakes?"

A gurgling sound escaped her throat as her body shook with another tremor. She elbowed his side. "Stop it."

He laughed again. A lightness that he hadn't felt for a long time filled his chest. It was freeing, and it loosened his tongue. Or maybe it was the fact that he'd admitted to Kennedy that he found her attractive, so he didn't need to be so nervous around her.

Either way, he wanted to know more about her, so he wasn't about to stop asking questions.

For the next three hours, they talked about anything and everything. Music, movies, hobbies, families. When their discussion turned to their heroes, Kennedy again talked about her dad. This time without the tears.

"I've named the tow truck at the shop Thomas after my dad." She said with a grin.

Scott looked sideways at her. "Our tow truck? I get that you want to honor your dad, but why name a tow truck after him?"

"Because Thomas always comes to the rescue and saves the day. My dad was always like that."

"Oh, that's pretty cool, I guess." Scott nodded. "What other things have you named?"

"Well, my motorcycle's name is Lily. It used to be Delilah—because my mom always called it his other woman. But after my mom passed away, he renamed his bike after her. That way it felt like he was taking a piece of her with him when he rode."

"Do you feel that way when you ride her?"

She nodded then ducked her head. "I know it's silly, but it's kind of like they are both with me whenever I ride."

"It's not silly at all. In fact, I think it's awesome that you have something that ties you all together like that."

"At T&J's I named the oil drain pan Silas."

"Silas? As in the boy who put bugs in your hair?" When she nodded, he grinned. "I guess it's an appropriate name for the dirtiest thing in the garage."

"Yes, but I have an even better name for the oil drain pan at Knight's."

"What?"

"Nate." She let out a giggle that made Scott laugh.

"No wonder you like doing the oil changes. I bet you get a sense of satisfaction every time you kick it under a car."

"Yep."

"Wait. Didn't you tell me a few weeks ago that you named the impact drill Tina? As in Tempting Tina?"

"One and the same. You should have seen the way she chattered and wrapped herself around Nate."

Scott laughed again and looked sideways at her. "I'd better be careful, or you'll give me a nickname."

An attractive blush covered her cheeks.

"What? You've already got a nickname for me, don't you?"

"Maybe." She bit her bottom lip but couldn't hide her grin.

Scott wanted to replace her teeth with his against her lip. He pulled away a little. Mostly so he wouldn't give in to the temptation to kiss her, but also to look her square in the eyes. "What's your nickname for me?"

"Try to guess."

Scott just stared at her with raised eyebrows and shook his head.

"It has something to do with your strength."

"Hulk?"

Kennedy burst out laughing. "Oh please. You're strong, but not that strong. I'll tell you, but first you have to understand something. You were so much bigger than I expected with the shoulders and the biceps…and you had that scruff of beard that made you look like a lumberjack. Then when I found out you used to work with the Forest Service, I couldn't help myself, the name just stuck."

"What name? Lumberjack?"

"No, silly, Paul Bunyan."

"Huh." Scott leaned back against the couch. It wasn't quite the compliment that Hulk was, but it was a lot better than any of the other nicknames she'd shared with him tonight. He pulled her back against his side. "You want to hear my nickname for you?"

"You have a nickname for me?" Excitement filled her voice as she turned toward him again. "What is it?"

"Initially it was Barbie, for obvious reasons."

"Wait! What reasons?" Now she was full on facing him.

Heat crept up Scott's neck. "You know, because of your…long blond hair and your…figure."

"I'm not sure whether to feel flattered or offended. You realize that sounds sexist?"

"I know, that's why I have a different nickname for you now."

"Well, what is it?"

"Ever since I saw you in that blue dress at the Labor Day barbecue, I think of you as Elsa."

"Elsa?" Kennedy's brows furrowed. "As in the ice queen? You think I'm cold? You were the one who ignored me that night."

"No, you're pretty like Elsa." Scott bit back a smile before adding the next bit. "And you get a little bossy and domineering sometimes."

"What?!" Kennedy grabbed the throw pillow at the other end of the couch and smacked him in the head with it.

CHAPTER 20

*K*ennedy became aware of the slight rise and fall of her head about the time an ache started throbbing in her neck. Instead of pushing herself upright like her neck screamed at her to do, she reveled in the fact that her head rested on Scott's hard chest.

Holy cow!

This man was built. But that's not what shocked her so much. She'd just spent the night in the arms of an incredibly handsome man. She should feel ashamed, but she didn't because nothing happened. Well, nothing inappropriate anyway.

Something had changed between them last night though. Scott said he just wanted to be friends, but he'd held her close all night. And he'd talked to her!

Well, he'd mostly kept her talking, but she'd managed to get him to talk about himself more than he ever had before. They talked about all kinds of things, easily shifting from one topic to another. He spoke more freely when she wasn't looking directly at him, which was fine because it was hard to look at his face with her head on his shoulder. He even told her a little more about Hannah, who'd been persistent in pulling him out of his shell.

Somewhere around two in the morning, Kennedy decided she

could be as patient and persistent as Scott's last girlfriend. Because that's what she wanted; to be his girlfriend. Scott may have a hang-up about working with women, but it wasn't because he thought they were inferior. He was simply concerned about their safety. And he was reluctant to get into another relationship for fear of losing the woman he loved again. She had a feeling he still suffered more than a little PTSD and anxiety over what happened to Hannah.

Not that she thought Scott was in love with her. Yet. But she often saw the raw desire in his eyes, right before he ducked his head or turned away. She'd glimpsed it last night before he became fascinated with her blank television screen. She'd thought he might give in and kiss her, and the disappointment had been powerful when he didn't, but then he'd pulled her close and she relished the contact.

Then around four a.m., they'd shifted for the second time to get more comfortable, laying out across the couch. And when he'd offered his shoulder yet again, she'd taken it. He grew quieter after that, and she'd quickly succumbed to sleep. She should have offered him her bed or at the very least, gone to her own bed, but there was something about Scott finally opening up to her that kept her captive.

Scott sucked in a deep breath that lifted her head, then he stilled. So much so, she wondered if he was still breathing. Finally, he let out a lengthy sigh.

She pushed upright and looked at him.

"What time is it?" His gruff sleepy voice sent shivers racing down her spine.

She looked through the dim morning light filtering through the thick curtains toward the stove. "Seven o'clock."

They'd slept for a total of three hours. They were supposed to be at Mary's in an hour. It wasn't near enough sleep for her, yet she felt oddly refreshed despite the crick in her neck. She looked back at him. Did he regret spending the night with her?

He smoothed the hair away from her cheek, sending little tingles shooting across her face and scalp. His lips turned up. "I have a feeling I'm going to feel a whole lot guiltier when I get that disapproving look from my parents than if I'd spent the night alone on your sofa."

She grinned. "As you should. I should probably feel guilty too, even though I don't have a judgmental parent to answer to."

"You don't feel guilty?" He held her gaze as he asked the question.

"No, I feel grateful. I needed comforting and a friend last night. You gave me both. Thank you." If she referred to him as a friend, maybe he wouldn't freak out over the fact that they'd just spent the night together.

He held her gaze for several long seconds before his eyes dropped to her lips.

Kennedy's mouth went dry. There was that look again; full of longing and desire. As much as she'd love for him to kiss her, she had major morning breath and couldn't let that happen. Placing a hand on his rock-hard chest, she pushed up the rest of the way and disentangled her legs from his.

He pushed himself upright too and quickly rose to his feet, clearing his throat as he did so. Then he sat back down and scrambled to find the big fuzzy bear feet—complete with claws—slippers that he'd worn over last night. When she'd given him a hard time about them, he admitted that this was the first time he'd worn them in the five years he'd owned them. An urgency fueled his movements that told her he'd be gone once he had both of his slippers on.

"Would you like to...stay for breakfast? I can make omelets or something."

He stood after slipping on the second bear foot. One hand rested on his hip while the other massaged his neck. He looked at her. "I'd love to, but I should probably get home and get changed before heading over to Mary's."

She understood his hesitation even if it disappointed her. At least, he met her eyes while rejecting her.

He broke eye contact as he stepped toward the door. "Maybe another time."

"Do you mean that?" She held her breath waiting for his response. The man gave her whiplash; he said he didn't want a relationship, yet he held her in his arms all night long. And now, he acted like he couldn't wait to get away from her while saying he'd like to have breakfast with her some other time.

He froze in the process of moving the chair away from the door.

"Don't toy with me, Scott. I've been jerked around enough by men." When he still didn't turn, she added, "We just slept together. Well, we didn't sleep together in the usual sense, but we spent the night together. And I know you want to just be friends, but please don't say things you don't mean. Or things that I might interpret one way when really, you mean them an entirely different way."

Finally, he turned and looked at her. "I like the idea of having breakfast, lunch, and dinner with you, but…"

"But what?" She refused to let herself get excited about what he'd just said before she heard the rest of his words.

"But I still don't think it's a good idea to date my coworker."

She stepped closer. "Because it's distracting and dangerous?"

"Yes."

She rolled her eyes. "Working with you already distracts me even though we're not dating. If we did decide we wanted a relationship, work wouldn't suddenly become more dangerous."

"I know but I…" he rubbed his thumb across the top of the chair. "I can't stop worrying that something might happen to you."

She closed the distance between them and grabbed the hem of his shirt to prevent him from retreating. "I'm going to say this plain and simple; I like you a lot. I'm interested in seeing where things could lead between us. I'm willing to take it slow, because I know you're dealing with a huge loss that still affects you, but maybe…" She paused, unsure of how he would receive the rest of what she had to say.

"Maybe what?"

She grimaced. "Maybe you should see someone about…your PTSD and anxiety."

Scott jerked back as though she'd slapped him. "What do you mean?"

Instead of pointing out how agitated he was when he told her about Hannah's accident and how stupid his reasons were for refusing to get involved in a relationship, she asked, "You worry about me and my safety even though we're not dating, don't you?" When he nodded, she went on. "Do you worry about your own safety?"

His brow furrowed as he shook his head. "No."

"But you could just as easily get hurt."

"I suppose, but I'm stronger and—"

She pointed a finger at him. "Don't you dare say more skilled."

"I was going to say more capable of looking after myself."

"Ugh. Now you sound like that jerk I met my first day at work."

"I'm sorry, Ken, but that's just how I feel. I mean, you called *me* for help last night, remember?"

That was the first time he'd called her by her dad's nickname for her. As much as she liked the familiarity, his last words doused any feelings of affection the nickname triggered.

"I called you because... Never mind." She turned away as tears stung her eyes. Of course, the guy who liked to keep to himself didn't understand what it felt like to need a friend. "I guess calling you was a mistake."

Scott let out a heavy sigh behind her. "Listen, I'm sorry. I'm glad you called me last night. I enjoyed spending time with you." His large, warm hand settled on her shoulder. "I'm sorry if you feel like I'm toying with you. That's not my intention, but I can see how I'm sending mixed signals. I guess I'm not really sure what I want right now. Can you give me some time to figure things out?"

Kennedy blinked away her tears before turning to look at him. She nodded. "Just don't say and do things you don't mean."

"Okay." He opened the door. "I'll come back with my dad and fix this." He motioned to the splintered wood. "Hey, don't hate me for this, but I don't think either one of us should use the power tools today. We didn't get near enough sleep to do that kind of stuff safely."

Kennedy wanted to argue that she was fine, but Scott was right. Besides, her emotions were a little ragged right now anyway. She nodded agreement.

He walked out, closing the door behind him, and Kennedy

dropped into the closest chair. Why had she let herself fall for another man who wasn't sure he wanted her?

Anxiety!

Scott climbed into his truck after cleaning up the flowerpot Travis knocked over and slammed the door. He started his truck and put it into gear. Kennedy might be right about the PTSD thing. He'd had difficulty breathing and his heart rate had remained elevated while he told her about Hannah's death. Talking about it had made him relive all the horror and helplessness of that day. That's why he avoided discussing it.

But Anxiety? He struggled with a lot of things, but anxiety wasn't one of them. Didn't having anxiety mean you constantly worried about everything to the point of not being able to function normally? The only thing he worried about was that Kennedy might get hurt while working in the garage. Accidents happened in repair shops all the time. Worrying about her safety wasn't irrational. It was normal.

Okay, so he worried about her working with power tools at Mary's too. And even though he thought she looked sexy riding a motorcycle, he feared she might get in an accident someday. But that kind of worry was normal when your loved ones rode motorcycles.

Scott's truck jerked to a stop in his parents' driveway.

Loved ones?

He wasn't in love with Kennedy, was he? Sure, she'd managed to draw him out of his shell, and he was attracted to all kinds of things about her, but that didn't mean he was in love with her, did it?

Kennedy had said she liked him a lot, but she couldn't possibly be in love with him. Not with the way he'd treated her during her first week of work. And of course, the mixed signals he'd sent this morning had ticked her off. No way was she in love with him.

He shook his head trying to dislodge all the crazy thoughts of love from his head as he let himself into the house. He was way too tired to think about such serious stuff.

"Ah, there you are." His mom rose from the table. "Sit down and I'll get you some breakfast. Or did Kennedy already feed you?"

Scott's gaze darted back and forth between his parents, searching their faces for the disapproval he expected to see there. Rudy sat at the table shoveling food into his mouth, so of course, they knew all about what happened last night.

"No, I haven't eaten. But sit down, Mom. I can dish up my own food."

Alice Wheeler loved serving her family and others. Arguing with her was usually futile, so they rarely did, but Kennedy kept giving him a hard time about his mother doing everything for him, and she was right. He was a big boy—just like he'd told her last night—and he could fill his own plate with food.

A mild look of surprise crossed his mom's face as she dropped back into her seat. "How is Kennedy doing this morning?"

"She's uh... She's fine."

She's ticked at me, but otherwise she's fine.

Rudy winked and gave him a knowing grin. Scott could tell his brother wanted to make all kinds of teasing comments—ones that might sound inappropriate—but because their parents were present, he kept his mouth shut.

Thank goodness.

Scott was not in the mood for teasing. He'd gotten way too little sleep last night to have to put up with his annoying brother today. Besides, Kennedy's comments about him having PTSD and anxiety had put him in a bad mood, because as much as he hated to admit it, she might be right.

"I'm glad Kennedy felt comfortable calling you." His mom met him at the counter and lifted lids off the frying pans as though Scott wasn't capable of doing it himself. "She must have been so scared."

"Yeah, she was." He meant it when he told Kennedy he was glad she called him. The thought of anyone else, including his little brother, comforting her made him want to punch something.

Mom patted his cheek as though he was a five-year-old boy. "I'm proud of you, son."

You're proud of me for spending the night with a woman?

And not just any woman. The woman he was falling in love with. Scott was glad he didn't have to defend his choices and actions, but his parents' lack of censorship didn't bode well for him being able to withstand Kennedy's charms.

After filling his plate with pancakes, eggs, and bacon, he sat at the table and looked at his dad. "Will you help me fix Kennedy's door frame this morning before we get started at Mary's?"

His dad nodded as he stood and carried his empty plate to the sink. "You better hurry and eat then, because we've got a full day planned at Mary's."

Scott shoved a big bite of pancake into his mouth. He didn't look forward to facing Kennedy again so soon. He felt bad for telling her he didn't know what he wanted after she'd admitted that she liked him, but his heart rate elevated every time he considered a relationship with her. It wasn't the good kind of racing though. It was the what-if-I-fall-in-love-with-her-and-something-bad-happens-to-her kind of racing. The kind that stole his breath and made him want to run away from the possibility of any conflict.

The kind of racing his heart was doing right now.

Blast! I think I'm already in love with her.

For some reason, instead of being excited by the thought, it scared him to death.

CHAPTER 21

Scott watched Ben pick up the paper he'd just signed and place it face down on top of the stack in front of him. He picked up the pile and tapped it on the table to straighten the pages. "That's the last signature. Congratulations, you just bought yourself a gas station and repair shop."

Scott dropped the pen and flexed his fingers. "Really? That's it? It's final?"

That's it.

Scott bit back a laugh. Like he hadn't just spent the last hour signing his life away on a hundred different documents. Talk about overwhelming. He was sure he'd pushed Ben and Andy's patience to the limits by requesting an explanation of every page he signed.

His thoughts jumped to Kennedy. She had been amazing these past few weeks; answering endless emails on his behalf to establish new contracts with the vendors and obtained business and liquor licenses, as well as a dozen other little things. She'd also helped him find an accountant and an insurance agent. Even when he felt like giving up, she'd worked tirelessly to help him get his new business off the ground.

My new business.

He liked the sound of that, but he didn't want it to be his alone. He wanted a partner. A partner willing to help where he was weak, like Kennedy did. He liked the idea of her being his partner inside and outside of the shop.

"Charity signed the paperwork for the repair shop and the diner back-to-back yesterday afternoon, so it's final." Ben held out a set of keys to him. "I know you already have keys to the repair shop, but now you have *all* of the keys for the garage and the convenience store."

Once again, a feeling of gratitude warmed him as he thought about all the people who had helped make this possible. His parents' unfailing support and encouragement meant the world to him, and Sherry's willingness to continue filling in for Mary as the manager of the convenience store, took a load of stress off him. He wasn't sure Mary would ever be able to return to work full-time, but Chase would be coming home soon, so that was a good thing.

Ben rose to his feet and clapped Scott on the shoulder. "I'm proud of you, man."

"Thanks." Scott was proud of himself too.

He couldn't wait to text his family to let them know it was official, but more importantly, he couldn't wait to tell Kennedy in person. She knew he was signing the papers today, but he looked forward to telling her it was final. Despite losing out on T&J's she still hoped someday to own her own shop, or at the very least, a partnership in one. He felt bad that his dreams were coming true when hers weren't, but he knew she'd be excited for him regardless.

He'd asked Kennedy for time to figure things out, and she had given it to him. Even though he'd realized he was in love with her weeks ago, he'd spent a lot of time thinking about what kind of future he wanted with Kennedy, and he repeatedly tried to convince himself that something bad wouldn't automatically happen to her just because they decided to date.

Yes, he planned to date Kennedy. But first, he needed to have a serious talk with her when he got back to the shop.

When he got to his truck, he posted a quick message in the family group chat, announcing his good news. It wouldn't be a surprise to anyone, but he was excited to share this accomplishment with them.

His phone started pinging with what he figured were congratulatory texts from his parents and siblings before he even made it back to the shop. After he parked, he scanned through the texts then climbed from his truck and jogged across the street.

He needed to discuss something with Amy.

KENNEDY PARKED the Nissan Sentra that she'd just replaced the spark plugs on and hurried back inside to close the bay door. Fall had arrived, and the air was nippier this morning than it had been all season. Of course, that was to be expected for mid-October.

She looked at the clock on the wall above the workbench. Scott would soon be done signing the paperwork that made him the new owner of the shop. Now he wouldn't just be her manager, he'd be her boss and landlord.

She was so happy for him. She recalled thinking how small the garage was when she first arrived, but now it felt quaint and homey. It was comfortable and cozy. The small town of Providence didn't need a large eight-bay shop like T&J's Auto Repair. Between her and Scott, they kept up with the repairs just fine despite spending hours and hours these last few weeks reviewing contracts and filling out a mountain of paperwork for licenses, permits, and insurance.

Things between her and Scott were amiable, but she wouldn't call them comfortable. She'd placed the ball squarely in his court when she told him how she felt, but until he was ready to make a move—if he ever did—she told herself to give him the space he'd requested and try not to get her hopes up.

She was still friendly and cheerful around him, but she'd stopped wearing lip gloss and body spray, and she never stood closer to him than the job required. Making an effort with her appearance only resulted in disappointment when he didn't give her the attention she desired.

He made eye contact quite often lately and talked more freely than he ever had before, but he seemed to measure his every move, as if he feared sending the wrong message. He'd hardly touched her these last two weeks, intentional or otherwise, and it drove Kennedy crazy. She couldn't wait for him to get over his stupid hang-up about women working in garages and realize a relationship between them wouldn't make work anymore dangerous than it already was.

Kennedy washed up and called the Nissan's owner, then she ordered the alternator for the Honda Accord that came in first thing this morning. She glanced at the clock again.

Scott should be back by now.

A sense of anticipation filled her. Or maybe it was excitement for Scott coupled with the fact that she missed working with him that gave her this fluttery breathless feeling. Falling for another mechanic that she worked with wasn't the smartest thing she could do, but she couldn't have stopped herself if she'd tried—which she hadn't. Something about Scott did crazy things to her insides, making her feel excited and hopeful.

She grabbed a broom and started sweeping the office. It wasn't that dirty, but she needed something to keep her busy. Anything to keep from worrying about Scott getting overwhelmed by all the paperwork he needed to sign.

The back door to the shop opened, and Kennedy froze.

He's back.

It had to be Scott. They were the only two who used that door.

He stepped into the doorway of the office, and that fluttery feeling rose from the bottom of her stomach and pushed up through her chest, driving all the air from her lungs on its way. She dropped the broom from her suddenly clammy hands.

Wow! The man looks great in a suit.

He smiled and raised a key chain and rattled it.

Pulse racing, she let out a squeal and launched herself at him. "Yay! I'm so happy for you!"

Scott wrapped his arms around her, and the air rushed from her lungs. She should be content that he returned the embrace at all, but it didn't feel like enough. She craved a deeper connection with him on this momentous occasion, so she pressed her lips to his.

His whole body stilled.

So much for giving him space.

Panicking, she abruptly pulled back. Heat rushed to her cheeks. "Sorry. I didn't mean…"

Scott's eyes darkened as he reached out and grabbed her belt loop before she could put much distance between them. He tugged her toward him with one hand while he tossed the keys in his other hand on the table. Then his free hand came up and gently stroked her cheek.

"You're so blasted beautiful." His whispered words were low and velvety.

A rapid pulse fluttered at the base of Kennedy's throat, and her breaths came a little faster. She didn't dare analyze what Scott's words meant or the message he sent by touching her for fear he didn't mean what she hoped. She simply reveled in the fact that he *was* touching her and looking at her with that heated, intense gaze. She'd longed for this kind of contact with him since he spent the night at her apartment three long weeks ago. She intended to enjoy every second of it.

"I want to kiss you." He dragged a fingertip across her bottom lip, making them ache with the desire to have his lips on hers. "But first, I want you to know I mean it. All of it. Every word. Every. Delicious. Moment."

A quiver of anticipation rocketed through her. She had no idea Scott could be so romantic. More than ready to have his lips on hers, she leaned toward him.

But he kept talking. "I'm still not sure a relationship between us is smart, but I'm tired of fighting it. I can't guarantee I won't freak out over your safety occasionally, but I'll try not to let my anxiety get out of hand."

Kennedy grabbed the lapels of his suit coat and closed the distance between them. "Just kiss me already." Her words came out breathy and rushed.

Scott needed no more invitation than that. His mouth claimed hers in a fervent and hungry kiss while his hands slid up her back, pulling her tight against his body.

A shiver of pleasure rippled through Kennedy, sparking all her nerve endings to life. She slid her hands up to play with the hair just above his collar as his lips glided over hers in a graceful dance. If she hadn't been so caught up in what his mouth was doing to hers and the sensations he evoked in her, she would've laughed at herself for comparing their kiss to a dance.

A well-oiled machine was more like it. There was no hesitancy or awkwardness in the way his mouth moved over hers. Just smooth, fluid movement, and her lips knew exactly how to respond. In fact, a humming vibration that she'd never experienced before coursed through her body like the purring of an expensive sports car.

Something that sounded like a mixture of a growl and a moan came from Scott as he tangled a hand in her ponytail. Kennedy loved that he seemed to be as affected by their kiss as she was. Just as she began to feel overwhelmed by the sensations rippling through her, voices rang out in the shop.

"Congratulations, Scott!" Rudy's voice shouted. Several feminine echoes followed.

Scott swore under his breath and pushed Kennedy away. His eyes grew wide as he stepped back. He gave a slight shake of his head before he turned and exited the office.

Kennedy struggled to catch her breath. What did Scott's wide-eyed look and head shake mean? Was it just surprise at almost being caught kissing her? Or was it a plea not to say anything about this recent change in their relationship status?

She waited until her disappointment subsided and her breathing returned to normal before she went out to join what sounded like Scott's whole family but turned out to only be his parents and siblings. Debbie had her three youngest kids in tow; the twins in a double stroller and the baby in a second stroller that Alice pushed.

Sheila and Joy shuffled the cake and balloons they carried back and forth as they took turns giving Scott a hug. Then the men's brief embraces included a hearty slap on the back. Rudy gave Scott a sly grin as he congratulated him.

Before long, the cake sat on the small table in the office, and Alice served up generous pieces on paper plates that Debbie pulled from her diaper bag. Because the office was so crowded, Kennedy hung back in the shop, watching Scott celebrate with his family.

She liked to imagine this is what it would have been like if she'd had siblings. Loud, boisterous, and supportive. That's probably why she and Eden were so close. They considered each other the sister they never had.

Rudy appeared in front of her holding two plates. He handed one to her then leaned back against the workbench beside her. He was in uniform, so he must be on duty, finally working days again.

"So, how are things between you and Scott?"

"What do you mean?"

"I mean, have you made any progress on getting him to open up to you?"

Kennedy wasn't sure how to respond. If their kiss was anything to go by, Scott had opened up to her in a big way, but she wasn't sure if that's what Rudy meant. Besides, she wasn't about to talk about their kiss with Rudy before she even had a chance to discuss it with Scott. It's not like she needed to analyze everything, but she sure hoped Scott didn't back off this time like he did after their last kiss.

Rudy speared a piece of cake with his fork but didn't put it in his mouth. "I keep trying to get him to talk about what's going on between you two, but he just gets grumpy and growly and tells me to mind my own business."

Yep, that sounds like Scott.

Kennedy wanted to tell Rudy the same thing, but she shrugged instead. "He's grumpy and growly around here most days too."

She'd like to think it was because he was as frustrated with their non-relationship as she was. Hopefully, that was all about to change.

Rudy angled his body toward her. "What about today? I bet he's excited today." He stared intently at her as though searching for something in her face.

Scott was definitely excited today. Hopefully, he wouldn't back off after the excitement wore down and decide he didn't mean it after all. Warmth swept over her at the memory of their kiss. She took deep, steady breaths, willing her cheeks not to turn rosy.

"Of course he's excited. He has every right to be."

"Yeah, but has it made him act differently?" Rudy still watched her closely.

"What do you mean?" She looked him square in the eyes, unsure if she should try to feign innocence or not.

Rudy leaned a little closer and lowered his voice. "Come on. I was the first one to enter the shop, and I saw the two of you kissing in the office."

"Oh." Now heat did rush to her cheeks.

"So, you can't tell me nothing's going on, but what I want to know is how long it's been going on?"

Rudy was friendly and fun to talk to but discussing her relationship with Scott with his brother felt strange, especially when she looked up and caught Scott watching the two of them. He held Kennedy's gaze for what felt like a long time for him, then he winked before turning his attention back to his dad.

Kennedy's heart did a somersault in her chest. He sure didn't act like he intended to back off. She smiled when she looked at Rudy. "It's a recent development, but I'd say things are going well."

"I KNEW you had it in you." Rudy elbowed Scott in the ribs as they stepped out of the office.

His parents and sisters had all left a while ago, but his annoying little brother stuck around to give him a hard time about the kiss he'd witnessed. Scott refused to discuss it with Rudy though, especially with Kennedy standing only a few feet away.

"I'm glad you came around and pulled your head out—"

"If you don't walk out now, Little Brother, I might break your arm." Scott clapped a hand on Rudy's shoulder and guided him toward the door.

Rudy snickered. "I'd like to see you try." Even though Scott was a little taller and broader than his brother, Rudy had the skills to take him down if he wanted to. Not to mention a stun gun and pepper spray on his belt.

"I'll get Kennedy to help me."

"Okay, now I'm scared." Rudy laughed and finally walked out the door.

Scott heaved a sigh of relief as the door finally closed behind his brother. He appreciated his family's enthusiasm over his accomplishment, but they'd interrupted something important.

He had things he needed to say to Kennedy, and if he didn't hurry and say them, he'd be interrupted by one of Charity's—or rather Amy's—waitresses when they delivered lunch. Or he might just chicken out. Praying he didn't bungle this whole thing, he turned to find Kennedy leaning against the doorway to the office, staring at him with those big brown eyes.

He studied her shirt for a moment until he read, *Here Comes Trouble*. The woman must be psychic or something because her t-shirts always seemed to fit the mood of the day. He'd never wanted to get into trouble so bad in his life.

He envisioned pushing her back into the office then pulling her into his arms again. He'd be sure to lock the door this time so they didn't get interrupted.

A surge of desire shot through him as he recalled their earlier kiss. Kennedy triggered a primal instinct in him. One fueled by passion and desire. He needed to be careful, or he'd cross a line neither of them intended to cross until they were married. Keeping his hands to himself now that he'd given himself permission to get involved with her would be a constant struggle.

He forced himself to stay on the opposite side of the garage. "Have I told you that I find you very distracting?"

Her face split into a grin, making the dimples in her cheeks dip. "I think you may have mentioned that once."

"Only once? That's remarkable since it happens on a daily basis." He should keep his distance, but he took a small step toward her.

She straightened from the door frame and took a step. "Hmm… that could be dangerous. You should try harder to focus on your work."

"It'd be easier if you didn't always smell so good."

"Sorry, but that would mean giving up my baths, and I just can't do that." She took another step toward him.

Scott shut down the image that filled his head of her taking a bath. He couldn't afford to go there. She was already too much of a temptation as it was. He took another step. "I suppose you can't tone down your looks either. Guess I'm going to have to learn to live with the distraction."

"If it's any consolation, you're not alone." She advanced again. "You look really hot in a suit."

"That does not help." His voice became something of a growl. The last thing he needed was her telling him how attractive she found him. He changed the subject. "I want to take you out tonight."

Her smile grew. "I'd love to go out with you tonight." She lengthened her stride with her next step.

"I'm afraid if we don't set some ground rules for working together though, we'll never get any work done."

Her eyebrows rose. "What kind of ground rules?"

They both continued to step closer each time they spoke. Soon, they'd be close enough to touch. He shoved his hands into his pockets to keep from reaching out and pulling her into his arms.

"No kissing at work." His words came out gruffer than he intended.

Her lips turned down in a dramatic pout. "None at all? Like not even a good morning kiss?"

"Okay, we can greet each other with a kiss in the mornings."

The closer she got, the harder it was for him to maintain eye contact, but he wouldn't let himself look away. He wanted Kennedy to see the sincerity in his eyes.

"What about at the end of the day?" The corner of her lips crept upward.

"Oh, there will definitely be a kiss at the end of the day, because I'll likely be spending every evening with you." He winked at her. "When I do something, Ken, I'm all in. If that's going to be a problem, you better say so now."

"No problem."

"Do you mind me calling you Ken? I know it was your dad's nickname for you." Scott inched closer still.

She shook her head. "I like the way it sounds when you say it. What will people think when they find out I'm dating my boss and landlord?" Her dimples returned with her broad smile.

"I don't give a da—" He cut off the swear word. "I don't care what people think."

"Is this a bad time to mention that my tub isn't draining well?"

"The worst time. We'll talk about that later."

Kennedy stood mere inches away now, and her fruity scent invaded his nose. "Can we return to the discussion of kissing at work?"

Scott bit back a groan. The woman was trying to drive him crazy. He was sure of it.

She grinned. "Waiting until the end of the day for another kiss might be rough. Can't we kiss at the end of our workday?"

His own lips turned up. He had a feeling saying no to Kennedy was going to be impossible, especially when she kept talking about kissing. Giving into the temptation, he pulled his hands from his pockets and slid them around her waist. She felt so good in his arms.

"Before work, after work, a greeting when I arrive to hang out with you for the evening, then a kiss goodnight when I leave. That's a lot of kissing." His voice grew deeper as he talked.

He curled his fingers around her ponytail and pulled it forward. Mesmerized, he watched the blond silky strands glide through his fingers. He loved everything about this woman. He wanted to tell her that, but it felt too early to say the L word. Besides, he was still getting used to the powerful emotions she triggered in him.

"It will be a lot of kissing," she agreed as she slid her hands up his chest to rest on his shoulders. "But I have a feeling I'm going to want more."

This time he made no effort to hide his groan. "You know, technically, my workday hasn't started yet, so I suppose I can kiss you by way of greeting." He tilted his head toward her, but she leaned away and grinned.

"If this is your greeting, then what was that last kiss?"

Reflexively, he tightened his arms around her so she couldn't escape. "That was purely celebration, of course. *This* is good morning, even though it's almost noon." He gave her only a moment to pull away before pressing his lips to hers.

A deep and contented sigh whispered out of him when her lips parted right away, inviting him to deepen the kiss. There was something about this woman that completed him. Holding her and talking with her felt freeing in a way that he had never experienced before. Not even with Hannah.

Normally, he enjoyed solitude, but not anymore. He didn't want to be alone. He only wanted to be with Kennedy. He wanted to work with her, talk with her, and play games or watch a movie with her. He didn't care what they did, as long as they did it together.

His hands stroked her back, gently sliding up then back down again as he enjoyed the feel of her in his arms. Her mouth moved in rhythm with his, fueling the chemistry that always sparked between them.

Her fingers caressed his neck, leaving a trail of fire in their wake. When her palms splayed across his chest under his suit coat, warmth shot through his veins. His mind immediately jumped to much more intimate activities he'd love to do with Kennedy, and he had to put a stop to the kiss.

With a soft groan, he pulled her hands from his chest and stepped back. He sucked in a sharp breath to steady his breathing.

"Ken, I'm eager to experience all the things that come with a relationship with you, but…" He took an additional step back, releasing her hands as he did so. He gave her a pointed look before continuing, hoping she'd get his message, so he didn't have to spell it out. "But you affect me too strongly and make me want things I shouldn't."

Her cheeks turned rosy as she ducked her head. "Sorry, I guess I kind of got carried away."

"We both did." He scratched his neck as the discomfort of such an intimate topic settled over him. "We should probably tone down the kissing while we evaluate what we each want from this relationship. Making out and spending a lot of time alone together might not be a good idea."

"You're right." She took a step back then gave him a smile that didn't meet her eyes. "And that kind of kissing isn't appropriate at work."

He nodded. "I'd better change my clothes so we can get to work."

He headed toward the restroom, but Kennedy stopped him. "Wait, I have something for you." She darted to the office and returned seconds later holding a black t-shirt with white lettering. "You should wear this today."

The t-shirt was much easier to read than most of the ones she wore, because it only had two words on it: *The Boss.* A picture of a tie hung below the O.

Kennedy had bought him a t-shirt. Something in his chest tightened. It was as if she had invited him into her personal, private world in a way that no one ever had before.

He grinned as he took the shirt from her and went to the bathroom to change. Several minutes later, he looked at himself in the mirror. The t-shirt was rather snug across his chest and biceps, emphasizing his muscles. Kennedy probably should have purchased size 2X instead of XL.

Oh well. If it distracts her, it's her problem.

He walked out to find her leaning against the tool bench wearing a similar t-shirt, except hers said, *The Real Boss.* The word *real* was in bright pink lettering, as was the bow that rested on the top corner of the B.

He burst out laughing. Trust Kennedy to find a way to make a simple t-shirt not only look sexy but also funny. Working with her would never get boring.

CHAPTER 22

"*K*ennedy!" Eden squealed as soon as the door opened. Kennedy found herself engulfed in a tight hug that she eagerly returned. It had been almost a month since she and Eden had been able to spend time together. It felt like they lived a thousand miles apart instead of only a hundred. And even though Scott had been occupying much of Kennedy's time, she still missed her friend terribly.

That was the only drawback to making her move to Providence permanent. She'd miss her best friend. But Kennedy had no desire to leave Scott and the small repair shop that had come to feel like home.

Eden finally released Kennedy after pulling her into the apartment. "Oh, my goodness! You are positively glowing."

Kennedy's lips turned up in a cheesy grin. She had been doing a lot of that lately. Grinning, not glowing. Although, being happy probably caused the glow.

"I just need to slip on shoes, then we can go." Eden hurried down the hall.

Kennedy waited in the small living room that looked much the same as it had when she lived here. She liked that, but it also made her a little sad. Eden needed to find someone who made her as happy. Like Scott did her.

Eden walked back out putting on earrings. "Are we still planning on going to Fernando's?"

"Yes." Kennedy had been craving the popular Mexican food, and if they didn't get there soon, the wait to be seated would go from thirty minutes to an hour and a half. The place was always packed, especially on the weekends. Hence the reason they were rushing out the door even though Kennedy just got here. They'd have plenty of time to visit during dinner and afterward, since Kennedy planned to spend the night.

Eden snatched her keys off the kitchen counter. "I'll drive."

Kennedy didn't argue since she'd driven her gas hog of a truck. She would have loved to ride her motorcycle, but the weather was way too cold nowadays.

On the drive to the restaurant, they exchanged small talk, discussing the weather, work, and some of their mutual friends. It wasn't until after they were seated and had placed their order that Eden brought up Scott.

"I just knew you were going to fall for him when I saw him in church that one Sunday."

"I think I had already started falling by that point. Which is crazy because I'd only known him for two weeks."

"Let's see, he's tall, strong, and handsome. Of course, you were bound to fall for him."

Kennedy couldn't argue with Eden's logic, so she laughed. "I remember thinking what a jerk he was when we first met, but he's really just a big teddy bear." She sobered. "Do you think it's bad that I got over Nate so quickly and fell for someone else so fast?"

"I think you stopped being in love with Nate about five years ago. I never understood why you stuck with him for so long when he wasn't willing to commit."

"I don't know why I did either. He was the only guy I ever crushed on through high school, so being with him felt like a dream come true."

Eden gave her a look filled with pity. "Except you have to admit your relationship wasn't very dreamy."

Kennedy lifted one shoulder in a half-hearted shrug. "I guess, I always thought we'd end up owning the garage together, so I just assumed we'd eventually get married."

Eden paused in the process of scooping up salsa with a chip. "I get it, and I'm sorry you lost out on the garage, but I'm so glad things didn't work out with Nate."

"Me too. I was too stubborn to admit that all those things you didn't like about him bothered me too."

Was that why it had been so easy to peg Travis as a womanizer? Because she'd seen it so often in Nate? The thought made her stomach roll. Why had she put up with him for so long?

Because I never knew anything different.

Her parents had a good relationship, but her mom had been gone for so long Kennedy didn't really know what a healthy relationship looked like. Maybe that's why she enjoyed spending time with Scott's family. His parents were still madly in love with each other after almost forty years of marriage, and all his sisters looked so happy.

Eden propped her elbows on the table and leaned forward. "It's more than that though. I didn't realize until just recently how bad Nate was for you."

Kennedy tilted her head and studied her friend. "What do you mean?"

"I mean something changed in you while you were with Nate. I didn't realize how drastic the change was because it happened gradually. But I look at you now... I wasn't kidding when I said you were glowing. You look so happy. You look like my best friend from high school again."

The cheesy grin returned until Kennedy dipped a chip and shoved it in her mouth. Had Nate really been that bad for her? She recalled frequently feeling inferior to the women he flirted with, and how he often gave her the impression that he found her lacking in the femininity department, but she hadn't realized how unhappy that had made her.

In contrast, Scott frequently told her how beautiful she was and how much he liked this t-shirt or those jeans on her. He also praised her often on her skills as a mechanic, which was the biggest compliment he could ever give her.

"So, you don't think it's a mistake for me to fall in love with another mechanic? One who happens to be my boss."

Please say "no."

Kennedy didn't think she could handle it if her best friend didn't like the man with whom she hoped to spend forever. Not that Scott had proposed or anything. It was way too soon for that, but she couldn't help hoping.

He did call her his partner once. She wasn't sure what to make of his casual comment, but she liked it. She didn't have the funds to buy-in to become an actual partner, but she liked the idea of working with him every day for the rest of her life.

Eden pointed a chip at her. "Not when said boss makes you this happy."

Kennedy leaned back in her seat and sighed. "I had no idea he could be so thoughtful. Did I tell you he still has lunch delivered every day? And he insists on opening the door for me any time we go out, even though I've told him it's not necessary." Kennedy continued to talk about all the little things she loved about Scott and how she loved spending time with his family. She especially loved how patient and tender he was with his nieces and nephews.

At first, Eden smiled, obviously happy for Kennedy, but then the smile faded, and her eyes glistened with tears.

"Hey." Kennedy reached across the table and clasped Eden's hand. "What's wrong?"

"Nothing." Eden chuckled as she dabbed at her eyes with her napkin. "I'm being sentimental, I guess. It just hit me that you're never coming back to Spokane." She waved her napkin in the air when Kennedy tried to interrupt. "You'll marry Scott and settle down in Providence and start having babies, while I'm stuck here, working for my dad and fending off guys like Tristan Jourdain."

"You're not stuck in Spokane, Eden. Nor are you stuck working for your dad. You have a degree and experience that could get you a job anywhere."

"Maybe, but to be honest, I'm not sure I enjoy working in the world of business and technology that much anymore."

"I thought you liked your job."

Eden shrugged. "It just feels like such a rat race lately. I think I'm just jealous that you're finding love, and I'm stuck with a cocky, billionaire playboy."

"I thought you were going to tell him to take a hike."

"I tried, but he's like a bad penny that keeps turning up. It doesn't help that my dad keeps doing business with his dad."

"You should come stay with me in Providence, then I could line you up with Rudy." Kennedy winked at her friend.

"Scott's brother? He's cute but he's also…" She held up a hand. "Don't be offended by this, but he's a small-town boy."

Kennedy chuckled. "He may be from a small town, but he's incredibly smart and fun to be around." She got a kick out of the way Scott and Rudy ribbed each other and envied his close relationship with his family.

"I'll take your word for it. Even though I've dreamed for years about us living next door to each other and raising our babies together, I don't think I could ever settle down in a small town like Providence."

A twinge of sadness filled Kennedy. She'd had similar dreams. Now, she felt torn. She didn't want to lose her best friend, but she didn't want to leave Scott and the beautiful little town of Providence either.

How do I start a new life with the man I love without distancing myself from my best friend?

CHAPTER 23

Scott grinned when Kennedy looked up after tightening the final bolts on the engine they'd just rebuilt. "Are we ready?"

She smiled back, exposing her dimples. "Let's do this. Then we can finish getting the truck put back together and get an early start to our weekend!"

He sucked in a sharp breath at the sight of her dimples and resisted the urge to pull her into his arms. The woman was a major distraction, and he loved it. He loved working side by side with her. He never knew he could work so well with another person. Even when they worked on separate projects, there was a harmony between him and Kennedy that made him want to do this with her for the rest of his life.

"So, what do you want to do tonight?" Scott asked as they attached the transmission back onto the engine block before lifting the whole thing with the hoist.

"I don't care. Playing games with your parents last weekend was fun." Kennedy helped guide the engine over the truck as Scott rolled the hoist into place.

"Yeah, but I want to take you out tonight. Maybe get dinner at a nice restaurant." He was ready to tell her he was in love with her, and he wanted to do it in a setting that was more romantic than his parents' dining room. He should have told her weeks ago, but part of him feared that making that admission would make the prospect of losing her in some freak accident become a reality.

"That sounds fun." She wiggled her eyebrows at him. "I'll dress up if you dress up. It's been a while since I've seen you in your suit."

"You saw me in my suit on Sunday."

"Sunday was a whole five days ago." She winked at him. "Like I said, it's been a while."

"I thought I could just wear the newest t-shirt you gave me," he joked.

Scott had laughed out loud when Kennedy pulled out the latest shirt she'd bought for him. It read, *Some people just need a high five. In the face. With a chair.* He could think of a few people that would be appropriate for. People like Travis Brooks, who'd shown up at the shop after he got out of jail. The jerk apologized to Kennedy then turned right around and asked her out on a date.

Sure, there weren't a lot of single women in Providence, but Travis had better stay away from his girlfriend or Scott would be the one getting thrown into jail. For assault.

"I'm still waiting for you to wear your 'morning people' one out in public," Kennedy said with a laugh. The shirt she'd given him two weeks ago said, *I don't like morning people. Or mornings. Or people.*

Even though she often made him laugh, apparently Scott hadn't shed his grumpy persona sufficiently, because Kennedy kept giving him shirts that emphasized his lack of desire to socialize with other people. But Scott didn't need a crowd of people. He only needed his family and Kennedy.

"Hold it right there," Kennedy said, referring to the hoist. "Let me get under the truck and guide the transmission into place."

Scott's stomach tightened as Kennedy slid under the truck. Watching her put herself in potentially dangerous situations never got any easier. She was a competent mechanic though, so he bit his tongue and let her do her work.

"Okay, let her down nice and easy."

The engine rotated a little as Scott slowly lowered the whole thing, and Kennedy guided the transmission into place.

They almost had the engine where it belonged when she said, "Wait a minute. It's not square and it's getting caught on the mounts."

Sure enough. The rebuilt engine wasn't settling into place like it should.

"I'm going to try to lift and shift it a little," Kennedy said from under the car.

"No, it's too heavy. You'll hurt yourself. Let me hoist it back up."

"Really?" The tone of her voice told Scott that Kennedy was peeved with him.

He looked down past the engine to find her beautiful brown eyes staring up at him.

"I'm not going to try to lift the whole thing, like you would, Paul Bunyan. I just meant I'd push it a little to see if I can get it shifted on the mount."

Scott should be the one under the truck, so he could do any heavy lifting that needed to be done, but Kennedy wouldn't appreciate him pointing that out, so he bit his tongue.

"Okay. Be careful."

If they switched places, she'd have to use a ladder to get the leverage he had. But using a ladder posed a whole different set of risks that Scott didn't want her taking either. It was stupid to be anxious about something so trivial, but he couldn't seem to tamp down that churning feeling that kicked up in his stomach every time Kennedy did something that could turn out to be dangerous.

He peered down through the engine cavity at her while she tried to shift the engine. He bit back a laugh when the tip of her tongue peeked out of the corner of her mouth.

Kennedy grunted, then her strained voice came up through the engine cavity. "It's not budging."

"Let me lift it a bit and try to shift it from this side." Scott moved the lever he'd been slowly lowering the hydraulics with back to the tube used to lift the hoist. He pumped once, twice, three times.

"Okay, that's good," Kennedy said. "Let it back down now."

Scott shifted the lever back to the shank and lowered the engine again, slowly, but after only half a turn, it stopped descending.

"Nuts! It keeps getting hung up on the mount, but it's still not sitting right."

"Here, I'm going to wiggle it." Scott grabbed a hold of each side of the engine.

"Wait—"

He jerked the engine to the left. The chain holding it rattled a little as several links twisted, and it shifted with a lurch.

"Ouch!" Kennedy's pained cry came from under the truck. "Fudge nuggets and peanut butter balls!"

Scott's heart flew to his throat, cutting off his air supply as images of Kennedy being crushed by the engine filled his head.

He made no effort to stifle the curse words that slipped from his mouth as he quickly shifted the lever again and cranked it as fast as he could. A cold knot the size of a diesel engine filled his core and radiated through his whole body. The terror pulsing through him mimicked the nightmare he endured with Hannah all over again. He didn't understand exactly what had happened to Kennedy, but he knew it was his fault.

What had she been about to say before I jerked on the engine?

"You can stop now," Kennedy said behind him.

Scott spun around. She'd rolled out from under the truck and gotten to her feet while he furiously cranked and battled the images that assaulted his mind of her profusely bleeding. He huffed out a deep breath and pulled her into his arms.

"Ow!" She pulled away, cradling her left hand to her chest.

Scott took in the stark white crease across her two middle fingers that were already beginning to swell. He swore again.

Blinking back tears, she gave him a wane smile. "I'm going to get some ice in the store."

"No, you're not. You're going to the hospital." His voice was sharper than it had ever been.

She scowled at him. "They're just pinched. They'll be fine after I ice them for a few minutes."

"There's no way they're not broken. Not with the weight of that engine on them." He started toward the back door. "Come on, I'm driving you to the hospital." When she didn't follow him, he turned back and glared at her.

She returned his glare for several long moments before a look of resignation settled over her features. Instead of following him, however, she walked over and flipped the lock on the front door. They kept the big bay doors closed most of the time nowadays, because it was too cold outside. He breathed a sigh of relief when she finally walked out the back door.

"I can drive myself to the doctor," she insisted as she passed him.

"No way. Get in my truck." His words were clipped and much harsher than necessary, but Scott couldn't seem to get the iceberg out of his stomach.

Tense silence filled the truck as he drove, but Scott's mind was in overdrive. "What happened? How did you get your fingers pinched?"

"The electrical wires had slipped down, and I wanted to get them out of the way before you went all Paul Bunyan with the engine." Defensiveness filled her voice as she spoke.

She had every right to be defensive, especially with the tone his voice had taken. Scott couldn't seem to let go of the fear that seized him when she yelled out from under the truck. He hated to think about what might have happened if the chains had slipped off altogether or the hydraulics had failed.

Her fingers could have been severed.

She wouldn't be able to do what she loved if that happened.

What if her hand was higher in the engine cavity? She could have lost her whole hand.

Alternate possibilities of Kennedy's injury—each one more dire than the last—continued to fill his mind on the short drive to the hospital, including the engine falling all the way through the cavity and crushing her. The knot in his stomach continued to expand.

A cold sweat broke out on Scott's brow as his heart beat a furious, irregular pattern in his chest. He had to protect Kennedy. He couldn't continue to put her in this kind of danger every day. He couldn't work with her anymore. His heart couldn't take it.

～

It was all Kennedy could do to keep the tears at bay on the drive to the hospital. She'd wanted to argue with Scott about the need to see a doctor, but she feared he was right. Her fingers were broken. That was the only explanation for the excruciating pain pulsing through her whole hand.

It didn't help that Scott looked angry, and his tone was sharper than she'd ever heard before. As though she'd intentionally gotten injured. She knew he was worried about her, but weren't people supposed to be sympathetic when they were concerned?

She watched him out of the corner of her eye on the short drive to the hospital. His shoulders remained hitched, and he repeatedly clenched his jaw. She wanted to assure him everything would be okay, but she was in too much pain. When the receptionist at the ER told them to wait in the waiting room, Kennedy thought Scott might punch something.

Thankfully, he chose to pace instead. The glare he sent the receptionist every time he walked in her direction had the girl leaving her post and retreating down the back hallway.

Kennedy had never been so glad to hear her name called as she was when a petite blond nurse stepped into the waiting room. Not waiting for an invitation, Scott followed her back to the exam room. Part of her was grateful for his support, but the other part feared his surliness and hunched posture meant he might explode at any moment.

His pacing worsened in the small curtained off exam room when the nurse gave Kennedy an ice pack then disappeared, saying, "The doctor will be with you soon."

The cramped confines seemed to enhance his agitation, like a caged animal getting ready to pounce at the first sign of danger.

"Good afternoon." A middle-aged man pushed back the curtain

and entered the cubicle. "I'm Dr. Henderson." With raised eyebrows, the doctor acknowledged Scott who shifted to the corner and stood with a broad stance and folded arms. He stepped to Kennedy's side. "Tell me what happened."

Kennedy was all too aware of Scott's hulking presence in the corner as the doctor poked and prodded at her throbbing fingers. He scowled every time she winced, and when she cried out in pain, she thought he might rip Dr. Henderson's arms off. Fortunately, he stopped a few feet away and kept his balled fists at his sides.

Dr. Henderson only smiled and quirked an eyebrow at Scott, but Kennedy made it a point to not vocalize her pain after that.

"Let's get some x-rays to see what we're dealing with, shall we?" Dr. Henderson finally said before walking out of the cubicle.

Fortunately, Paul Bunyan stayed behind when Kennedy was taken down the hall for x-rays, but he was right back to pacing when she returned.

A nurse carrying a small container with a pill and a cup of water pushed her way past the curtain. "Here's something to help with the pain."

"What is it?" Kennedy asked.

"Percocet."

"No," Kennedy held up a hand. "I don't like how Percocet makes me feel. Can I just have some Motrin or something that's not a narcotic?" She needed to keep her wits about her if she had any hope of convincing Scott to let her help put the engine in and finish putting the truck back together.

"You should take the stronger pill, Ken." A hint of concern laced Scott's words, but there was still a gruffness in his voice and finality to his tone that irritated her.

"No, I just want Motrin or ibuprofen."

The nurse left, and Scott glared at Kennedy the whole time she was gone.

Well, this is going to put a damper on our Friday night date.

A tense silence filled the air as they waited for the nurse to return.

When she did, Kennedy glared back at Scott as she took the proffered medicine.

Once they were alone again, Scott resumed his pacing.

She'd had enough. "Will you just sit down? Your pacing isn't going to make this go any faster."

"I can't." He shook his head. "I can't just sit there," he pointed to the lone chair against the wall, "when you're in pain."

"It doesn't hurt all that bad anymore," she lied. "The ice has helped." She tried for a smile, but the deepening furrow between Scott's brows told her he didn't believe her for a second.

He pushed both hands into his hair then interlocked his fingers behind his head. He looked up at the ceiling as his jaw continued to clench. "I shouldn't have let you get under that truck."

"What? Of course you should have. Our only problem was not communicating well with each other."

"No." The word was deep and gruff. "I should have gotten under there."

"Then you'd be the one with the broken fingers."

He shook his head as he looked at her. "No, I would have been able to shift the engine myself the first time it got hung up."

A flash of irritation drove up Kennedy's heart rate. "Are you saying my fingers got broken because I wasn't strong enough to do the job?" She wanted to remind him it was his impatience that broke her fingers, but she bit her tongue. There was already enough tension in this small space. Instead, she glared at him, daring him to say yes. If he did, she'd lose it and tell him what he could do with her job.

The curtain slid back, and Dr. Henderson entered again. "Looks like the middle and ring fingers are indeed broken." He did an excellent job of pretending the small cubicle wasn't charged with tension.

Scott stepped in front of the doctor. "Will there be any nerve damage or long-term problems?"

Dr. Henderson ignored Scott and looked at Kennedy. "Would you like me to make him leave?"

Kennedy gave Scott a warning glare that said, "behave," before shaking her head.

With a nod of acknowledgment, Dr. Henderson turned his back to Scott as he spoke to Kennedy. "Fortunately, your tendons and nerves appear to be undamaged."

"So, she'll make a full recovery and have full use of her fingers?" Scott still towered over the doctor.

Kennedy bit back a chuckle when the good doctor scowled at him before speaking to her again. "You're looking at four weeks in a cast, but you should make a full recovery."

Paul Bunyan seemed to deflate in that moment. His shoulders dropped, and he let out a lengthy sigh as he sank onto the chair. Relief filled his face, but his lips formed a tight line, and a glint of something —determination or defiance—lingered in his eyes.

Dr. Henderson explained, "Normally we splint and tape a broken finger to the one next to it, but since it's broken too, and the breaks are in the proximal phalanx…" He indicated the bone closest to the knuckle, we'll have to cast them and the whole hand."

Scott stayed silent with his elbows on his knees and his head bowed while the nurse put the cast on Kennedy's fingers and hand. His anger seemed to have dissipated, but he still looked upset and resolved. As if he had an unpleasant task he needed to face.

He's probably dreading finishing putting the engine in.

Kennedy had a feeling he'd refuse to let her help finish up the truck, but she planned to fight tooth and nail, if necessary, to get him to let her continue doing anything and everything she could with one and a half hands, since she still had the use of her thumb and two fingers on her left hand.

Scott continued to glower and remained quiet on the drive back to the shop.

"It's a good thing I broke two fingers instead of one," Kennedy said in an effort to lighten the atmosphere, "or I'd be flipping everyone off for the next four weeks."

Nothing. Scott didn't even crack a smile. A less obvious, but more dangerous, tension seemed to have built inside him. Kennedy didn't look forward to spending the evening with this extra broody version of the man she loved.

It was after six by the time they made it back to the shop, and Kennedy was ready to call it a day, but they needed to get Mr. Tibbet's truck put back together. He was the cutest, little old man who'd driven the same truck for thirty years. She skidded to a stop a few feet from the back door when Scott turned to face her.

He spread his feet and folded his arms across his chest, effectively blocking the back entrance to the shop. "I can't have you working in the shop anymore. It's too dangerous."

Kennedy let out a little growl of her own. She had a feeling this would happen. She'd seen it in his demeanor at the hospital and on the drive home. She wanted to lash out at him, because she was tired of having to fight for her right to work in her chosen profession. It especially hurt coming from Scott. The one man with whom she thought she'd found total acceptance. But she also knew that because of a past tragedy, he was in pain.

"It was just a little accident. It could have happened to anyone. You heard the doctor; I'm going to be fine."

"It could have been much worse! You could have had your fingers severed or even your hand."

"You're being overly dramatic." Kennedy stepped toward him, intent on shouldering her way into the shop.

He shifted to block the door. "No, I'm not. Next time, it could be much worse." Scott's usually gruff voice was much deeper than normal. "But I refuse to let there be a next time."

She gave him a gentle smile and put a hand on his arm.

"There's still plenty of work I can do with only one hand that's not dangerous."

He shook his head before she even finished speaking and shook off her hand. "No, I can't work with you anymore."

Ugh. He's demoting me to office work again.

Kennedy stared at him while debating whether to argue with him over her responsibilities or agree to stick to the office work for a while, giving herself time to remind him what an asset she was in the shop.

"Fine, I'll stick to the office work, *for now*." She added emphasis to those last two words so Scott would know she wasn't totally giving in.

"No, you won't, because you're fired." That glint Kennedy had seen in his eyes at the hospital was more prominent now. Pure determination.

Heat flared in her chest. "What? You can't fire me over a silly little accident that was technically your fault."

"Yes, I can," Scott's voice grew in volume just like hers. "Because I own the shop now. And I'm well aware this..." he pointed to her injured hand, "was all my fault, and I refuse to let it happen again. I can't lose the woman I love again!"

Kennedy froze. "You love me?"

"Blast!" Scott shook his head and scratched at his neck, as though he regretted his declaration. "Yes, I love you. That's why I can't put you in a position where you can get hurt again."

Kennedy always thought when she heard those three words from a man they would fill her with joy. Instead, she felt the urge to grind her teeth together, much like Scott always did. The tightness in her chest and abdomen made her want to lash out at him instead of telling him she was in love with him too—which she was. She couldn't tell him that, though, not while he was firing her. It made the rejection that much more painful.

She took a deep breath to steady her emotions. "You're not responsible for my welfare. I am, and I intend to keep working at the shop." She stepped toward the door, and again he blocked her way.

"No, you won't, because you're fired. As of right now, there will be no more women working in this garage." He softened his voice a bit before going on. "Don't worry, you can stay in the apartment as long as you want. Rent free."

Kennedy should have been happy for that concession, but heat flared inside her chest. Scott's rejection was much more personal than his simply laying off a coworker. He'd rejected her as a woman, as his girlfriend. A heaviness settled over her. He said he loved her, but he had a stupid way of showing it.

"How generous of you." Sarcasm filled her voice. "Are you going to gas up my truck and buy my groceries too?"

His voice was much softer than hers when he spoke again. "I'll help you with whatever you need."

"So what? I'm just supposed to become your kept woman?"

"No, I'm sure you'll find another job in no time. I'll gladly give you a reference as a hard worker, Ken."

How dare he call me Ken after firing me?

"But not as an excellent mechanic?" The tears were threatening to fall now, which only made her angrier, because she felt like the weak, weepy female Scott saw her as.

"I don't want you to work in a garage again. It's too dangerous."

"What about what I want? I thought you loved me."

"I do," he said, but his actions belied any conviction in his voice.

"Then why are you taking away the one thing that means the most to me?" Technically, he was taking the second most important thing too. He was the first, and her job as a mechanic was the second. She swallowed the lump in her throat and furiously blinked back the tears that filled her eyes.

"I'm trying to protect you."

"That's a load of crap, and you know it. You're trying to protect yourself because you don't want to admit that you have anxiety and PTSD after what happened to Hannah."

Scott reared back as if she'd slapped him, but Kennedy didn't regret her words. She saw his shoulders bunch every time she got under a car. If Scott couldn't get over the past and forgive himself, there was no possibility of them having a healthy working relationship. Unfortunately, that destroyed a personal relationship too.

Now the tears did fall, and Kennedy swiped angrily at her cheeks. "Fine. Let's see how long you last working by yourself. Good luck finding someone to replace me." She started up the stairs to her apartment. She needed to get away from him before she had a total breakdown. At the top, she looked down at Scott. "I bet Travis Brooks would love to come work for you. Oh, and by the way, in case it wasn't clear, I'm breaking up with you. Not only will I find another job, I'll find another place to live."

Scott would never hire Travis, but he needed to realize his options were limited.

Good luck finding someone who's willing to relocate to this small town.

Kennedy stepped inside her apartment and slammed the door. She'd never understood why women threw themselves on the bed and cried after a break-up. All she wanted to do was punch something, but the stupid tears coming from her eyes made it difficult to see. Besides, she didn't have anything in her apartment that would make a good punching bag.

Grabbing a paper towel off the roll on the counter, she wiped her eyes and blew her nose, all the while trying not to remember how gentle and caring Scott was the night Travis tried to break in.

With no physical outlet for her emotions, Kennedy turned to the next best thing. She packed a bag and donned her leather riding gear. Riding a motorcycle without the use of two good hands was stupid, but she needed that connection to her parents right now, never mind that she'd probably freeze to death. Shifting the clutch with her left hand would hurt like crazy, but it couldn't be any worse than the pain in her heart.

CHAPTER 24

*K*ennedy rolled over and groaned. She flung an arm over her eyes to block the beam of direct sunlight filtering through the crack in the curtains. If the sun was at that level already, she'd slept most of the morning away.

It's a good thing Eden hadn't gotten around to finding a roommate yet, or Kennedy would be sleeping on the sofa.

A soft knock sounded on the door before it opened. "Are you going to get out of bed today?"

Kennedy didn't bother moving her arm from her face before speaking. "The prognosis doesn't look good."

She'd wiled all day Saturday away either in bed or on the couch watching Netflix. Yesterday, she let Eden drag her out to church, but it only reminded her of how much she'd enjoyed attending church with Scott and his family the past few weeks. Alice always invited her over for Sunday dinner, and she spent the evenings surrounded by his family. She knew the names of all his nieces and nephews now.

"I made breakfast," Eden said in a cajoling voice.

Kennedy peeked out from under her arm. "What did you make?"

Despite Mrs. Watson, Eden's nanny and housekeeper, insisting she learn to cook, her friend had never quite mastered that skill. Her pancakes either turned out runny or as thick and dry as a brick. Her eggs were rubbery, and she couldn't seem to cook bacon without burning it.

"Okay, so I didn't actually cook. I ran out and bought breakfast burritos from your favorite drive-thru and picked up some chocolate muffins at the bakery."

My favorites. Eden is either planning to kick me out or tell me to get a job.

Kennedy threw back her covers with one arm while removing the other from her face. "Looks like I'm getting out of bed today."

It wasn't until she was settled at the table with a glass of orange juice, a giant chocolate muffin, and an even bigger breakfast burrito that she realized it was Monday. She looked at her best friend who sat across from her. "Shouldn't you be at work?"

Eden shrugged. "I took the day off."

"For me?" Tears filled Kennedy's eyes again. She was surprised there were any more left in her. The tears she'd cried over the past few days could fill a reservoir.

Eden put a hand on her arm. "I'd do anything for you, Ken, you know that."

Kennedy sniffed and nodded. "I do. Thank you for letting me crash here, and thanks for breakfast."

"I want to say anytime, but I hate seeing you hurt like this."

Eden had been nothing but sympathetic since Kennedy showed up out of blue Friday evening. She'd made Kennedy tell her the whole story before taking her side and determining Scott was an idiot. She offered to drive to Providence and tell Scott what a blockhead he was. When Kennedy rejected that idea, she pulled out a wad of cash from the hidden stash in her underwear drawer and offered to hire some thugs to beat him up. Like Eden knew where to find thugs for hire.

"I can't take tomorrow off, though, so you're on your own." Eden picked up her burrito and took a big bite.

Kennedy plucked a chocolate chip from her muffin and plopped it in her mouth. "I should probably go home soon."

Eden froze. "Home as in…"

"Back to Providence." Kennedy wasn't sure when she'd come to think of the small town as home, but it was where she wanted to be. Even if she didn't have a job there anymore and needed to find somewhere else to live.

Eden's face fell. "Oh, I thought with a little time, you'd be ready to look for a job here."

Aha, so she was prepping me to find a job.

"I don't want to work in a big shop anymore where the customers and their cars are like cattle being pushed through the auction. And even though I've gotten over Nate and come to terms with losing out on T&J's, I'm not interested in working for anyone who associates with them."

After working these past few months with Scott who personally knew the owner of every car he worked on, she'd come to realize small town shops had an integrity that was often absent in larger shops like T&J's.

Kennedy lowered her gaze to her casted hand in her lap. "I belong in Providence."

"I was afraid you'd say that." Eden set down her burrito. "I'm not gonna lie; it makes me a little sad, but I want you to be happy. So, what are you going to do for a job?"

"I don't know, but I'm not ready to give up on me and Scott yet." Kennedy pinched off another piece of muffin and put it in her mouth. "When things went south with Nate, and I lost any chance of owning a portion of T&J's, I ran away. I didn't stick around and fight for what I wanted. I'm not going to do that again."

"Now, that's the Kennedy I know." Eden grinned and pointed a finger at her. "You never loved Nate like you do Scott."

"Exactly. That's why I have to go back. What Scott and I have—" Kennedy corrected herself. "What Scott and I had was the real deal. I'd be as big of a fool as he is if I just gave up and walked away from that."

"Is he likely to come to his senses and ask you to come back?"

Kennedy chewed on her bottom lip. "I don't know. He's pretty stubborn, but I refuse to give up." Having made that decision,

Kennedy picked up her burrito and took a huge bite. She barely took time to chew it before speaking again. "I might have to enlist Rudy's help, but I'm going to wear Scott down."

CHAPTER 25

*S*cott looked up as Rudy stepped out of the office at the garage and stretched. "Done already?"

"Already?" Rudy said with raised eyebrows. "I've been here for two hours. There's probably still more that needs to be done, but your parts are ordered, and your invoices are ready for the next few days. As far as I can tell, Kennedy had everything in order with the finances before you *fired* her." The emphasis Rudy put on fired let Scott know his brother didn't approve of what he'd done.

No one did. But they didn't understand that what happened to Kennedy could have been so much worse. He'd fired her to protect her. He couldn't lose her in another horrible accident like he did Hannah.

He'd done what was best for Kennedy, but he'd lost her anyway. Ignoring Rudy's comment, he ducked his head back under the hood of the Taurus he'd promised to have ready first thing tomorrow morning.

"I'm not a bookkeeper," Rudy said. "So, I don't know what needs to be done in that department."

It was another not-so-subtle reminder that Scott needed to find some help. Soon. This was already the second time Rudy had come to help him out since Scott fired Kennedy ten days ago.

Rudy picked up a ratchet wrench and spun it around, making an annoying buzzing sound. "I heard Kennedy found a temporary job out at the Double Diamond, repairing equipment."

Scott's stomach coiled so tight he felt like a strut ready to snap. Farm equipment could be dangerous. What was Jake Winters thinking hiring her?

The Double Diamond's equipment shed was top notch, but it was open on one side. It wouldn't protect Kennedy from the temperatures that dropped a little lower each day. The thought of her working out in the cold made him feel as agitated as the ratchet Rudy spun. If his brother didn't stop, Scott might throw something at him.

"I'm sure she'd come back in a heartbeat if you asked her to." Rudy dropped the ratchet on the workbench with a clang. "Although, if she's smart, she'll make you apologize and grovel a little—"

"I can't." Scott lifted his head and pinned his brother with a glare. "It's too dangerous for her here." This wasn't the first time they'd discussed this, but Scott was ready for it to be the last.

Rudy snorted. "Too dangerous for her? Or too dangerous for your heart?" When Scott didn't respond, he went on. "Why can't you admit that what happened was an accident that could happen to anyone, and the real problem is with you? You've been anxious about Kennedy working here since day one."

"Yes, because I knew she could be hurt. And I was right."

Rudy scoffed. "It was two broken fingers. They'll heal. You on the other hand... You're carrying scars that I'm not sure will ever heal if you don't get some help." His brother shook his head. "Would you have fired Kennedy if the roles had been reversed and she was the cause of you getting your fingers broken?"

"Of course not." Scott knew what happened to Kennedy could have happened to anyone, but the fact that it happened to the woman he loved, and it was his fault...

He couldn't do that again. He couldn't be responsible for something bad happening to the woman he loved again.

"So, you're punishing her to assuage your own fears?"

"I'm not punishing her. I'm trying to protect her," Scott snapped.

"I doubt Kennedy sees it that way." Rudy shook his head. "What happens next time when you're the one who gets hurt, and there's no one here to help you?"

"I don't need help."

It was a bald-faced lie, and they both knew it. The fact that Rudy had spent two hours doing paperwork and the lot outside just kept getting more crowded attested to that.

"I'll remind you of that next time you need help with the paperwork." Rudy stepped closer, getting right in Scott's face. "You better pull your head out soon before Kennedy picks up and leaves Providence. If that happens, you might never get her back."

Rudy's words pierced Scott's heart. He'd lost so much more than a bookkeeper and mechanic. He'd lost his partner, in the shop and in his life. He'd never loved a woman so deeply. Not even Hannah. Compared to how he cared about Kennedy, what he shared with Hannah had been little more than puppy love.

Scott used to have a hard time catching his breath anytime Kennedy was around, but now, without her here, he felt like he was breathing through a coffee stirrer full of Jell-O.

Rudy clicked his tongue in disappointment when Scott didn't respond. "I can't keep this up forever, bro, especially with the extra bookkeeping required, now that you own the shop."

"I know." Scott's words came out all grumbly because he couldn't keep up this pace either. Despite working twelve-to-fourteen-hour days, he was more behind than ever.

He needed help in the shop and in the office. He needed Kennedy in his life, but he couldn't let go of the fear that gripped him every time he thought about how badly she could have been injured. Until he did, he couldn't ask her to come back. No matter how badly he wanted to. Not until he could stand to let her work in the garage.

He doubted Ben would be eager to run another job listing. Not when the perfect candidate lived right upstairs.

"Well, I need to get to work. It's going to be a long night." Rudy opened the back door and walked out.

"Thanks," Scott called before the door closed behind his brother. He turned back to the Taurus, preparing for another late night himself. Even the convenience store was closed already.

Thirty minutes later, he let out a soft string of swear words as he rolled out from under the Taurus for the third time. Even though Kennedy wasn't around, he still tried not to swear out loud like he used to before she came into his life.

He pushed to his feet and grabbed a wrench with a longer handle and a hammer for good measure. The nuts he needed to remove to replace the rack and pinion system on Mr. Gibson's car were being stubborn, just like every other nut and bolt on the twenty-year-old rust bucket.

All this work to fix a leak in the power steering fluid.

That was the problem with old cars though. You go to fix one thing but end up having to replace others because they are in no better shape than the part you started out fixing. Kind of like relationships. If you neglect the little things, they become big things.

He tripped over a bad jack stand on his way back to the car, adding to his frustration.

Blast! I forgot to ask Rudy to research new jack stands.

The last set he'd purchased less than a year ago had been recalled last week when it was discovered that the ratchet teeth on the lifting extension didn't engage deeply enough on the pawl to keep it from dropping under pressure.

Yet one more thing I need to worry about.

Having an extra set of hands would make this job so much easier. Kennedy could work on one side while he worked on the other. He let his mind linger on what happened on occasion when they worked under the same car together. Despite his insistence about the need for safety, he and Kennedy had shared more than one kiss under a car.

It was always only a quick kiss though. Just a peck really. Unlike their morning greetings or their goodnight kisses that were long, lingering, and passionate.

He gave himself a mental shake. He wouldn't be bumping heads or brushing arms with Kennedy anymore, so he needed to get her out of his head.

Unfortunately, his heart refused to read the memo, and his thoughts quickly returned to her. His chest grew tight as it did every time he thought about how badly she could have been injured that afternoon. He'd blown the whole thing out of proportion. He could see that now, but at the time, the only way he could think of to protect Kennedy was to keep her out of the shop. If he asked her to come back, he'd be putting her in danger again.

Getting her off his mind would be much easier if she wasn't right upstairs. Well, not at the moment. She must be working late too. He always heard her truck or motorcycle return home, except for those three days after he fired her.

He'd nearly had a heart attack when he heard her take off on her motorcycle only minutes after they returned from the hospital. She was too upset to be riding her bike. Besides, it was too cold out.

When she didn't return that night or the next day, or the next, he'd almost started calling all the hospitals in the state. He managed to convince himself she was visiting Eden, so he could stop worrying. But then he feared she might never return. Firing her hadn't made him stop worrying about her, it had only increased his anxiety.

When she finally did come back, something relaxed inside of him. Until he looked up and saw her standing inside the back door of the shop. The air rushed from his lungs at the sight of her, and his chest squeezed tight. She looked so sexy with her hair in braids and wearing her leather riding gear.

She gave him a small smile. "The lot's looking kind of full. Do you want some help?"

Guilt clawed at Scott's insides as he looked at her left hand. A firm and sharp, "No," came from his mouth before he could stop himself.

The dejected look on her face before she turned to walk out the door twisted his insides, but he couldn't make himself go after her.

Scott rolled out from under the Taurus yet again to get a shorter wrench this time. One that would allow him to get into the tight spots. He really needed an extra set of hands. Exhausted and frustrated, he dropped back onto the creeper and shoved back harder than necessary. The corner of his creeper hit the jack he'd used in place of the fourth jack stand.

He swore and cringed, bracing himself. Slowly, he turned his head toward the jack to make sure it still held steady before checking each of the other three jack stands that kept the Taurus suspended above him.

With the recall of the newer jack stands, he'd been forced to use his old stands, one of which had been faulty in the past, hence the reason he'd bought new ones. It was stupid to use a jack in place of the fourth stand to support the car, but he couldn't wait days or even weeks for new jack stands to arrive. He needed to get Mr. Gibson's car finished tonight so he could move on to the next car in the line-up that was too long to think about.

If Kennedy were here, she would have already researched the stands, found the ones with the highest ratings, and ordered new ones.

But she's not here, and she never will be again. Unless I can figure out how to rein in my fears.

Kennedy and Rudy were right; he needed help. Professional help.

If he weren't so swamped, maybe he could look into talking to Dr. Emily Winters, the psychologist at the hospital. The thought of discussing the feelings of apprehension and foreboding swirling around inside him made his stomach twist into knots. It would be worth it though, if it made it so he could work with Kennedy again without freaking out.

Ken's worth it. The cars in the lot can wait. I'll call tomorrow and schedule an appointment.

Or maybe he'd ask his mom to call; she'd be sure to get the job done. Either way, he'd climb the back stairs first thing in the morning and apologize to Kennedy and offer her job back.

No, I'll do it tonight. When she gets home.

Having made up his mind, he focused on his work. Another flash of irritation shot through him when he realized he needed to remove the sway bar to get to the final bolts on the tie rod ends. He expected some release of tension when he removed the first sway bar link, but he was completely unprepared for the second rusty link to snap, allowing the torsion-spring sway bar to fly out. Right at his head.

Scott jerked sideways to avoid being struck by the airborne metal. The end of the creeper under his thighs slammed into the jack, sending a reverberating shudder through his body. A loud pop echoed under the car as the jack gave way.

A cold chill ripped through him as he watched the car shake then drop. Unable to move fast enough to get out from under it, he squeezed his eyes closed and turned his head away from the two tons of metal coming at his face.

Excruciating pain ripped through his thigh just above the knee. He cried out in agony, stopping abruptly when the effort created such pressure in his chest, he feared he might suffocate. Expecting to have his whole body crushed, Scott's shocked brain scrambled to process what had happened.

Cold, grimy metal pressed against his cheek, preventing him from turning his head, but because he was conscious and breathing at all, he deduced that the old jack stands still held most of the car off the ground. And judging by the agonizing pain in his left thigh, his leg held the rest.

Grimacing, he looked up at the corner of the workbench where his cell phone sat. As the direness of his situation settled in, the throbbing of his pulse reverberated through his head and chest, blurring his vision.

Blast!

Doing his best to ignore the ringing in his ears, he pulled in a deep breath against the crushing weight on his chest and yelled for help. His scream sounded like little more than a feeble yelp, and the effort only increased the pressure against his ribcage. It didn't help that no one was around to hear his yell.

Desperate to free himself, he attempted to wedge his hands by his sides and lift. Despite the adrenaline coursing through his body, making his heart race like a V8 engine topping two hundred miles an hour, the effort only intensified the pain in his thigh.

Scott groaned and swore under his breath. He would have cursed out loud if it didn't take so much air. Shadows floated around the edges of his vision, threatening to drag him into unconsciousness. He blinked a few times and focused his gaze on the oil drain pan under the workbench. The one Kennedy nicknamed Nate.

Kennedy.

If he hadn't been such an idiot and pushed her away, she would be here right now to help him. Instead, he might die here alone because he was too afraid to let himself love a woman that he could lose someday. Pushing her away hadn't made him stop loving her though.

He'd always love Kennedy. Until the day he died.

Which, thanks to the car sitting on his chest and crushing his leg, might be much sooner than he'd like. He hated to think how quickly he could bleed out if the artery in his leg ruptured.

No. I can't die. Not today. Not until I fix things with Kennedy.

She needed to know he loved her and was sorry for the way he'd treated her. He needed to tell her he wanted her to be his partner. He wanted her by his side both at work and at home. Feeling a renewed surge of adrenaline, he tried lifting the car again. Just enough to get a little more air into his lungs.

"Help!" The plea came out louder this time. Trying to ignore the searing pain in his leg, he yelled a second time. "Help me!"

Ceasing his efforts, Scott gasped for air as the car settled back on his chest.

Where's Kennedy? Surely, Jake isn't requiring her to work this late.

Needing something to focus on besides the pain and darkness that pulled at him, he pictured a life with Kennedy as his wife. The joy of working side by side with her each day was eclipsed only by the thought of spending the nights with her in his arms. They would quickly outgrow the apartment upstairs because he wanted to have a family with Kennedy.

The image of a little blond-haired, brown-eyed girl filled his head as darkness overcame him.

KENNEDY NOTED Scott's truck and the garage lights as she parked her truck behind the shop and pulled her groceries from the back seat.

He's working late again.

Just like he had every night since he fired her. Except Sunday. Even then, he took Thomas the tow truck out shortly after church and came back with a pickup truck that needed repairs.

She scanned the side lot after she climbed from her truck. Eight vehicles. Two more than yesterday. A few of them were different vehicles though, so Scott was getting the cars fixed. Just not fast enough. If he kept this up, he'd start losing business. Anyone who could still drive their cars would take them to the Tri Cities area for repair.

Kennedy hesitated as she reached the stairs that led to her apartment and looked at the back door of the shop. She wanted to offer to help Scott again, but she recalled the vehemence in his "no" the last time she offered. She was better off going upstairs and taking a hot bath than to subject herself to his rejection again.

It's going to take a lot longer to get him to come around than I thought.

She'd just started up the stairs when someone called her name. She froze, listening.

Hearing nothing but the wind, she convinced herself it was just wishful thinking that Scott would call out to her, asking her to come back and help him. She'd fantasized about that more times than she could count over the past week and a half.

Shaking her head, she continued up the stairs. She'd only taken two more steps when she heard her name again.

"Kennedy." It was definitely Scott's voice, but it sounded muffled and far away. "Help me."

The anguish in the words she'd longed to hear turned her blood to ice.

Something's wrong.

Kennedy turned and raced down the stairs to the back door of the shop. Dropping her groceries, she flung it open and darted inside.

With her heart lodged in her throat, she skidded to a stop at the sight that greeted her; every mechanic's worst nightmare.

Legs clad in navy-blue work pants stuck out from under a car that sat precariously perched on three supports. The only thing that kept the fourth corner off the concrete floor was Scott's leg.

For the second time in her life, Kennedy swore out loud.

"Scott!" She dropped to her knees and lay down on the floor, expecting to see Scott's head crushed by the undercarriage of the car. Relief flooded over her to see his hazel eyes looking at her. No blood or worse stuff marred his face or stained the cement.

Her eyes darted around taking in the jack that had failed and the three stands. The two back ones seemed to be holding, but the one beside Scott's head looked off kilter. If it slipped any more, Scott would be crushed for sure.

"Ken." He sighed her name, making it sound like a caress. "You're sso blasssted beautiful." Scott's quiet, slurred compliment was punctuated with a wince.

"Hang on. I'm going to get this car off you."

"No!" He hissed out a breath and squeezed his eyes shut. The rest of his words came out labored as though he couldn't get enough air into his chest. "Call 911 firsst. I might be bleeding. You know, i-internally."

"Right." Kennedy choked out the word. The thought of Scott bleeding internally caused a painful tightening in her chest. It's a good thing she lay on the floor already, or she might have collapsed.

Scott could die from this, and I'll never get the chance to convince him we're supposed to be together.

Emotion clogged her throat as she pulled her cell phone from her back pocket. Her hands shook so badly she dropped her phone on the concrete floor. Her voice trembled as much as her hands as she talked to the dispatcher. She didn't even attempt to stop the tears that ran down her cheeks.

"Hey, don't cry." Scott's hand reached out from under the car.

Kennedy clasped his hand in hers. "You're such an idiot." The fear arcing through her made her words come out harsher than she intended.

"Excuse me?" the dispatcher said in her ear.

"Not you. Sorry. I'm talking to Scott."

"He's lucid? That's good. Keep him talking. An ambulance is on the way."

"I *am* an idiot," Scott said softly. "I shouldn't have...fired you. I'm sorry. You're the best thing..." He struggled to bring in enough air to finish his sentence. "...that ever happened to me. I ruined it."

More tears filled Kennedy's eyes, blurring Scott's face.

This was not how Scott's apology was supposed to happen. This sounded too much like a deathbed confession.

"I forgive you, and I insist you give me my job back to make amends, so something like this doesn't happen again."

"I love you, Ken." Scott closed his eyes for several long seconds.

"I love you too." When he didn't open his eyes again, she squeezed his hand. "Hey, stay with me."

His gorgeous hazel eyes opened. "I wanna have...your babies."

Relief filled her, and she laughed through her tears. "You mean you want me to have your babies?"

Confusion filled Scott's face before he gave a crooked grin. "If you insist."

Kennedy pulled the phone from her ear and checked the time. She'd been on the phone with the 911 operator for a minute and a half already.

Where is that ambulance? This is a small town. It shouldn't take them so long to drive two miles.

"I need...you wanna...be my sunshine?"

Kennedy grinned. "Yes, Mr. Grumpy Paul Bunyan, I'll be your sunshine."

"Wanna park...with me?"

Kennedy had no idea why he was asking her if she wanted to go parking with him, but she was definitely game for a make-out session with him in a parked car. "I'd love to go parking with you after we get you out of here."

Scott's brow furrowed as confusion again filled his face. "No. I mean… Parmesan…parade…para—keet?"

Kennedy's smile faded as each word became quieter and more slurred.

Scott wasn't making sense. That wasn't good. Was he having a stroke or something?

Maybe he's bleeding internally, and he's lost too much blood.

A cold chill swept over her despite the perspiration dripping off Scott's brow. Kennedy had never been so glad to hear the sound of sirens as she was at that moment.

She didn't want to leave Scott's side, but she needed to open the garage door and get this car off him. "Help is here, Scott." She gave his hand a final squeeze before letting go. "You hang on, you hear me? It's all going to be okay."

Kennedy wished she believed the words she said to Scott. But while she'd lain on the floor holding the hand of the only man she'd ever truly loved, fear had settled deep in her core. Her heart raced so fast, she feared it might explode, and her legs didn't want to cooperate as she crossed the shop to open the garage door.

Rudy rushing in, swearing and calling his brother an idiot, did nothing to help Kennedy's frazzled emotions.

The next fifteen minutes felt like an eternity as the paramedics struggled to find a solid spot on the chassis to brace the jack so they could lift the car off Scott since the front axle rested across his chest.

When they asked her to work a second jack on the side of the car as an added precaution. She shouted, "Yes."

Anything to keep her from feeling so helpless. Her shaking limbs struggled to perform their assigned tasks, however, especially when Scott cried out in pain with every movement of the car.

The paramedics repeatedly asked Kennedy questions she didn't have answers to, and Scott wasn't lucid enough to answer clearly. The stress and worry nearly caused her to break down sobbing.

Finally, Scott was free, and the paramedics hovered over him, blocking Kennedy's view.

"Is he going to be okay?" Kennedy and Rudy asked in unison.

The paramedics ignored them while they took Scott's blood pressure and worked to splint his broken leg. Then the older of the two put in an IV and said something about administering what sounded like an awful lot of morphine.

Kennedy hoped it alleviated Scott's pain.

"His blood pressure is dropping," the younger one said less than a minute later. "We need to go, now!"

Kennedy sank to the floor in front of the workbench, tears again filling her eyes. What did it mean when a person's blood pressure dropped too low?

"Hey." Rudy crouched in front of her. "They're waiting for you."

"What?"

"You should ride in the ambulance with Scott."

"Me? But I need to…" Kennedy's mind and heart felt like they had been put through a paper shredder. She struggled to form a clear thought. "The car…isn't secure."

"I'll get some blocks from out back to put under it." Rudy pulled her to her feet. "Get in that ambulance with Scott."

The ride to the hospital passed much faster than the time spent waiting for the ambulance to arrive, and Kennedy soon found herself alone in a waiting room while Scott was rushed off for x-rays and an MRI. It wasn't long before his parents joined her, and she broke down in Alice's arms, blubbering about how she should have been there for Scott.

"I shouldn't have let him fire me. I should have kept showing up for work and demanded he at least let me do the office stuff. Then I would have been there."

"Now, now. You can't blame any of this on yourself. He's a stubborn man."

"I know, but I can't lose him." She looked at Alice with imploring eyes. "He's going to be okay, isn't he?"

"I hope so, honey." The words weren't spoken with the confidence Kennedy needed to hear.

She wrapped her arms around herself as a blast of cold air rushed into the room with Rudy.

"Any word yet?"

She shook her head right alongside Bill and Alice.

More cold air filled the room as each of Scott's sisters arrived separately but in quick succession. No one acted surprised to see her there. In fact, Debbie and Sheila hugged her and told her they were glad to see her. It brought tears to Kennedy's eyes all over again.

She watched the slow tick tick tick of the clock, willing the door to the ER to open. When it finally did, she jumped up hoping for good news, then sank back down in disappointment when it turned out to be a janitor pushing a mop bucket.

The two-hour wait was almost as bad as the one she endured at the hospital in Spokane after her father's stroke. Except this time, she had Scott's family.

Everyone breathed a sigh of relief when a nurse named Sylvia finally came out to inform them Scott was stable. His parents and sisters asked questions all at once, but Sylvia raised her hands, palms out.

"I understand your concerns, but unfortunately, I don't have the answers. Scott is still receiving imaging, and we're still running tests. He's in good hands. Either Dr. Young or Dr. Henderson will be out to talk to you as soon as they are able."

Everyone's spirits lifted at the news that Scott was stable, but Kennedy knew there would be long-term complications for Scott.

He could lose his leg.

The thought caused a painful twisting in her chest. How would he continue doing what he loved if that happened?

Kennedy was jumping to conclusions, but she couldn't help herself. She couldn't rid her mind of the image of the brake drum crushing Scott's leg or the axle pressing so tightly against his chest that he could barely breathe.

During the next hour, the seven of them took turns pacing and sitting. They talked a lot and cried a little. While they waited for more news, Kennedy heard more stories about Scott's childhood than she had in the weeks they'd dated. She enjoyed learning more about the grumpy giant of a man that she loved, but the humorous tales did little to dispel the worry coursing through her.

Those who were sitting sprang to their feet when a weary-looking doctor entered the waiting room. He shook hands with Bill and Alice and gave Scott's siblings a nod before turning and introducing himself to Kennedy, who was apparently the only one who didn't know him.

"I'm Dr. Young. I understand you're Scott's girlfriend."

Kennedy wasn't sure where the doctor—who looked like an older version of the attorney who interviewed and hired her to work at Knights—got his information, but she was more than ready to resume the role as Scott's girlfriend.

She nodded as she shook Dr. Young's hand. "Yes. I'm Kennedy McGregor."

"It's nice to meet you." Dr. Young turned to face Bill and Alice. "Your son is one lucky man. He has a compound fracture in his femur, for which he's going to need surgery. He also has three broken ribs and a fractured sternum from the weight of the car. The injuries to his torso should have been much more severe, but the real miracle is that there's no internal damage and more importantly, no internal bleeding."

Relief flooded over Kennedy's body, weakening her limbs. She sank down onto the chair behind her and blinked back the tears. The surgery Scott faced could still pose a danger with his bleeding disorder, but he was going to be okay.

As soon as the fear dissipated, anger rushed back in.

Scott should have known better than to get under that car with a jack in place of a stand. What was he thinking? He could have been killed.

Kennedy shook her head. Now she understood why Scott got so upset and fired her after her accident. She wanted to do the same to him. Or at the very least forbid him to ever get under another car, especially when he was alone in the shop.

Being in love with someone and agonizing over their well-being was torture.

CHAPTER 26

A hand on Kennedy's shoulder shook her awake.

"Scott's out of surgery," Bill said. "He's still pretty groggy, but he's asking for you."

How she'd managed to doze off on the uncomfortable chairs in yet another hospital waiting room, she didn't know.

Yes, she did. She'd hardly slept last night, because she couldn't get the image of Scott's body trapped under that car out of her head.

Kennedy stood and followed Bill to Scott's room. She'd readily accepted when Alice invited her to come with them to Kennewick this morning for Scott's surgery. Being with his parents meant the hospital staff treated her like one of the family. Girlfriends didn't always get that consideration.

Her heart rate kicked up a notch when she stepped into Scott's room to find him smiling at his mom. A sudden lightness filled her as the tension she'd carried since last night—no, longer than that— melted away, leaving her feeling giddy.

Scott's coloring looked so much better than it had last night when she'd had a brief chance to see him before Rudy drove her home at one a.m. He'd still looked rather pale this morning before his surgery, especially in contrast to the purple bruises on the side of his face.

With all the bruising caused by broken blood vessels, it was a miracle he hadn't bled to death.

Despite being heavily medicated, Scott had been lucid enough to make her promise she would be here when he got out of surgery.

"I promise," she said, pressing a kiss to the edge of his mouth. But it had ended up being one of those times when the girlfriend got relegated to the waiting room.

Now, looking at Scott, propped up in the hospital bed, she was ready to promise him a whole lot more.

Alice stood when Kennedy approached Scott's bed. "Bill and I will go find some lunch and give you two some privacy." She leaned over and planted a quick kiss on Scott's forehead before walking out of the room.

It really was adorable that this big lumberjack of a man was still mama's little boy. Kennedy kind of hoped that never changed. A man who treated his mother well treated the other women in his life well too.

Kennedy slipped her hand into Scott's then leaned over and pressed a quick kiss to his lips. "How are you feeling?"

"Like I've been run over by a truck." The words were little more than a mumble.

"Close. You were crushed by a car." Kennedy repressed a shudder as images from last night filled her head. "Do you remember what happened?"

"Yes." Scott's eyes drifted closed, and he slowly sucked in a deep breath before wincing. "I was afraid…"

"I'll bet. I would have been terrified if I'd been trapped under a car."

Scott squeezed her hand then slowly opened his eyes and met her gaze. "I was afraid I'd never get the chance to make things right with you."

"Oh." Kennedy didn't know what to say to that.

"Thank you, Ken, you saved my life." His hand tightened around hers.

She loved it when Scott called her by her dad's nickname for her.

His eyes drifted closed again. "Did I tell you last night that I love you?"

"Yes." When his eyes didn't open again, she asked, "Are you okay?"

He peeked out of one eye before closing it again. "I'm fine. Just sleepy still. Did I tell you last night how beautiful you are?"

Kennedy grinned. "Yes, apparently, I'm so blasted beautiful."

Scott's lips turned up at this. "You are."

"You also told me you wanted to have my babies."

His grin grew, but his eyes remained closed. "I do. Well, I would if I could." He finally opened his eyes and studied her face. "I want you to be my wife and the mother of my children. I can't face the future without you. I don't want to do it alone."

"Do what alone? Work or life?" It wasn't fair for Kennedy to pressure him while he was still groggy from the anesthesia and pain meds, but she needed to know if he was going to allow her to work with him again.

"All of it. I don't want to do it without you by my side. I need you." His gaze shifted to his leg. "Now more than ever."

"Good, because I need you too. But I also need to work on cars, which is exactly what I'm going to do while you recover."

Scott's eyes drifted closed again, so Kennedy stopped talking. He squeezed her hand again. "Keep talking. I like the sound of your voice."

She hooked her toe around the leg of a chair and pulled it closer so she could sit down. "Well, Ben has already offered to help me at the shop as often as he can, and I have a feeling if Debbie and Austin have their way, you won't see a single medical bill."

Scott's brow furrowed with a scowl.

"There's no point in fighting her, you know that. She's still sore you wouldn't let her lend you the money to buy the shop."

He opened his eyes. "I know, but I hate feeling obligated to people."

"You'd better get used to it, because you're going to be laid up for a long time."

Scott turned the scowl on her. "I know," he growled.

Kennedy laughed. "It's good to know the accident didn't affect your grumpy nature."

Scott didn't laugh with her. He didn't even smile. Kennedy worried he was in pain.

"I'm not going to waste my time, Ken. I'm going to go to therapy."

"Yeah, the doctor said you'll likely have to do physical therapy for months."

"No, I mean…counseling."

Tears pricked Kennedy's eyes. They seemed to be doing that a lot lately. She rose to her feet again and leaned over to look him in the eye. "You're going to go to counseling?"

His hand tightened around hers. "I love you, and I want desperately to be the man you deserve. But I need help to get over my anxiety and fears concerning you working in the garage."

"I'm glad you're willing to get some help."

"I'd do anything for you, Ken. The way I see it, I'll never be able to pay you back for saving my life."

She leaned a little closer. "In that case, I'd like you to kiss me."

"Gladly." Scott brought the hand with the IV in it up to cup the back of her head and gently pulled her toward him.

She tried to keep the pressure of her lips light for fear of hurting him, but Scott wasn't having it. He claimed her mouth with an intensity that surprised her, all signs of grogginess gone. He'd obviously missed her as much as she missed him.

The knots in her chest and stomach smoothed out, and Kennedy felt like all the little pieces of her broken heart had mended. Stronger than ever.

She had just stopped worrying about hurting Scott and given into the passion that always flared between them when an alarm sounded. Before she could question what was happening, a nurse burst into the room.

She scowled at Kennedy before pushing some buttons. "It's not good for his heart rate and blood pressure to spike right now. If you keep that up, I'll ban you to the waiting room."

Kennedy couldn't help herself, she burst out laughing. "It was his fault."

Scott's laughter joined hers for a moment before he groaned and pressed a hand to his chest. He winked at her. "It's a good thing we have the rest of our lives to kiss."

CHAPTER 27

*S*cott lifted his head from under the hood of a Toyota Corolla at the sound of air brakes outside of the shop. He pulled off his gloves and wiped suddenly clammy hands on his pants as his heart rate kicked into high gear.

Kennedy darted to the window in the office. "It's here!" She squealed and clapped her hands. "It's finally here."

It's here alright. Today's the day my life changes forever. I hope.

As he stepped into the office, Scott's gaze followed hers to the semi-truck and crane parked outside the garage.

Thank goodness they kept the new sign covered during transport.

A thrill of excitement shot through him, warming him on this freezing January day. Or maybe it was the two shirts he wore that made him feel so warm. Not even the dull ache in his thigh, triggered by the cold weather, could dampen his spirits today.

He patted the small ring box in his front pocket then walked up behind Kennedy and wrapped his arms around her. "Have I told you thank you, lately?"

She leaned back against him with a sigh. "Yes, you told me yester-day. And the day before that. And the day—"

"But I haven't told you today?" He loosened his arms and turned her to face him as he clicked his tongue in regret. "I'm slacking. Thank you. For all the big and little things you do to help me each day." He stroked a finger along her jaw. "Have I told you how beautiful you are?" He looked into her gorgeous brown eyes. It was much easier now to look at Kennedy when he talked to her. Now that he was comfortable with her and knew he could trust her with his heart.

Knowing those things didn't make what he planned to do today any easier.

Kennedy slid her arms around his neck. "Hm… I don't believe you've told me that yet today." Dimples lined her cheeks.

Scott sucked in a deep breath. He hoped he never got used to the effect this beautiful woman and her dimples had on him. "You have the prettiest eyes and a gorgeous smile."

He pressed a kiss to her forehead. He wanted to kiss her lips, but if he did, he'd never want to stop. It hadn't been that long since they ended their good morning kiss, and it was almost ten o'clock.

"Have I told you that I love you?" Kennedy beat him to his next question.

He pretended to ponder her question. "I think I recall you saying a time or two that you love me more than baths, your silly t-shirts, and even chocolate."

It had become a game between them to come up with silly things to compare their love for each other to. Scott hoped to win that game today once and for all.

A man wearing insulated overalls and heavy winter gloves walked through the glass door to the left of the first bay. "Scott Wheeler?"

Scott pulled away from Kennedy and walked out of the office. "That's me."

"I've got a sign here for Ke—"

"You've got the right place." Scott cut him off. He practically shoved the man out the door before Kennedy could ask questions.

After conferring with the team that would soon take down the Knight's Repair Shop sign and replace it with the one Scott ordered, he headed back inside the garage and out of the freezing weather. He felt bad the crew had to install the new sign in such horrible conditions, but the three men seem to have come prepared with heavy winter gear.

While Kennedy hovered near the window, Scott alternated between checking the progress of the sign installation over her shoulder and pacing around the shop. He had no idea the process would take so long. There was a strong possibility he might hyperventilate before the sign was up. Replacing the starter on the Corolla would help kill the time, but he found it impossible to concentrate.

Every time he wandered away from Kennedy, it wasn't long before he found himself back at her side. She was like a powerful magnet that drew him in. He hoped he'd always have her by his side. Forever.

He recalled the day he asked Charity to sell him the shop. She'd told him the story of how Rich had surprised her by building the diner across the street, so they could work close to each other every day.

Scott cast a glance at Kennedy, praying she'd say yes when he asked her to be his partner for life so they could work side by side every day.

"Hey, are you okay?" She gave him a concerned look. "Are you worried about the guys putting up the sign? They're wearing harnesses, so I'm sure they're perfectly safe."

"No, I'm not worried about them." He worried a lot less about accidents and a lot of other things now after visiting with Dr. Emily Winters every week for the past two months.

She'd helped him realize there were some things he simply couldn't control and that trying to do so was not only damaging to his mental and emotional health but it also affected his relationships with others. She'd also assured him that it was perfectly normal to be nervous about proposing to his girlfriend, even though he was certain she was the love of his life.

"What are you worried about then?" Kennedy put her hands on his shoulders and gently kneaded the muscles. "You're all tense."

"Nothing." The word came out more tersely than he intended. He feared she'd feel the extra shirt he wore under his work shirt and his plan would all go south before he had a chance to carry it out.

She rolled her eyes. "Whatever, Paul Bunyan."

Kennedy always called him that when he got growly and tried to distance himself from people. In return, he called her Elsa anytime her bossy, feminine side took over in the shop. It was another silly game they played, but it brought a little joy to each day. Or maybe it was simply Kennedy that filled his life with joy.

When it looked like the sign was finally up, Scott grabbed the extra t-shirts he'd stashed that morning on the upper shelf above the workbench. He stuffed the blue one into one back pocket and the ugly, rust-orange one into the other.

Kennedy rocked up onto the toes of her steel-toed boots and let out a squeal. "It's up. They'll take the cover off soon. We should have invited your family to come witness the unveiling."

"I did. They're all over at the diner."

"Oh, good idea. That way they can stay out of the cold, and it won't be so crowded in here."

He nodded even though that's not why he told them to stay at the diner. He did it because he didn't want an audience or their heckling —in Rudy's case—when he proposed to Kennedy. He resisted the urge to swipe at the perspiration forming on his brow.

Kennedy pulled her phone from her pocket. "Should I go outside to video this?"

"No. Through the window is fine. It's too cold out there."

If they went outside, his whole family—and half the town who'd parked their cars along main street to see what was going on—would see him get down on one knee.

Kennedy held her phone up and pressed record. "Here we go."

Scott didn't even bother to look outside. Instead, he stepped away from the beautiful blond at the window and unbuttoned his shirt as fast as he could, fumbling button after button in his haste.

Blast! Why am I all thumbs?

Silly as it sounded, he'd practiced stripping last night. Finally, the last button was free, and he yanked the tail of his work shirt from his waistband and tossed it on the floor. He smoothed down the t-shirt he still wore and pulled the ugly orange shirt from his pocket and laid it on the nearby table so the single, two-letter word on the front was visible. Then he pulled the ring box and blue t-shirt from his pockets before dropping to one knee.

Ignoring the pain that shot through his thigh, he sucked in a deep breath and held it, waiting for Kennedy to turn around.

KENNEDY LET OUT a little squeal as the tarp covering the sign lifted. She was so excited for Scott.

Wait... The sign's not supposed to say Ken's Auto Repair. It's supposed to say Wheeler's Auto Repair.

The colors, the font, the words looked exactly like she and Scott had designed together, but they'd never discussed putting her name on it. Kennedy had tried to get Scott to put his first name on the sign, but he insisted he wouldn't be the only Wheeler working there—yes, they had been talking marriage—and she couldn't be happier, but she never expected this.

"Scott, what did you—" Still holding her phone in front of her, she turned to find him down on one knee behind her. Her heart leaped to her throat, thudding hard, threatening to shut off her air supply. Her mind reeled as she took in the scene.

Scott held an open ring box containing a gorgeous, wide, white-gold band with delicate engravings and small diamonds inset in it, but it was the words across the chest of his blue t-shirt that drew her attention. *Marry me?* Out of all the t-shirts she'd seen him in, she loved this one the most.

Then her gaze jumped to his other outstretched hand which held a matching blue t-shirt with one word emblazoned on it. *Yes.*

Just as she was about to let out another very feminine squeal, something on the table caught her eye. A hideous orange shirt that also had one word on it. *No.*

Kennedy repressed a shudder. Not only was the t-shirt her least favorite color ever—which Scott knew—there was no way she'd ever consider saying no to this incredible man who went to so much effort to make her feel loved, cherished, and welcomed in a man's world.

She let out a little laugh. "Thanks for giving me a choice, but there is no way in H-E-double hockey sticks I'll ever wear that shirt." She pointed to the table. Scott grinned and started to rise, but she stopped him. "Wait. Just because you know my answer, doesn't mean I'm letting you off that easily." She pointed at the words on his chest. "You need to say the words yourself."

Realizing her phone was still recording, she shifted her camera to Scott's face. She loved the idea of documenting this moment forever. Just like she had proof that Scott had once stuck tampons up his nose. Of course, she hadn't dared admit that to him yet. Maybe on their first anniversary.

With a grin, Scott tossed the blue t-shirt over his shoulder and took her hand. Her heart did a back flip when his heated gaze met hers. He'd come a long way when it came to communicating.

"Kennedy Elyse McGregor, you have encouraged me to chase my dreams and stood beside me even when I'm grumpy. You've helped me through some difficult trials, and you've inspired me to strive to be better and do more. You're patient, constant, and faithful. You're the sunshine that lights my day. Thank you for never giving up on me."

Scott would never be an eloquent orator, but every once in a while, the words that came from his mouth turned her to mush. Today was one of those days.

"I love you, Ken." He grinned and winked at her. "I love you more than my mom's cooking, more than this shop that I've worked so hard for, and more than life itself. Will you please marry me and be my partner forever?"

The band of muscles around Kennedy's chest squeezed tighter and tighter with each of his declarations, making it difficult to breathe. She chuckled, however, when he mentioned his mom's cooking. Scott was definitely making a sacrifice there. Her heart raced so hard by the time he got to the part about marrying him and being his forever partner that she feared she might pass out.

"I will." She threw herself at him. "I'll marry you and be your forever partner."

Scott managed to keep them from toppling over and brought them upright with a grunt. His arms tightened around her as his lips claimed hers in a passionate kiss.

Warmth and utter contentment filled her. When she left Spokane six months ago, she wasn't sure she'd ever figure out who she was or what she wanted for her life, let alone find a place where she felt like she truly belonged. A place she could call home.

She'd found both with Scott. He loved her for who she was; a tomboy who loved working on cars, taking baths, and wearing colorful t-shirts with silly sayings. A woman who was most comfortable in jeans, but who also loved dressing up occasionally just to see that fiery look in his eyes.

Oh, how she loved this grumpy-growly, mountain man of a mechanic and the way his kisses drove her crazy. The rest of her life wouldn't be near long enough to spend with him.

Distant whistles and cheers broke through the haze that Scott's kiss created in Kennedy. She pulled away from him to find his whole family—grandkids and all—huddled outside the window with half a dozen phones poised. Laughing, she waved for them to come in out of the freezing cold. She was getting a lot more than a husband and a shop out of this deal, and she couldn't be happier about it.

Scott didn't get a chance to slip the beautiful yet practical ring he'd bought onto her finger until his family had gathered around. The kiss that followed was much briefer and more chaste than she would have liked, thanks to their audience.

After putting on the blue t-shirt and receiving dozens of hugs and congratulations, Kennedy snatched the ugly orange-brown shirt off the table.

"What are you doing with that?" Scott asked.

She quirked an eyebrow at him as she walked over to the desk and grabbed a pair of scissors. "It'll make great shop rags."

EPILOGUE

*R*udy checked his watch one last time before walking in the back door of Debbie's house and down the hall to the master bedroom. He found Eden's dad, Oliver Du Pont, in the hallway checking his own watch.

"Are they ready?" Rudy asked.

"Eden assured me a little while ago they were." The older man smiled.

"Well, let's get this show on the road then." Rudy knocked on the bedroom door.

His mother opened it and slipped out. "Is it time?"

"It's time. Joy sent me in to come get you all. She's adamant we stick to the schedule."

Mom stuck her head back into the bedroom. "There are a couple of handsome men out here waiting to walk you ladies down the aisle."

A little squeal from Kennedy floated through the open doorway. "I'm finally getting married!"

Rudy laughed. She sounded as eager as Scott. His brother just showed it differently. He'd become surlier than ever. Rudy suspected it was the buildup of sexual tension, and Scott's impatience to make Kennedy his wife already.

"I'd better get the twins headed out with the flowers." Mom hurried down the hallway.

His nieces Lucia and Mia were playing the part of flower girls again, just nine months after Debbie and Austin's wedding. They were adorable in their ruffly mauve dresses. The ring of delicate white flowers in their curly dark hair made them look like little princesses.

Kennedy's best friend, Eden Du Pont, stepped out of the bedroom, and all the air rushed from Rudy's lungs. The slender, dark-haired woman looked beautiful in her burgundy dress. A sweetheart neckline and fitted bodice emphasized Eden's assets. The high-low skirt showed off shapely, well-toned legs, and purple toenails peeked out of her high-heeled sandals. A delicate diamond necklace and earrings completed her ensemble, creating a very attractive package.

Eden held her arm out. "Are you walking me down the aisle or am I walking you?"

Rudy gave himself a mental shake and gave a dramatic bow before offering his elbow. "At your service, ma'am."

"Oh please. I'm all for chivalry, but don't call me ma'am. That makes me feel old."

"Madam?"

She grimaced. "Ugh, that's even worse."

"How about milady?"

Eden snickered. "Does that make you my prince? Or my knight in shining armor?"

Rudy shrugged. "Take your pick."

Oliver cleared his throat behind them. "Do you think we could *get this show on the road* sometime soon?"

"Come, milady, the guests await."

Eden chuckled again as she tucked her hand in his elbow. They had only taken three steps before she stopped. "Wait, I forgot my bouquet." She darted back into the master bedroom, reappearing a moment later with a pretty arrangement of fresh flowers, consisting of white and dark dusty pink roses with a few tiny pale pink roses and baby's breath mixed in.

They stepped off the back porch just as Lucia and Mia reached the front of the aisle. Mia peered into her little white basket that still held rose petals. Shrugging, she turned it upside down and dumped the remaining petals in a pile on the grass. Lucia studied her own basket for a moment before following her sister's example.

Laughter rippled across Debbie's backyard.

Eden leaned her head toward Rudy's "Those two are so adorable!"

Her warm breath tickled his neck just below his ear, sending a zing of warmth shooting through him. There was something about Eden that did things to him that no other woman had for a very long time.

He'd always found Kennedy's friend attractive ever since the first time he saw her at church with Kennedy months ago, but he'd recognized her high-maintenance type right away and had no interest in going there. Scott and Kennedy had been trying to line him up with Eden for months now, but things never seemed to work out. For which, Rudy was grateful.

Eden was pretty and fun to be around—as he'd learned these past few days. She was exactly the kind of girl he could see himself falling for, but he wasn't interested in a long-distance relationship with a wealthy socialite. Girls like that didn't fall for small-town cops.

Despite it being early April, the weather had turned out even nicer than the meteorologist had predicted. Debbie and Austin's backyard gazebo made the perfect setting for a simple, yet classy, wedding. When his sisters helped Kennedy organize a simple ceremony and reception, they'd planned to do it in Debbie's game room. But when the weather report predicted unseasonably warm temperatures in the high seventies, the family all held their breath that it would be nice enough to have an outdoor wedding.

They were halfway down the aisle when Eden shrieked, jerked her hand from his arm, and did a little flailing jig before throwing her flowers on the ground.

Rudy grabbed her shoulders to still her as exclamations and murmurs swept through the crowd of gathered guests. "What's wrong?"

"A spider crawled out of my flowers and up my arm," Eden said in a hissed whisper. She shuddered and swiped at her right arm again.

"It's okay, it's gone now," Rudy said in a hushed voice before bending to pick up her flowers. He gave the bouquet a good shake, just to be sure, and inspected the flowers before handing them back to Eden. "No more spiders."

He feared she might refuse to take them, and he would have to carry them down the aisle. Finally, she reached out a shaky hand and took the flowers between her thumb and two fingers. As they continued their walk, he expected her to drop the bouquet again since she barely had a hold on it.

When they reached the top of the aisle, he made it a point to walk through the pile of white rose petals to scatter them. Eden grinned and did the same with the second smaller pile.

When Rudy stepped to Scott's side, his brother turned to him. "What was that all about?"

"Spider," Rudy said out of the side of his mouth, because the bride and her stand-in father had started their walk down the aisle.

Scott chuckled but then his laughter died when he caught sight of Kennedy. "Isn't she so blasted beautiful?"

It was Rudy's turn to chuckle. His brother was so whooped.

He felt bad that Kennedy's own father wasn't here to walk her down the aisle, or her mother for that matter. Thankfully, she had a good friend like Eden whose father gladly stepped in. The Wheelers had totally taken Kennedy in and welcomed her with open arms. Now she had parents and siblings, as well as nieces and nephews.

Mr. Du Pont planted a kiss on Kennedy's cheek before placing her hand in Scott's.

Rudy did his best to focus on the couple and the ceremony taking place, but his gaze kept drifting to the vision in burgundy behind the bride. Eden's cheerful smile eventually faded, then she began discreetly wiping at her tears. Even crying, she looked pretty.

The back of Scott's hand smacked Rudy's chest. "Where's the ring?"

"Sorry." Heat filled Rudy's face as he scrambled to pull the ring from his pocket. He'd been so distracted by Eden he'd missed half the ceremony.

As Scott placed the ring on Kennedy's finger, a movement behind Kennedy caught Rudy's eye, and once again, he was right back to staring at Eden. She stepped sideways and flailed her arms, now holding Kennedy's bouquet as well. Then repeated the motion in reverse.

Had another spider crawled out of her bouquet?

Eden's motions grew more frantic when the pastor told Scott he could kiss his bride.

Rudy stepped behind the bride and groom toward Eden, hoping to keep her from making a scene and ruining the wedding.

She continued to flail as the happy couple ended their kiss, and the crowd cheered.

"What is your problem?" Rudy hissed as he approached Eden.

She swung her arm, nearly hitting him in the face with Kennedy's bouquet. "Bees. I'm allergic."

Just as she said the word, a buzzing sounded near his ear. He ducked and swung his own arms in the air. "They want the flowers. Drop them."

Eden hesitated only a moment before following his instructions. She swung her arms a few more times for good measure.

Debbie's big backyard had gone silent except for the noise he and Eden were making. He forced a smile. "Sorry, everyone. Just a pesky bee. Congratulations, you two." He stepped over and gave Kennedy and Scott a hug before shoving them toward the aisle.

More cheers filled the air as husband and wife made their way up the walkway, and Rudy turned his attention back to Eden. "Are you okay?"

Looking more than a little ruffled, she nodded.

Rudy nudged the bouquets further away with the toe of his shoe then offered her his arm again to escort her back up the aisle behind the happy couple.

The afternoon was spent eating delicious food, making toasts and dancing. Eden cried through most of her toast, but she left everyone believing that Scott was getting an incredible woman. Rudy did his best to keep his toast lighthearted and make the guests laugh. He succeeded, but he also got choked up at the end when it hit him that yes, he was gaining another sister, but he was also losing his best friend in a way.

When the dancing started, he wanted to applaud Kennedy for getting his brother on the dance floor. Scott had changed over the last few months, especially where Kennedy was concerned. He was still grumpy and growly most of the time and preferred to avoid people in general, but he was putty in Kennedy's hands. He would do just about anything for her.

His mom nudged his arm after she finished her dance with Scott, and other couples—mostly his sisters and their husbands—began filling the dance floor. "Go ask Eden to dance."

Rudy looked over to where Eden stood by her dad. She'd already danced one dance with her dad, and now she fidgeted.

He wanted to refuse, but that would be rude. He didn't want to dance with Kennedy's pretty maid of honor, because he feared he'd enjoy it too much. After a second nudge from his mom, he crossed the dance floor to stand in front of Eden.

"Would you like to dance?"

She grinned. "Sure."

She put her soft hand in his, and warmth crept up his arm. This was why he kept telling himself to avoid Eden; she affected him too strongly. He hadn't been this attracted to a woman since he dated Alice back in high school. But Alice had only ever wanted one thing; to get out of this one-horse town.

The music changed from an upbeat song to a slow, romantic song as he pulled Eden into his arms. She stepped closer than he anticipated, and he found her body almost flush with his. Her sweet floral scent filled his nose and heightened his senses. Her perfume smelled amazing and expensive. It was probably made with exotic flowers like jasmine or gardenias.

Rudy was too distracted by the feel of Eden in his arms to focus on leading her through the waltz or any other dance steps, so he gently swayed side to side, turning them a quarter turn every so often.

Needing something to focus on besides how good it felt to hold

Eden, he watched Scott and Kennedy. "She's totally got him wrapped around her finger."

Eden's gaze followed his. "I'll say. He's hardly said more than a dozen words to me in the months I've known him, but Kennedy keeps telling me how they talk about all kinds of things, and I have a hard time believing it."

"Me too."

When the song ended, Rudy wanted to insist she dance another one with him but figured that was asking for trouble. Eden was great and all, but she was a wealthy businesswoman who would never be interested in sticking around a small town like Providence.

"Mind if I cut in?" Violet, Eden's cousin, grabbed Rudy's shoulder and spun him toward her.

Rudy turned an apologetic look on Eden but found her giving him one instead. He recalled a few of the stories Kennedy and Eden had shared about Violet. The woman was rather brash and had poor social skills, often saying and doing things that were inappropriate. She was also rather large.

She pulled him close and locked her arm around his neck in a vice-like grip, crushing her ample chest so tightly against his it felt indecent. Her perfume wasn't nearly as pleasant as Eden's. In fact, Violet smelled of something cloyingly sweet like cotton candy mixed with body odor.

The woman talked non-stop about herself as she pulled Rudy around the dance floor. Occasionally, she threw out a compliment about how attractive or strong he was while stroking his shoulder or bicep. Her hand even found its way to his chest at one point. He quickly shifted it back up to his shoulder and prayed for the song to end already. Her words and actions were so overt, he felt like he was being molested.

He pushed back as soon as the song ended.

"How about another one?" Violet reached for him again, but Rudy sidestepped her.

"Sorry, I promised my nieces I'd dance with them." He spun around, searching the crowd for his teenage nieces.

Savannah was the closest.

He hurried to her. "Please save me and dance with me?"

Savvy laughed as he pulled her onto the dance floor. "Was that the cousin Kennedy and Eden were talking about the other night?"

"Yes, and she's every bit as…interesting as they said." He wanted to use a much stronger word, but he shouldn't speak so negatively in front of an impressionable seventeen-year-old.

Before the dance with Savvy ended, he'd located Aubrey. He dragged her out to the dance floor next. Before asking Brooklyn to dance, he hurried over to Dallas and Cody, keeping an eye out for Violet.

"You guys should ask Kennedy's friend Eden to dance."

He would have asked her again, but he feared it would only make his attraction toward her grow. And that wasn't smart considering she'd be leaving town tomorrow.

"Ew. No." Dallas's face looked like Rudy had just suggested he eat Brussel sprouts.

"Come on." He pointed at Eden. "Doesn't she look lonely, sitting there in the corner all alone?"

Both boys shook their heads.

"If you boys each ask her to dance one time, I'll take you for a ride in my police car."

Cody's eyes grew big. "Can we turn on the siren and the lights?"

"Absolutely!"

"Can we handcuff Dallas in the back seat?"

"What? No." Dallas shoved Cody, almost knocking him off his feet.

"Tell you what…" Rudy grinned. "Whoever asks Eden to dance first gets to put handcuffs on his brother."

Debbie and Austin were going to kill him, but at least he wouldn't have to feel bad about ignoring Eden all night. The bribe was effective; Cody hurried over to where Eden sat.

Rudy spotted Violet headed his way again. He quickly looked back over his shoulder at Dallas as he walked toward Brooklyn. "I'll let you handcuff Cody too, if you ask Eden next."

Fortunately, Brooklyn agreed to dance with him without needing a bribe, and thirteen-year-old Lizzy practically paced the edge of the dance floor, waiting for her turn.

Dallas and Cody must have decided dancing wasn't all that bad because they both now shook and shimmied with Eden to the upbeat song.

When he ran out of teenage nieces to dance with, he rounded up the twins. No way would he wait around for Violet to accost him again.

After dancing with a two-year-old on each hip, he was breathless and making plans to ask each of his sisters to dance. Anything to keep from having to dance with Violet a second time.

The DJ announced that it was time for all the single ladies to gather on the dance floor for the bouquet toss, saving Rudy from more dancing. Good thing because he was tired.

Kennedy grabbed his arm. "Make sure Eden catches the bouquet."

"What?"

"Don't let Violet shove her out of the way. She can be rather violent when it comes to these things." Then she hurried to the head of the dance floor.

Rudy caught sight of Eden hanging back and went to stand beside her. She didn't look at all eager to catch a bouquet.

He nudged her forward. "Kennedy told me to make sure you get up there with the girls."

The girls consisted mostly of his nieces and a few friends and cousins on the Wheeler side.

Eden cringed. "I hate doing things like this when Violet is around."

"I'll run interference. Kennedy wants you to catch the bouquet."

Eden rolled her eyes. "I just hope Violet doesn't trample one of the young girls."

Beyoncé's song *All the Single Ladies* started playing and the gathered ladies crowded closer together as Kennedy eyed the group before turning her back to the room. The last place she looked was at Eden at the back of the crowd.

Violet must have noticed because she hiked up her skirt and darted in Eden's direction.

Kennedy threw the bouquet, sending it right toward Eden.

Violet shrieked, "It's mine!"

Rudy stepped into Violet's path so Eden could have a chance at catching the flowers. He must have underestimated Violet's momentum and his own positioning because the next thing he knew, flowers hit him in the face, and he was knocked off his feet.

His elbow smacked something sharp on the way down, and a loud "Oomph," came from Eden followed by a groan. He'd taken her down with him.

Violet grabbed the flowers off the floor and jumped to her feet with a cheer.

Feeling horrible for knocking Eden down, Rudy rolled off her, pushed to his feet, and extended his hand to help her up.

When she pulled her hand away from her face to take his, bright red blood flowed from her nose.

Great! I've just assaulted my new sister-in-law's best friend.

.

ACKNOWLEDGMENTS

Special thanks to all the awesome writers in the three different critique groups that I participate in. You guys always help make my stories better, and this one was no exception. Your words of encouragement definitely keep me going.

Thank you to Kelli Ann at Inspire Creative Services for yet another awesome cover. You always know how to bring my stories to life with amazing covers. Tia Taylor, your cute little artwork at the beginning of each chapter helps give my books a little something special. And thank you to Megan Walker for dropping everything and making my story a priority once I finally got it ready for proofreading.

And as always, I'd like to send out a great big thank you to my awesome husband who does so much work behind the scenes to keep me sane and makes it possible for me to follow my passion. He truly is the best!

ABOUT THE AUTHOR

JILL HAS always been an avid reader, and romance has always been her favorite genre. If she's not writing or folding laundry her head is usually in a book.

When her father told her, "I've got a story I want you to write," she didn't think she'd ever actually do it.

But after twenty years of being a stay-at-home mom with seven children, the idea of writing and publishing a book sounded less terrifying than entering the workforce again. Boy, was she wrong!

Keep in touch with Jill Burrell
www.jillburrell.com

amazon.com/author/jillburrell

facebook.com/authorjillburrell

goodreads.com/authorjillburrell

bookbub.com/authors/jill-burrell

www.ingramcontent.com/pod-product-compliance
Lightning Source LLC
Chambersburg PA
CBHW070809180626
46818CB00001B/174

9 781955 507110